FACES IN THE CROWD

FACES IN THE CROWD

WILLIAM MARSHALL

THE MYSTERIOUS PRESS
New York · Tokyo · Sweden · Milan
Published by Warner Books

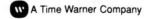 A Time Warner Company

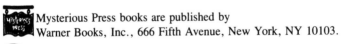Mysterious Press books are published by
Warner Books, Inc., 666 Fifth Avenue, New York, NY 10103.

A Time Warner Company

Printed in the United States of America
First printing: July 1991

10 9 8 7 6 5 4 3 2 1

Library of Congress Cataloging in Publication Data

Marshall, William Leonard, 1944–
    Faces in the crowd / William Marshall.
        p.   cm.
    ISBN 0-89296-367-0
    I. Title.
    PR9619.3.M275F25   1991
    823—DC20   90-84899
                                                                  CIP

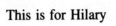

This is for Hilary

FACES IN THE CROWD

1

New York City:
Sunday, April 13th, 1884

MR CASHIER,

SIR:

After considering my deplorable circumstances I am convinced that this life is not worth living without liberal means and therefore I am resolved to make one more effort on the high road of self-help to sustain my miserable existence by asking you to kindly hand over all the money in your possession.

Should you not comply with my demand I am compelled to employ my last remedy, a bottle of nitroglycerine, and to bury myself and you under the ruins of this building, blasted to everlasting nothingness.

Yours, respectfully,
A Despondent Man.

In Grammelspacher's Shooting Gallery, 234 The Bowery at 10:08 P.M. Sunday, April 13th, 1884, there were a lot of guns shooting. Through the smoke and fumes, flashes and flames, there were a lot of people shooting them. In Grammelspacher's, on the noisiest street in the world, with the steam engines of the Elevated running on both tracks north and south outside thirty feet above the sidewalk every two minutes, there were clerks in tight suits shooting .25 Stevens at mechanical Indians that went "Ugh!" when hit in the heart, country boys firing Flobert Five Millimeters at flashy farfarooms that flew to fragments, wanton women and their wastrels whamming Winchesters at whirring windmills, diving ducks being powdered to pumice by Peacemakers, and, at every second booth along the

1

walls of the gaslit place, S & W .32 Number Twos being shot and shooting things to shards by anyone who could get their hands around them two at a time. Everything moved, spun, turned, ducked—everything ran by steam. The excess pressure ran a small calliope in the corner that shuddered and shook as it blasted out patriotic airs full volume a penny a time.

In Grammelspacher's, the Despondent Man paused for a moment by the calliope to adjust his clothing. He was sweating; he put three fingers of his right hand in under the second and third buttons of his ankle-length coat and flapped at the material to make a breeze. He had a long black beard with giant moustaches; he put the back of his other hand that held the note under the whiskers below his chin and flapped there too. The spectacle frames that held the whiskers on around his eyes had started to itch and he shook his head to reset them. He had a black patch on one eye. He had an oversize derby hat pulled down over his patch. He had a fake wart on his nose.

He was in disguise.

It was a good disguise.

There was an alcove with a door behind the calliope leading to the gallery office and counting house, and, completely inconspicuous, nodding to himself as he went to it with a terrible, foot-dragging limp, the Despondent Man drew his little bottle from an inside pocket and, holding it up above him like a flambard, limped, shuffled, shambled, itched and sweated his way down the corridor to hand it in.

Juggling the note and the bomb, flapping at the coat and beard for a little more air, the Despondent Man drew from inside his coat a small brass ear trumpet and, holding it hard against his ear like a bellflower, remembering to keep limping, continued on his way down the corridor toward yet another carefully conceived, wonderfully executed, sure triumph of the criminal mind.

LARGEST   SNAKES
In The World!!!
EXHIBITION AT THIS MUSEUM
These Extraordinary
M O N S T E R S
Swallow at a Sitting 8 pigs and 3 rabbits
And Are
EXPECTED HOURLY TO FEED!
Bunker's Bowery Dime Museum
Dante's Inferno Done With Real Fire
SINNERS BURNING TO DEATH!
PLUS ARTIST'S MODELS IN EFFIGY
AND BEWITCHING FEMALE BATHERS IN REAL WATER!
(For Educational Purposes Only)

On the noisiest street in the world, outside Bunker's, the conductor on the 10:08 P.M. uptown, clanging at his bell above the racket of bars, saloons, beer halls and bordellos, yelled at the top of his voice to his carload of country boys in from the New Jersey ferry, *"All out for the whorehouses!"* In the center of the street there were carts and wagons, pushcarts and peddlers; there were hawkers and harridans, white men, black men, yellow men and brown men; there was gunfire from the shooting galleries and smoke from the oyster bars and chop sellers, there was the shouting of auctioneers on the sidewalks, the patter of three-card monte men in checked suits and the roars of approval or disapproval of their customers and the smell of pigs' knuckles boiling hot in basins, there were jizz bands from the brothels, minstrels from the nickel theaters. The conductor, roaring above it all, clanging at his bell as the 10:09 P.M. downtown train on the El thirty feet above him shook the entire street to its foundations and filled his mouth with soot and steam, yelled, "Naked Can-Can dancing to the left, Lively Flea to the right, Hotel Nymphomania three doors up at number 297!" There were hand-held placards in the street, waving, beating in the air like wings—

TOBACCO JUICE IS THE SPITTLE OF SATAN!

**THE MISSION OF GOD
IS A SALVATION ARMY**

**THE SHAME OF OUR CITY!
D R I N K !**

The conductor yelled, clanging, "—Do-gooders everywhere!"

*"We will come rejoicing,
Bringing in the sheaves . . ."*

The conductor yelled, "Make sure you try the clams at Nelson's Clam House, guaranteed finest in New York!" A peddler, a woman in rags carrying a basket, made for the horsecar.

"CLAMS! CLAMS!
Here's your fine Rockaway Clams!
Here they G-O . . ."

On his step, the conductor gave her a kick. The conductor, clanging his bell to drown her out, yelled, *"Nelson's* for clams!" The conductor, ringing at his bell rope to set the car off again, yelled, "Tell them Nelson sent you!"

"ROSIE—!" There was a lewd in the center of the street near someone wreathed in smoke selling hot potatoes from a stall. Drunk, she was weaving and bobbing, trying to focus on something.

The conductor saw the country boys all in their best tight suits stop. The horsecar was moving, clanging.

The conductor yelled, "Best lewds at Nelson's!" The lewd was staggering, reeling toward him, "Indoor lewds! Scarlet sisters of every persuasion! Fallen flowers from the garden of Eden!" She was coming toward him. The conductor screamed in the chaos to impart a final word of fatherly advice to the bucolic band, "At Nelson's, our ladies eat only our clams to keep their energy up!" The conductor roared, "Beware the perambulating solitary Strange Woman of the streets for she will rob you blind!"

He sighed. He stepped back from the step to let the gaping goobers out and pulled the horsecar door shut behind him.

On the street of sin, the avenue of avarice, the road to ruin, he rang the driver's communication cord three times to show they had an empty car, and, brushing at his moustaches, sat back in a rear seat to smoke a cigar until they got to the depot at Houston Street to change horses and, until his shift ended at 3 A.M., make the little round-trip journey for the convenience of the traveling public three times more.

It was a nice cigar, a thirty-cent Cuban.

Snipping the end off with a gold clipper, setting his little official pillbox cap beribboned with the toil of thirty years unstinting service to the public beside him on the seat, he lit it carefully with a match from a silver and gold match case with a single diamond set in it, and settled back, safe from war, pestilence, depression or famine, to savor it.

In the pine-lined room at the rear of the shooting gallery—the office—there must have been a thousand shooting medals pinned and hanging down from the ceiling. The medals were silver, bronze, round, octagonal, cruciform with ribbons and chains and colored braid hanging down from them, all in the name of Peter Grammelspacher, all in German, all first and second and occasionally third prizes from shooting fests in Switzerland and Germany and, here and there, emblazoned with the gilded embroidery of horses and wagons and kegs, from American beer companies. There was a collection of Scheutzen rifles on a rack of antlers on the far wall of the windowless room and stuffed dead animals from mountains and alps and forests on all the others. They were all Grammelspacher's. The two men in the room reading the note at the blackwood desk all carved with hunting scenes were also Grammelspachers—they had what looked like shooting competitors' wooden nameplates pinned to their suspenders, "Luther"—he was the big, red-faced one, a real sauerkraut eater if ever there was one—and "Ludwig"—the little one with spectacles: some sort of midget Black Forest gnome.

They were cousins, or brothers. In the gaslight flickering at all the black glass eyes of the dead animals on the walls, they looked hard at the note and blinked. They were stupid Germans. The Despondent Man, holding the glass phial of death a little higher as they finally got to the end of the first paragraph of the communication and looked at each other, said warningly, *"Hargg!"* With his long coat, his hat down hard over his forehead, his patch and one good eye, his ear trumpet and nitro, he was a creature of terrible aspect.

They looked back to the note for paragraph two.

The Despondent Man said like a clock ticking off the remaining seconds to eternity, *"Haarrmmm—!"*

He forgot to favor one leg.

He favored one leg.

The Despondent Man said, *"Haarrr!"* He did a little fast demented breathing. He fixed them with his glittering eye. He glanced at a framed painted target on the wall to one side of the staircase to the outside roof. The target was a picture of a circle of birds in a tree with the words *"Bild Dir anfs Treffa net allzubiel ein; Es waar ja leicht mögli dahs Zufall kunnt sein"* painted around it in old German, and under it in English, the translation "Do not be proud when you hit; It may be only by chance" and the printed emblem of Neidermayer and Hoffman's Beer Company, New York. It was a nice example of draftsmanship, very artistic.

They were taking a long time to read a short letter.

The little one—Ludwig—his eyes were moving along the lines quickly, then back again. Thickhead—Luther, the big one—was moving his orbits at the speed of dead mutton.

The Despondent Man said, *"Raggh!"*

He was the criminal mind honed to ultimate perfection, confident, in command.

The Despondent Man said just to remind them he was there, *"Raggh."*

He watched.

He waited.

He glanced, to while away the time, with passing interest at the hanging, glittering shooting medals on the ceiling.

* * *

"—Rosie!"

She was an Abandoned Angel, a Daughter of Damnation, a gilded, powdered, rouged, short-skirted Siren of Sin.

"Rosie—!"

She was drunk, or mad, or both.

"—Rosie!!"

Pushing off drunks and soul savers, in the center of the street, with tears running down her face, she stared vacant-eyed up at the roof of Bunker's Dime Museum next to Grammelspacher's, shouting the name as if it was a prayer, an orison, an entreaty, without ceasing.

The Despondent Man said politely, "Um . . . you do speak English, don't you?" They were standing there behind their desk looking at him with no expressions on their faces at all, merely staring at his boots and working their way up the oversize tattered coat to the beard and to the eye patch and then to the hat.

They looked at his brass ear trumpet and then, sadly, at his one good eye.

He didn't speak German. The Despondent Man, holding the glass phial of nitro up in front of his good eye to catch theirs, said, "Um . . ." The Despondent Man said, *"Cash up or die!"*

Luther looked at Ludwig.

The Despondent Man said, "I know you've got money! I've been checking this place out for a week! It's a gold mine! I know you've got the weekend's takings still on the premises! I know you don't go to the bank until Monday—" The Despondent Man said, "I'm a desperate individual! I'm liable to do anything!"

They whispered something to each other.

The Despondent Man said, "I can see you whispering!" He raised his eye patch quickly and fixed them with both his glittering eyes.

Luther, the big one, said softly to Ludwig the little one, "Ludwig . . ."

The Despondent Man said, *"I'm not deaf! I can hear what you say!"*

Ludwig, the little one, nodding, said softly to Luther, *"Ja . . . ja . . . die Ende . . ."*

He caught *"Ende."* It was the same word in English. The Despondent Man, nodding himself now—he could nod too—said, "Yes! That's right!—the *end!"* The Despondent Man said, "This is three ounces of nitroglycerine held six feet above a hard wooden floor by a desperate man!" He took a step forward on his bad leg and stamped it hard to get their attention, "Don't think you're dealing with an amateur here! I've done this three times before in the last month!" The Despondent Man said—

The little one, Ludwig, reached into an open drawer of the desk and brought something out. It was paper, it was money—it was an envelope. He looked for a moment at his cousin or brother or whatever the hell he was and held it out for him to touch it.

Luther sniffed. He put out his hand gently to touch the envelope and a large round tear rolled down his face and fell onto the desk. The Despondent Man said—

Ludwig said in a soft, lost, sad voice, *"Auf wiedersehen,* Luther, mein old friend . . ."

Luther made a burbling sound. He patted the thick white envelope gently on the flap.

The Despondent Man said, "Give me the money!"

Ludwig said in a whisper, "So close, Luther . . . so close, but the Fates . . ."

"Just give me the money!"

Luther nodded. He was in tears. They were giant's tears. They rolled down his face.

"The Fates, Luther, for little men like us, are not kind."

The Despondent Man said, trying to catch their attention for a moment, "The money . . . !" The Despondent Man, reaching out and taking the envelope where Ludwig put it gently on the desk, said, "Thank you." The Despondent Man said because he was not a cruel man, "Now you're going to live." It would be nice if they bothered to look at him occasionally. The Despondent Man, opening the unsealed envelope with the hand holding the ear trumpet, said soothingly, "It's not your money anyway! It's Grammelspacher Senior's!" The Despondent Man, pulling papers from the envelope, said in a sudden nitroglycerine-armed anger, "This isn't *money!* This is two first-class tickets on Friday's sailing of the German Lloyd Steamship Company's ship *Ariel* to Hamburg!"

"Auf wiedersehen, Luther!" From the drawer suddenly, holding one in each hand, Ludwig had two tiny bottles of greenish liquid. Each of the bottles had a small white rectangular label on it. The labels read in an identical hand in red, POISON. Below each word on each bottle there was a hand-drawn skull and crossbones. Each of the bottles was corked.

At attention, Ludwig pulled his cork with his teeth. He handed the second phial to Luther.

"Danke, Ludwig!"

"A toast, Luther."

Luther, his head stiff, his own cork pulled, his eyes raised a little to Heaven, said, *"Ja."*

The Despondent Man said—

Ludwig said, "To Headquarters City Detective Virgil J. Tillman of the New York Police!"

Ludwig said, stiffening his spine, *"Prosit!"*

Luther said, *"Prosit!"*

They both said together, *"Prosit!"*

In the pine-lined room, the gaslight throwing yellow light and shadows on all the medals and trophies, stiff with decorum and determination, simultaneously, they raised up their drams to drink, and die.

She wore no rings, nor earrings. She wore around her neck a tiny oval of black obsidian on a silver chain with the outline of a lily picked out on it in silver.

It was a rebus of her name—Lily.

> "Strawberries! Here's Strawberries!
> *Fine ripe Strawberries,*
> *And Hautboys so fine,*
> *Eat them with relish*
> *With sweet cream or wine!"*

"Rosie—!"

On the roof above Bunker's, above the gas lamps, all she could see was darkness.

> "MATCHES!
> *Fine matches! Good matches!*
> *Will you please have any,*
> *In pity do take some—*
> *Three bunches a penny."*

"Rosie—!!"

> "HOT CORN!
> *Here's smoking hot Corn,*
> *With salt that is nigh,*
> *Only two cents an ear—*
> *O pass me not by!"*

It was a rebus of her name—Lily.

Holding it, gripping it hard in her hand like a single, thin thread holding her on the edge of an abyss, suddenly grasping it hard in both hands, squeezing it, crushing it, her talcum face powder dark and running with tears, passing through the melee of humanity like a Dement, she ran, still screaming, for the wooden fire stairs at the south side of Bunker's, for the roof.

It was the worst disguise on Earth. It was so bad it was insulting.
And, before he died, Ludwig had just a few things he wanted to say.
And he spoke English all right; he spoke great English.
Ludwig, his face a mask of hatred, speaking wonderful English, said with his hands shaking, his eyes burning at the Despondent Man, "Tillman, I hate you. I hate you with a hate that knows no forgiveness. I hate you with a hate that is implacable, that is eternal, that ranks with the great hatreds of all time—I hate you with a hatred that is a burning coal fire deep in a pit that turns all the landscape around it primeval and barren and smoking with little brush fires. I hate you with a hate that puts the sun forever into shade, a hatred of eternal night and burning winds, a hatred that turns the seasons off, a hatred that makes the world itself into a desert, a rock, a swamp, a mire—a hatred that hates because it hates you, hates every living thing in the world, every tree or flower or blade of grass because it is a walking or crawling creature on the same planet as you or it is a tree or a blade of grass that lives as you do." He had the Despondent Man's eye and patch held in an unblinking stare, "I hate you more than any man in the history of the world has ever hated another." Ludwig said, "And Luther—Luther hates you too." He looked at Luther.
Luther's English wasn't that good. Luther, nodding, said, "*Ja.*" Luther said, "*Ja,* Herr Tillman, you have not been kind to us."
Ludwig said, "You have been the epitome of cruelty! You have been the Spanish Inquisition, you have been the rack, the burning oil, the thumb-screw, you have been the medieval torturer in the black mask and you have laughed while you did it! For four long weeks you have pierced us with daggers and flayed our flesh with whips and now, now desperate that your pathetic prisoners, your victims might escape into the light of life and freedom, now you stoop totally *sans honneur* to this!" He sneered. Ludwig said, "Well, now you have your victory—you have our tickets home . . . we can resist you no longer and, in a moment, you will have our lives—but you have not won! You have not triumphed—because you will never, never get that which you crave most, the pinnacle of your perfidy, the Matterhorn of your malevolence, the diamond of your duplicity—you will never get the fifty-five thousand two hundred and thirty-seven dollars we have stolen from our uncle Grammelspacher over the last three weeks because it has already been sent out of the country ahead of us to Europe!"

Luther said, nodding, "Ha. Ha."

Ludwig said, "The Courts would give you no search warrant for our homes and premises because you had no evidence, so you come in here like a sneak in that pathetic disguise to guile us into giving it to you for free!" Ludwig, shaking his head sadly, said, "Well, in a way that probably means something to a man as low as you, you have beaten us and we are too weary to go on . . ."

Luther said, still nodding, "We drink up the poison, Mr. Detective Tillman, and maybe at Headquarters they think you give it to us."

Ludwig said, "Even as much as we loathe our wives and children we would have made arrangements for them to be provided for by regular remittances from Switzerland."

Luther said, "You have spoiled that also." He raised up his phial to drink.

Ludwig said, "Tillman, you are a swine on every count!"

Luther said, "Lower than a swine!"

Ludwig said, "You are a boil, a carbuncle upon the face of humanity! You are a *wart!*"

Luther said, *"Schweinhund!"*

Ludwig said, "A scurvy! A scab! A stain! And, most of all, Mr. Headquarters City Detective Virgil J. Tillman—" His lip was curled in loathing.

Ludwig shrieked, "And most of all, by denying it as you are about to do—by denying it—you, Tillman, are a goddamned, low-down *liar!*"

From the third-story brick-parapeted roof of Bunker's, it was as if she looked down into a long, deep tank of gaslit yellow water swirling with life. From the darkness on the roof lit only by the moon, the Bowery was a golden track of light two and a half miles long running from Chatham Square at the Brooklyn Bridge to the junction of Fourteenth Street and Fourth Avenue where Governor Peter Stuyvesant of New Amsterdam once had his gubernatorial farm or *bouwerie.*

"Rosie . . . ?"

The roof was empty, silent, deserted. The sounds of the street came up muffled and she was alone.

There was a wind blowing through the black-skeleton framework of the elevated railway above the building. She touched at one of the bricks of the parapet encrusted with a layer of black soot and the brick, shuddered at fifty times a day as the trains thundered by, came out loose in her hand.

"Rosie . . . ?"

Across the street through the black girders of the railway she could see all the lights of the garrets and attics in the brothels and hotels of happiness. She could see her own room in the Lively Flea.

> ". . . 'The wind blows East,
> The wind blows West,
> The wind blows over the Cuckoo's Nest;
> Shall he go East?
> Shall he go West?
> Shall he go under the Cuckoo's Nest?
> Hon-pon-kuck-a-da-hook!
> Hon-pon-kuck-a-da-hook!' "

"Rosie . . . ?"

On the roof, alone, weeping, remembering her girlhood, she sang. On the roof, clasping her hands hard together in front of her, turning slowly in little circles looking, looking down hard at the soot-encrusted roof for a hon pon rectangle drawn on the old city streets when she had been a girl and played with her friends, she sang.

"*Rosie . . . ?*"

There was a little brick stile between Bunker's Museum roof and Grammelspacher's next door and, looking, clasping her hands, wanting to dance, humming to herself, she crossed over to it in the darkness.

The Despondent Man said, "*I'm the authentic Despondent Man!* I'm not someone called Tillman! I'm not a cop! I'm—"

Ludwig said, "The authentic Despondent Man, the original Despondent Man, is *deaf!* It was in all the newspapers when he robbed Oliffe's Pharmacy!"

"It's a *disguise!*"

"What is?"

"The ear trumpet! Being deaf!" The Despondent Man said, "If I was really deaf do you think I'd advertise it on a job? I'd disguise myself by pretending *not* to be deaf!"

He thought about it for a moment. Ludwig said coldly, "No, you are not the authentic Despondent Man, you are Tillman! Tillman is *not* deaf! Therefore, to disguise himself as either the not-deaf Despondent Man or even as the truly deaf Despondent Man, Tillman, as you have done, would disguise himself as deaf!"

Luther said, "*Ja.*" He looked at the ear trumpet. He thought he understood. Luther said, "Tillman is also not blind in one eye." He looked at the patch. "Are you blind in one eye?" Luther said slowly looking at

Ludwig, "Tillman is not blind in one eye, but if this man is blind in one eye then—" He asked directly, "Are you blind in one eye?"

"Of course I'm not blind in one eye! I only want people to think I'm blind in one eye!" He ripped off his patch to show them he wasn't blind in one eye. Tillman wasn't blind in one eye either. The Despondent Man said suddenly, "Look! Take back your tickets, and give me some money and I'll go!" The Despondent Man said desperately, "Look! Look!" He pulled off his beard with his free hand and held it up in the air with the nitro, *"Look! Am I Tillman?"*

Luther said in a growl of recognition, *"Tillman—!"*

Ludwig said, "How I hate that face . . ."

"How can you say I'm Tillman when I'm not Tillman?" The Despondent Man, not favoring one leg, said with one last effort at reason, "Does Tillman limp? I don't limp—look!" He jumped up and down, the nitro in his hand sloshing, "Well? Well? *Does he?"*

Ludwig said, "No. He does not."

"There! You see?"

Ludwig said, "Neither do you."

"It's a disguise!" The Despondent Man shouted, "Look! Look at this face—it's the real, undisguised face of the authentic Despondent Man!"

"Tillman, we have seen you for days following us."

"I've been following you to con the place!" The Despondent Man, starting to hop up and down, said with his hands crushing at the beard and the bomb, "That's what I do! I follow the owners around and I—" The Despondent Man said suddenly, *"Ahh!"* A number suddenly lit up in his brain. The number was fifty-five thousand two hundred and thirty-seven, with a dollar sign. The Despondent Man said in triumph, "Wrong! Wrong! Wrong!" He had it. It was all clear. "You think I'm Tillman because you've been embezzling money from your cousin—"

Ludwig said, "Uncle."

"Uncle. And because you've seen me following you, because I bear some passing resemblance to this fly-cop Tillman, because of that, your consciences—" He was happy. It was how all progress was made: by genius slicing surgically through the foliage of verbiage. "Your consciences have created an entire fantastical world of a determined police dog relentlessly hounding you through Eternity and you have—" The Despondent Man said, "But you are wrong and you can live! You can go home to Europe and the hearth fires of your heart's happiness because—"

Luther said with his eyes wide, "Because . . . ?"

"Because I am *not* Tillman!" The Despondent Man said, "Live! Put down your poison *and live!"*

Luther said in a whisper, "Ludwig . . . ?" Or was it too much to hope for?

"*Luther . . . ?*"

"Ludwig . . . ?" A tear formed.

Ludwig said in a gasp, "*Luther—?*"

The Despondent Man said, "It's true! It's all true!"

Ludwig said, "But the nitro, the disguise, the—"

"All I wanted was your payroll!"

Ludwig said, "But all our fears—"

"*Groundless!*"

"Our desperation—"

"*Precipitate!*"

"Our final self-destruction in the face of our enemy—our suicides to keep the good names of our families from scandal and—"

"*Unnecessary!*"

Luther said in sudden hope, "Ludwig! The mountains of home! The alpenhorns on the Alps in winter! The inns and bierkellers of Europe! The serving girls!"

Maybe, maybe there was just the faintest glimmer of hope. Faintly, he glimmered. Touching at his mouth with the hand that did not hold the poison, Ludwig said in a whisper, too good to be true, "Never to look upon the faces of my revolting wife and children again . . . never again to be crushed by nagging, never again to be driven witless by whining . . . Freedom—! —*Liberty!*"

The Despondent Man said happily, "All yours!"

Ludwig said, "We have perhaps two hundred and fifty dollars in coin in the safe—"

He handed back the tickets. He put back on his beard. He reset his eye-patch. He remembered to favor one leg. The Despondent Man said firmly, "Keep it." He, unlike Ludwig, did not glimmer. He glowed. The Despondent Man, shaking his head, said softly, "No, there will be other successes for me of the monetary kind, but a success of the heart, the touching of a fellow human creature in desperate plight—*two* human creatures in desperate plight—how often may a man achieve that sort of conquest?"

"God bless you, sir." His voice had gone hoarse. He was affected. Ludwig said blinking back the tears, "Luther! *Free!* And we owe it all to no one but our friend here—"

The Despondent Man said modestly, "The Authentic, Original Despondent Man, criminal genius, New York City, United States of America."

Luther said thickly, "Oh, thank you, Herr— Oh, thank you, thank you . . ."

Ludwig, his eyes soft with adoration said in a whisper, "But the dangerous life you lead, my friend, the path of peril . . . To walk the streets with nitroglycerine against your breast, not knowing whether at any moment, it might . . ."

He was happy beyond words. *"It's just oil and water!"* The Despondent Man, flailing his arms, replete with joy, surging with goodness, smashing the phial to shards on the ground at his feet, said in the final triumph, *"It's nothing but oil and water and it works every time!"* The Despondent Man, reaching out to take Ludwig's hand, said, "Edward George Evans, stable owner, 31 Charlton Street." The ceiling was full of honors and medals. His soul was full of joy. The Despondent Man said, thumping his chest with the ear trumpet, "This police dog, this wonderful policeman, this master of disguises and indomitable, celebrated Headquarters City Detective Virgil J. Tillman, just who, just who *is* this great Tillman?"

There was a silence.

Ludwig said softly, "I am." The oil and water mixture lay in pools harmlessly on the floor. "And you, Edward George Evans, are *under arrest!"*

He saw the Despondent Man's face. He saw him tense, and, leaping the desk and flying toward the turning man, dashing down his poison phial of placebo, reaching into his pockets for his badge and handcuffs, he ordered Luther—Plain Clothes Patrolman Edward Patrick Muldoon of the Strong Arm Squad—"Ned! Ned! Quick, club him before he gets to the stairs to the roof!"

"Hon-pon-kuck-a-da-hook . . .
Hon-pon-kuck-a-da-hook . . ."

On Grammelspacher's roof, by the doorway to the stairs, for all that once she had been, she was dancing.

"Rosie—!" She heard sounds, noises, voices. She heard, from downtown, the El train coming. She heard all the rails and girders shake. She heard in the darkness— She saw—

"Rosie—!" There were shadows at the door to the roof, one man, then another, a huge ox of a man catching at him and throwing him to the ground, and then there was the figure of a smaller, slighter man, and she—

There was the thundering and shaking of a train coming.

On the roof, Lily shrieked to them, to the shadows, to the lights, to everything that was lost, "Rosie's *dead!* Rosie's *dead!"*

In the doorway, pinned like a butterfly to the top step, the Despondent Man said, "Ow!"

"Rosie's dead and drowned—murdered! I saw her die and she's dead and—" The roof was shaking with the approaching train, all the bricks in the parapets and walls loose, raising dust and soot. "I saw her die! I saw her die and—" She was hunched at the parapet pumping her hands up and down. Everything, everything was gone: what once she was, what— Lily shrieked at all the lights of the attics and the garrets and all the lights of the street, "It's all gone! Everything I dreamed of— Everything! There's no redemption, no forgiveness—everything is a *lie!*" She was sobbing, pumping up and down, nodding, her wits flown, the sound of the approaching train like thunder on the rails and girders and crossbeams.

"Wait! Wait there!"

She touched the parapet with her hand. The train was raising soot and dust, swallowing her up. Lily said to someone, to something, "No, oh, no . . ." Lily said, starting to push at the bricks, "No redemption for whores, no forgiveness, no—" She shrieked. She shrieked above the approaching sound, "Rosie came back! Dead, she came back! There—" She was pointing with her finger across the abyss to the lit rooms of the brothels and bordellos on the other side of the street, "There! I saw her from there! She stood here with a lamp and beckoned me and I saw—"

He had the Despondent Man on his feet in cuffs. Muldoon, jerking the man to one side to see the rising soot and dust, yelled, "Virgil—?"

On the roof, moving toward her, Tillman, his hand out, yelled, *"Wait—!"*

Lily screamed, "I saw her *ghost!*"

She was dancing, humming, singing. She sang, lost in the thunder of the train, "Hon-pon-kuck-a-da-hook . . ." She smiled sadly at all the games she had played when she had been a little girl. She thought, smiling, for a moment of a spring day so long ago on a sidewalk with a hon pon square and a— She thought . . .

On the roof, running, everything around him shaking and reverberating with the train, Tillman, his hand outstretched to get her, yelled, "Wait! *Wait—!*"

In the earthquake of the train, she brushed against the bricks on the parapet above the street, only, it seemed, lightly, and she was gone over.

It was the 10:32 uptown, ablaze with lights.

On its elevated tracks, the train passed with a rain of falling bricks smashing to powder on the sidewalk.

2

Muldoon said, "It's those astro-psychic fortune-telling crones they all go to who send wretched girls like Lily into fairyland." He had his neck snugged down deep into the collars of his topcoat. Only his eyes showed. Plain Clothes Patrolman Ned Muldoon said, "That and reading sensational novels."

They were riding back from the Bellevue Hospital Morgue in the back of a horse-drawn Health Department ambulance on its way back to its Worth Street depot. In the open rear of the vehicle there was no room for his feet on the floor. And it was 7:15 A.M. with a wind blowing down Houston Street from the East River, and it was cold. Muldoon said, "It's all to do with the moon and lunacy, and—you know—women."

He glanced at Tillman. He didn't feel the cold. There wasn't enough meat on him. He was about five foot four, built like a whippet and he wasn't even wearing a coat over his buttoned suit. He was looking out at Houston Street, watching the morning traffic and the women in the tenement buildings stacking their families' bedding and linen out on cast-iron balconies and on ropes to air them. Muldoon said, irritated, "The way they put the bodies on marble slabs in that place and play water on them from the ceiling to keep them cool: it's a miserable sight to start anyone's day with." In the cab of the ambulance, separated from them by a waterproofed black canvas curtain, the ambulance driver was dozing, letting the horse find its way. Muldoon said, "It's a hard thing when all a dead human being has to leave behind her is a cheap locket with a lily on it."

City Detective Tillman said, looking out at the street, "There's Onions—" Standing in the doorway of a cheap lodging house next to Charlie Hester's House of Happiness Bar there was a bent-over wizened figure unfolding a large dark handkerchief and glancing furtively up and down the street. Still watching, he unlocked a clasp knife, took an onion from his pocket and, slicing it in two, set both halves into the material and folded it up. It was the beginning of his workday: he put the kerchief to his eyes and nose, drew in a deep breath, produced a howl of terrible human agony and, ready for a day's begging, broken, weeping unconsolable soul that he was, went off shuffling with a terrible shuffle in the direction of Mulberry Street.

Muldoon said, "Are you listening to me, Virgil?"

"Yes."

In the street, all the doors of the shops and warehouses were opening. There were handcarts and wagons starting to appear from stable doors and lanes, smoke from fires and small steam engines from the sweat shops smudging smoke and hissing. From around corners and alleys there were men coming pushing barrels or carrying boxes or crates. There were women in shawls, children. There were people lighting fires in the street to set up their food stalls. There were sounds, noises, the commotion of the day beginning. Tillman said, "Look! Murky Adams!" He was up from a manhole cover in a miasma of effluvia looking around the street like a sharpshooter in a rifle pit looking for someone's business to ruin by blocking their sewer, or, for a small consideration, unblocking the sewer of someone's business he had already ruined during the night. Tillman said, his eyes flickering from one end of the street to the other, "Look! Adenoid Annie, Ten Thousand Rabbits Robinson and, look there, the Roaring Gimlet, the only human alive who can sing in three keys at once!" She was coming out of a basement under Parson's Potables pinning her black straw hat to her hair with a seven-inch hatpin, on her way to the stores of the Ladies Mile uptown to see what the storeowners might pay her for a performance or lack of one. Tillman said, "And there, Lucifer Johnson!" Tillman sang softly,

> *"Grandpa had a candy store,*
> *It was not doing well,*
> *Johnson put a match to it,*
> *The Insurance cannot tell—"*

Muldoon said firmly, "Virgil, it's not your fault the damned parapet on Grammelspacher's roof gave way!"

He would not look at him.

Muldoon said, "And all this business about someone called Rosie being murdered—"

"Stop!" On his bench, leaning suddenly forward and grasping the dozing driver by the shoulder, Tillman said in a whisper, "Stop!" He was looking out at something, at a horse-drawn wagon carrying four-gallon glass carboys of kerosene plodding its way past what looked like a little family group of human cockroaches, father, mother, three small children and a baby. Tillman said with his eyes suddenly bright, "Look! *Look!*"

It was the morning. It was light. It was a new day.

Tillman, shaking at the driver, trembling, pointing, renewed, *alive,* said, "Ned! Look! Look— *It's the Horrible Houlihans!*"

Horrible Houlihan shrieked, *"Aarghh—!"*

Fallen down near death on the roadway in front of the kerosene wagon Horrible Houlihan yelled, "Oh, Jaisus, Mary and all the Saints in Heaven, *it's taken a chunk out of me aarum the size of a number-ten shoe!"* He was some sort of revolting, pinched-face creature who smelled like he never took his collar or boots off. On the ground, grasping his arm, staring up at the horse, Horrible Houlihan shrieked, "I just went by on me decent and lawful occasion crossing the street with me family and yer nag bit me on the arm!" There were six of them in the Houlihan hearth: Horrible Houlihan himself, his wife the Horrible Houlihan harridan, Horrible Harry Houlihan aged twelve, Horrible Henry, ten, Horrible Henrietta aged eight with a face like a snake and the baby in the Horrible Houlihan harridan's hands, Fred. Horrible Houlihan, convulsing like a swatted fly, squeezing at his arm through the filthiest coat on Earth, shrieked, "Look! *Blood!*"

The hand-painted sign on the wagon read, *Poditz, Carrier.* He was a thickset man wearing a full-length carrier's apron and a derby hat. Poditz, not speaking a word of English, said to his daughter on the seat next to him, *"Vos—?"*

She was twelve years old, his *mizinikil*—his youngest child. "The *mizinikil,* starting to get down from the seat, said in English, "What's—"

There was a commotion, a scream. Houlihan yelled, "More blood!" Horrible Houlihan shrieked, "Holy Mother, it's bitten me poor Henry!" They were milling around the horse. Someone hit the horse. Houlihan shrieked, "And Harry! It's bitten Harry too!"

"What's—" She was getting down from the seat. Her father held her. Her father, his eyes wide, shaking his head, said in Yiddish, *"Vos rep ir epes?"*

The *mizinikil* said in alarm, "What are you talking about?"

"I'm talking about me poor family!" He was up on his feet, but staggering, drawing his little children about him, his eyes wide at the sight of his own blood dripping down his wrist. Houlihan shrieked, *"Yer horse has bitten all me children for no good reason!"* Horrible Houlihan, wrenching at Harry and almost ripping the sleeve of the unidentifiable garment off his arm to expose the teeth marks, said in horror, "Look! Look!" His eyes went absent. He almost swooned. For the sake of his little

ones, he pulled himself together. Houlihan said, "We're all going to die—"

On the seat Poditz said, *"Vos—"*

The *mizinikil* said in Yiddish, "Serge has bitten him and his children!"

Poditz said, *"Zol Got mir halfen*—Oh, God help me . . ."

Horrible Houlihan said in a howl, "Oh Christ, it just had a go at baby Fred!"

Poditz said, *"S'teitsh?"*

His *mizinikil* translated, "How is this possible?"

Horrible Harry, looking at the teeth marks and the blood on his arm, said, "Aaarrgghh—*me hopes for a career playing the violin to get me good family out of poverty are ruined!"*

Henry said, also dripping blood, "Am I going to go to Heaven with the angels, Father?"

The Horrible Houlihan harridan, Daddy too busy writhing and starting to froth at the mouth to speak, said to her dear one, "Yes, Henry, yer little life on Earth is over."

Poditz said, *"Oi gevalt! S'iz oys! Zol got mir halfen!"*

The *mizinikil* said in English, protesting, "Serge wouldn't—"

"Serge? Is that the name you give this wicked animal?" Horrible Houlihan, drawing back his fist to kill the offending beast and then withdrawing it because his heart was too kind and full of sorrow of his dying children, demanded, "What sort of horse is this? *Is this the horse the English used to ride across the heart of Ireland? Is this the horse—"*

The *mizinikil* said, "It's a good horse! It's a gentle horse!"

Her father said with his head in his hands, *"S'iz oys*—it's over; it's gone." Her father, shaking his head, starting to thump his breast said weeping, *"Groisser fardiner.* Big breadwinner! *Groisser k'nacker!* Big shot!" Everything he had hoped for in America was gone, *"Ver volt dos geglaibt . . ."*

"Yer horse must be destroyed on the spot!"

The *mizinikil* said, "No! He's a good horse! *Wu tut air vai?"* She was speaking Yiddish. She had forgotten her English. The *mizinikil,* trying to get down, but held by her father, said, "Where does it hurt you?"

"Me arm and the bodies of me babies are gnashed to pieces by a nag with choppers the size of Lucifer's trident and you ask me where it hurts?" Harry had fainted. He lay crumpled out on the roadway with his mother looking skyward to Jesus kneeling beside him in desperate prayer. Henry was starting to sway. The baby, Fred, decided to start screaming. Houlihan, with the last of his strength before he too shuffled off the mortal coil, said, "Only expensive medical treatment can hope to save us! Only—" A voice beside him said, "My God, *Equinetridiomonocyanosis!"*

and Houlihan, looking up and seeing a small man in a suit with his face covered by an infectious disease mask, said, "What? Who the hell are *you?*"

He was the surgeon from the ambulance parked across the street. He was— The masked man said in a gasp, "Special Surgeon Sims of the Pittsburgh Plague of '78 fame." He was at the horse in an instant, prying open its mouth, peering at its teeth, "My God, equinetridiomonocyanosis! And advanced!" Sims said with his eyes darting to Houlihan and the bodies on the roadway, "My God, man, if this reaches contagious level there won't be a carriage horse or a cavalry mount left in the country!"

Houlihan said mildly, "It bit me on the arm."

"Instant destruction!"

She translated it for her father. Her father, weeping, said, "Oi . . . oh . . ."

"Now, hold on a minute—"

"Instant destruction!"

Houlihan, recovering fast, said reasonably, "Now, it's not as if—"

"Instant—*destruction!*" The eyes above the gauze mask glittered. They were hard. They were unyielding. They were the Eyes of Surgeon Sims. *"Police! Health Department!"* Surgeon Sims, summoning up as if from nowhere a huge ox of a man from behind the ambulance, called out, "You, sir! You, there! Are you a policeman, sir?"

Muldoon said, "I am!"

The *mizinikil* said in tears herself, "Oh, please don't—"

"Mr. Policeman, it's the terrible disease of Equinetridiomonocyanosis!"

Muldoon said in horror, "It isn't!"

"And advanced at that! The germs and infection have probably already taken hold and are this very moment coursing through the bloodstream and—"

Muldoon said, *"Instant destruction!"*

Sims said, "Right!" He patted the horse. He covered his eyes with his hands. Sims said, "Quick—that entire family there—destroy them!"

Muldoon said, "Right!" He looked at Horrible Houlihan.

Muldoon said, "My pleasure entirely."

He reached inside the pocket of his coat for his gun.

"You're going to shoot an entire household of Christians dead on the street and let the horse live?"

Surgeon Sims said, "Of course. Horses are valuable beyond gold. Did you know that the entire equine population of the world stems from but a single pair of hardy mountain ponies caught and domesticated millennia ago on the Russian Steppes? Did you know that in all our great nation, before the Spanish came with but a single breeding mare, the previous lords of the land, the Indians, had to walk everywhere they wanted to go? Did you know that in—"

The *mizinikil* said with tears in her eyes, "He's a good horse, a docile horse!" She translated into Yiddish for her father.

Surgeon Sims said, "He is. I can tell. That is why we must halt the infection he has received before he carries the contagion to all the good horses all over this country." He patted the horse. He almost touched Horrible Houlihan and then changed his mind. "This man is a walking extinction for all the horses of the world—look, see the lividity and blotches already on his arm from the disease!"

Horrible Houlihan said, "That's not lividity or blotches—that's dirt!"

Sims said to the girl, "Fear not for the life of good Serge. We will save him. No expense will be spared." He said to Muldoon, "You haven't shot them yet."

"Fred is yet only a babe in arms!" It was the Houlihan harridan.

"He is." Sims, the soul of compassion, said, "Which is why we will not let him live on as a poor unwanted orphan, be assured." Sims said with a trace of irritation in his voice, "This horse must be quickly taken to a horse hospital, but I cannot do it until these people are shot." He ordered Muldoon, "So shoot them."

"Henry wasn't bitten by the horse!"

Sims said, "Alas, madam, the blood on his filthy arm shows he was."

Horrible Houlihan said reasonably, "Now, now, now, now—now, look, a few carboys of that kerosene will see our suit settled nicely, and—"

Sims said, "You have no suit. The policeman here is going to shoot you."

"Me husband wasn't bitten by the horse!"

"Ah, Madam—"

"Harry wasn't bitten by the horse! No one was bitten by the horse!"

The *mizinikil,* translating instantaneously as her father suddenly stood up on his seat to speak, said in a desperate voice, "Don't shoot the poor people! Shoot if you must poor Serge, but let the people live!"

The Houlihan harridan said, "Listen to the good man now!"

Poditz said, *"Mizinikil?"* He asked in Yiddish, "And you?"

The *mizinikil* said with tears glistening in her eyes, "Yes. Shoot poor Serge."

Sims said with a sigh, "Ah, the innate kindness of the true horse lover. It shines through the avarice and venality of common humanity like a beacon—"

Poditz shouted in Yiddish, "Cossacks! Murderers!"

The Houlihan harridan shrieked, *"Houlihan, tell them the truth!"*

Houlihan said, "One carboy of kerosene then—"

Surgeon Sims said to Muldoon, "Shoot him."

The *mizinikil* cried, *"Serge! Shoot Serge instead!"*

"Half a carboy . . . a few drops for me lamps—"

Henry said, *"Da—!"*

The Houlihan harridan said, "Houlihan, I'll make your life—"

Muldoon said. "Houlihan, prepare to meet your God."

Sims, patting the horse, said, "Good horse—"

"A single *drop* of kerosene just to save face with me—"

"Not a—"

Houlihan said, "Sure, sure, sure . . ." He looked at the *mizinikil* and her father. Houlihan said with a smile like a graveyard of broken tombstones, "God in Heaven, what a fine man and his girl they are to sacrifice their livelihood to save a little family from a different race, a different—" Houlihan said, "Sure, it makes a man want to do no less. Sure, it—" Houlihan, avoiding his wife's eyes that could slice a man in half like scalpels, said in an abundance of Christian love, "Sure, it makes me glad that I can reciprocate and—"

Sims said to Muldoon, "Shoot him!"

"—and tell you, dear child and your good father, that your horse has no disease at all!" Houlihan said, "For—"

Sims said to Muldoon, "Shoot him now!"

"—for, the truth is"—maybe there was one last possibility—Houlihan said, "A thimbleful of kero . . . ?" He saw his wife's face. He saw Muldoon's hand go deep into his pocket. "For the truth is that *it was I and not the horse who bit all me family and meself!"* Houlihan, pulling out from his filthy coat something made of bone and metal and wood that looked like a bear trap said, "You see, you have here not a murderer of horses—I'm an Irishman and like all me race I truly love horses—but just a common criminal with a homemade set of horse dentures loaded with a spring who bites himself and his family on the arm with it and then threatens a suit if the horse owner doesn't come up with a little pacifier!" Houlihan, happy, said, "I am no carrier of contagion, *merely a criminal!"* Houlihan said in relief, his career choice vindicated, "Ha, ha, ha, ha—I'm just a *crook!"*

He had almost made a terrible mistake. Surgeon Sims, his hand flying to his gauze mask, said aghast, *"Good God!"*

"We crooks, we Irish crooks, would never hurt *a horse!"*

He was overcome. Sims said in a whisper to Muldoon, "Oh." Sims said, "Almost a terrible mistake."

Houlihan, hopping up and down in happiness, said, "Ha, ha, ha, ha, ha!"

The *mizinikil* said, "No one is going to be shot?"

Houlihan said, "And Serge will live to serve you for many a year yet!"

Poditz, listening to the *mizinikil*'s translation hard, said, *"Danken Got!"*
Thank God! *"Got tsu danken!"*

Muldoon said in disappointment, "I don't get to shoot them?"

Surgeon Sims said softly, "No." He removed the gauze mask.

Houlihan said in horror, *"Tillman!"*

He was a horrible, pinched-faced cockroach of a man, with his cockroach family, and he smelled like summer garbage.

Tillman said softly, smiling, "Houlihan." He nodded.

As Poditz whispered questions in rapid Yiddish to the *mizinikil* and shook his head in wonder, on the street full of life and activity and the sounds and sights of morning, he patted the revolting creature over and over on the back like an old friend, full suddenly, full—blessedly, again—of joy.

3

For each of the last three years the immigrant ships had disgorged a thousand people a day onto the end of Manhattan Island at Castle Garden. This year, 1884, they were unloading and the New York Immigration officers were processing over three thousand a day.

They were from Bohemia, Italy, Poland, Russia, Ireland, Denmark, Germany, England, Greece, Portugal, Spain. The wealthy ones—the ones with the fare—went onto trains that took them to the West. The poor, the people with nothing, went homeless, penniless, jobless into the city because they were within walking distance, to the Lower East Side and below Canal Street near the Tombs Prison, where already the population density was five hundred and twenty-two people per acre. They went into the tenements, and, if they were lucky, to the sweatshops for work.

On the Bowery, at 9 A.M., it seemed that all of them—everyone who had come in rags for the last three years—were milling in the street, walking, shouting, dragging handcarts, babbling and bargaining in their own language, filling the sidewalks and spilling out onto the road, but it was not all of them. Merely some of them.

The others—all of them—moving, spread out, were in all the other streets, in the lanes, in the alleys and the tenements and factories in all of the island's twenty-five thousand acres, like ants, *everywhere*.

But not in the Lively Flea. Slamming the engraved glass and carved mahogany double doors to the great reception room at the top of the flight of marble steps to the place, she shut them out.

She was the most famous madam in New York: the original Santa Fe Sal who had kept a brothel by the Santa Fe railhead where visiting engineers and signalmen had left their red lights to show where they were and coined the term *Red Light District*. She was at least in her late fifties or early sixties. Dressed in a puffed-sleeve green full-length silk gown, standing straight as a ramrod, her black hair in a bun, she looked like the Queen of

Troy. She wore no jewelry, only a thin black ribbon around her neck above the high-cut collar of the gown, and a silver chatelaine of keys at her waist. She had eyes like black onyx. Santa Fe Sal said, "No vulgarity or non-English speakers allowed in this establishment whatsoever." All the doors on the first floor and the second facing the triumphant cedar and mahogany staircase were open for airing or cleaning. Santa Fe Sal said, "Every conceivable pleasure on Earth available for the asking!"

Muldoon said in a whisper, *"God . . . !"*

Everywhere there was gilt and gold and damask and silk, and cut glass and crystal and marble statues and a Persian carpet so thick his boots sank into it. There were people in aprons cleaning, polishing, sweeping, dusting; there was a Negro boy in full livery at a barrel of apples—kept for the horses of gentlemen customers—polishing each apple from the barrel with a silk cloth. There was the sound of waterfalls, train wheels clicking on rails, there was a full string orchestra playing somewhere out in back, there was the smell of incense in the air. There were great hanging chandeliers tinkling a teardrop at a time as young girls in aprons dusted at them with extended feather dusters, there was the sound, somewhere, of chains and apparatus, of leather being stretched and groaning, of something whooshing that sounded like a brazier full of red-hot coals.

Santa Fe Sal said, "We offer our Nymphs and Shepherds scene complete with real flowers and grass and aromatic scented soil, well-mannered life-sized mechanical deer and soothing waterfalls. We offer our Turkish harem with incense and silk tent and desert breezes, our private train car with sounds of real travel and choice of destinations, octoroon ladies from New Orleans for our slave scene, a tastefully appointed dungeon with the complete contents of an original medieval torture chamber from a castle in Europe, a room of home and hearth with obedient wife and maid and complete selection of discipline, beating and chastisement devices, a Red Indian encampment of squaws in rawhide dress who long for their long-gone braves, various other moveable scenes that may be varied to personal taste and, for long-term, favored customers of good standing, a complete system of credit ticket accounting and a choice of letterheads for the discreet mailing out of accounts at the end of each month." In the converted ballroom off the reception room of the four-story, seventeen-room mansion, there were rows of girls in skirts and blouses and sleeve protectors tapping at brand-new-on-the-market Remington Gun Company typewriters a key at a time. Santa Fe said, "Every room or scene fitted with an untamperable time clock for time in and time out. All credit tickets coded merely with numbers and abbreviations for complete privacy." She nodded in at the girls. "All computations and accounts done by the girls themselves who have consulted with the clients whose cards they calculate, the master mailing list known only to me."

Tillman asked, "Your girls can all read?"

"They can." She looked at Muldoon and summed him up. "No sensational novels allowed." She threw him a bone, "Full facilities for up to thirteen private carriages in the stables with complete blacksmithing service, plus fifteen supervised hitch post places on the street, at no cost." Santa Fe Sal said, "For all-night gentlemen a complete clothes pressing and bootblacking service, and—if required—assisted, scented bathing facilities." She stood almost six feet tall. She had a spine as straight as a ramrod. She looked at the two policemen with her glittering black eyes. "And a complete, paid-for guarantee of continuing tranquility for both our staff and clientele that ranges from two dollars a night left out on the top stair of the stoop for the passing policeman on the beat to special disbursements of roughly one hundred times that paid into private accounts each week to other persons." She looked meaningfully at Tillman, "Including, once a year, special dividends paid to—"

Tillman said, "Miss—"

Santa Fe Sal said, " 'Madam.' I am referred to by clients and visitors as madam. Only staff and personal associates may call me miss." Her life meant something. Santa Fe Sal said, "When I die, the girls and my many friends will have me interred in a marble mausoleum in the tranquil Twenty-third Street cemetery uptown. They have set up a fund which they have been voluntarily contributing to for many years." She nodded to herself. "The tomb is in the finest Florentine stone incised with cherubs and angels and the motto 'A Good Friend to All' incised above the door, and it will feature a small white gaslight on either side of the portico that will burn gently but eternally." Her eyes did not seem to have any pupils. "The funeral cortege making its way there at measured pace will be of thirty-one great eight-person carriages drawn by matched white horses with black cockades. I will be buried on the first fine day after my demise to the sounds of an orchestra, and the motto above the mausoleum bed on which I shall slumber through eternity will say, in complement with the legend above the portico, 'Ever Kind.' " She glanced up in the direction of the nymphs and shepherds room with waterfall. "A small fountain shall bubble peacefully outside, and there will be always bouquets and beds of tended flowers."

Tillman said quietly, "About Miss Lily—?"

Santa Fe Sal said, "Just Lily." She had a pocket in the gown behind the silver chatelaine. She reached in and took out a brown card with numbers and letters stamped and typewritten on it. "Lily Seymore, aged 32, born Brooklyn, live-in labor, attic room number three. General services. No specialty." She looked down at the card, "Her log tells me she has not worked often in the last week due to illness."

He knew about women. Muldoon, nodding, said sagely, "Ah, feminine problems . . ."

Santa Fe Sal said, "Gin."

Muldoon said, "Oh."

Santa Fe Sal said, "I have collected her possessions and left them in her room." Santa Fe Sal said, "I have the key. I will accompany you. Everything she had is there, less various items of clothing and three towels, which were tools of the trade and therefore revert to the employer upon cessation of service." In Santa Fe, there were no bubbling fountains and quiet gardens of eternity on Twenty-third Street. There, in the old days, they buried whores out in the hard ground on the edge of town with no marker. Santa Fe Sal said, "She was a nice girl, a pleasant girl, popular with a certain class of customer of limited imagination who only wanted a little relief from the daily round of toil and the responsibilities of his family."

Tillman said quietly, "Did she contribute to your funeral fund?"

"She did. Only a little, but then she had not been with us a long time."

"And her friend Rosie, what about her?"

"Light me." From nowhere, she had a small black cheroot in her hand. Santa Fe Sal, faintly smiling as Muldoon hurried to light it for her with a lucifer, said with a shrug, "My only vice."

She drew in the smoke and, for a moment, her eyes closed in pleasure, savored it. Santa Fe Sal said thoughtfully, "Rosie?"

"Yes."

She thought about it for a moment. It was a little after 9 A.M. and she smelled, set off by the acrid smell of the cigar, of eau de cologne. She thought through the sounds of the waterfall, the chains, the soft sounds of the orchestra somewhere, the whisking of the feather dusting and the steady slapping of the Negro boy polishing at the apples for the horses. She thought, more and more as she grew older, of eternal rest and a life crowned by marble and beds and bouquets of ever-tended flowers.

Santa Fe Sal, drawing in on the cigar, touching at her chatelaine of keys to find the right one, shaking her head, thinking of other things, said firmly, "No. The name means nothing to me at all."

She asked, "Why? Did she claim to know me?"

It was a tiny twelve-by-ten low-ceilinged room at the front of the house on the fourth floor with a corridor leading away from it toward other rooms at the rear, containing only a stripped iron bed, a washstand, a plain chamber pot under the bed, a high-backed chair for gentlemen's clothes by the tiny window facing the street. There was faded flowered wallpaper on the walls, and a single gas lamp set high above the bed with a brass chain to raise or lower the illumination, and no apparent way to turn it on or off. There were two cupboard recesses set into the side walls, both with matching flowered curtains, both open, both bare.

There was no room for three people in the room, and Muldoon waited outside and read the inspirational signs set along the walls of the corridor. The signs, all hand-painted or needleworked, hung in gilt frames, read, DECIDE, THEN PERSERVERE; IF AT FIRST YOU DON'T SUCCEED, TRY, TRY AGAIN; NOT TOO MUCH CAUTION, SLOW BUT SURE IS THE THING; and, done in curlicues of colored thread, STOUT HEART, MY SON, AND ALL YOUR BATTLES WILL BE WON . . . They were in even arrangements of four: four where the wall of Lily's room was, four farther down where there was another door to another room, then four more.

He craned. He read one with a border of palm trees and some sort of desert flowers that read, BE BOLD. BE RESOLUTE. STEP BY STEP WE MOUNT THE PYRAMID, and then part of another decorated with daisies that said something about acorns and oaks, and another that read— He said softly, "Holy Mother of . . ."

In the corridor, stepping back, he touched at the wall and moved the sign that read about Deciding. It was hinged. It swung out to uncover a time clock and a switch. He counted the slots in the time clock for cards. He counted, all along the corridor where the rooms were, the hanging signs.

Muldoon said in a whisper, "God in Heaven—"

He touched at a button on the clock and, simultaneously, making no sound at all, all along the corridor, all the signs slid down, and revealed, all along the corridor, four for each of the rooms, peepholes in the walls for watchers.

In the corridor, Muldoon said in a gasp, *"Jesus, Joseph and Mary—!"*

Outside that room, Muldoon touched at the switch on the time clock and, with no sound at all, together, all the signs slid back into place.

All there was, all she had had, was in a single frayed carpetbag set in the center of the mattress of the stripped bed.

At the open bag, Tillman, taking the items inside out one by one, asked, "Is this everything?"

She was at the tiny window looking out across under the El to the roof of Bunker's Dime Museum and Grammelspacher's Shooting Gallery. From the street, in a babble of tongues, she could hear the dangerous classes in the streets. Santa Fe Sal, turning with a fleeting look of anxiety on her face, said, "Yes." She saw Muldoon at the doorway and could not read his expression. She nodded in the direction of the open cupboard recess. "The items and tools of the trade that were supplied by this establishment as part of her situation and duties have been removed for cleaning and resupply." She could not make out the look on the big one's face in the doorway. "Specialty clothing, shoes, stockings, parasols, unmentionables, and various other effects."

At the open bag, carefully taking out a cheap folded linen dress and matching coat and placing them neatly to one side on the bed, Tillman asked, "Where are her toiletries?"

"They were part of her situation. Rouge, powder—supplied."

"Her hairbrush and mirror?"

Santa Fe Sal said, "Supplied."

"Hair clips? Jewelry?"

"Supplied."

All there was in the bag was the cheap suit of clothing, two pairs of cotton stockings, one of them darned at the heels, a small sewing kit, two plain cotton blouses and two pairs of gloves, both cream, neither quite matching the color of the linen suit. Tillman said, "Where are her shoes?"

"Shoes wear out. They are replaced."

"She was wearing opera slippers when she died." Shoes had to be earned or paid for. Tillman asked, "Where are her private pictures and mementos? Things she had on the wall?"

"There are uplifting portraits all through the house." She looked at Muldoon. He was a little inside the doorway reaching out with a huge hand to the edge of the open door and touching at the doorknob. Santa Fe Sal said, "Her empty gin bottle, for the sake of her reputation, has been disposed of."

Tillman said, "And the glass she drank from?"

"Breakables are not permitted in the private rooms."

"She had no personal decorations? No earrings? No—"

"She had a locket."

"She was wearing it when she died." He ran his hand along the bottom of the bag. "Where are her papers, her documents? Her birth certificate?"

"She was an orphan. Her family died in a house fire. All her papers, I assume, were destroyed."

"Who are her friends?"

"The girls here are not encouraged to form—"

"What are they encouraged to do?"

"They are encouraged to *work!*"

"To work?"

"Yes!"

"Hard?"

"Yes!"

"Without stinting?"

"Certainly!"

"I see." There was nothing in the bag. In the hall, Muldoon, swinging the door a little on its hinges by the knob, had a strange, bewildered expression on his face. He was thinking something through. He thought it through and the expression changed. Tillman said, "What she did in this place, with no respite, with no extravagance—with utter frugality—was *work*. Am I correct?"

Santa Fe Sal said, "You are."

He took his hand out of the bag. It was all there was. It was everything. He held her eyes. He knew what the look on Muldoon's face was for.

Tillman said suddenly, hard, holding her eyes, "Then tell me, where the hell is her goddamned *money?"*

Muldoon said in a fury, "There's no lock on this door! Did the poor creature who lived here have no privacy *at all?"*

Tillman demanded, "Who owns this place?"

"Important people!"

"What important people?"

"Important men! Men with importance! Men with gold watch chains and uptown houses and—"

Tillman said tightly, "Where are her friends? Her mourners? Where are her—"

"It is not the policy of this establishment to—"

"Where did she *bathe?"*

"She bathed in the communal wash house in the basement!"

Muldoon said with his voice shaking, "And is there a peephole there too, me darlin'?"

"It is not what I or the staff wants, it is—" She was at the window. "It is—" Outside, she could hear the babble of voices, of shouts of the streets, "All the girls here—"

"Who was her friend Rosie?"

"It is not the policy of the house to allow our girls to associate with the lower classes! The clientele of this house is a select one, composed of men of worth and quality seeking relief from life's daily toil in the brief dalliance with a female of obliging nature and—" She could hear the voices on the street, every day, louder and louder. Santa Fe Sal said, "When a whore died in Santa Fe they took her body and disposed of it out in the wilderness in an unmarked grave so the decent people of the town—"

"Where is her money? Her wages?"

"There are expenses that must be met!"

"There is not even a one-cent coin in her bag!"

"Her situation was a good one! She was an orphan! She had no one. Everything here is all-found. It is a life of—"

"It is not a life at all! She is dead!"

Muldoon said softly, "You vile hag, you took all her wages . . ."

"In life, she wanted me to—"

Muldoon said, "You took it for your goddamned funeral!"

"She wanted me to!"

Tillman said evenly, "Who is Rosie?"

"Our girls do not associate with common street harlots! It is not permitted! The men who own this place do not permit it! Our clientele is select and our girls exclusive!" Santa Fe Sal said suddenly, "I will not die like an old cur-dog in the street! Whores die like that! I will not die like that! I will have my place next to respectable people! I will have my flowers and my monument! I will have my inscriptions!" She was an old woman. Under the face powder, she was lined and old and she no longer stood straight and upright, and at night, when she was alone, she had begun to ache. Santa Fe Sal said, "I have worked hard all my life, giving pleasure to strangers, ministering to them, soothing them, listening to them and I will not die cold and alone! I will not be disposed of in an unmarked hole in the ground like a pauper with no coffin, for the animals to disinter!"

Tillman said quietly, "Lily will be thrown into a hole in the ground like a pauper."

"She was young! She had nobody." She was an old, old woman who felt, more and more each day, the ice moving in her veins. Santa Fe Sal said, "My girls spend their lives in luxurious surroundings supplied by me, provided by me, freely given by me, and, in return, my girls will see me sent off properly, with carriages and flowers and the singing of hymns!" Santa Fe Sal said, "No man ever came to a whore's funeral! My girls must see to it that I am rewarded and recognized for what I did for them!" Every day, she heard the people in the streets fighting for their place in the New World. Every day, she could hear them getting louder, closer.

Tillman said quietly, "If you tell me who Rosie is, I will give you a dollar."

Muldoon said in horror, *"Virgil—!"*

Outside, she could hear them swarming, like ants. Santa Fe Sal said, "Two! Two dollars!"

"A dollar fifty."

"One dollar seventy-five."

"A dollar sixty and that's my final offer!"

"One dollar and—"

Muldoon said, aghast, "For the love of Jesus!" He had his club at his belt. His hand went in under his coat for it. Muldoon said, advancing, "You vile, unchristian spider of a woman—!"

"Done! One dollar sixty—and no paper money—in coin!" Santa Fe Sal, reaching out for it as Tillman put his hand into the pocket of his vest, said, "Done! Done!" She had only one life. In all her years, she had never met anyone who had had two. "Done!" She offered to a select clientele exclusive services. She ran a whorehouse.

Santa Fe Sal, reaching out for the money, said in an old woman's voice, "Thank you. God bless you." She had the money. She closed her hand around it.

Santa Fe Sal, turning to Muldoon, halting him, making it clear, explaining it to him, said, shaking her head, "She was no good anyway, Lily. She was not a good girl—"

Santa Fe Sal said to teach him about living long, getting old, "Up here, alone, after hours, *she drank gin from a bottle!*"

4

On the sidewalk outside Belligerent Smith's (Late of Pugilistic and Fistic Renown) Bowery Physiognomic Restoration Rialto and Emporium of the Tonsorial Arts (Twenty Chairs, No Waiting), Belligerent Smith shouted at the top of his lungs, "I don't give a Continental about Mr. Alexander Graham Bell or the Electric Speaking Telephone, or the New York Telephone and Telegraph Company, or progress, or what you say, Billy Jenkins! What *I* say is that the first man who gets up onto my roof with that infernal wire comes down half a head shorter!"

In the roadway, his kerosene wagon stopped by the lines of cables and wires, the reels and wagons, Poditz said urgently to his *mizinikil* in Yiddish, "What's happening?" There were men in white coats in the street and on the sidewalk holding porcelain knobs like surgeons and glancing up at the sky at the tops of buildings. There was wire everywhere. There were ladders on the wagons. In the hand of the huge, bow-tied coatless giant of a man outside the barber's establishment, there was an axe. And there was the Law. The Law was a six-foot-high clean-shaven man with no pockmarks on his face, in full uniform, wiping at the inside of his helmet with a white-gloved hand. And, on the other sidewalk, outside a house that looked like a mansion, a lady dropped her parasol on the sidewalk and nobody passing by—no man—stopped to offer to pick it up for her.

On his wagon Poditz asked his daughter in Yiddish, *"Voz iz di untershteh shureh?*—What's it all about?" He glanced at the lady on the sidewalk. Her skirts were short, but it was America, and perhaps she was respectable. Poditz asked his daughter, "What's happening?" There was what looked like a string running from the ebony handle of the folded parasol to the leather purse the lady carried in her left hand. Poditz said, "What's the wire for?"

"Telephones." She had read about them.

The big man at the front of the establishment had his hair parted in the middle and slicked down on his head. In the pocket of his striped shirt he carried what looked like steel instruments. Poditz asked, "Is he a surgeon?"

Jenkins, putting his helmet back on his head, said reasonably, "Now, look here, Smith—"

Belligerent Smith said, "Mr. Smith to you, Patrolman Jenkins! Mr. bloody free haircuts and shaves and rosewater Smith to you, *copper!*"

The *mizinikil* said in a whisper to her father in Yiddish, "He's a barber." Her father nodded.

The *mizinikil* said, "They're two different professions here in America."

Her father asked, "What's a 'Telephone'?"

The Law took a pace back. Billy Jenkins, raising his hands to smooth the situation, said mildly, "Now, look here, George, now you and I grew up together . . ."

Belligerent Smith said, "Goddamned birds are going to roost on those goddamned wires! All downtown is already covered by the damned things like an old maid's knitting, and it isn't enough that you can't see a decent patch of blue sky for them, goddamned birds roost on them and shit on people's heads!" He folded his arms across his chest. He was a rock. Belligerent Smith said so all of Mr. Bell's employees could hear him, "This establishment will refuse to cut the hair of any man who comes in here covered with bird shit!"

Patrolman Jenkins said as an order, "Mind your language, you intemperate man!"

The *mizinikil* said in a whisper, "It's an instrument for sending voices through wires."

Poditz said, "Oh." The lady on the other sidewalk had no knight to pick up her parasol. Poditz said, "Why won't anyone help that poor lady?"

"She's a Bowery Electric Girl, Papa." The *mizinikil*, twelve years old, said without looking at the wicked woman, "She has a battery in her bag so that anyone who touches the handle of her parasol is electrified and cannot move."

Jenkins said, "It's progress! You can't stop progress!" He glanced at the axe.

Poditz said, "Why? For health?" He had once seen an advertisement in a scrap of newspaper on the street with a drawing of sparks jumping down wires from a machine to a man's (covered) herniated testicles.

"So she can then rob them, Papa."

He had immediately torn the scrap to shreds so children would not see it. He could read not one sign in the street. Poditz said quickly to change the subject, "Why would a voice be improved by sending it through wires?"

"It's for talking with. It's for talking across the city without leaving your home."

The streets had not been paved with gold. "Why would—?" He was a grown man, a father, a breadwinner, asking his twelve-year-old daughter about life.

The *mizinikil* said, "It's for—"

"Why would a man like a barber want to talk to people far away?"

Jenkins said, "George, be reasonable—"

The *mizinikil* said, "It's not for barbers. It's for rich people in big houses."

Poditz said, "Ah!"

"And the wires have to go over all the roofs of the ordinary people to connect the rich people—"

Poditz said, "Ah!" That he understood.

The *mizinikil* said, "At school, Mr. Bell sent papers showing how his instruments work." The *mizinikil* said, "By 1886, everyone in New York will be able to talk to everyone else!"

He wanted to ask how they would be able to understand each other, speaking different languages.

The *mizinikil* said, "By Electricity!"

Billy Jenkins said, "You can't stop progress with an axe!"

On the sidewalk the lady picked up her parasol carefully and put it under her arm.

He did not want to shout—there was a policeman about. Poditz said in a harsh whisper, *"How do you know these things?"* The books and papers she brought home from school had no pictures in them, so he had no idea what she was learning. Poditz said, *"Why did the two policemen in Houston Street pretend to be horse doctors?"*

"To help us."

"They were secret police! Detectives without uniforms!"

"The secret police here are to catch criminals."

"They let the criminals go!"

"Perhaps they felt sorry for the large family—"

Poditz said, "He has an axe, that barber. Why doesn't the policeman shoot him?"

The *mizinikil* said, "I don't know, Father."

Belligerent Smith roared, *"I don't see Mr. Benefactor Bell paying me anything for the rent of my roof!"*

"Mr. Bell only wants the air around your roof!"

"Then let him attach his junction boxes to a *cloud!*"

He was getting sick of it. Patrolman Jenkins, drawing a breath, said finally, "Now, George, don't make me run you in—"

The Bowery Electric Girl—if that was what she was—turned and began walking south toward Canal Street. Her skirts were short, but in America maybe she— Poditz said softly, "I don't know what's happening!" Poditz said, "I work. I deliver. I heft weights on my shoulder. *Why in the name of God am I asking my little child to lead me through life?*" He had come, penniless, with not high hopes but only the hope that, in America, he and his family might be allowed to live. In all the street, for as far as he could see, there were painted words and signs and orders and ukases and he could not read one of them. Outside the barber's, for some reason, because of something, the barber and the policeman were shaking hands.

He spoke only Polish and Yiddish. He knew only Poles and Yiddishers. He knew not at all what each day, word by word, letter by letter, maybe even secret picture by picture, what things his children were learning about. He had thought there were things that, like Serge, like the power of the muscle of man and horse and hard work, were eternal.

"Papa . . ."

On the wagon, looking away, shaking his head, Poditz said softly, *"Nein . . ."* He looked at the woman with the umbrella walking away with no man to escort her on the street, to the wires and the wagons, to the railway that ran above the streets, to the sky that was no longer still and silent, but ran and hummed with voices.

"Papa—" She touched at his hand, but he brushed it away.

He could read not one word of all the words on the street. He delivered his carboys of lighting kerosene from a map drawn by the distributor and marked with house numbers and the numbers of carboys to be delivered to each address.

"Papa . . ."

She was his favorite.

"Papa—" As she touched at his hand, she had the kindness of her mother's eyes.

He spoke, in silence, only to God. In prayer, Poditz, mouthing the words, asked God in Yiddish, *"What is this place? This city? These streets?"*

The policeman in the center of the road stood six feet tall, glittering with all his buttons and insignia of rank and service polished to gold. He was clear eyed, American, with no pox marks on his face and a figure that had never known hunger or cold.

"Papa . . ."

As he waited, Poditz, bowing his head slightly, touched at his derby hat with his finger out of respect, but the policeman was watching the wires and the reels and the porcelain objects in the hands of the important men on the sidewalk, and acknowledged the salute—from a mere nobody—not at all.

5

On Crib Alley, off the Bowery, the air was full of the stale smell of hops and malt from the Croton Brewery on Chrystie Street a block east.

On Crib Alley, a subsiding, sinking grassy track in a valley of blackened derelict buildings, the air was full of mosquitoes and flies.

In the street outside number 21½, halfway down the alley, Muldoon, watching where he put his boots, said in irritation, "This is crazy." Whatever his boot landed on, it scurried away. "All these infernal women are crazed from gin and separation from the Church, and here we are, a couple of rational men obligingly trotting off at the first whistle like a pair of trained dogs to make sure one of them hasn't been murdered!" Muldoon said, "These women get murdered all the time! And if they don't get murdered they work themselves up into a fit of sentimentality about the children they never had or children they think they've had but misplaced somewhere and chuck themselves into the East River with their eyes rolling up to Heaven like plaster saints and half drown some poor copper who tries to pull them out!" He touched at the wooden gate to the yard of number 21½. The hinges were long gone and the door, merely pulled shut, tipped over at an angle and then fell down. Muldoon said, "The infernal girl is probably in there now, alive and kicking, doing things that I for one don't want to see this early in the morning without food or strong drink in my stomach!" He said with disgust, "Rotary Rosie—what a name! Can you imagine what that means in her trade?" He looked at Tillman thumbing through a little gray book he had gotten from some hideous establishment three doors down from the Lively Flea where the India rubber goods and the latest Paris illustrated magazines were sold. "Have you found her yet?"

Gentlemen's Guide To Gotham—15¢
THIS BOOK MUST NOT BE MAILED!!!!

To know the right from the wrong, to be sure of yourself, go through this little book and read it carefully, and when you visit the great Metropolis you will know the best places to spend your money and time, as all the BEST sporting houses and ladies are advertised. Read all the "ads."

He had only the address and her first name. Tillman, shaking his head, said, "No."

This book contains nothing but Facts, and is of the greatest value to Strangers when in the city. The Directory will be found alphabetically, under the headings "White" and "Colored," from alpha to omega. The names in capitals are landladies only.

The Best of Everything
"OUR MOTTO"

Everybody who knows today from yesterday will say that the Gentlemen's Guide is the right book for the right people.
"Honi Soit Qui Mal y Pense."

He was trying to get a picture of her and her surname. He had found three Rosies, but they were all in the better uptown houses around Fourteenth Street, and under the final heading in the book at the end of the Colored section ("OCTOROONS") there were only two names—*Williams, Pinky,* and *Piazza, Juanita*—and they were both listed as working out of Josie Arlington's Sporting House at 567 Franklin. Tillman said, "She isn't in here. She must have worked the streets without a protector." It was a horrible little rag, printed on cheap paper, and in case somebody did post it and the Postmaster General Anthony Comstock got hold of it under the new Federal laws against obscenity, had no publisher's name or return address in it. Tillman said, "If she lived down here she was probably a thief and no respectable Madam would have admitted in print she had her in her house anyway."

The yard had once been the vegetable and goat-grazing area of a brick tenement built in the 1830s to house the families of Irish laborers brought over to swell the ranks of the city's Democratic voting electorate in the time of the first great potato famine of the nineteenth century. They had swelled it, voted their own kind into power, and prospered. They had prospered and moved away. Tillman, crossing the overgrown yard and peering through a smashed filthy window, said without surprise, "Everything's burned away in there." He said, nodding, "Maybe you're right. Maybe we should just hammer on the door of the basement if there is one, and if we get no reply, assume she's off happily drunk in a gutter somewhere and let the whole thing go."

"Right." He had a swig from his hip flask and felt a warm glow of philosophy. Muldoon, looking down at something horrible his right shoe had missed by an inch in the sodden, unpaved ground, said, offering the flask to show his concern, "Your trouble is that you were brought up in a Home as an orphan and you think that everybody is equally important to the world." Tillman took a swig. Muldoon took a larger one. Muldoon, licking his lips, not swigging, but quaffing, said to educate him, "Look on life the way an Irishman with a big family does and you'll be a happier man. An Irishman with, say, seven or eight or nine or ten sisters and brothers as well as a mother and father and a few uncles and aunts and cousins thrown in, looks on life in the same terms as a farmer looks on his herd of cows or sheep or horses. Statistically the farmer knows that because he's got, say, fifteen or sixteen or seventeen animals—*statistically*—that a few of them are going to get consumption and die in childhood (say, three), that, say, one or two of them are going to be idiots (say, for the sake of argument, one), in a good family one is going to end up in prison or on the gallows, an ugly one with no prospects is going to be a nun, one or two will disappoint you whatever you do just because of their nature, and at least one other—"

He lost count. He thought in a family of ten, he had already reached eleven. He took a swig from his flask to clarify his calculations. Muldoon said, "Anyway, the point I'm making is that only God watches every sparrow that falls and even for Him it's a full-time job." It was a little Celtic wisdom worth passing on. Muldoon said, "And apart from that, the basement is probably full of rats and disease and Rotary Rosie or whatever her name is, if she's in there, is as sloshed as a frog."

Tillman said quietly, "If she's in there why is the door boarded up?" He was standing above the hole in the ground that led down the two steps to the splintered wooden door of the basement area below ground. Tillman said, so softly Muldoon had to come over to hear him, "If she isn't in there and she simply secured the door while she was away how did she manage to do it with broken beams of wood that no woman could even lift?" He sniffed. Tillman said, "I can smell something in there!"

Muldoon said in a whisper, *"Oh, God . . ."*

Tillman, going down the steps and putting his ear to the door, said, "Listen! Rats. And they're active."

Muldoon said softly, "Oh, Jesus, Mary and Joseph . . ." They were going to go in. They were going to take down the planks and the beams and they were going to go into the filthy place like cockroaches. Muldoon said—

Tillman said, "Look! Her name!" It was on a filthy little piece of pastecard stuck to one side of the door, half hidden by a beam. It was in a child's printed hand. Tillman said, *Seymore.* He was like a ferret at a rabbit hole. He was like some tiny, obsessed animal with bright, burning eyes. Turning back to Muldoon like a discoverer of a continent, the bright eyes blazing, a look of triumph on his face, Tillman said in a gasp, "Seymore: Lily and Rosie—*Seymore!*" Tillman said, "There, on that roof—she saw her ghost! She said she saw her die. She said she saw her ghost calling her." Tillman said, *"Sisters!"* He was at the boards and beams, pulling them away until he got the broken door loose and ajar and could see into the blackness. He had a lucifer out. He got it lit and, holding it ahead of him into the passageway beyond the door, peered in after it.

Seymore.

They had been, at the very least, *sisters*.

He could not be stopped.

Tillman, peering into the dark, holding the match high, his face half lit by it as he turned to pull Muldoon closer in, looking like a small, mad, unstoppable creature digging at the burrow of its prey, said in a voice trembling with vindication, "Look! Look in! Look! It's all true!"

He stepped back. He waited while Muldoon lit his own lucifer and, maneuvering himself, peered in.

It was all statistics, life.

In there, by the light of the flickering match, he saw where one of those statistics, a human being, mercilessly, had been killed.

New York Immigration Center
Literacy Test (Polish Language)
READ THIS TO YOURSELF:
Every applicant for admission must demonstrate his ability to read. To prove that you can meet this test, place both hands upon the table before you, palms down, and tell the inspector in what city you expect to live.

The inspector at Castle Garden had worn a shining silver badge with words and a motto on it in English and, laying his hands palm down on the table and looking hard into the inspector's eyes, he had not been able to read a word of what the badge said.

All he read in English, because they were the same, were numbers, and he was not sure of all of them. He had heard that, in America, the sevens and the ones looked the same and that Americans—to be different, to make it impossible—did not cross their sevens and so you could not tell the difference.

He read Polish. He read Polish words.

In English, all he could read were the numbers. On his wagon, Poditz looked at the map the kerosene distributor had drawn for him for his deliveries and counted out the marked stops on his route.

Seven. Eleven. The *mizinikil*, at school, would have learned that American secret also, but he did not ask.

Numbers. He read the numbers.

He read them now.

Patting the *mizinikil* gently on the hand, Poditz, reasssuring her about something, being her Father, flicked again at Serge's reins and, going in the same direction as the disappearing Bowery Electric Girl, went on toward Crib Alley, the delivery stop marked #6, to the left of the Bowery above Canal Street, number . . . 27½.

He watched.

Belligerent Smith had gone back inside his barbershop to get drunk with his friends and customers and to lay aside the axe, and, standing in the center of the roadway amidst the wires and cables and reels, Patrolman Billy Jenkins watched as the Bowery Electric Girl, her folded parasol under her arm, went down the sidewalk on the far side of the street toward Canal Street.

He touched at his chin and pursed his lips.

He ran his white-gloved finger across his mouth and, if he thought something, none of the telephone men in their white coats around him could tell what it was or thought from his face that it was important.

He was sorting in his mind all the photographs of all the Bowery Electric Girls in the Rogues' Gallery Headquarters at 300 Mulberry Street that had been sent down to the 5th Precinct at Leonard Street over the years, trying to remember who she was and where she lived.

Six feet tall, thirty-nine years old, and hale, the brass buttons and badges on his uniform catching the morning sun and flashing, the sentinel of the city, Patrolman Billy Jenkins, with an expression on his face that could not be read, touched at the side of his face with his fingers and thought about it.

In the narrow, cave-like passageway that led from the boarded-up door through to the basement room beyond, there was a five-foot-long, scoop-shaped japanned tin bath full of water. The water was stagnant and brown and green, kaleidoscopic colors of yellow and blue lying like islands on its surface, the tin at the low end of the vessel dented and misshapen where whoever had been held under and drowned in it had kicked and drummed and convulsed with their legs and feet in their death throes.

The colors on top of the water were garish fallen dyes from a woman's clothing.

The water from the threshing was in puddles on the stone floor, the colors lying on top of that too.

It was only a five-foot-long bath: at the end of it all the tin had been dented and buckled as someone small, small enough to almost lie out in it full length, had gotten their shoes to the end of the vessel and, their knee and thigh muscles pumping like pistons, had kicked and smashed at the tin until it bulged out and bowed, but did not break. There were stains around the side of the bath at the head end and rust where the arms and elbows had fought. It was blood. In the still deep water, with the colors of the dye, there were little circles and swirls of darkness—sodden, matted clumps of human hair. There was a crushed tin bucket someone had used to bring water to the bath from the pump in the yard. There was no sound at all in the passageway, no rats or mice or insects moving, only—as Tillman and Muldoon stood looking down into the drowning box—only the faint hissing of masonry dust and powder falling from the brick ceiling and pattering on the surface of the water and the matted clumps of hair like rain.

The bath sat flat on the floor. With no legs to it there was nothing under it and, apart from the stove-in bucket, no other object anywhere near it in the corridor.

There was the silence. Like the discoverers of an ancient tomb they stood still above the awful object and, not looking at each other, gazed down at its surface.

He reached down gently with his fingers outstretched and touched the surface of the water. It was cold and oily with dye. Tillman said softly, glancing back, "Lily must have seen it happen from the top of the steps in the yard."

He glanced back. Muldoon, looking back at the open door to the yard, said nodding, "Yes." He glanced at the thick water of the bath and the dented tin and thought how long it took to drown something. He thought about the sounds it must have made. Muldoon, because he could think of nothing else to say, said again, "Yes."

"Then she ran, and then whoever did this, not seeing her at all, took the body of her sister out of here, laid it on the ground outside, and boarded up the door. Or she waited, hidden out there in one of the buildings at night while her sister lay small and drowned on the ground." Tillman said, "She must have waited, watching the body, hoping that it would breathe, knowing that if it did whoever it was who had killed her would stop there in the yard and kill her again." Tillman said, "He must have taken her away in a wagon or a cart or a carriage and buried her or thrown her body into the river." He saw again Lily's eyes on the roof of Grammelspacher's. Tillman said softly, "Ned, go into the next room, find a lamp, and see what you can find in there." The dust was falling like fine rain. Tillman, taking off his coat and, finding nowhere to hang it, handing it to Muldoon, said quietly, "I'll stay here." He was undoing the cuff link on his shirt, rolling up the sleeve.

"All right." He thought of ghosts. He had Tillman's coat over his arm. It rested against the side of his own. Compared to his, it looked like the garment of a small child.

Muldoon, turning, going the three steps down the corridor to the open door to the room where Rotary Rosie Seymore had lived, not looking back, said tightly, "Yes, I'll do that."

He did not want to, but he could not help himself from listening, and he heard it.

He heard, in the awful, still, dead place, Tillman's hand and arm go full length into the thick, terribly colored water to feel about at the bottom of the bath to see if anything was there.

At the southern end of the Bowery, following his map, Poditz, flicking gently at the reins, turned Serge into Crib Alley, glancing at the number written on his map to make sure he had it right—number 27½.

It was a shoe.

He had thought, when his fingers first touched it, that it was something else. He had thought when he felt its skin, felt it pliable and soft, that it was a rat or—but it was a shoe, and it had come out dark and soft and sodden with all the high buttons on it broken and torn away and the heel, as it had drummed in a final panic against the inside of the tin, off at one side and hanging by only a single bent-back nail.

It was a lady's white Blucherette, with a pointed, patent silver tip—a whore's walking-out shoe, and as he withdrew it from the bath, where it had kicked and fought against the containing tin, the silver tip fell off and he had to reach out to catch it with his other hand before it sank back into the mire again.

On his knees at the bath, his naked arm dripping water and running and stained with the dye and clumps of hair, Tillman said in a whisper, "God Almighty . . ."

He had thought at first that what he had felt, because of the soft leather of the shoe, was a rat. He had thought for a moment, as his fingers had closed around it, that perhaps it had been alive.

"Virgil—"

Kneeling at the tub, putting the broken object to one side on the floor, he reached in to see if there was anything else.

"Virgil—"

At the end of the passageway, looking up, he saw the glow of an oil lamp, then as the lamp was turned up full, the room filled with yellow light.

"Virgil . . ." He heard Muldoon's voice. With his hand in the slime, his fingers moving across the bottom, his eyes closed two inches above the awful smell of the surface, the voice seemed to be coming from a long way away.

Nothing. He felt nothing. There was nothing else down there. He opened his eyes and saw Muldoon's light, heard his voice; standing up in the corridor with his arm stinging as if it had been in acid, he saw him standing inside the doorway with a lamp in his hand looking at something in there.

Everywhere, like a rough-opened tomb, the dust from the ceiling was falling.

He had nothing to wipe his arm with. At his wrist, hanging like a tendril, there was a matted length of hair.

Muldoon, at the door, holding up the lamp to see him, said suddenly, suddenly shouting in the corridor so loud it was deafening, "Virgil! Jesus, Joseph and Mary—Holy Mother of God, *come and see what the hell is in here!"*

6

Muldoon said in a steady, even voice, "Virgil, I want to get out of here."
There was no tremor in his tone: it was steady, matter-of-fact. It was a
statement. Muldoon, holding the flickering lantern at his side, the darkness
all around its halo glittering with little points of yellow light, said calmly,
evenly, "I believe there are some places a good Christian shouldn't find
himself. I believe there are some places God doesn't want people to go."
The lantern was not steady. It was trembling. "I believe there are some
things that are best left alone in the scheme of things and that—"

"Hold the light up." Everywhere on the stone floor and in the
pitch-black room, there were little points of yellow light. Tillman said,
"They're rings. Hundreds of them. Wedding rings. They're all over the
floor." He picked one up: a thick man's gold band, scratched and dull with
age. Tillman said, "They're—"

"I know what they are!" Muldoon, standing his ground, only raising the
lantern and aiming it to the far end of the room, said as a piece of
information, "And over there there's a wooden bed with a straw mattress
on it. And, lying on its side with more rings around it, there's an open
carpet-bag like the one at the Lively Flea with clothes and shoes in it."
Muldoon said, "And on the floor, around the rings, there are more clothes
and clips and paper." His voice was wavering, losing its strength, "And
under those clothes and paper there are more rings." Muldoon said, "There
are at least two or three hundred wedding rings on the floor and on the bed
of this place and I think, now, what we should do—" He caught Tillman
in the light. Muldoon said, on the edge, "Your goddamned arm's still
dripping from that bath!"

"There was nothing in the water but a shoe." Tillman, going to the man
and putting his hand gently on the lantern, said quietly, "Give me the
lantern."

Muldoon said, "On the floor, everywhere, there are papers. There's
brown shop paper and bits of newspaper and documents and what look like

bits and pieces of old books that have been ripped up and—" Muldoon, gripping the lantern hard to keep it in his hand, said, "I'm a Christian man, Virgil, a Catholic—there are things good Catholics leave alone. There are things that shouldn't be thought about. There are things—"

"It's just the room of a dead woman!"

"Then where's the body?"

"The body was taken away and then the outside door boarded up." Tillman, trying to get the lantern, moving it, making the gold on the floor flash like stars, said roughly, "Pull yourself together! All it is is the room of a dead woman who thieved a lot!"

"There are thousands of rings in here! And spots of lamp oil on the ground that go nowhere!" Muldoon, wrenching back at the lantern, holding it up, said, "Look! Look! There are drip spots from an oil lamp all around the room that come from under the bed and don't go anywhere and there are no burned matches on the floor from where it was lit!" Muldoon, starting to shout, said, "I found this lantern in the doorway! It's a small room—it doesn't need two lamps! This lamp takes kerosene! The spots on the floor are whale oil and there isn't any whale oil lamp here!"

"It was taken out when—"

"There weren't any whale oil spots in the corridor! There weren't any rings! There weren't any papers!" Muldoon said, "Lily said she saw her sister's ghost! Her sister's ghost was carrying a lamp!" Muldoon, losing control, shouted, "She didn't say her sister's ghost was only wearing one shoe!"

He was at the bed, pulling at the carpetbag and reaching in. Tillman, holding up a fistful of papers, said, "They're papers, birth certificates, newspaper clippings—"

"Something came in here after she was dead and it wasn't human!" Muldoon, rooted to the ground, said in a strange, faraway tone, "On the battlefield at Chancellorsville, when I was wounded, after all the guns stopped, I heard the moans of dying men and the sounds of their hands beating on the earth and on their rifles and then, after a while, there was silence, and I heard their ghosts leaving their bodies in the long grass and rustling, and I—" Muldoon said, "Whoever died in that bath, whoever was held down kicking and fighting and drumming with their boots on the metal—whoever was suffocated alive under the water in that coffin—" Muldoon said in the darkness, "In the terror of battle, the ghost can leave the body shrieking!"

"Nonsense!"

"It isn't nonsense!" He crossed himself. In the darkness, his hand shaking, his eyes wide and unblinking, going dry, Muldoon said for everything his religion had ever taught him, "If it isn't true that the ghost leaves the body—the soul—*how can we have any hope of Heaven?* What do you think sits on the seats of Paradise near the throne of God? *Our withered bodies from old age?* The shot-through carcasses of soldiers blown to tripes by artillery fire? What sits with God is the soul!" The rings and papers were everywhere. He heard them start to move. Muldoon said warningly, "I fear no living man, Virgil, but I—" They were rustling, the papers, moving against some of the rings hanging precariously in the cracks on the stone floor, making little jingling noises as they tipped over or rolled, "But I—"

Tillman said, "It's the wind."

"The door at the end of the corridor is five feet below ground! There isn't any wind!"

"Then it's—"

"Look." The papers were starting to move, to roll, to lift up a little from the floor. Muldoon said, "Look. When I came in—"

"Then it's from a window."

"There isn't any window!" The papers, rustling, were moving, starting to lift up and circle. They were starting to roll, to flap, to turn over against themselves and move the little glittering rings. Muldoon said softly in a chant, "*Holy Mary, Mother of God . . .*"

There were oil spots all over the floor, at the foot of the bed and by the walls and under the bed. Tillman said, "It's a hole in the wall somewhere!" He saw, as Muldoon for some reason moved and threw a pool of light against the far wall behind the bed, a shape, a shadow, a darkness different to the darkness everywhere else in the awful place. Tillman said—

"*Oh Jesus!!*" He saw, all at once, all the papers in the room, as they had done when he first lit the room, take flight and begin spinning in circles above the floor like whirlwinds.

Tillman said, "It's a tunnel! It's a tunnel behind the bed! It's another way out and in!" He saw, at that tunnel, everywhere flying out from it, papers. He saw the glitter of gold. Wrenching at the lantern, getting it, going with it for the mouth of the hole under the bed, Tillman, reaching for any paper he might catch on the way, ordered the man now standing in pitch darkness, "Ned, light a lucifer! Light a lucifer and wait out here for me in case I call you!"

He heard a scratch. On his hands and knees, crawling in, he heard the sound of a match burning into life.

Everywhere in the tunnel on the stone and earth floor there were the thick parallel marks of a leaking oil lamp, coming in and going out.

In the tunnel, coming hard from somewhere, he felt a wind on his face.

He heard the rustle of the papers rising in the room behind him.

He heard, as he heard also Muldoon's sudden gasp, the sound of the lucifer too wet to catch, fizz and go out.

She paused, looking about.

She was hungry. She had, in the satin bag where the battery for the parasol was, no money at all.

One street up from Canal the Bowery Electric Girl, seeing some Jew's wagon delivering fuel turn into Crib Alley, seeing no other likely marks about anywhere, went, checking the power left in her battery, after him.

He heard a sound. He heard a click. He heard the sound of footsteps on soft earth. He heard something coming, heavy and unhurried, getting closer. He was in the darkness with the dead lucifer still in his hand, his hand shaking, his eyes looking straight ahead to the wall in the darkness.

All around him the papers were blowing, rising, swirling, falling away, touching, rustling, plucking at him like a banshee.

He heard a click. He heard, from where Tillman had gone, no sound at all.

He heard something outside, in the passageway, coming in.

Muldoon, rooted to the spot, his legs turned to stone, his mouth too dry to pray, heard something coming.

"Damn!" At the corner of the Bowery and Crib Alley Patrolman Jenkins, seeing her move quickly from side to side in the alley behind the rear of a kerosene delivery wagon, said, "Damned slut!"

He saw the Bowery Electric Girl's skirts fly up as she ran, as she scuttled over the ruts in the road like a rat and then, peering in at something in a yard, stop at number 15½. He saw her duck down in the shadow of the broken gateway there to get in.

His hand, at his mouth, had become a fist. It shook.

He saw, on the seat of the delivery wagon, the driver rein in his horse for a moment as the little girl or boy or whatever it was next to him leaned over with what looked like a piece of paper in her hand and seemed to point something out on it.

He saw the driver, after a moment, shake his head.

He saw—

He saw the Bowery Girl with the electric parasol not at all.

"Damn! God— God—*damn!*" He was shaking, trembling, the fist at his face tight and punching at his chin with pent-up power.

He glanced back to the Bowery and saw no one anywhere who saw him.

All the buttons on his uniform polished and glittering in the light,

Patrolman Billy Jenkins began running down the alley, his hand at his hip pocket for his gun, watching for the rat-girl loose in the yards.

In the center of the room, with all the blood drained from his cheeks, Muldoon waited, but as the light filled the room, all that crawled out of the tunnel was Tillman, and, as he got to his feet, his arm still dripping from the bath, all the papers in the room stopped swirling.

He was standing stock-still in the center of the room, still holding Tillman's coat, still holding the dead lucifer in his hand by his side. He stood like a slab of dead, cold meat. Muldoon asked, "Is she in there?" Muldoon, trying to sound calm, asked, "How far did you go?"

"She's not in there."

"How far did you go?"

"All the way." Tillman, watching the man's face, said, "It's a thieves' tunnel. It goes through the double walls of this building along a sort of ventilation passage into the building behind and it comes out through another hole in there into another basement." Tillman said with concern, "Are you all right, Ned?"

"I'm fine." Muldoon, glancing up at the ceiling, asked with no expression on his face, "And what then?"

"Then it goes up a flight of wooden stairs to the first floor and then—and then, I imagine, outside into another alley." Tillman said, "It's for wood. It's for stealing wood. All the buildings around here are derelict and the basement is full of broken laths and planks for wood." The man would not look at him. "For the stove there. To cook her meals—for heat."

"Good." He wanted to go. He turned to go. Muldoon said, "Well that's okay then, isn't it?"

Tillman said, "It's just a tunnel to steal things from the building next door."

"Fine." Muldoon said, nodding, "Fine. Good. Fine."

"It isn't anything—it's just a passageway that's probably been here since—"

"—forever. Right?" Muldoon, his voice very soft and calm, still looking at the ceiling, said like a child, "My lucifer went out. I didn't have another."

"Ned . . ."

His mouth was suddenly wet. He wiped it with the back of his hand and his hand came away wet. Muldoon said, still wiping at it, "I'm dribbling, Virgil! It must be the air in here. I'm all wet and dribbling like a kid!"

"There are no ghosts. It's just another way out to an ordinary basement room in—"

He was still brushing at his mouth. He could not understand where the moisture was coming from. His throat was dry as a desert.

"It's just a poky little tunnel between two buildings so she could get into the next building and steal wood for her fire!"

"Is that all?" Muldoon, nodding, said, "Oh. Is that all?" Muldoon said suddenly shouting, "What the hell are all these wedding rings? What the hell are all these papers everywhere? What the hell is—"

"The papers are her life! The papers are documents and clippings and postcards and bits and pieces of—"

"Of a dead woman whose ghost is still in here!"

"No." Tillman, still standing in front of the tunnel, still holding the lantern, said, shaking his head, "No. No, what it is, is—"

"The soul is supposed to leave the body, Virgil!" Muldoon, starting to shout, said with his breath coming fast, not to be swayed, "But it didn't leave her! It's still in here! It's in here dripping that slime from the bath from her mouth and nose with a look of horror frozen on her face and her hands out and clutching and it's—"

"No." He came forward. Tillman, shaking his head, said, "No." All around him, as he cleared the tunnel entrance, the papers started to fly up in the wind.

"Don't touch me!"

Tillman said as an order, "See what I found."

"I don't want to see what you found!"

"Look at it!" It was a yellowed piece of paper, half folded back, flat. "I found it halfway along the tunnel with more rings where, terrified, scrabbling and crawling along the tunnel in a panic, the person who came back in to get it from in here dropped it." Tillman, pushing it forward, said, *"Read it!"*

"No!"

"It isn't written in blood! It isn't some communication from the Devil of your damned Irish Schoolboy's Book of Martyrs—it's an advertising flyer!" He pushed it forward, shoving it into the man's hand, *"Read it!"*

Tillman, trying to bring him back, seeing him starting to sway, grasping him hard by the shoulder and pushing the single sheet of paper under his nose, said, "Ned! Ned! It's about her! It's about Rotary Rosie Seymore! *Read it!"* Tillman, losing him, shouted in the awful, still room with the papers starting to swirl around him, "Ned! Ned! All this! The person who came in here after the drowning—all this . . . it was *her!"*

He held the man's shoulder, pressing with all his strength.

Tillman, pressing, hurting, trying to bring him back, starting to shake him, said directly into his face, "Ned, it was her. She isn't dead! She came back! Listen to me! Read it! *She came back!"*

Looking back over the glass carboys at the rear of the wagon from Number 27½ Crib Alley he thought he saw a shadow behind the broken fence at Number 21½ Crib Alley.

27½. It was the wrong number. In America . . . It was the wrong number and he should have delivered it to 21½.

On the wagon seat, the *mizinikil*, the little map in her hand, had eyes full of the softness and kindness of her mother. She said nothing at all, neither in English nor Yiddish.

She touched only at his hand.

There was no room to turn Serge around until the end of the alley, and as her father got down from his seat to walk back to 21½ to carry back the carboy by hand, the *mizinikil* clasped her hands together in her lap in front of her to be a good girl and kept her eyes straight ahead.

She was afraid she had done something wrong, but she did not know what it was.

On the wagon, to please him when he came back, she sat very still and straight and demure, like a lady.

HALF-FISH! HALF-WOMAN!
Never Before Recorded in Scientific Annals!
EXCLUSIVE TO BUNKER'S DIME MUSEUM FOR 1881
ROTARY ROSIE SEYMORE
The Astounding, Astonishing Gill-Girl
Who Can
HOLD HER BREATH UNDER WATER FOR A FULL
ELEVEN MINUTES!!!
No Trickery! Any Test Invited! Transparent
Glass Vessel Sealed By Padlock!
BUNKER'S DIME MUSEUM, The Bowery
Exhibited All Over The World!
(No Naked Flesh Displayed)
SUITABLE FOR ALL THE FAMILY
Educational. Amazing. Scientific.
A Modern Wonder of Bodily Training And—

Tillman said softly, "It was her. She came back. She came back for all this. She came back in the lamplight through the tunnel from next door and she got at her bag of belongings and she—"

"*Jesus . . . !*"

"And she took everything she could carry off—the rings, money, papers, clothes, anything that might—" Tillman said, "There are no photographs here, Ned. There are postcards and documents and—but there are no photographs or portraits of what she looked like or—"

"*Jesus!*" On the floor, the papers were still swirling. In the corridor where the bath was, he could hear noises, but they were only the noises of . . . And the papers were the wind and . . . Muldoon, his arms tingling, said in a gasp, "Jesus—!"

Tillman said tightly, "It was her. She came back. She came back down that passage and she—"

He heard a sound. It was nothing. The paper was shaking in his hand.

"It was her. She came back." Tillman, holding the man's eyes, seeing the focus come back, seeing the blood warming his face, hearing him start to expel a breath, said, "She lived through it. No one holds anyone under water for eleven minutes. She lived through it, and afterward, after she was taken away and thrown in the East River or half buried, wet, soaking, bloody, covered in slime and muck, she came back here through the tunnel to get what was hers, for her money and—" Tillman said tightly, triumphantly, "Ned, on the roof, on Bunker's, what Lily saw—the figure with the lamp—it wasn't her ghost, it was her! She's out there! Rotary Rosie Seymore—she isn't dead at all! Out there somewhere, hiding from whoever killed her, *she's still alive!*"

"Jesus, Joseph and . . ."

. . . and in that instant, turning to see what the noise was in the doorway behind him, he saw her.

"*Jesus!*" He saw her standing in the corridor in the light, glowing with the lantern light. He saw her raise a parasol and he saw—he saw at the end of the corridor in the broken-down doorway someone with something raised above his head, a glass kerosene bottle and he saw it was—

"*Look out!*" He saw the Bowery Electric Girl's parasol spit blue flame as she lunged in with it. Muldoon, pushing Tillman aside, the spark crackling in the room, yelled, "*Look out!*" He saw, for an instant, someone in the corridor dressed in blue with all his buttons gleaming, and he heard a scream as he slammed the door hard in the girl's face, and she fell backward and collided with the man behind her. He heard a commotion, then glass smash.

He heard a man's voice howl in pain as the four-gallon carboy of kerosene he held ready to throw smashed against a wall with the impact of the girl against him and then he heard a crackle, a crack, as the parasol, charged with electricity, scraping and splintering along the wall, flashed power.

He heard in that instant, out there in the darkness, Patrolman Billy Jenkins, saturated in kerosene, catch fire and burn.

7

He was burning like a straw scarecrow. His head and shoulders, saturated by the kerosene, were on fire and he was in the center of the open yard with his head and hair and shoulders on fire, flailing with his gloved hands, his gloves disappearing into the flame, themselves burning at his palms and the end of his fingers. The fire had already burned away his tongue, blinded him, deafened him, and, turning in circles, his arms out and smashing against his body and his head like a whirligig, he was turning, spinning, burning. His shoulders were gone: you could see the bones—he was in the center of the yard turning and flailing and burning. There was kerosene everywhere on the ground, burning in spots, dripping from him, running down his uniform and lighting, flashing, catching, then going out or exploding in a blue and yellow flame. In the yard as he moved the fire was fanned and roared like the furnace in a boiler. He was a flare. The flames at and above his head were four feet high and he was burning like a dry stick with smoke going upward from the roaring blaze.

The Bowery Electric Girl was on her knees at the broken boarded-up doorway, her dress smoldering, beating it out with her hands, pulling the hem up to get at the petticoats before they caught. She was in a circle of broken glass from the carboy, blood running down her face from the shards that had exploded when the carboy had smashed against the wall of the corridor and burst. The Bowery Electric Girl, her eyes mad with terror and the horror of the yard, shrieked as Tillman and Muldoon got past her in the corridor and out into the yard, "He tried to brain me with the bottle! He—" The Bowery Electric Girl, pulling away as Muldoon reached down and wrenched her up to clear the door, shrieked, "I'm only a thief! I wasn't doing anything! I only came to thieve!" and the burning man was upon them, flailing, reaching out from the top of the steps in his blindness with his burning hands, his fingers opening and shutting like claws, and then as she shrieked in terror, he was staggering, turning, going back whirling into the yard, and then he was out in the yard again, going somewhere, spinning, turning, teetering, reaching out.

He hit against the fence to the alleyway and spun back. In the roar of the fires he was making sounds, but they were not human sounds. Blind, deaf and mute, all the skin on his shoulders gone and showing white bone, his gloves dripping off him in droplets of liquid fire, the inferno at his head and face roaring with the movement, he was grunting like an animal, like a steer.

He hit the fence and staggered back. In his darkness, in his black, silent, burning world, he crashed back at the obstruction. His hands were down by his sides, the sinews all gone, and he was butting at the fence with the flames and his forehead.

Like a top, like a gyroscope, unhuman, unstoppable, like some dumb, dying beast, he butted at the fence, was thrown back, and then, burning, lowing, thrust himself at it again and was thrown back.

Somehow, he had his arm up, reaching out. He had the fence against his palm, burning at it with his palm.

He was grunting, lowing like a beast.

Burning, burning through, he was hard against the fence, smashing his forehead through the flames against the wood to break through, his knees starting to go, inside his body, down all the bones and muscles and sinews, burning away.

Like a top, like a gyroscope stuck spinning in a rut it could never escape from until it ran down and stopped, Patrolman Billy Jenkins, burning from inside like a chimney, smashed and battered at the wall to get free.

The hand pump in the yard was dry, used-up, empty, unprimed. There was a fire plug out in the alley with maybe some pressure, and Tillman, running toward it across the yard, ordered Muldoon, trying to put the fires out on the door above the Bowery Girl with handfuls of dirt from the floor, "Water! There's water in the bath and a bucket!" The smoke from the burning man was swirling in the yard, "Get what you can and—maybe we can—" He was drowned out by the shrieking of the girl as one of her petticoats caught fire and she beat at it with her hands and, as she scrabbled to wrench it off, something like a fireball touched at her and covered her with smoke. It was Jenkins' helmet, the felt burned through. The Bowery Electric Girl, getting to her feet, shrieked, "I'm on fire!" The Bowery Electric Girl, slapping at her dress, screamed, "I didn't do anything! I crashed into him and all the kerosene exploded on him!" She reached down for her parasol, but it was broken into spokes and burning like a stave. The Bowery Electric Girl, screaming at Muldoon as he raced by her back into the corridor for the bath, shrieked, *"I didn't do anything!"*

It was one of the old eighteenth-century fire plugs, a wooden water pipe plugged with a tampion. In the alley, Tillman, wrenching at it, pulled the tampion free and the line was dry.

In the corridor Muldoon shouted, "The bucket's stove-in and broken!" He tried to get water out of the bath a cupped handful at a time, but it was no good. Muldoon, in a panic, yelled, "I lost the lamp when I—I can't see into the main room to find another bucket!" and as he ran back into the yard to help Tillman with whatever he had found, there was a crash as the fence came down and Jenkins was out into the street, buckling, starting to fall, and the flames at his head suddenly died, had burned away everything there was to burn, and what there was there, for a moment, was a man with no face or hair. It stopped him. It halted him. Muldoon said in horror, *"Oh my God!"*

"Papa!" Her father was running back down the alley with his apron flying, going toward the burning man and the two men standing on either side of him in the smoke. Standing up on the wagon the *mizinikil* screamed to stop him, *"Papa—no!"* and the burning, smoldering man was down on his knees, starting to crawl, his hands out in front of him, then dropping like a marionette with no strings, then jerking up again.

"Oh, my God, oh, my God—" There was nothing left of the face and hair. It was white bone, and the eyes were gone, burned away, were darkness, and he was crawling in silence with God only knew what tiny moving muscles of life left inside him, jerking his hands out and then back again, and then he was down, fallen down like a plank onto the flagstones in the road, rocking, rolling over, the ghastly white skull fallen back on the neck muscles and the burned-away windpipe, his hand a claw slapping at the top of his leg for something, seeking it, grasping for it, getting it away from his body and onto the roadway.

"Papa!" It was a gun. She saw it glitter on the road as it fell. She saw it happen so quickly it was as if it did not happen. She saw the two men by the terrible thing on the roadway—she saw a small coatless, hatless man with one shirtsleeve rolled up with his hands out, reaching for the dying man—and she saw the big ox of a man shaking his head as he moved with the crawling creature on the ground—and she saw her father, not stopping, unstoppable, become part of it and she saw—

The claw was rubbing on the ground, pumicing at the stone to find something, to make contact with the earth. He saw their faces: the face of the little man with his eyes full of horror and shock. He saw the face of the big one not wanting to see it, seeing it, shaking his head to make it end, to go away, and he saw—

"*Papa—!*"

He knew nothing about letters or numbers or words. He knew only, from a life full of hardship, about pain. Running, getting there, he heard the creature on the ground gasp with his last breath like an animal. He saw him try to reach out. He saw him, broken and shriveled, all his face gone, contract, bend like an insect. He saw—

He saw the broken, twisted thing on the road curling like a scrap of charred paper, the head going back from the neck, all the muscles burned away. He saw the white skull where the hair came out in clumps, and he saw the scalp. There were no eyes, but the eyes were going up, the head falling back, the mouth open in an O, the claw up, reaching, moving like a pendulum, and he saw—

And he had him. He was on his knees on the ground in front of the falling, reaching man and he had his fist gripped around the cloth of the tunic at the chest and he was pulling, pulling the man closer, reaching with his free hand for the gun on the roadway.

"*Virgil!*" He could not see Tillman. He had his hands to his face, his elbows coming together in front of his eyes, and he could not see Tillman. Muldoon, frozen to the spot, the smell from the awful, burned-through, falling flesh from the face making him gag, screamed, hiding his face, not looking around, "Virgil, where are—"

"*Alivei! Halevai!* God will it—" He had the pistol from the ground in his free hand. On his knees he was pulling the terrible unhuman face closer to his, saying something in Yiddish, his head shaking, not looking away, trying to stare into the dead, burned-out eyes.

"*Alivei . . . Halevai . . . !*" and the gun was coming up, going out to the head where the temple was, the barrel convulsing, held in a grip of iron, the hammer coming back with a click.

"*Aaahhh . . .*" There was no windpipe left, and it was only the sound of air in the lungs.

He was kneeling, facing him, holding him, the gun out and hard against the white skull, the burned and dying man like a monkey with the arms loose and hanging down, swinging, the head rolling back, the sound of the air in the lungs like the gasping of a machine, the mouth open in a terrible O—

"*Papa—! Papa—!*" She had her hands on the side of the wagon, shrieking, her legs gone at the knees. He was like a rabbi, a priest, holding a sinner in a terrible embrace, like a surgeon with a terrible, glittering tool in his hand looking for the exact spot.

He had done it three times in Poland. He had done it on one terrible morning at his brother's house when the lancers had swept down to burn all the houses out in his brother's village. He had, on his knees, shrieking to God, done it with a shotgun.

"—Papa!"

"*Alivei! Im yirtseh Hashem! Alivei! Halevai!*"

He had done it three times before. He had done it for his brother and his brother's wife, and, forever in his nightmares, he had done it for the baby after the ulans had speared it through with one of their lances and thrown it back onto the burning straw of the roof of his brother's house.

He knew nothing about letters or numbers or words.

He knew only everything there was to know about pain. What he was was all he would ever be. He knew nothing about words or letters or numbers or America at all. It hurt that he believed, alone in his bed at nights, that all his children were ashamed of him.

He had no notion at all what the policeman holding his shoulder like a vise said.

He did not look away from the face.

He blinked hard because, for a moment, he could not see for the tears and he did not want to have to shoot again.

He had no idea, after it was over, what the policemen were going to do to him.

In Crib Alley, on his knees, Poditz, *Carrier,* drawing Jenkins suddenly toward him like a lover, pressing the muzzle hard against the center of the head, pulled the trigger of the little silver gun.

There was no windpipe left, and it was only air in the lungs.

In the roadway, like the wind, maybe not even there at all, there was only—as the burned, black thing fell forward onto its knees—the gentlest of sighs.

He handed the gun to the little man, but did not look at his face. Poditz, his hands empty, standing as if he was naked, said, "I—I—" He had no English. He looked at the big policeman next to the little man and saw his mouth moving as if in prayer. Poditz, waiting, with no words, said with his hands out to explain, "I—I—" He was afraid of what he had done. He had no English. Poditz, touching at the apron on his barrel chest, said quietly to tell them who he was, "Poditz."

On Houston Street with the Houlihans, he had not looked into the carrier's face at all. Tillman, looking at him now, looking into his eyes, said in a whisper, "Virgil Tillman."

"Poditz."

Muldoon said, "Ned."

"Poditz."

Muldoon said softly, "Yes."

The little girl at the wagon must have been his daughter. He glanced at her for a moment, but he did not want to take his eyes off the man's face, and he looked back. Muldoon said again, touching at his chest to make it clear, "Ned Muldoon." All there had been after the shot had been the gentlest of sighs. All there had been in the single moment of mercy when the poor dying creature had been eased to his Redeemer had been— The Bowery Electric Girl was at the broken-down fence to the alleyway and Muldoon, not wanting her to sully something, not wanting her to see the tears on his face she had done nothing to earn, ordered her in a roar, *"Get back behind the fence out of sight!"*

"Poditz." He was afraid for his family. He wanted them to know it was only, solely, him.

Tillman, taking the man's hand in his, looking down at the dead thing on the roadway, said formally, "Yes." The man's child was by the wagon at the end of the alley watching, and he thought for a moment to go down there and tell her what a good and kind, merciful, brave man her father was.

He saw her face.

She already knew.

"My God . . ." He had no words. In the awful place with the desolation of abandonment all around, with the terrible dead thing on the roadway, with the smell of wet and ruin and dark, hidden places all around him, Muldoon, consumed in that moment with a feeling that had no words, staring hard into the man's face, moving Tillman's hand from the man's paw so he himself could take it, said like a child, like a lover, like a listener to music he thought sometimes only he could hear, "My God, man—"

Muldoon said in admiration with his eyes brimming with tears, "My God, man—my God, you make me proud to be an American!"

8

The sign on the smokestack said THE KING OF THE SEA was BACK IN SERVICE!

Fish fled.

Seagulls skedaddled.

On both sides of the Buttermilk Channel of the East River, from the windows of their shoreside houses on Brooklyn and Manhattan, brave souls winced.

On the great Brooklyn Bridge the jammed traffic stopped trying to unjam. People lined the walkway.

At 7 A.M., for its first trip of the day, the death ship of the East River, festooned with bunting, its aft deck lined with mermaids and a German lederhosen band and Neptune covered in seaweed holding his trident, sailed from its Whitehall pier with a full complement of 120 passengers and interested parties.

The full complement of 120 passengers and interested parties were being towed behind in eight lifeboats.

Nothing in this world, or more likely the Next, would persuade them to set one foot upon that terrible deck. They couldn't have gotten a seat on any of the other Manhattan–Brooklyn steamboat ferries for love or money. And they had tried. The other ferries, safe in dock, were waiting for the *The King of the Sea* to blow to splinters, or sink without a trace, or catch fire like paper, or any of the above. They were packed to the gunwales with spectators.

Neptune—C.K. Cooder of the Unique Steamboat Line—waving his trident, shouted at the top of his lungs to them, and to the rats, the mutineers, the deserters in the lifeboats, "Cowards! Turncoats!" He shouted to the salvage steam tugs circling the awful hulk like vultures, "Hyenas!" *The King of the Sea* was a little out in the stream, its sidewheels slashing foam against the running-out tide. C.K. Cooder, appearing and disappearing in the billowing smoke from the boiler fires, screamed,

60

"Fogeys! Antiques! This ship has been fitted with the latest Watson vertical beam engine! This vessel can do fifteen knots against a ten-knot wind!" Cooder, wrenching a speaking horn from the leader of the lieder—a happy, smiling man in short leather pants who, blissfully for him, spoke not a word of English, bellowed—"This vessel has a proven hull speed of twelve knots—the lifeboats have a hull speed of six! You'll all be dragged down to the depths like dolphins and drown!" He was from Boston. He had thought it was the business opportunity of a lifetime when he had bought the boat sight unseen. Cooder, starting to hop up and down, waving his trident, thinking of his wife and children, shrieked, "I hired a band for the maiden trip. The band is all set to entertain you for the seven minutes—the mere seven minutes—it takes this great vessel to whisk you from one shore to another!" Cooder shrieked, "The Ride of the Valkyries!" He said to the horn-less singer who turned to open his mouth to let fly the opening notes, "Shut up!" Cooder shrieked, "No charge for the first ten men who board! And a lucky lifetime pass for as long as the lucky winner lives!"

On that vessel that might not have been long. She was a two-hundred-foot sidewheel paddle steamer that had always been fitted with a Watson vertical beam engine. She had always been fitted with it because—after she had been launched in November 1879 and immediately blown up in midstream, been refurbished and caught fire in April 1880, been refurbished and run down a schooner in February 1881, been refurbished, lost power and floated out into the Atlantic (twice) in September and October 1882, caught fire, blown up, lost power and floated upstream to Hell Gate and been beached in December—there had been so much refurbishment that no one had been able to take the engine out except Watson and he had become a broken man after the minor catastrophes of January 1882, April 1882, January 1883 and lately, March 1884, when she had, respectively, splintered one of her paddlewheels to toothpicks and circled around in an ever decreasing circle off Coney Island until her other wheel splintered, rammed the coal barkentine *Ann Eliza* in dock, set fire to her own smokestack and the sails of six oystermen foolish enough to be on the same ocean as she, and had her keel drop off in a gale with an excursion of lunatics from Blackwell's Island on board.

The lunatics had taken flight and escaped.

Watson had taken poison and died.

As business opportunities went, C.K. Cooder had the volunteers-only concession on the passage across the River Styx.

On the aft deck, as the lieder band, shrugging, dismissed, went below to get drunk, Cooder, a modern budding captain of industry, knowing that all it took to sell the public was a little subtle advertising, screamed through the voice horn as the ghastly ghost ship began its terrible trip, "Cowards! Jellyfish! Funkers!"

The salvage tugs were circling, the captains, thinking of all that nice wood and brass and iron.

C.K. Cooder shrieked, "*In Boston, they make better men than you!*"

C.K. Cooder shrieked, "All right then . . . ! *Full speed ahead!*"

In the last lifeboat, Muldoon, huddled by the helmsman at the rudder, said quietly, "You don't suppose his church will refuse to bury Billy Jenkins in consecrated ground because we said he killed himself, do you?"

Tillman said, "No." This morning, with *The King of the Sea* underway in a torrent of foam and abuse, it was easy to see why anyone might have death on their minds. Tillman, his hat pressed down hard on his head, looking small in the back of the boat next to Muldoon and the gigantic standing helmsman, said softly, "No."

He was thinking of the little room beyond the hall where the bath was. Muldoon, looking up and wiping spray from his face as *The King of the Sea* put on pressure to drag them all under, said "I'm no coward, Virgil. You know that."

"I know that."

Muldoon said, "I'm an Irish Catholic. Even though Billy Jenkins, with a name like that, has to have been an English Protestant, there are some things that—"

He had his leather pocket notebook open on his knees. There was a list of property taken from Rotary Rosie's rooms written on the first page. Tillman said, "Whoever drowned her didn't finish the job and after they took her away she came back through the tunnel from the other building into her room and took everything she thought was important." He could feel the thumping of the vertical beam engine of the ferry in the water under the flat keel of the lifeboat. "What Lily saw on the roof of Bunker's wasn't a ghost—it was Rosie trying to signal her with the same lamp she used when she went back into her rooms through the tunnel."

"I would have put my hand into that bath water—"

"All there was in there was a shoe." He looked down at his list, "And, in the room, leaving aside the scraps of fire-lighting paper and the furniture, wrapping paper from Hewitt and Company's Drapery Store on Broadway and—"

Muldoon said tightly, "And one hundred and eighty-seven wedding rings."

"And one hundred and eighty-seven wedding rings." Tillman said, "That had been wrapped in Hewitt and Company's paper." He saw Muldoon's face, "The paper was split along the folds where she must have dropped it and it broke open." Tillman said, "And a clipping from an old newspaper of twenty years ago about a fire in a house near Prospect Park that killed the father and mother of a family called Seymore and left their two girls, Lily and Rosie, orphans." He looked down at his list, "And nothing else." Tillman said, "The shoe was average cheap but serviceable quality, bought anywhere. There was no money hidden in the room because when she came back she took it all with her." Tillman said to finish it, "The Bowery Electric Girl only came in because she saw the open door and she thought there might be something to steal."

There was a crash as two of the lifeboats at the end of their lines astern must have collided, then a wave that rocked the stern of the last boat on the line—Tillman's and Muldoon's—and made the standing helmsman sway. Muldoon said tightly, "In Ireland souls and spirits—"

Tillman said, "Rosie wasn't a spirit. Rosie was a whore who was half drowned and then, presumably, taken away in a wagon or a carriage and thrown into the river to be picked up the next morning by the River Police or a passing fishing boat. Lily falling off the roof at Grammelspacher's was an accident."

"And the Bowery Electric girl, and Poditz delivering to the wrong address was a coincidence—"

"Yes, it was."

Muldoon said tightly, "The Theoretical Detective."

"The Theoretical Detective."

"In Ireland when I was a boy we didn't believe in theory and coincidences! In Ireland we believed that God sees everything and that He has a plan for us all and that—" He was getting wet. Muldoon, kneading at his fist, wanting to get onto dry land, afraid to look up, shaking his head against the smoke billowing back from the chugging, beat-missing Watson vertical beam engine ahead of them, said with his voice rising, "I knew Billy Jenkins, Virgil! I knew him when he was with the Strong Arm Squad, and then later, when he went to the Steamboat Squad I used to see him sometimes at the pier near the Customs House." Muldoon said to speak for him, "They put him back on the beat at the Fifth Precinct because he wrenched his back pulling a poor sailor off a burning wheat boat in the North River!" Muldoon, trying to catch hold of the side of the lifeboat to steady himself, said angrily, "Billy Jenkins was a good, old-style copper who never used his club if he could have a quiet word with you—" Muldoon said, "I don't want to have it on my conscience that he's in Hell because of what I said!" Muldoon, getting furious at the swaying, scudding boat and clenching his fist to give it a jab in the timbers, said with no room for argument, "I don't want to see him buried in unconsecrated ground because of a lie of mine!"

"Explain it to his Church if you feel you should."

"Don't think I won't!" Muldoon, shaking his head, said so the other passengers in the boat, huddled like soldiers, turned to look at him, "I'm no coward and I'll face even Chief Inspector Byrnes—the Big Finger—I'll face even him and tell him that I lied if that's what it takes to see Billy right!" Muldoon said, "Oh, I won't compromise that good man who helped—I'll say I shot him—but Billy . . . Billy Jenkins . . ." There was another crash and spray came over the bow and soaked him and silenced him. Muldoon said sadly, nodding, "You've read his file, haven't you? On the next page of your notebook you've taken down everything about him from his file at Headquarters, haven't you?" He was no coward, but there were some things he could not face. Muldoon said, "But I knew him! I knew when I saw him there behind the Bowery Electric Girl in the doorway—I saw him with the carboy of kerosene—" Muldoon said, "And he knew me."

"Yes."

Muldoon said quietly, "God has a plan for us all, Virgil. I believe that."

"I know you do."

"And I'm no coward. I'm not the sort of man to run—I'm not the sort of man to—" Muldoon demanded, "Have I ever let you down? Have I?"

"Never."

"I saw his face. I—" They were a little over halfway to Brooklyn, halfway there, as the steam whistle on *The King of the Sea* began screaming at them in defiance. Breathing sea air and getting wet, Muldoon said "I—he—"

He looked away. He was shaking, trembling, his fists knotted. He was no coward. He knew what he had seen.

"Virgil . . ." Muldoon, his jaw tight, looking Tillman straight in the face, holding his gaze, said suddenly, "Virgil, that place, that place under ground, when you went into the tunnel with the lantern—when my last lucifer went out—all those rings, all one hundred and eighty-seven of them—" Muldoon said, trembling, "Virgil, I swear to God, all of them, like something unholy—" Muldoon said tightly, "Virgil, on that floor there, in that place, all the rings, all of them—Virgil, I swear just for a moment, I saw them *glow blue in the dark!*"

Advertising. It wasn't so much that you had to convince the buying public that what you had was so wonderful, it was that you had to convince them that what the other fellow had on offer was worse.

The King of the Sea was burbling along beautifully, thumping thunderously, its twin wakes washing over the lifeboats. The German band, down below, drunk, was singing, serenading—they were full of smiles and suds.

C.K. Cooder, King Neptune, hurt, roared out over the foaming wakes to the crouching cowards, "I had plates of nibble treats for you! I had anchovies and tunafish and oysters and clams and crabs!"

That was what he had had on offer.

What the other fellow had on offer, wheeling and soaring high above the little wagon train of lifeboats, was seagulls.

What Neptune had was a two-inch-bore muzzle-loading, percussion-cap-fired line-throwing gun. What seagulls had was a stomach retention time between imbibation and evacuation of about one point zero seconds.

All the lifeboats were open.

Old merry King Neptune was a man who knew how to give orders. He gave four of them.

He ordered the white-coated Mess Boy on the upper deck, "Fish bits!"

He ordered the First Mate by the wheelhouse, "Line-throwing gun!"

He ordered himself, "Load . . . Aim!"

He ordered himself, ". . . Fire!!"

He was a man who knew when his first job was his last. He was a huge, hulking longshoreman wearing a turtleneck sweater and derby hat. At the helm, speaking up so everyone in the boat could hear him, the helmsman asked pleasantly, "Parasol hire, anyone?"

Tillman said, "Thanks." The helmsman had a score of them wedged in flat under his seat. At a quarter, the price seemed more than reasonable. Tillman, huddling with Muldoon as the air around them turned white, reading from the second page of his notebook, said, "Jenkins, William John, present age 39, born New York City, 1844. Father, George Edward Jenkins, stonemason, emigrated to the United States June 1837, deceased. Mother, Elizabeth Jenkins, née Hopkins, also deceased." He had gone back over everything Headquarters had had. "Metropolitan Police, January 1867, after Union Army garrison duty, port of New York with honorable discharge. Enlisted as probationary officer. Confirmed in the rank of Patrolman, July 1867, posted to Eighth Precinct, 128 Prince Street."

The plopping on the parasol was like rain. The Eighth in those days had been Captain Charlie McDonnell's precinct. He had been a good copper, McDonnell. He had been a man who liked a drink, but he had been a good copper to all his men. Muldoon said, "Things aren't black and white. For all we know, Billy Jenkins might have just seen the carboy of kerosene in the yard and, thinking he'd do the householder a good turn, picked it up to bring it in and—"

"The householder was Rotary Rosie."

"Well, maybe he didn't know that! Maybe he thought—"

The seagulls were wheeling, shitting. Tillman, ducking as he moved to turn the page in his notebook and was missed by a falling fish-ball, said looking at Muldoon, "He was the cop on the beat." He had it all written down on the little lined page in his notebook in what looked like some sort of shorthand. At first, at Headquarters, and then at the Fifth Precinct, it had taken him all night to get it. Tillman said evenly, reading from the hieroglyphs on the page, "No adverse reports, three accusations of bribe-taking found to be not proven and one complaint of brutality dropped, number of arrests in years 1867 through 1872, two hundred and twenty-three; number of successful prosecutions leading to imprisonment of suspect, eighteen; number of fines levied against suspects, forty-three. Sergeant's exam sat for, January 1872. Failed. Transferred to Steamboat Squad, Whitehall Street, the same year." Tillman said, "Commended for bravery, February 1873. Sergeant's exam sat for second time February 1874. Failed. Not promoted. Two allegations of taking money from dock pirate gang not proven when witnesses failed to appear at Administration Tribunal to give evidence. Charges dropped."

"Everyone gets charged with bribery at least once! It's the nature of the job!" Muldoon said reasonably, "It's like being caught in a bar in uniform—the rules say a cop shouldn't be in a bar in uniform unless he enters it because of a disturbance, but—"

Tillman said, "And the standard reply is that he went in there because he was disturbed. He was disturbed because he needed a drink." His face was set. Tillman said softly, "Who do you think took the pile of coins Santa Fe Sal left out on the steps of the Lively Flea each night? It was Jenkins' beat. It was Jenkins."

"For all we know he went into the hallway at Rosie's because he saw the boards on the door had been taken down!"

"Then if he was only being helpful and delivering the kerosene to the owner, why hadn't he been helpful a little earlier and taken the boards down to see what had *happened* to the owner? He was the one who put the boards up. He came in because they were down." Tillman said tightly, reading, "Involved in minor accident North River docks, December 1876, back injury, put on light duties. Transferred to Twentieth Precinct, West Thirty-fifth Street as enquiry desk assistant and records clerk, February 1877. Third attempt at sergeant's exam. December. Grade insufficient for promotion." Tillman said, "His third attempt and last. Remained on light duties until December 1879. Applied for transfer to Fifth Precinct, Leonard Street. Transferred January 1880 and returned to patrol duties Bowery–Canal Street beat, and then—"

He waited.

Tillman said, "And then, nothing. Arrests leading to successful prosecutions: none. Applications for transfer: none. Promotions applied for:

none. Age at transfer: thirty-six; rank: patrolman; yearly salary: eight hundred and fifty dollars a year; commendations or awards or adverse reports: nil. Injuries, sick leave or special mentions or circumstances: none."

Muldoon said shrugging, "He gave up. He couldn't make the sergeant's exam and he gave up."

Tillman said, "Seniority rating at January 1880: thirteen years. Place on list of automatic promotions in Precinct: number one. Desk sergeant rank offered May 1881. Refused. Reason given: recent relocation of accommodation from Manhattan Island to Brooklyn and difficulty of travel for split shifts required by promotion." He looked up. They were only three minutes out from the shoreline. Tillman said, "Previous accommodation: room in Water Street. Home address as from February 1880, care of Post Office box number 45, Brooklyn Post Office." Under the edge of the umbrella he could see the docks and piers of New York's second city. He could see, up on the heights, the tree-lined avenues. He had only one more line of symbols on the page, "Marital status: single. Debts and obligations listed on file: none." Tillman said tightly, "Salary: eight hundred and fifty dollars a year. Extras: *none.*"

Tillman said, "Total salary earned during thirteen years of police work: plus or minus eleven thousand dollars—"

"Everyone takes bribes, Virgil—everyone! No grown man can live on a patrolman's salary with a wife and family and—"

Tillman said, "Marital status: *single.*"

"—or resist the sort of temptation that comes a beat copper's way every day!"

"—Allowing for frugality and or bribe-taking: approximate value of assets—" He looked up.

"What assets?"

"P.O. Box 45, Brooklyn Post Office." He was still looking up from under the corner of the parasol. "I had the Post Office records department in Brooklyn telegraphed to see what P.O. Box 45 represented." He was looking straight ahead and up. Tillman, pointing, said, "It represents that." He was pointing up from the shoreline, to something high on the heights overlooking the water where the trees and avenues were. "That asset! Patrolman Billy Jenkins, silent and content for the last four years . . ." He was pointing, his arm outstretched, stiff, trembling a little, a look on his face of pure, unalloyed hate.

Tillman, uncaring of the bird shit as it fell like snow into the water all around the little, bobbing boat, said with his voice full of anger, "Jenkins, that good and honest and plodding patrolman who tried to fry us and everyone in that room to hell with kerosene—since February 1880 when suddenly all his ambition and money worries fell from his shoulders as if by magic—that bastard Jenkins has been living *there!*"

She was a great, wonderful white lady slicing through the seas.

She was freshly painted, polished, all her flags and bunting flying, her trusty paddlewheels making foam and spume and a mockery of time and distance and the separation of cities. She was his. She had cost him his life's savings. She was polished, pristine, provisioned. She was *The King of the Sea*. She was a maritime machine of mellifluous melody. She was the joy that filled his heart and brought tears to his eyes.

She was the dream of all his days and the nectar of his nights. She was a two-hundred-foot long, twenty-eight-foot beam, eight-hundred-ton vertical beam, side paddlewheel *steam*boat.

She was a two-hundred-foot long, twenty-eight-foot beam, eight-hundred-ton vertical beam, side paddlewheel steamboat towing a hearse line of little scows growing black parasols like toadstools.

His gun was out of ammunition.

His galley was all out of chopped-up fish.

The weeds were falling from his kingly crown and, downstairs, all the Prussians were pie-eyed and, to anyone from New York, it was clearly the end.

He was not, however, from New York.

He was from Boston. They knew how to treat people who didn't like boats in Boston.

On the aft deck, with all the grace and charm of the inhabitants of that great maritime tea-drinking town, C.K. Cooder shrieked without benefit of voice horn to anyone on board who might have an axe, "Swines! Bastards! *Cut the rotten bastards' tow lines!*"

In the sterns of each of the eight lifeboats, each of the eight helmsmen enquired pleasantly, "Mast and sail erection, anybody? One dollar."

It seemed, to each of the one hundred and twenty passengers, at approximately six cents, plus tip, an extremely reasonable fee.

He looked up. He saw the house.

Muldoon said in a gasp, *"God Almighty—!"*

"Cowards! Fools! Traitors to progress and civilization!" It was *The King of the Sea*'s maiden voyage under new management.

She was there, ten seconds away from the long wooden pier jutting out from the shoreline, a symphony of grace and speed. She had not burned. She had not blown up. She had not lost her rudder or her sidewheels. She had collided with no one, drifted nowhere.

She roared. She thundered. She foamed with the reverse thrust of both the great sidewheels turning astern under the force of the live steam scalding in her Watson vertical beam engine. She had made it, come through. She was a great, white bird slicing through time and space.

She was eight hundred tons of solid wood and brass and iron.

"Fogeys! Know-nothings! New Yorkers! *You'll need to beg on bended knee to ride this great vessel now!*"

It was a wonderful day for a triumph.

Triumphantly, as the ghost of Watson laid an icy finger on the levers and stopped the engine in midstroke, *The King of the Sea*, the great white painted lady, hit the end of the pier head-on and mowed it full length to matchwood.

Muldoon said softly, "God in Heaven, Virgil . . . !" He was looking, not at the Specter of Death as it turned oak into oakum or pylons into pulp, but up at Jenkins' house on the hill.

"Beach landing, anyone? Fifty cents."

He watched opened-mouthed all the way as, off to the little tasks of their daily round, ducking and avoiding falling, burning parts of boat and pier and what looked like segments of a seaweed crown, one hundred and twenty people, gently, safely, with the dignity and confidence that only canvas and God's own soft wind on the sea could bring, sailed safely, gently onto the shoreline of the great, sylvan, sleeping city of Brooklyn.

9

It was a wonderful, wonderful, two-story brick house on the heights below Furman Street overlooking the river across to the shoreline of Lower Manhattan.

Surrounded on all sides by latticed verandahs, it was a modern copy of one of the great houses of the early Dutch merchant-settlers built amid stands of shading trees and bushes, with a mock brick tower with a railed-in widow's walk above it and, in respectable salute to the merchants who had once lived in houses such as this one and watched for their trade ships entering and leaving New York harbor, a flagpole for their company's standard.

There was a white picket fence running the perimeter of the entrance to the house from the tree-lined avenue it stood in. Standing at it, Tillman and Muldoon, a small, sparrow-like man and a huge ox, both in bowler hats and suits that felt a little too tight and shiny, looked up to the open doors of the place behind the front verandah.

Muldoon said in a whisper, *"God preserve us—!"* He smelled everywhere, the smell of flowers and new-mown grass.

Muldoon said, "God . . . ! In that carriage house—" He could see it sticking out a little from the open doors, shining with newness. Muldoon said, "God Almighty, there's even a brand-new big-wheel fifty-dollar Columbia bicycle in there!"

It was a mansion. It had cost, even empty, a minimum of twenty thousand dollars.

It was set on a full two acres of flowers and trees and bushes.

It was where Patrolman Billy Jenkins of the Fifth Precinct lived.

There was someone at the open door, waiting for them, watching them—an old woman in a dark dress. Gingerly, so as not to strain the hinge or make it creak, Tillman and Muldoon pushed open the little wooden gate to the place and, watching where they put their boots on the laid

70

cobblestone path through the perfume of all the flowers and trees and stillness and silence, went in.

She was Jenkins' housekeeper, nothing more.

She had had the news last night at midnight, telegraphed from the owl shift at Headquarters to the Joralemon Street Police Telegraph Office in Brooklyn and delivered by a patrolman from the First Precinct Station in Atlantic Street, and after the patrolman had left she had begun cleaning the house from top to bottom in preparation for the morning. Standing in the main drawing room of the place in a plain gray dress and shoes, with her hat and purse ready on the sidetable outside in the hall, with the heavy carpets and the oil paintings, the gleaming, polished mahogany and oak furniture around her, she was perhaps sixty-six years old with her skin dried and pale from a lifetime of toil, her hands red from hot water and housework. Mrs. Gillon said, "If there's anything else in the house I can show you—" She had the keys in her pocket. She held them up.

He shook his head. Tillman, gazing at it all, said softly, "Not at the moment."

They had walked through all the rooms on the first floor. It was a museum, dustless, untouched, all the paintings arranged and hung straight in lines and rows, the billiard table in the games room at the back shining and smelling of polish and new baize, all the balls in their rack bright and unused, the cues shining with their original varnish, the little squares of chalk for the tips still wrapped in their original packets, the decks of cards and bottles at the card table and in the drinks cupboards unopened and laid out like exhibits in a time capsule, all the chairs and sofas in the sitting room and on the verandahs uncreased and un-sat in, all the china and glass in the kitchen stacked still with protective sheets of cardboard between plates and bowls as it had been delivered from the store, still with the original price tags. Mrs. Gillon said, "Anything you want to inspect I can show you."

He wanted to say something. Muldoon said, looking around, feeling huge in the room, "It's a credit to you, ma'am, this house. In the old houses in Ireland when I was a boy, the lords and ladies used to crow about their furniture and how good it was, but it was the servants over generation to generation who really kept it looking—" The house was fully lit by electricity. It had indoor plumbing. Outside, in a little room off the rear verandah, there was even an indoor privy with automatic chain-flushing sewerage. He ran out of words. Muldoon said to compliment her, "And I'll wager too you're the hard-worker in the garden who's responsible for all those beautiful blooms we saw on the way in, aren't you?"

She had lived upstairs in the house for almost four years, for almost as long as Jenkins had owned it. Mrs. Gillon said, "Yes." She paused a moment. She asked Tillman respectfully, "Did he have any relatives, sir? Mr. Jenkins?"

Tillman said, "No."

"Perhaps in New York City or—"

She was, like the furniture and the house, after the death of the owner, disposable.

Tillman said, "He had a cousin in England, but that was a few years ago according to his record. Whether or not his cousin is still alive, I don't know." He asked, "Did anyone come here—his friends? People he knew here in Brooklyn, or people he worked with or—"

Mrs. Gillon said, "No." She was wearing a plain gray walking-out dress and her hat was on the sidetable in the paneled hallway with a little cloth pocketbook. Upstairs, in her room below the widow's walk, all her bags were packed. Mrs. Gillon said, "Mr. Jenkins was hardly ever home. He took his meals in New York or, if he was off duty, at Gage and Tollner's restaurant here in Brooklyn. Sometimes if he went outside to the verandah to smoke a cigar he took coffee, but he always made it himself, in a saucepan." Mrs. Gillon said, "The first year I served him, he used to take his carriage out to the stores, and I helped him arrange the furniture and things he bought, but after a while, when there was no more room for anything—" Mrs. Gillon said, "He sold the carriage and he used to walk to the ferry to Manhattan in the mornings and walk back when he got in late at night." Mrs. Gillon said, "He wasn't at first, but after a while he became a very quiet man at home."

Mrs. Gillon said, "At first, Mr. Jenkins took an interest in the garden. At first, a lot of people from the stores came to show him how to arrange the rooms and what to buy from their catalogues—the carriage man came by one Saturday with six carriages drawn by pairs of horses so he could choose which one he wanted—but after all the rooms and stables and sheds were all full, and there was no room for more, they stopped coming." She glanced at Muldoon, "A horticulturalist came all the way from Pennsylvania to landscape the gardens and the lawns and eight gardeners came to dig the grounds and set out the paths—but that was years ago."

Mrs. Gillon said, "Mr. Jenkins was happy to let me tend the flowers, and a local man mows the lawn once a week." Mrs. Gillon said, "Mr. Jenkins took no interest in the grounds. He never walked in the garden."

Muldoon said, "What did he *do* here then?"

"He sat on the verandah smoking a cigar."

"There aren't any cigars in the house."

"There are a dozen boxes of Havanas in the dining room in the brandy cupboard." Mrs. Gillon said, to prove she had stolen nothing, "With the receipt from the tobacconist. They're unopened. Mr. Jenkins always brought his own cigars home with him from New York in the pocket of his tunic."

Tillman asked, "You did his washing and pressing?"

"And his cleaning and provisioning, and sweeping and—"

"Was there ever anything in the pockets of his uniform when you cleaned it?"

Mrs. Gillon said quickly, "Oh, no. Mr. Jenkins was always careful to take out his pistol and his club and his handcuffs before he gave me his uniform to clean." Mrs. Gillon said, "His billfold and loose change I left for him on his bedside table."

Tillman said easily, "What sort of cleaning did his uniform require? Did you, for example, ever have to remove bloodstains from it?"

"Oh, no." Mrs. Gillon said, "Just ordinary marks. I used Robbins' Clean-All on it. It was a little more expensive than ordinary cleaners, but when I explained to Mr. Jenkins that it made the cloth smell nicer because it didn't have ammonia in it, he said to buy it." Mrs. Gillon said, "I made the man at the store give me a receipt."

Muldoon said, "Your husband must have been a well-looked-after man when he was alive." He smiled at her to show that as a man he appreciated what a good, honest women could do for a man when she set her mind to it and she was treated with a little respect.

He was a policeman. His bulk filled the room. Mrs. Gillon said, "I'm not a married woman, sir. I've never been a married woman. It's just the form."

Tillman said, "A week ago, did you remove any stains from Mr. Jenkins' uniform?"

"I didn't use the Robbins' Clean-All. They were just water stains so I washed the tunic in suds and then wiped it off and left it on the clothesline in the sun to—"

"What sort of water stains?"

Mrs. Gillon said, "Freshwater and salt. And little bits of enamel paint like paint from a bathroom fixture or a stove. Salty water like the harbor because after I brushed the cleaned coat off there were little bits of sand still on it." Mrs. Gillon said, "I mentioned it to Mr. Jenkins and he said it was part of a silly ceremony at a secret society he belonged to." Mrs. Gillon said, "I didn't ask him because it wasn't my place, but Mr. Jenkins said that was where he spent most of his time at nights: at his society." She said, still serving him even after he was dead, "Mr. Jenkins was an *oubliette* in his society."

Muldoon said, thinking she had got it wrong, "An oubliette is something in a castle the lords used to throw their enemies into—it's French. They had one at a castle in County Meath in Ireland near me when I was a boy. It's a bottomless pit. I learned about it in history at school. It means a Forgettor."

There was a framed Currier and Ives print of Custer's Last Stand at the far end of the wall, the only picture in the room of no value or quality, the only picture hung not from the picture rail running the length of the wall, but apparently screwed directly into the plaster, the only picture that, perhaps, the experts he had paid to tell him what to buy and what to hang and what to have, had not told him to have or hang. Tillman asked, nodding at the heroic scene of the beleaguered Custer battling the Indians in the last great victory of the Red Man eight years ago, "Behind that picture of Custer, is that—"

Mrs. Gillon said, "Mr. Jenkins was a very patriotic man."

"—is that where the safe is?"

Mrs. Gillon said, surprised, "Yes." She had been right to tell the truth about everything. They were policemen. If she did not tell them, they would find out. Mrs. Gillon said, "But I don't have the key and I don't know what's in it except Mr. Jenkins' telephone. I heard it ringing once and he told me that he—"

Muldoon said in astonishment, *"He even had a private telephone in here?"*

Mrs. Gillon said, "But I don't know where the key is."

"I have the key." Tillman, taking Jenkins' keys from his pocket said, "They were removed from his—I got them at the hospital after— Wait outside in the garden." Tillman, smiling, nodding at her to dismiss her, said, "Thank you."

She paused. She was dressed and packed in the extinct, dead place. She was ready to go.

Tillman said to her, "Wait in the garden. If we need you we'll call."

At the swung-back picture of the last stand of the Seventh Cavalry, Muldoon said as Tillman selected the right key from Jenkins' key ring, "He drowned her in the bath and threw her body into the harbor, didn't he?"

"Yes."

Muldoon said sadly, "It was him, wasn't it?" The print was full of light and color and glory and death. The room it faced was full only of death. It depressed him. Muldoon said, "Billy Jenkins—it was him, wasn't it?"

"Yes." He had no idea at all, apart from the telephone, what he would find in the space behind the secure steel door in the wall behind the picture. He had only ever once seen a telephone before in his life, and that was the Police Telephone at Headquarters in Mulberry Street, and he had no idea what a telephone for a private person would even look like.

Fitting the key carefully into the lock and turning it once to release the tumblers, he reached for the handle on the one-and-a-half-inch plate-steel door to find out.

In the garden, she was sitting not on one of the ornamental cast-iron seats or on the unpainted ship's timber benches built around the great trees, but on the grass.

She had been working from midnight when the patrolman had come, cleaning the house.

Everywhere around her, there was the smell of flowers and fresh, new-mown grass.

On that grass, amid the flowers, Mrs. Gillon waited.

"So that's what an electric speaking telephone looks like!!" Muldoon, taller by a head than Tillman, pushing in to get a better look at Man's latest attempted usurpation of God's previously sole right of Creation, said, stunned, "Look at the complication of it!" The object filled the entire two-foot-square opening behind the steel door in the cavity, a polished wooden box banded in brass with bells and earpieces and levers and winders and funnels and wires—wires everywhere. Muldoon said, "It must weigh thirty pounds!" Muldoon said, reading from the brass hand-engraved plaque set in the center of the horrible contraption, *The Metal Tympanium Electro-Magnetic Telephone Company, New York, Instrument Model I.* " Muldoon, shaking his head, something deep held inside him confirmed, said with his finger pointed like a priest giving a sermon, "And to think God built all of Man out of a lump of clay!" He touched at the instrument. It was wood and metal and wire and, inside the wood and metal and wire . . . Muldoon, shaking his head, said in horror, "Virgil, when they finally build an electric man he's going to need two steam trains to pull him!" Muldoon said with his fingers drumming on the glittering beast to tell it it was a failure, "In my humble opinion—" Muldoon, starting back as the entire object came at him with a *ping!* from one of its bells, yelled, "It *moved!* It's *alive!*"

"It's on hinges."

"I knew that!"

"—there must be some sort of electric charge still left in one of the bells."

Muldoon said, "I knew that!"

"There's something in the safe behind it."

"I knew that!" He saw Tillman, with no fear at all, put his hand in behind the swung-out instrument into the darkness of the safe and feel around. Muldoon said, "I knew that! It's just a box of bells and brass and wires—I knew that!"

He too was brave. He stood his ground and tried to peer in.

Muldoon said, bravely, in spite of himself, with no tremor in his voice at all, "So? So what's in there?"

She was ready to go.

Outside, on the grass, her hat and purse in her lap, Mrs. Gillon rubbed at her hands.

In the garden between the empty, lifeless house and the street—the tree-lined avenue that now went nowhere—opening her purse, she took out her walking-out gloves and put them on.

It was money.

At the safe cavity, Tillman said in a whisper, "God Almighty . . . !"

It was money in wads. It was money in stacks of gold twenty-dollar pieces and wads of bills, money in rolls and bundles, money in sheafs and in bales, money held together in paper wrappers or loose, money folded and shoved in where there was no more room for money—it was money pressed in so tightly in the confined space that it was a wall of money, a barrier of money—it was so much money it spilled out at a touch and cascaded to the carpeted floor, and when Tillman reached in to scoop the remainder of it out, there was still as much as had fallen, and then, this time as he tried to get it out in a solid lump, behind it, there was even more money.

It stilled him to silence. He wanted to say something, had it in his mind, but it did not come out, and he merely stood openmouthed, staring.

Muldoon said, fighting to make the words, ". . . My God, Virgil . . ." He saw as he turned to look back at the room the walls and the pictures and the carpet and the furniture. Muldoon said in a gasp, "My God, Virgil—" The floor around him was layered in engraved bills—twenties and fifties and hundreds. They covered his boots like leaves. Muldoon, trying to take it all in, slapping his hand against the side of his head to jolt his brain, said in a gasp, "Houses, horses, servants, bicycles . . . !" Muldoon, looking down, looking everywhere at what Jenkins had, said, "My God, *why did he stay a cop on eight hundred a year for another four years if he had all this when he came here?*" He said as Tillman reached in and removed from the glory hole not more money, but something else, "What's that? What have you got?"

It was a parcel wrapped in thick brown paper eight inches long and six inches thick tied together with string. As it came out, it was heavy.

His brain had ceased to work on the level normal men's brains worked at. Muldoon, slapping his head again with his palm, hoping to shake something loose to work on a level of existence it had never worked at before, said, expecting it to be true, "My God, what the hell's wrapped in there? *Diamonds?*"

In the garden, Tillman said softly to the woman sitting on the grass with her gloved hands in her lap, "We've searched his desk in the billiard room, but all we found were his various birth and police documents and receipts for the house and the furniture." He saw her hope for a moment, "There's no will or anything about you or any special instructions in the event of his death."

Mrs. Gillon said, "He died young." She glanced at her hands.

"There's nothing about any secret society or, so far as we can find, any sort of Masonic regalia or correspondence." He had the rewrapped brown parcel in his hand. Tillman said, "Mr. Muldoon is putting a few things back in the safe. He'll be out in a moment."

He had in his hand the eight-inch-long, six-inch-thick packet tied with string held by the side of his coat. Tillman said gently to Mrs. Gillon, "Mr. Jenkins gave you no character in any of the papers we found." She was sixty-six years old, unmarried, with no one. She was ready to go. Tillman said, "So I have. I've written a letter for you to take to the Brooklyn Police stating that I have seldom before met a woman of such unveering honesty and application and I have asked the Inspector In Charge as a courtesy to the Detective Bureau to allow you to stay on here as caretaker until an heir to the estate can be located, and, after that, to commend you to the future owner in the position of housekeeper." In all the house, in the hours between the time the patrolman had come from Joralemon Street and the time they had come, she had stolen nothing. Tillman said, "I hope it puts your mind at rest about your future."

He had, held loosely in his hand by his side, the packet of two hundred and forty blue and white stereoscope views of Rotary Rosie Seymore, naked, posing with her breasts bared, and in two views each of the eight cards that made up each of the thirty complete sets in the packet, completely naked, lying full length on a carved ottoman couch amid brocaded cushions, smiling, with her legs open before the camera.

He had in his hand the rewrapped packet from Jenkins' safe.

"*Rosie—Ready*" It was the legend on each of the views. It had on it, no photographer's name at all.

He laid his hand lightly on the woman's shoulder as she looked up at him from the grass.

Tillman said softly to the servant obedient and loyal beyond questioning, grateful only for her position and the hope it gave for her old age, "My God, woman, didn't you ever wonder though? Didn't you ever once wonder what Patrolman Jenkins—for all this—*really did?*"

10

Slipping a slide of the Wonders of Egypt into the portable T-shaped viewer on the rack, the big man, jolted to astonishment by the sudden sight of the Sphinx in full living three-dimensional color only inches from his eyes, said, "Oh! *Magical!*"

They looked as if they had recently completed some terrible sea voyage. Their clothes were still wet. You could tell they were sailors by the revolvers stuck in their belts.

In Quinney's Photographic and Three-Dimensional Hand-Tinted Stereograph Studio at 108 Broadway, Tillman, rolling a little as he walked among the racks of stereo views, gazing first at Blondin Crossing Niagara on a Tightrope and then, barely half a rack away—the wonders of the modern shrinking globe—to a view of Mexican Peasants Planting Corn, said proudly to Quinney, "This here be Cap'n Richard Moby, Master Mariner!" He raised his starboard flipper to introduce the great man beside him. Tillman, a mere dwarf in the presence of the looming lobscourer he had the honor to accompany, said, "No need for formality with me. I be but the Cap'n's humble Mate." Tillman said, "Call me Ishmael."

A tear came to the eye of the noble Nautilus. Muldoon, swinging his great davit down to embrace his sterling subordinate, said to Quinney with a heave and the distant look of a man who had seen sights and seas seen by no mere land-living man, "I love this little fellow, Mr. Quinney." He fixed Quinney with his glittering eye. (He only had one. The other seemed permanently closed, probably from some terrible encounter with a sea monster.) Muldoon, gazing at the slight man in his artist's smock and fingers stained brown from the mysterious process of photography, said with his paw still on the shoulder of the diminutive deckie, "A happy ship is a futtock-fine furler!"

"The Cap'n, he look after his crew." Tillman, the happy helmsman, said with his eyes sparkling like a child's at Christmas, "The Cap'n, he buy from his own duffle bag, a skittles set for the crew!" He jerked his thumb out the open door of the place toward the street. Obviously, the skittles set was being transported by wagon or on the backs of a line of waiting, smiling Jolly Jack Tars doing the hornpipe in pleasure. Tillman, shaking his sail, said, "He buy for the crew from Messrs. Harpers and the Enquiring Publishing Company, all—all—the newest volumes in the set of the Enquiring Soul's Starter to Self-Education!" Let no man spare the kindly commodore's blushes. Tillman, not to be stopped, telling the world, looking around in the deserted gallery for human ears, said flying the little flag of his finger, "For his crew—for our coming voyage—the Cap'n—he bought a harmonium!"

"A singing Schooner is a—"

Tillman said, "Now 'ee buy three hundred stereo views and viewers for all!" Little Ishmael was almost beside himself. He touched at the mighty hull at the shoulder and scraped it clear with his palm.

The Cap'n said, "And fiddles for to play Irish jigs on the foredeck!" It was the New Age. The Cap'n, looking down at Quinney said happily, "A skittling, singing, sight-seeing—" He was an old salt who had seen many sights. Muldoon, gently removing the scraping palm from his paintwork, said seriously, "Hanging doesn't work, Mr. Quinney, and flogging has been a failure. Keelhauling merely slows progress and shooting, ah, shooting . . ." Muldoon said, "No, this next great Circuit . . ." He gazed off into the distance. The Cap'n, grinning to himself, glowing with expectation at a jolly good jink on the dancing Drink, said in spite of himself, "Damn it, sir, have even purchased for my men this day a box of penny whistles and two cases of pencils and sketching materials!"

The grinning gob said in his delight, "And we will have funny paper hats for the passing over the plinth line of the Pacific!"

"And you will have funny paper hats for the passing over of the plinth line of the Pacific!"

"And ribbons for our hair!"

"And ribbons for your hair!"

"'Broidered bunks for our backs!"

"You shall have *tapestry,* honest sailor!"

"Oh, Christian Commodore!"

"And, I shall rush out, the moment this present transaction is completed and purchase, for each man, soft slippers!" Cap'n Moby said, "Money is no object. I shall even purchase in advance, for each man who has signed on, the services of a full-time Turkish masseur in each port along the way!"

"Oh . . . !" He was beside himself. Tillman, starting to swoon, speaking on behalf of all those who sweated before the mast and the lash and the gun, trilled, "Oh Heaven-sent humanitarian! Benign benefactor!

Outstanding altruist! Grand Goodheart! He was in ecstasy. He danced a little hornpipe. Tillman, as happy as a moth, said to Quinney in joy that knew no bounds, "This be a happy ship, Mr. Quinney. This be a singing sampan, a whistling wherry, a contented cockleshell. This be—"

Mr. Quinney said mildly, asking the Captain, "This be . . . ?"

He was proud of her. Cap'n Moby said, "This be the good ship *Der Fliegende Holländer*! And she sail in the morrow on the tide!"

Oh, slightly mixed-up matelot. Ishmael, still grinning, slapping the great man gently on the chest, said happily, "Oh no sir, she be gone, that ship. I served on her and she—why she down there in Davy Jones' locker these days with her cargo of coal oil that exploded-like and—"

Cap'n Moby said in an even tone, smiling, "She has been salvaged and refitted."

Oh, humorous Helmsman. Ishmael, shaking at the shoulder from the Captain's little joke, said, "Ha, ha, ho, ho, ho, sir, that was a good one!" Ishmael said, "Ah, sir, we be a crackling carrick this trip—the *Fliegende Holländer,* she went to smithereens with the soul of many a good man and she—"

Muldoon said, "Mr. Mate, she has been made good again!" He seemed happy at the news.

"—and she carry more coal oil, aye, sir?" Oh, he were a jolly joking jasper all right. Ishmael said, "Ho, ho, ho, ho! By the blazing fire in the galley when I fun with the fellows, how they will laugh at that one, sir, and split their—"

Cap'n Moby said in a voice of iron, "No naked flames allowed."

"Ho! Ho! Ho! *Ho!* Oh, Have-a-Laugh, Lads, Ha-ha." Ishmael, positively shaking with glee, said, almost unable to get the words out for his merriment, "Ah, Mr. Quinney, my Cap'n, he be making a little sailor's reference to the blackhearted Blighs of the Briny who secretly sign their crews onto death ships and fake illness at the last moment and leave their First Mates to either make the voyage with dangerous cargos and remit them the profits or to die like the poor lads on the *Fliegende Holländer* and be made rich on shore by the insurance!" He glanced at the Prince of the Poop Deck. He glanced at the good man's face. He glanced at his good eye. He glanced at the other good one that he had never noticed was no good before. Ishmael said, "By the slide show of the magic lantern, how the gobs will guffaw!"

"No magic lanterns."

"On the singing deck timbers, how the nails in our boots will strike sparks of delight from the iron fastenings on the—"

Cap'n Moby said as an order, "No nails in boots. No iron fastenings in the decks. No—"

". . . as we smoke our clay pipes in the moonlight and . . ."

"No smoking. No matches. No tinder." He touched at his eye. Cap'n Moby, glancing at Quinney, said as if it was a sudden thought, "How my eye troubles me this day. I do hope it is recovered sufficiently for me to take command of my vessel tomorrow and not entrust it to—"

Ishmael said, *"What?"*

"My eye. It—"

Mr. Quinney asked politely, "The *Fliegende Holländer* . . . ?"

Cap'n Moby said proudly, "Salvaged, serviced, resealed and ready for sea!"

Ishmael said, *"—What?"*

"Ready with her cargo for the continuance of commerce!"

Ishmael said in a soft voice, "Murderer—"

Cap'n Moby said, "Mr. Quinney, for the joy and comfort of my crew, whether I be fit enough to accompany them or not, or whether I must sleep secure in my shore bed at night knowing my dearest friend Ishmael leads in my stead, I will take one thousand of your slides and a portable viewer for each man!"

Ishmael said, *"Assassin—!"*

It was as if he heard not a syllable. Cap'n Moby said, "Let us have uplifting and educational views produced for our inspection by the score!"

"Butcher—!"

He touched at his eye. Poor fellow, obviously it was getting worse. But he bore up bravely. He had a noble face. He rested his kindly hand on Mr. Quinney's shoulder. Really, at the rate Mr. Quinney monopolized a conversation, it was a wonder he ever got any business done at all.

"—Widow-maker—!"

Kindly Cap'n Moby said, leading the man, "Come, sir, have you not a back room here—your studio perhaps—where you might not have a comfortable chair or ottoman for a fellow with a sore eye to sit on while he makes you a tidy sum from the profits he intends beginning to make tomorrow on the tide delivering his cargo of forty tons of loose gunpowder to the Lava Belt?"

Ishmael said softly, *"Hangman . . . ! Executioner . . . ! Axeman . . . !*

Ishmael, not so softly, his eyes wide and staring, his fists clenched, giving Mr. Quinney such a shock that he almost collided with a rack and sent the sets of the poor Mexican peons planting in the plot tumbling to the floor, screamed at the top of his voice, *"Villain! Vulture!"*

Ishmael shrieked, *"—Sea Captain!!"*

In the center of his studio, ripping at the top buttons on his full-length artist's smock, Mr. Quinney, also shrieking, screamed, *"Don't hang yourself here! Please!"* The little man was on top of a four-foot-high hinged wooden egg Quinney used to photograph newborn infants for their doting parents. Over a rafter hanging with swords and bludgeons, battle-axes and blunt instruments he used to photograph educational scenes from English history, the sailor had thrown a stout rope (used to photograph tightrope walkers and occasionally restrain the newborn babes and infants and players in medieval scenes from English history gotten a little out of hand), and in that rope he had tied a noose. Quinney shrieked, "All the knives and swords are blunt! We couldn't cut you down before you throttled!"

He had a comfortable corner of the carved ottoman in a corner of the room where the Arabian tent scene was. The Cap'n, reading from the little advertising booklet he had found by the campfire of the Western scene on his way to Arabia, said with interest, "Oh, I see how it works now. The two photographs on the viewing card are pictures of the same scene or person taken by two different lenses two and a half inches apart—the same width as the eyes on the human face—and the brain, looking at the resulting prints puts the two slightly different images together in the brain as one picture with foreground, background and subject!" The Cap'n said, impressed, "Mr. Oliver Wendell Holmes, the inventor of the modern portable stereograph viewer, calls the subjects viewed in this way 'pages ripped from the book of God's recording angel.'" Muldoon said, "Fascinating!" The Cap'n, glancing up from a page thick with optical equations, focal lengths and long discussions of the mechanism of the human brain, said to allay Mr. Quinney's concern, "Ignore him. He'll come down."

Mr. Quinney said as an order, "The Captain says to come down!"

"Hell-ship!" The eyes were rolling. He was very small and slight. Maybe he was a foreigner. Maybe he might do it. Mr. Quinney looked at the Captain. The Captain was reading. He turned a page and crossed his legs and followed the equations with his finger. Mr. Quinney said, "Now, listen to reason—!"

"All in a hot and copper sky . . ."

Mr. Quinney said, "Quite."

"All the boards . . ."

"Yes?"

The eyes came back. They were mad eyes, "They did *shrink!*" He was reeling on the point of the egg, the noose tight around his neck, his shoes starting to slip, *"Water—!"*

Quinney said, "I'll get you some!"

"—everywhere, and not a drop to drink!"

Quinney said, "I think I heard of this disaster at sea somewhere myself—!"

Tillman, on his egg, said helpfully, "It was in all the papers at the time." Tillman said, *"The crew! The crew!"* Tillman said with the eyes gone again, "Captain, my Captain—" His hands were wandering in the air like crabs, his voice gone to a whisper. *"The crew! The crew!* All the lost souls of the hollow-eyed crew dragging, dragging their chains and bony feet across the ghost of that doomed ship!"

"They'll have their fiddles to play and their slippers to—" The egg shifted. Quinney, reaching for his flowing hair to tear it out in clumps, screamed through clenched teeth, "Oh, please! Please—in the name of—*please come down from the egg!"*

"Devils! Devils in seamen's boots! Wild-eyed, hard men with knives and marlinspikes—the foul, fated *Fliegende Holländer* mad mutineers bent on treasure and piracy with only little me alone against them!"

"Pshaw!" In his comfortable billet, Cap'n Moby the Cruel said without looking up, "Let them look at stereoviews!"

"Ah—yee!" He made a sobbing sound. He made a gulp. He said, reaching up to center the noose around his windpipe before launching himself into black and pitiless Eternity, *"Goodbye!"*

"I have views of stirring Germanic military parades from the Franco-Prussian War I can let you have at the same price as the regular portraits of flower and forest views and the Mexican planting corn!"

There was no hope. "On board, we have Frenchmen from the lowest dives of Marseilles with stiletto knives!"

"I have a series of the great victories of Napoleon reproduced from the finest oil paintings in Paris!"

"We have Prussians with clubs!"

The Cap'n, not looking up from his mathematics, said in a gentle but firm paternal tone, "Just so long as you don't have any naked lights on board."

"Representations of Greek and Roman statuary!"

"Made of stone?"

"Yes!"

"As in 'sink like a stone'?"

"Mountains!"

"We have Swiss with secret crossbows in the sleeves of their sailors' coats!"

"Perfect then!"

"We have a flatlander Austrian who hates the Swiss!"

"Scenes of a *Christian* nature?"

"As in *Fletcher* Christian?" It was all too much. Ishmael said, tensing, "Betrayed. Blown up. Bludgeoned. Murdered. Marooned. Mutinied against—" Ishmael, looking down, bending the knees for the last setting of the sail, the Great Drop, the Last Leap, said in the final torture, "Goodbye! I go to the soft glow at the edge of the horizon to be with my band of—" Ishmael said, "Hsst! Do I hear them call me? Do I detect a seaweeded phantom finger beckoning me from the Vast Bottom? Yes! I hear!" He wasn't going to jump; he was going to merely, slowly, sadly lean off the top of the egg into eternity. Ishmael, cocking his hand to his ear, said, calling back, "I come . . . I come . . ."

"I have things that will keep even the vilest beast openmouthed in amazement while you pilot your ship from here to the Lava Belt!"

Muldoon said, "I like the idea of the Mexicans planting corn. That's educational for a multinational crew. I'll take forty sets."

"Plotting . . . plotting against me like rats in the bilges, honing their knives to needle point, dulling their clubs . . ."

"I have views for private circulation only!"

"Gabbling, jabbering, whispering—all conspiring against me in their native tongues . . ."

"I have views that *need* no common language!"

"Ghosts of drowned mariners, here I come!"

"I have views of *women* hidden here in my studio!" Even the Cap'n looked up. Quinney, starting for a locked cupboard against the wall, reaching into his pants pocket for the key, said, "Yes! Even the Captain looked up at that one!"

He paused in the business of self-suspension. Ishmael, looking interested, said, "Women with no . . . *Naked* women?" He thought about it. He looked hard at Quinney, "Women with no— *Young* women? Women with thighs and ankles and—?"

"Completely fully equipped women! Women who once reclined upon that very ottoman in this very studio! Women who—" He was a genius, and it was going to cost a hell of a lot more too, "What honest sailor worth the name of old, lascivious salt will care whether he sails on fair ship or foul with his own library of—" He was at the cupboard, working the key. Quinney, a true artist, a manipulator par excellence of both mannequin and men, said, reaching in for a bundle, "Pictures of naked women the like of which you have seen nowhere on all the seven seas of the world! Pictures to drive men into a state of aphrodisiacal automatism! Pictures to swoon before! Pictures—" He had the first bundle. He was inside the open cupboard ripping at the paper wrapper that secured it. "Pictures like—"

He heard a sound behind him. Quinney, turning, said with his voice changing, suddenly weakening, running out of strength, "Pictures . . ."

Tillman said softly, an inch behind him, "Pictures like this?" He had, held up, a picture of Rosie naked on the ottoman. Tillman said with Muldoon standing stock-still beside him like a statue with his kindly

Captain's face tight and hard, "Your name isn't on any of the photographs, but you used the same ottoman for all your seated poses of Scenes from the Shakespearean Plays and Famous Actors. Copies of them are in all the retail stereograph stores up and down Broadway, everywhere."

Tillman said in a voice that chilled the smock-coated man to the bone, "Nice pictures of a naked, young, willing woman. Tell me—*do you have any more?*"

He was wearing heavy boots to protect his feet against the corrosion of the chemicals he used in his developing work. In his studio, Quinney gave the ottoman a single kick and smashed one of the legs off. Quinney said with triumph, "Now it isn't the same ottoman!"

He was at the open secret cupboard taking out the wrapped packets of cards. There were none of Rosie. Tillman, turning back and glancing at the damage, nodding, said agreeably, "Right."

The big one, planted in the center of the room, blocking off the exit to the gallery and the street, did not move. Quinney said, "All I have to say is that someone brought these pictures in and I was so shocked that as an act of public good I confiscated them and put them there in the cupboard where they'd be safe from the eyes of women and children and the mentally enfeebled until I had the time to take them out somewhere and destroy them!"

He was taking the pictures in piles to a workbench at the back of the room and stacking them. Tillman, turning back, being polite, nodding, said, "That's a good idea."

"I'll say that's why they're in unopened packets—because I either confiscated them entire or bought them as a lot as a public duty!" He was like a rat, sidling, testing the space, watching Muldoon watching him. Quinney, stopping, holding his ground, nodding, said, "That's all I have to do!"

"Sure."

"I'm a charter member of the Society for the Suppression of Vice. I've been seen *publicly* raiding barbers' shops and other places that sell rubber goods under the counter to degenerate men! I've been seen! My name has been in the newspapers! I'm publicly one of the foremost campaigners against lewd modern novels in free public libraries for the poor!" Quinney said, "The police—"

Muldoon said quietly, "We are the police."

"I have friends in the police! I'm a heavy contributor to the Democratic Party and the police and the Courts—"

Tillman said, "Right." He had the last of the piles on the workbench and was examining something else, turning it over on the top and looking at it.

"The Anti-Obscenity League will take my side!"

"Absolutely."

"The Anti-Obscenity League has people in it who—" He changed his mind, "I'll go to the Anti-Obscenity League and tell them that—" He could not get out. He was heading into a corner by the medieval set. Quinney, halting, looking around, moving back across the room toward the egg for the photographing of newborn babes, said, "I'm a member of the congregation of Trinity Church! I'm a well-known pious man! I have a wife and three children!"

Muldoon said, nodding in admiration, "Good man yerself."

"So there's nothing you can do to me!"

Tillman said, "That's true."

"And they'll certainly believe me over two policemen who are obviously unmarried and—" He paused, "And, *and* for all I know . . ."

There was a deep rumbling somewhere, like thunder. It still seemed a little way off. It was only a little way off. It was Muldoon-thunder. Muldoon, taking a step forward, said warningly, touching himself on the chest, "This man you're speaking to is an Irish Catholic from an honest family of twelve children . . ." Trinity was Protestant. Quinney was an English name. Muldoon, fixing him with his glittering eye, said adding a little lightning, "You're the sort of snotty-nosed little Englishman who evicted my honest family from their land and then—"

"I'm an *American!* I'm a good, moral, clean-living family American with"—he remembered—"with a wife whose maternal uncle just happens to be a friend of the chief judge at the Police Court at the Tombs, and the stories he tells of the police and the way they work—"

He couldn't have been more right. Tillman, unwrapping a wad of the pictures and laying them out unseen on the worktop, waving his hand in the air to show it was as accurate as that the sun rose in the morning, said in total agreement, "Couldn't be more true."

"I had those filthy pictures in there away from prying eyes because I couldn't trust anyone who wasn't armored with the strength of a proven and public reputation as a tireless warrior against the tide of moral decay to get rid of them without having the beast in him aroused and becoming a danger to women and children and himself!"

Tillman said, "Wise thinking." There was a thumping sound on the workbench, and then another. Tillman said, "Ah, poor helpless women and children . . . Little do they know the perils that everywhere secretly beset them."

Quinney said, *"Right!"* He was right. Any moment now he was going to simply walk past the big man in the center of the room, take back his pictures, and he was going to— Quinney said, steeling himself, *"Right!"*

There was another thump. Tillman, using Quinney's rubber stamp and pad to carefully emboss the name and address of the studio on the back of each of the disgusting views, said, smiling, "Well, fear not, your onerous burden of disposal shall be shouldered by us." Tillman said, still smiling, "Ned, take a handful of these cards, would you, and discard them for Mr. Quinney out his open door onto Broadway"—he looked up, still smiling amiably to Muldoon—"Oh, an' Cap'n, if'n ye spy with yer one good eye a person or two of the respectable female persuasion-like, or their little children—cabin boys and girls—tell 'em they're treasure from Mr. Quinney 'ere."

He saw Quinney's face. He rubbed his hands in anticipation. Ishmael, kindly old shellback that he was, stooped down a little like a hunchback, said out of the side of his mouth, grinning horribly, "Ah-ha, Mr. Quinney, 'ow I likes to see the faces of women and little children and fathers light up before a good, well-taken, signed picture!"

Ishmael said in his simple glee, "Ah-ha, just like 'anging a pirate from the yardarm, it warms me from fore to aft—"

11

What do you want?" He was stopped, standing rigid and stiff in the center of the room. Quinney said, "I have three hundred and twelve dollars from the till in the gallery and I have stock worth another fifty or sixty dollars and the views which you've already got, and I can get maybe another—" Quinney said, ashen, "What do you want?"

Tillman said, "I want Rotary Rosie Seymore."

Quinney said, "21½ Crib Alley, off the Bowery—"

"I want to know how you got her name in the first place."

He was shaking. His voice was a whisper with no tone in it. It was a recitation. "I consulted the lists of fallen women who had posed for such pictures before in the files of the Society for the Suppression of Vice. Then, I went to the League Against Lewds and I got her address. Then I waited one evening at the end of the alley and engaged her in conversation and set a price and she—" Quinney said, "She came back with me to my studio and I took the photographs and I paid her her money and she left."

"How did you sell them?"

"I sold them to gentlemen who wanted them!" He answered a question that had not been asked, "I began this side of my business three months ago. I contacted eight women. Each of the series of views has twelve poses to it and I made twenty sets of each series." Quinney said, "I sold the complete series for ten dollars each." The views from the hidden cupboard covered his desk. Quinney said, "You can check the figures! From the total of one thousand nine hundred and twenty views, from the total of one hundred and sixty sets I have sold forty-seven sets"—he said to Muldoon looking down at them on the worktop—"I have made a total of four hundred seventy dollars gross minus my costs of sixty-three dollars for materials and payments of five dollars to each woman which is net three hundred sixty-seven dollars." Quinney said, "I have three hundred and twelve dollars from it in cash. The other fifty-five dollars I used to

89

purchase paint to redecorate the outside of my house." Quinney said, "Take it all! I'm happy for you to have it!"

"Who did you sell the views to, and where?"

"I sold them to people in the congregation at Trinity Church—men I knew. And men who came here to arrange portrait sittings or to purchase travel views of Mexico or Niagara Falls or the Wonders of Egypt for their collections." He looked at Muldoon. He had seen the interest he had shown in the wonders of the great sandy kingdom. He smiled ingratiatingly at the man. The man did not smile back. "Men who—" Quinney said, "Men, like me, who were dying by inches, shriveling up with the weight and worry of their responsibilities to family and—" Quinney said desperately, "Men whose dreams were all done and dust and worn to care by a life of correctness and politeness and duty and the flabbiness of their wives! Men whose last mad dream of women with their hair loosened and their faces bright and willing and— Men who—"

"You made twenty sets of each girl?"

"I did. Of Rosie Seymore and Mabel Tilley and two octoroon women named Elizabeth Lapierre and Constance something, and—"

"We are only interested in Rosie Seymore."

"I made twenty sets of her."

"Two hundred and forty exposures in all—all three-dimensional stereo-scopic views suitable for a hand-held viewer?"

"Yes."

"And you sold them?"

"Yes."

"To who particularly?"

He had forgotten he had answered. His neck was shaking with tension. "Yes."

"To who particularly?"

"To the congregation at Trinity—men I knew from church. And men who came here to arrange portrait sittings or—"

Muldoon said, watching the man, "The pictures were found in Brook-lyn."

"There may have been people from Brooklyn who—"

Tillman said, "The entire run of two hundred and forty views of Rosie Seymore was found intact in Brooklyn, still wrapped in a brown paper wrapper!" The man was trembling from head to foot, starting to sway, "Can you explain that?"

Quinney said in a whisper, "No."

"You can't explain why all the views—the entire run—was found in one place in the possession of a single owner? Pictures worth, according to you, net—what?"

Muldoon said, "One hundred twenty dollars less five dollars for the woman who posed for them, less approximately eight dollars for materials." He had been working it out. Muldoon said, "Net one hundred seven dollars." Muldoon said tightly, "Minus one-eighth the cost of painting a house exterior equals seven equals one hundred dollars exactly."

"Is it?" He held Quinney's eyes. Tillman said, "Mr. Quinney, do you belong to a secret society of any kind?"

Mr. Quinney said, "No."

"Mr. Quinney—" Tillman said, "Mr. Quinney, apart from waiting around on street corners, do you spend much time on the Bowery?"

Mr. Quinney said, "No!"

"How about the Fifth Precinct area?"

"I don't even know where it is!"

"How long have you been married?"

Quinney said, "Twenty-three years."

"How many children do you have?"

Quinney said, "Three." He was gasping, his chest beginning to heave. He was planted on the floor with his legs stiff, holding him up. He was swaying, the eyes going.

"Mr. Quinney—" He watched him. He watched the eyes going. He listened to the monotone of the voice. He listened to the answers. He saw the fear. Tillman, taking a step forward, dropping his voice, said softly, intimately, "Mr. Quinney—"

Tillman said tightly, his voice so low Quinney had to draw toward him to hear the words, "Mr. Quinney, what's an *oubliette?*"

"Oh, my God—you're *with them!*" There was a hammering outside on the gallery door to the street and then an impatient rattling as someone wanting a sitting tried the lock, and he thought the sound was inside his own head. Quinney, losing his balance, swaying, his chest heaving, trying to catch his breath, repeating, hiccuping said like a small child terrified beyond thought, reciting, " 'It's a hole in the ground into which you'll disappear. It's a deep bottomless hole full of dank bricks and stones with no air where you'll fall dead like a doll until—' " The eyes were gone, the chest heaving and repeating, the air in his lungs unable to stay down and hiccuping back up in his throat, " 'I am Death. I am the worst death in the world. I am the nightmare of all your nightmares. I am all the horrors that crawl in your mind. I am a killer of men, a sealer-in, a burier of minds—I am the man who buries you alive in an empty field where no one will ever hear your terrible cries from the coffin. I am—' "

"Where did you hear this?" The hammering and trying of the door stopped. The man was swaying, collapsing. Tillman, reaching out for him, ordered Muldoon, "Ned, grab him before he falls!" He was stiff, falling like a tree. Tillman, reaching out and shaking him by the shoulders as Muldoon held him upright in his arms, demanded, *"Where did you hear this? Who said this to you?"*

"'And your children . . . each of them, and your wife . . .'" Quinney, lost, sinking in Muldoon's arms, living the nightmare, said with his eyes full of tears, "I'm only a little man. I'm nothing! I'm not even successful at what I do! I'm not a great inventor or progressor. I don't travel with my camera with great expeditions or to strange lands and continents, nor to wars or great ancient monuments—I have no plans for my life—I'm—" Quinney said desperately, "I'm a little man like the little men I sell my pictures to—I live days one by one until they become a year! *I'm a little man!*" Quinney said haltingly, slowly, blinking at it, his chest heaving, "He put the barrel of the gun into my mouth and then he drew back the hammer and my eyes hurt staring at the cylinder where the heads of the bullets were and I—" Quinney said, weeping, "Men shrivel. They shrivel day by day. They become dry and made of dust and all their dreams—all their dreams *shrivel!*"

"Was it a policeman who said this to you?"

"They . . ."

"Did he come here for the pictures of Rosie Seymore?"

"You're with them!" He was weeping with no sound, standing up, unaware of Muldoon holding him.

"And did you give them to him? All of them? Did you give them to the policeman?"

"He said if I ever spoke a word about it to a living soul . . . !"

"Quinney!" Tillman, an inch from his face, shouting at the eyes, demanded, "Quinney—was it a policeman from the Fifth Precinct, in uniform?" He saw Muldoon feel every pulse of the man's body through his encircling arms. He saw Muldoon shake his head.

Tillman, shouting, trying to be heard, demanded, "Quinney—! Quinney! *Was it Police Officer Billy Jenkins from the Fifth Precinct?*"

"I don't sell the pictures anymore!"

"You were going to sell them to *us!*"

"I thought you were *sailors!* I thought you would take them to sea and—" Quinney, his fists clenched, hunching his shoulders down to hide in the hole that Muldoon's arms made around his chest, said, still hiccuping, "Suddenly he was here. It was the end of the day, about five, and suddenly he was in here in his uniform and he had locked the door, and for a full five seconds he just stood there looking at me as if I was some sort of insect and he was deciding whether or not to crush me under his boot, and then he brought me in here and he—"

Tillman said slowly and clearly, "Police Officer—?"

"Yes!"

"Billy Jenkins—"

"*Yes!*" Quinney said, "Like a—I was like a—"

"When? When did he come here? Did he come here a week ago? Was it a week?"

"Yes. And he—"

Tillman said, *"Why?* Why did he come?"

"For the pictures! To get the pictures of Rosie from me! To destroy any trace of her very existence!"

"He knew her by name?"

He had gone sad. He was reliving it. Quinney said softly, "Yes." Quinney said, seeing it again, "So I opened the cupboard and I told him to take what he wanted, but he—but he said he didn't do things like that. He told me I was to do that. I was to sort through the pictures, not him. He told me he didn't lower himself to do things like that, and when I got them for him he didn't even look at them to check I had the right ones—he just stood there looking at me as if I was something noxious and he—" He was trembling again, *"And he glanced out into the gallery to the front door to check there was nobody about and he drew his revolver to kill me!"* His eyes were rolling back, then refocusing, then rolling back again. Quinney, his chest heaving, everything inside his body trying to explode, to get out, said in a shriek, "And then he took his gun out and, holding me by the back of the neck, smiling, with his eyes staring into mine, he put the barrel in my mouth and cocked the hammer and said, 'Listen to me . . . listen . . . Listen to what I say . . .'"

Muldoon said tersely, "He was enjoying it, Jenkins, he was enjoying what he was doing."

" 'I am death.' " Quinney said, "He said, 'I am Oubliette. I am Death. I am the worst death in the world—' He had the gun in my mouth! He said, 'I am the nightmare of all your nightmares. I am—' " Quinney said, "And then he stopped. The game was all over and he said—" Quinney said, "I lived from second to second and I—" He had been terrified beyond bearing. He was weeping. Quinney shrieked, "I'm a little man! I might as well not have been there! It was as if God was in the room pondering great matters and I was a fly, a gnat to be swatted without thought—my life was only the merest caprice!" He was sobbing. Quinney said, "When I looked at the heads of the bullets in the cylinder of the gun I went *cross-eyed!*" Quinney said, "I was nothing! I am nothing. I'm a little man, gone to dust." Quinney said, "And he knew! He knew! He said, 'I know what you did.'" Quinney said, "He was God."

"What had you done?"

Quinney said, "I—"

"What had you done?"

He shook his head. He was still reliving it. He relived it every day. Quinney said, shaking his head to stop the tears, "I—I—"

"What had you done with the pictures of Rosie that he wanted them back?" Rotary Rosie Seymore: she had been able to hold her breath for eleven minutes. She was, wherever she was, holding it now. Tillman, laying his hand on the man's shoulder, asked him tightly, "What had you done with the pictures of Rosie Seymore?"

"He said—"

Tillman said, *"Who had you shown them to?"*

"He—"

"Who had you offered to sell them to?"

"And then he laughed. He took the gun out of my mouth and he stood back from me and he inspected me to see how his little game had gone and he—laughed!" Quinney said, "And *I still didn't know if he was going to kill me even then!"*

"You showed them to someone, didn't you? You showed them to someone powerful at Trinity Church or in the Society for the Suppression of Vice or—" Tillman said, *"You showed them to someone who—"*

"Yes!"

"Who?"

Quinney said softly, "My friend. My fellow parishioner. My friend at the church." He had learned the day Jenkins had come that the world was not as he had thought it was. Quinney said, "The friend in the church I sang with in the choir and socialized with after services. The friend I talked with about the day's news or great events, the friend who arranged with me for a portrait sitting and an entire series of pictures of his establishment if the quality of my work was—as he said laughing—of the same quality as my fellowship, the friend who—" Quinney said in a torrent, "He came here to make an appointment and we got to talking and I showed him the pictures and he—and he asked me, as a friend, for her address and offered to pay and I said—" Quinney said, "And in the name of friendship—"

Quinney said, "Rosie— On the way out Jenkins said that he was going now to kill her and he—" He said, "He did, didn't he? She's dead, isn't she? That's why you're here—he killed her and she's dead!" Quinney said, "I thought he was a nice man, my friend, but the power—the power he has—"

"What power?"

"The power to control people like Jenkins! The power to—"

Tillman said evenly, "Jenkins is dead."

"The power to—"

"Police Officer Billy Jenkins is dead!"

"The power to treat people like—the power to—" Quinney, sinking down, going loose, said with the tears rolling down his face, "When he went I was so afraid I lost control of my bowels and soiled all my clothing! I was so afraid I lost control of my bowels and after he went, after I had stopped shaking, I had to get down on my hands and knees naked with the stink of my own body wastes filling the room and clean it all up like a *dog!*" Quinney said, shrieking, "I'm a little man! I'm a nothing! I'm a boring, unimportant little man in a great age of progress where even my God-sacred soul is a joke!" Quinney, pleading with them, said, "What I am—what I am—is nothing but a *cur!*"

"Stand up!" In the room, Tillman ordered Muldoon, "Let him go." He saw the man sinking. Tillman ordered him, *"Stand up!"* Tillman said as a statement of fact, "Jenkins is dead."

"I'm nothing, a little man . . ." He was staggering, going down.

"Jenkins is dead!" Tillman, wanting to reach out for him, but instead standing back, said with no room for argument, holding his eyes, "Police Officer Billy Jenkins is dead! He was killed. He was killed yesterday afternoon and he is now cold and lifeless and silent in the Bellevue Mortuary and he is *dead!*"

Quinney said sadly, shaking his head, "No . . . no, he isn't."

"Yes, he is! He is dead. Whatever he was, whatever pleasure he got from torturing you, whatever cruelty he had eating away at his brain, all that is gone and he is dead, and maybe he should have killed you when he had the gun in your mouth but he didn't and that was a mistake on his part! It was a mistake because he, not you, was the little man! Because he had nothing but the pleasure your pain and fear gave him, and like a small boy he let you live like a spider in a bottle so he could come back and relive that pleasure again! Because he—"

"I soiled myself in terror after he had gone!" Quinney said, "He killed Rosie Seymore!"

"He did not kill Rosie Seymore! Rosie Seymore is still alive!" He was reeling. Tillman ordered him, "Stand up!" Tillman said, "You are not a little man because of your fear, you are an ordinary man. You are an ordinary man as every man is an ordinary man!" Tillman said, "And Jenkins is dead!"

"I could have *fought* him! I could have—"

"You could not."

"Then I could have refused him the pictures! I could have told him nothing! I could have died with dignity and—"

"And be as dead as he is."

"But I thought of my wife and children!"

Tillman said, "I believe you."

"I did! I swear to God, I did! I did think of them! I thought of them being left alone if I did anything to resist and I thought—"

"Yes."

"I thought, not of myself, but of my wife and children. I thought of them!" Quinney said suddenly, "They love me. They never asked that we live in a better billet! They never asked that we should have our house painted better than any of the other houses where our friends live! They never asked that they have more—" He looked down at the pictures. "They never asked that we should know better people, because I had something they wanted! They never— My children—" Quinney said, "They would have wept for me in their love!"

"Patrolman Billy Jenkins is dead. He was killed on the street by a man littler, so he would have said, than any man in this room." Tillman said, "He was killed by the smallest of men."

Muldoon said softly, "He was killed by a kind, good man as an act of mercy. The man did not know what sort of person he was, but even if he had, he would have still been merciful."

Quinney said, not taking it in, "You killed him? You killed Jenkins?"

"Who did you show Rosie Seymore's picture to at Trinity Church?"

"You killed him? You two—you killed him?"

Tillman said firmly, "Yes."

He was limp. He was standing up looking at them. Quinney said suddenly, "I showed the pictures to a man who came to my studio to see if my work was good so he could commission me to photograph both him and his business establishment—his store. He was an unmarried man." Quinney said, "I think, after I gave him Rosie's address in Crib Alley, he went there and took her to his place to make love to her." Quinney said, "Hewitt. T.G. Hewitt from the congregation at Trinity!" Quinney said, gazing at them hard, "T.G. Hewitt from the great firm of T.G. Hewitt and Company, Warren Street and Broadway." Quinney said, "—T.G. Hewitt of the great and rich and respectable firm of T.G. Hewitt and Company, Broadway and Warren Street: my friend— He sent Jenkins here like an obedient, snarling, rabid dog *to kill me!*"

12

"Don't be an old maid, Mol-ly,
Make up your mind to-day.
Sweet-heart, 'twill be no fol-ly
When you are old and gray—
Love's Summer days are jol-ly;
Sweet-heart, thou cannot be—
—Don't be an old maid, Moll-ee!
Just take a chance with me!"

On the three-person-wide driver's seat of the 2:05 P.M. Lower Broadway to Uptown stage the Black and White Minstrels troupe of Muldoon and the colored stagecoach driver were singing a duet at the top of their voices to the accompaniment of iron wheels a-clanging and a-crashing and a-grinding on the still cobbled street, to the mellow background of rearing horses, cursing cabmen, dodging pedestrians, weaving wagons, careering handcarts, occasional big-wheel bicyclists, and the pathetic inaudible whispers of elderly persons who should have been at home anyway trying to cross the street.

With Tillman bent over his open notebook on his knee as the stage rocked and swayed on its springs over first one pothole, then another, Muldoon and the uniformed and silver-nameplated driver, Mr. Lemuelson, harmonized:

"Say, Mol-ly dear, let's be sin-cere,
I know that you're far a-bove me—
But if you try, then by and by
May-be you will learn to love me!
Girls good as you are mighty few,
But that is not reason to tarr-y—
—It's not safe to wai-t . . .

It may be too la-te . . .
To wait, Molly, dear, to mar-ree . . ."

There were no horsecars allowed on Broadway. There were no rails. No one could close the street long enough from the traffic to lay them. The empty eight-passenger coach was the highest perch in town, and with its white paint and coachwork and gilt-edged route—BROADWAY TO 33 ST—freshly painted along its length and gleaming in the afternoon sun, Muldoon in rich, deep bass and the driver in tenor, swelled:

"Don't be an old maid, Mol-ly,
Make up your mind to-day!
Sweet-heart, 'twill be no fol-ly;
When you are old and gray!
Love's Summer days are jol-ly;
Sweet-heart, thou cannot be—
Don't be an old maid, Moll-eeee!!
—Just take a chance with ME—!!"

Muldoon said in delight, "Damned good!" He clapped Mr. Lemuelson on the back. Muldoon said, "Damned good, Lem!" There was a brief pause in hostilities on the road and Lemuelson got the horses into a good clip through a break in the surging tide of human, cabman and horseflesh across the intersection of Carlisle Street.

Muldoon, getting Tillman's attention, said with pride, "Lem here served in the war. He's an old soldier like myself—the Colored Regiments." Lem was brushing at his blue uniform with its silver buttons and humming "The Battle Hymn of the Republic." Muldoon, touching at his locust wood club under his coat, said happily, "That was a bit of my old clubbing song. In the Strong Arm Squad in the old days all our clubs had names. My club's name was Molly." Muldoon said, "That fellow, Quinney, him we should have clubbed the living daylights out of, and before you say that you can't go around walloping people just because you don't like them, I'll tell you that in the old Strong Arm Squad in the old days we used to go around doing it all the time." Muldoon said, "And then burned all his dirty pictures and then, for good measure—" He heard the humming. Muldoon said, "They don't write songs like that anymore!" Muldoon said to the driver, "I don't know about you, but I don't hold with all this modern thinking about things. In the old days . . ."

Mr. Lemuelson said, "In the old days . . ." Mr. Lemuelson said softly, pointing, "Liberty Street to the left there—laid out in 1690 as Tienhoven Street by the Dutch, then fifty years later changed by the British to Crown

Street, then, a few years after the Revolution that freed us from the British, changed to Liberty Street to celebrate the victory." He seemed happy about something. "One street back from that, Cedar Street, originally called when New York was New Amsterdam, Smith or Schmidt Street, then, in 1728, by the British, Little Queen Street, then again—in 1776—Cedar Street—"

Muldoon said, nodding, "Right!" He turned to Tillman reasonably, "All Billy Jenkins was was a blackmailer. He caught this fellow Hewitt poking old Rotary Rosie and he got hold of all the pictures her pimp Quinney had of her and he trotted along and threatened to tell Hewitt's select, upper-crust clientele about his private painted dove and he—"

They passed over the intersection of Liberty. Lemuelson said, "The site of the Old Dutch Middle Church later taken over as the first New York Post Office, then replaced in 1875 by the ugliest building in the world near City Hall where on the day shift a minimum of one thousand seven hundred mail sorters work twelve hours a day, where business may be transacted twenty-four hours a day six days a week and where, these days, mail is delivered all over the city every hour on the hour from seven-fifteen A.M. to seven P.M. at night, and on Sundays from eight P.M. to twelve."

Tillman asked mildly, "And did what? Got paid off in so much cash he couldn't spend it all? Then, at Hewitt's bidding, cutting his own throat, obediently trotted down to Quinney's to slaughter the goose that laid the golden egg?" He was glancing down at his notes, "Or did he get paid off in wedding rings?"

"The wedding rings were wrapped in Hewitt and Co. paper!" He hadn't understood the mathematics of stereoscopy in the book. He hadn't even understood the pictures. Muldoon, putting his hand on Lemuelson's shoulder, wanting to sing a little more, said, telling the colored man something, "They were better days, the old days. They were the days when a man was a straightforward creature and a life of good fellowship and strong whiskey was enough to keep him smiling—"

Tillman said, "Hewitt and Company is a draper's store. They don't sell wedding rings."

"Then he traded some drapery for some gold and he—"

"As well as the cash?"

"Nobody killed Jenkins, Virgil, but us! And Jenkins didn't—for all his talk—do anything to Quinney except frighten him. And, for all we know, nobody killed Rotary Rosie Seymore and—" Muldoon said lightly, "And maybe all this secret society business—" He had a thought. Muldoon said, "We found no regalia or tasseled aprons or badges or emblems or funny hats in Jenkins' house at all. What sort of secret society is it that doesn't go in for all those sort of things to dress up and playact in?"

Lamuelson said softly, almost to himself, "Dey Street. Originally called *Dye* Street because it was where all the dyers of clothing plied their trade, but called in their accent 'Dey' Street by the English Cockneys fleeing the oppression at home and, blessed in America by the sacrament of the ordinary working man, consecrated and kept." Mr. Lemuelson said, smiling, "Six streets back—Rector Street, called once Auchmuty Street for Dr. Samuel Auchmuty, the rector of Trinity Church, but too hard to say for the ordinary people and changed to—"

Muldoon said, "Beer and fellowship, that's what a man needs!"

Tillman, looking up, asked the man, "When did your people come here, Mr. Lemuelson?"

"With the Dutch." He had nothing of a Southern black accent. "With the Dutch in 1690. My family served them, and then the English and then—" He dared put out his hand and shake Muldoon gently on the shoulder, "And I fought for the Union." Lemuelson said, "I live now in Broome Street—in the district called Africa—where landlords fight each other for the honor of having black families—the cleanest and most honest types in the city, their words, not mine—to tenant their houses, and I—"

Tillman said, smiling, "Is this your first day on the job?"

"Yes, sir, it is."

Muldoon said, "Well, good man yourself!"

Lemuelson said, "I am the first colored driver of a stagecoach on a main route in the city. I know everything there is to know about the route by heart because I learned it." Lemuelson said proudly, "And today, I have sung a duet with an Irish policeman!" Lemuelson said, "I'm fifty years old. I am traveling up Broadway singing. I am traveling up Heere Straat, Heere Wegh, Heere Waage Wey, I am traveling in the Wide Way, on Broadway, on . . ." He could not contain himself. Lemuelson, grasping Muldoon's shoulder so hard it hurt, said in litany, counting off the streets, the generations, "Rector! Carlisle! Albany! Cedar, Liberty, Cortlandt! Dey! Fulton! Vesey! Barclay! Murray! This day, this first day— This day what I travel on is the Freedom Road—!"

—the shots were booming, roaring, echoing in the canyon of the street, the first poleaxing the left-hand-side horse dead in its harness; and as he went down with the coach smashing to splinters around him, as the living right-hand-side horse, kicking and bucking, caught in the traces, delivered Lemuelson a blow that split his head open and spilled his brains out onto the street, he thought—in that instant—he thought as his race had thought for generations—that he had said too much and been knocked down to the ground by his betters for his insolence.

13

The street was full of crazed and rearing horses wrenching loose from their traces and catching in shafts and buckles, neck yoke straps and choke collars. There was another shot and in the center of the street a roan horse pulling a black canvas-covered furniture wagon exploded blood from its neck and went down turning the wagon over and spilling the shouting driver out onto the street with a load of wicker chairs. Lemuelson was dead, caught under the dead horse, the still living one, dragged down, kicking and biting at its harness, its eyes wide and white.

There was a madman shooting horses from a window. The street was full of women and children—boys in sailor suits and little girls in pinafores—being pulled to safety by their screaming mothers. There were men in shirtsleeves and red kerchiefs about their necks—a construction gang from somewhere—there was a shot as they ran as a group across the roadway and then a medley of screaming and panic as a hansom cab, its horse shot through the neck in a gout of blood, went down as if clubbed and pulled the cab up and over and smashed it to matchwood with the driver rolling and scrabbling onto the road. There was a madman shooting horses from a window. Tillman, wrenching Muldoon's legs from under the dead horse in the traces of the stage, yelled at the swirling, running crowd, *"Go back!"* The shooting was coming from the far side of the street: he saw a puff of smoke from the fourth floor of a massive stone building at the corner of Warren Street. His hands were covered in blood. It was blood from the horse. The street was running with it. There was another shot, and then another—he heard children screaming—and then there was a wounded animal stampeding loose toward him and he yelled at the nearest kerchiefed man, *"Go back! Get those people back!"* and the escaped horse was clubbed by a shot like a buffalo and was down on its side, dead before it hit the ground.

The gunfire was coming from Hewitt's store. Pulling Muldoon free, he saw a blast of fire and smoke and powder come from the far window at the southern end, and then there was an unearthly sound as the bullet tore through the hindquarter muscles of an animal somewhere and it collapsed kicking and biting at its own wound. It had been pulling an immigrant wagon—a four-wheeler—there were screams and shouts in some language he did not recognize, then another blast made the animal's head jerk, killed it, turned the wagon onto its side and there were men in tight suits and dark peaked caps running among the women and children and shouting.

Muldoon, out and free, roared in a voice that sounded as if he used a voice trumpet, *"Get off the street!"* and he was into the midst of the running people, towering above them, pushing at them, shoving them, running them to the safety of the far sidewalk. There was a child running loose—a small boy in knickerbockers and new, shining shoes. A shot ripped apart something on the street near him, tore into the canopy-top surrey he seemed to be running for, and Tillman, running to him, scooping him up, screamed at the man and woman in their best clothes on the driver's seat, "Get off! Take cover! Get off the street!" He saw their faces: he saw the man in a fine new derby hat and the woman in a long satin dress with her button shoes showing on the footrest and a new, Egyptian lace bonnet on her head—he saw their eyes. Then there was a shot he did not even hear and the surrey was going down, still moving as the derby-hatted man tried to whip it up and there was a gout of blood from the shot-through horse pulling it and the surrey was jerked forward onto its shaft and destroyed and the man and woman, with looks of terror and surprise on their faces, were going down, and were on the roadway rolling over and over, the new bonnet flying loose and spinning into fireworks of blue ribbons and bows.

He had no idea if it was their child or not. He was on the sidewalk with the boy, shoving him hard up against the wall of a building, the angle too acute for the shooter above to take aim. There was a horse-drawn fire engine from nowhere suddenly out on the street—come from a Station somewhere—the brass-hatted crew pulling at their heavy coats to get them on and then, as they crashed into a spinning delivery wagon with no driver on board, falling and tumbling back onto their own hoses and getting tangled up in them. There was a shot that blasted at the driver's seat, then another that killed the front horse on the four-team rig, and then, as the appliance began spinning, all the crew leaping off to abandon it, a bullet tore through the gleaming brass boiler at the back of the engine and blasted a stream of steam straight up. Another shot directly into the pressurized boiler would turn it into a bomb. There was someone working at the boiler—a fireman—pushing and fighting with kerchiefed men who thought his uniform offered protection, and then, as the shots went on and on, there was a blast of superheated steam as the fireman got the emergency valve open on the boiler and vented all the steam and pressure out into the air.

It was like a battlefield. There were dead horses everywhere, as if hit by artillery fire and bursting cannonballs. The panic had turned the people into a mob. The mob was running, stampeding like cattle for the safety of the sidewalk, and Tillman, seeing Muldoon for an instant with a child in each hand, carrying them like firewood, yelled above the blasting of the steam, *"Ned—!"* There was a mounted policeman—a trooper from the Broadway Squad—riding like a cowboy at full gallop into the center of the melee and Tillman, getting into his path, raising both hands up to him to stop him, shrieked, *"Clear these people! Clear these—"* and then the horse, in midstride, was struck down and the uniformed man was flying at him through the air like dead weight, his white-gloved hands going up to protect his face and neck, striking the cobbles, and breaking his shoulder bone with a snap that was audible through the shrieking. He was a huge man—someone from the elite street patrol squad Tillman did not know—a man made of solid gristle, and he was up before he had stopped rolling, bent to one side with his hanging right arm, his intentions all martial, but his eyes rolling and lost like a child's.

Reaching for his badge, not finding it, Tillman shouted at him, "Headquarters Police Detective Tillman from Mulberry Street—*get to a police telegraph and call for help!"* He outranked the man. The eyes registered it. The eyes registered an order, a task, and in the midst of the firing, he tried to raise his right hand in salute.

Tillman shrieked, *"Get help now!"* He heard bells ringing and thought it was a fire alarm gone off with the steam on the fire engine, but the bells were louder, coming from somewhere else. He saw Muldoon on the sidewalk, looking to him, and, reaching inside his coat to pull his Colt Lightning free from its leather holster, screaming at Muldoon to come with him as the shots blasted out over and over into the street, as the cobbles ran slippery with blood, as the shooting from the window went on and on and on, he ran for the arched entrance of T.G. Hewitt and Company and, passing under the carved and friezed thirty-foot-high triumphal arch that celebrated seventy-five years of service and drapery supply to the citizens of New York and their wives, burst in.

"Stay in the store!" The shots were echoing in the great vaulted, pillared place like dynamite charges going off in a mine. All the voice tubes in the place were open and there was the sound of bells—tinny, insistent bells—shrilling without ceasing. There were people everywhere—all the right people in their satins and suits and silk hats with shopping baskets and wrapped parcels, and all the wrong people, kerchiefed street workers and women of bad repute in rags—fighting and shouting at each other and with

the aloof, suited floorwalkers trying to separate them and push them out.

There were people coming from everywhere. At the far end of the floor the two Otis elevators were open, disgorging people, the uniformed elevator drivers punching at the controls, pulling at the levers to make the things rise or fall, then ducking and shouting as the circuits went and spewed electrical sparks which jammed both the doors inoperably open.

The bells were ringing. Through every corner of the vast, mahogany-lined emporium they were shrilling like the presages of doom, like the call to arms for some shattering volley to cut advancing enemy soldiers down like chaff. All the voice pipes that communicated throughout the entire store were open and the building, all marble and high ceilings like a pharaoh's mausoleum, was ringing with them. The blasts, nonstop, unstoppable, relentless, set the chandeliers tinkling and swaying. There were hanging pennants advertising Hewitt's Spring Sale of imported fabrics for the season and bargains on overstocked lines, and, with the reverberations of the gunfire they were swinging and fluttering like flags from the brass ceiling fittings that held them.

Someone screamed, "My wife!" as a woman must have fainted and been trampled, and then, by the elevators a man rose up out of the crowd punching and swinging, trying to clear a space for her to breathe, and then two of the kerchiefed mob were by him pushing and shoving a space for him, and the man, his clothes all expensive and select, looking surprised that the kerchiefed common scum were on his side, bent down quickly to sweep his wife up in his arms and catch hold of his children. There was someone at a giant gleaming counter cash register, punching at the keys, trying to get it open and the kerchiefed man, stopping only to clap the well-dressed man on the shoulder to encourage him, was at the register clubbing a pinched-faced man to the ground. It was Horrible Houlihan—he was not the being clubbed, he was the clubber. Clubbing the vile thief away from the honest-earned machineful of money, he looked, briefly honest and pleased with himself, then remembered who he was and began, himself, wrenching at the drawer and keys to get it open. A floorwalker the size of Jake Kilrain swatted him to the ground like a fly, then turned around with terror in his eyes as the rest of the Houlihan brood, there to protect Daddy, flew at him.

Out in the street, the shots were booming, detonating, killing without stopping. The bells, shrilling, paralyzed thinking. At the jammed and open elevators there were people crouching down, terrified of the sparks of electrical fluid cascading out from the mouth of the new-fashioned things like fireworks.

The shots were booming, detonating, echoing through the insistent ringing of the bells. There was a space of light through the crowd at the sparks—a doorway, a gap of light and shadow—and Tillman, turning to gather up Muldoon to take him with him, yelled, "The stairs! The stairs are there!" and, with his gun still out and in front of him like a lantern, people on either side seeing it and shrieking, he got a way clear and went through the door and up the stairs for the top floor two at a time.

He was twenty feet around the corner of Broadway, in Warren Street, working the police telegraph with his left hand, his face white, shaking with the pain of his shattered shoulder.

It was a Gamewell Police Telegraph—a mechanism enclosed in an iron box on top of a green-painted cast-iron pillar five feet high set on the sidewalk, for a man in his senses simple to use—child's play—a simple dial like a clock face with a single metal lever to be moved in turn to each of the numbers on the dial.

It swam before his eyes and he had to reach out and grasp hold of the side of the pole to steady himself.

2,7. He moved the hand to the number and pressed at a key to send the location along the wires. *2,7: Corner of Broadway and Warren Street.*

He heard nothing but the gunfire. He heard, as perspiration stood out on his forehead, the screaming of children.

Officer Reporting: that was next.

He had to look at the badge number on his uniform to see it. *456: Broadway Mounted Patrolman Jack Bayes.* He sent *4, 5, 6.*

He swayed and thought he would not finish.

Next was: *Nature of Disturbance.*

Assistance Required. That was . . .

Or, it was . . . He was going, sinking.

He swayed and thought he could not finish.

He moved at the hand on the dial and pressed at the key.

He sent: *Corner of Broadway and Warren Street.*

456 Broadway Mounted Patrolman Jack Bayes.

He sent—

He could not remember.

9, 9, 9, 9—

—Murder! Murder! Murder! Murder!

He pressed the key and sent it.

People had fled down the stairs, clerks and salesgirls and messenger boys and wrapper-uppers. There were bolts of cloth, string, wrapping paper dropped or thrown away as they had run after someone on each floor, had opened the intrastore brass speaking tubes to ask what the first shot had been, pulled the plug out on its little brass chain and heard the fusillades.

Tillman was at the second-floor landing, Muldoon crashing, coming up, a step behind him. The oak and glass double doors to the floor were open—the floor was deserted, all the cloths and materials and silks laid out on the counters and in showcases under the white light of the electric chandeliers like winding cloths in an Egyptian burial tomb. Through the open tubes, reaching into every corner, the bells were shrilling nonstop, the gunfire from somewhere upstairs heavy and booming.

On the third floor, the double doors were wide open, the floor deserted and still, the elevator doors there were closed and silent as the electrical contagion downstairs jammed all the controls. There was no one on the floor—only, reaching into every corner, the sound of the bells. There was a closed wooden door at the top of the stairs marked in black PRIVATE. DO NOT ENTER, and Tillman, his gun out and cocked, ready to break it down, yelled to Muldoon two steps behind him, *"Top floor!"* The door was unlocked and he got through onto another staircase, going straight up, and he was suddenly climbing up through a white-painted wall on a metal staircase of bucolic cast-iron lacework with white painted cherubs cast into it and there was, at the top of the stairs, light from the sky, and he was out onto the roof, and it was a garden full of flowers and arbors and hedges and statues of nymphs and shepherds and more cherubs and, fed from a pump somewhere, or a tank, set in the carefully laid out, pathed areas of earth and grass, fountains.

"Where the hell are we?" The screaming from the street was faint, a long way down, a long way off, happening somewhere else, in another field. Muldoon, his pistol ready, looking around for something to shoot, seeing shrubs and statues, fountains and flowers, demanded, *"Where the hell are we?"* They were on a little winding cobbled path. On either side of it beds of flowers grew amid shrubs and miniature trees in oaken tubs, little cast-iron seats and benches with more cherubs cast into them, the smell everywhere of jasmine and flowers and herbs, the sound of the bells a long way off, muffled, coming from somewhere else, from behind a closed door. Muldoon said, *"Where the hell are we?"*

There was no more shooting. There was a sound like a door closing and, turning on the path by a profusion of hedges seemingly growing wild, but clipped into wilderness, there was, across the roof garden, a window and then another, and another: an apartment. There was the sound of a door opening and closing, or closing and then opening again, as if someone came out to look. There was the sound—that stilled them—of a lever-action gun being cocked. Muldoon, moving up behind Tillman, towering over him as the little man moved forward with the Lightning cocked in his hand, said in a whisper, *"Where the hell's the Broadway Squad?"* The shooting had all stopped. It had come from the roof. He could still smell the smoke. He heard, in his mind, the screams of the horses. Muldoon, moving forward, said in a whisper—

He saw him. He saw him as a shadow at the door to the private apartments at the far end of the roof: he saw him move in the light from the open door. He saw him as a shadow peek out from the open doorway and then come out. He saw the gun. It was a huge Whitney lever-action repeater with a 30-inch barrel, a .50-90, a buffalo gun, a horse killer. He saw the shadow lift it up. He saw— The scent of flowers was everywhere, in his nose, heady, making him blink. He saw the figure come out like a ghost and look around. He saw that he wore a silk hat and frock coat and spats from the 1860s and he thought, for a moment, inching toward him, that perhaps he was—

He saw—

The man in the frock coat and top hat and spats, seeing them, said raising his hand with the gun in it, *"Ah!"* Suddenly, in that instant, all the bells stopped.

He had the Lightning aimed, from less than twenty-five feet away, directly between the man's eyes. The eyes were like opaque brown beads with no light coming from them.

The man said, *"Ah!"* He seemed irritated. The huge gun was hanging down by his side as if he had finished with it. He seemed relieved. The man said, introducing himself, "Mr. Thomas G. Hewitt, Junior." He saw the Lightning and Muldoon's Smith and Wesson not at all. Hewitt said, "About time, *about time!*" He peered at them, "You are the men from Cotterill's, aren't you—the undertakers?" Hewitt said, "I thought you couldn't get through all the traffic with your hearse so I cleared the street of all the other vehicles for you." He was a thin man in his sixties. He seemed suddenly weary; the rifle, having done its work, heavy in his hand. Mr. Hewitt said, "Good! About time too!"

Mr. Hewitt, turning to go back inside his door, sighing a little, making disapproving tsking sounds, said with the blank, mad, brown bead eyes seeing them not at all, "I've been dead now for over a week. Really, I don't know what the world's coming to when it takes this long for the undertakers to call around to remove the body—I just don't know what things are coming to at all!"

14

He came at the gallop and reined back amid a clashing of metal, striking sparks on the cobbles in the middle of the street. He was one of the great German knights of the Mounted Broadway Squad. On Manfred, his snorting, dancing cavalry horse, Sergeant Fritz Engle, his sword glittering in its scabbard near the French polished butt of his .44-40 Winchester, glittering silver spurs flashing in the light, bareheaded, but with moustaches the size of the wings of a stone angel, roared across Broadway to his platoon of dismounted men, "Picket line, men!" He pranced across the street and stopped the traffic past the fallen horses and the smashed stagecoach. He saw Lemuelson and the police horse dead in front of him. He sat stiff in the saddle with his back as straight as a ramrod, all the medals and ribbons on his tunic stiffened with cardboard or held firm in little invisible pocket incisions put in there by his tailor. He saw Lemuelson and knew what he was.

Engle, making the horse turn and dance in the street as he took in the scene, roared as an order, "That poor beast is Jack Bayes' horse Monty!" He was a good, fine old beast due for retirement. He stiffened his lips. He hated to think how Bayes would weep for it.

Engle, each of his troop over six feet tall, the epitomes of discipline and authority in a world gone increasingly mad, shouted, wheeling and prancing, to the nearest man, "Corporal Norwith! There's a police horse down here!" He thundered down at the saluting trooper, "Get something to cover the open eyes of this poor dead animal *now!*"

In his madman's room Hewitt, still carrying the rifle, cocking and uncocking the hammer with his thumb as he moved, said, shaking his head as he picked his way across the floor, "Such a nice clientele we had once. Such good and courteous people, people who were a joy to serve. People who'd been customers of my father's for twenty, thirty years, people who—" The floor was littered with smashed furniture and glass and fired cartridge cases that had burned holes in the thick carpet as they fell, "People who came from only the best backgrounds . . ." There was ash everywhere on the carpet, around the shells and smashed glass from the hanging lamps and overturned display cabinets. It was burned money, in wads, in bales. "Hewitt's has been here over seventy-five years— presidents have shopped here and royalty—" There was a picture on the floor, torn down from the wall, a six foot by six foot copy of Mulvany's 1881 painting of Custer's Last Stand. "But now—" He turned around suddenly, the eyes beads, "But now, now everything is Broadway Quality at Bowery Prices!" It was hot in the room. Only the tiny window overlooking the street was open. His face was running sweat. "Now, a man has to scrabble like a street vendor to make a living and service, oh, service is something no one wants to pay for now that everything is cut-price and shoddy and discounted and Jack can be as good as his master when it comes to buying drapery!"

He was following him, picking his way carefully through the debris so as not to tread on something and make a sudden sound. Tillman, holstering his Lightning under his coat an inch at a time, said in a whisper to Muldoon and his Smith and Wesson Number Two, "Don't shoot him. Keep your gun out and ready, but don't shoot him unless you absolutely have to." The madman's eyes were staring at him, but they did not see him. There was a click as the thumb came back on the hammer of the big Express rifle and cocked it, then another as it was let down again. In the musty room there was the faint smell of urine. Moving on the thick carpet, there was no sound at all as Hewitt half turned and continued toward the far wall. Tillman, not wanting to take his hand from the butt of his half-holstered gun, forcing himself to take it away, said in a whisper to Muldoon, "Watch the rifle, just watch the rifle . . ."

He cocked it suddenly. Hewitt, turning back so fast it made Muldoon start, said to explain it, *"I died when they told me!* I had lived my life for fifty years in the shadow of my father, and when I became—when he passed on and everything was mine—when I was the Hewitt of Hewitt's—" Hewitt, looking up at the electric chandelier he had smashed to pieces with the barrel of the rifle before he had begun shooting horses, said with his mouth slack like a dead man's, "I died when they told me what they did! I explained to them that I was a man alone and sixty-one years old! I explained to them she was just a little thing to soothe my nights and I—" He was talking about Rosie. "—and when they told me what they did I felt my heart stop in my chest and at that moment, *I died!"*

The barrel of the gun was moving, coming up and down. It was a .50-90, a Dangerous Game rifle—a weapon guaranteed by its makers to be able to kill with one shot any creature on the planet. Muldoon said in a whisper, "Virgil . . ."

There was a click as Hewitt thumbed back the hammer, then another as he let it down again. Muldoon, moving to get a clear shot to the head, said in a whisper, "Virgil, this is . . ."

"I was lonely and alone and my father had passed over and I never understood the accounting because it was something he always kept for himself! And now, now that he's gone—" Hewitt said, "Broadway Quality at Bowery Prices—I did it for the money! I did it because times will change and service will come back!" Hewitt said, "He never let me do anything more than manage the second-floor curtain department! I don't know if it's me or the times, but the people who used to come when my father was alive just won't come back even though I grovel to them!" Hewitt said, "My father used to be asked to read the lesson in Trinity Church on Sundays and the rector would have him stand by the door on the way out to shake the hands of the congregation after service, but all I ever was, was—" Hewitt said, smiling, "I saw her picture at Quinney's Studio and I—" He could not weep because he was dead. He was in Hell and all he could do was suffer. "She thought I was such an important person! She thought I was—" He cocked the hammer of the gun and cradled it across his chest like a backwoodsman. Hewitt said, "She thought I was—she thought what I could give her was so much compared to what she had. She thought that I was—"

Tillman said warily, "Rosie Seymore is dead. Billy Jenkins drowned her in a bath in Crib Alley."

"I died when they told me what they did!"

"Jenkins is—"

Hewitt said reasonably, "My father talked to the English Prince of Wales once and he told my father that his mother Victoria would probably reign forever—he was pleased about that, of course, because he was a loyal Englishman—but that— Well, he said a little sadly that he had received no training at all for the day when reluctantly, but loyally, he would have to be King on the demise of his good Mother." He uncocked the rifle and then cocked it again. He was shaking. Hewitt, still staring up at the ceiling, said in desperation, "My father told the story at the dinner table and, not for an instant, not for a moment, did he understand the irony of what he was saying and I—I—*I sat there obediently and said nothing!*" Hewitt said, "It wasn't much to ask to have someone one night to ease my suffering! It wasn't much to ask to give her things that were nothing to me and that to her were riches, were wealth, were—" Hewitt, turning back, his thumb still on the hammer, his other hand slapping at the stock of the giant weapon hard, said to the wrecked and dank room, *"I died when they told me what they did!"* His eyes came back. For an instant, there was light in them and they saw the two men facing him. The hammer on the gun was still cocked. He saw the men from Cotterill's, the undertakers.

Reaching down for something, still grasping the gun, taking up something white and folded from on top of the torn-down painting of Custer at bay against the Sioux, Hewitt said, "Here, look—a quality shroud—from Hewitt and Company, Warren Street—the one you are to use for me, please, nothing cheap if you don't mind."

He sat down on the edge of an overturned sofa and put the folded winding sheet carefully on his knees under the gun.

He looked up.

He looked irritated.

Hewitt, wanting service, expecting it after such a long delay, said, demanding it, "Well? Where is it? I cleared the entire street of other traffic for you so you could get through, so where is it? Why isn't it here? *Where's my coffin?"*

In the street, Bayes, staggering, his arm hanging down and bloody, shrieked from Hewitt's doorway, "Fritz! In here! In here! The shots came from the roof in here!" He saw Sergeant Engle, wheeling on his horse, see him. Bayes, fighting to stay conscious, yelled, "Fritz, in here!" Inside the store he could hear people screaming in panic, fighting and trampling each other to get out. Bayes yelled, "A man with a gun—up there! In here!" The troop, as Engle roared out an order to them, were mounting. Bayes yelled, "In *here!"* He saw poor Monty lying dead in the street with a horse blanket covering his head.

Bayes, as Engle charged past him with his sword coming out from its scabbard in a flash of polished steel and silken hilt knot, yelled at the top of his voice, sinking down, fading, "Up there, boys! Up there on the top floor—he killed my poor horse! Kill *him!"*

"What's an Oubliette?" He was squatting, tensed, a foot from the man with the gun, speaking in a whisper. The eyes were blank, opaque. He reached out and almost touched Hewitt on the knee. He withdrew his hand. Tillman, in a whisper, a murmur, said with Muldoon moving around behind him with no sound at all, "What's an Oubliette?"

Hewitt said, "Jenkins is."

"Jenkins is dead." He watched the eyes.

The eyes were blank. It was as if, on the bank of the river to Hades, he was already staring into Eternity.

"Is it a killer? Is an *Oubliette* someone who does the killing?"

He nodded. He was explaining it to someone, perhaps his father. Hewitt said, not to Tillman, "I never knew what they did. I never asked."

"Did you tell Jenkins to kill Rosie Seymore?"

Hewitt said sadly, "No."

The Smith and Wesson felt insignificant in his hand. It was a .32, a peashooter. One shot to the body would not do it. Muldoon, moving around, watching the eyes and the long thin fingers resting loosely on the hammer and stock of the rifle, thought he would have to hit him between the eyes with the first shot. Moving around the room for a direct line of sight, like a butcher in a slaughter yard, he measured the distance.

"After you got Rosie's address from Quinney did you go to her address?"

Hewitt said, amazed at it, "The things I had were things she had never had! She thought, in return, she gave me nothing!"

"Did you tell Jenkins to kill Quinney too?"

His hands were sweating on the butt of the pistol but he was afraid to let go of it to wipe them. Muldoon, thinking of the bullet piercing the bone of the forehead, took a single pace to the left into another clear line of fire. He thought he might not be quick enough. His hands were wet and slippery. He could not let go of the gun. He thought he felt droplets of sweat dripping out from inside his closed palm on the gun butt. He thought he heard them fall.

"Did Rosie come here—to this room—with you?"

"Yes." He said it so softly.

"Did you give her things? Gifts?"

"She was . . ." Hewitt said softly, "I'm sixty-one years old. My father lived to be ninety-three and I lived in his house until I was fifty-seven. He read the lesson at Trinity Church and shook hands with the parishioners at the door with the rector. I was in the choir." Hewitt said sadly, "I never had a woman until her."

"All the money on the floor you burned. All the money Jenkins had—where did it come from?"

"*I wanted to show her that I was important!* I wanted to show her that I was a man of mystery like the handsome young men in the plays at the theaters. I wanted to—" Hewitt said, "I showed her things!" He shook his head, "I showed her things I shouldn't have shown her!"

"Did you give her gold wedding rings?"

Hewitt said, "No."

"They were wrapped in your store's paper."

"No." Hewitt said sadly, "No, she stole them. She—"

"Stole them from where?"

He fell silent.

"What secret society did you and Jenkins belong to?"

He was thinking of Rosie. He merely sat on the edge of the broken sofa and shook his head.

"What is it called?" Tillman said, "Where does it meet? Who are the other members? What does it do?"

"Where's my coffin?" He looked up. He saw Muldoon.

"Where does all the money come from?"

"Where's my coffin—?"

"What did Rosie see? What did you tell her? What did Rosie Seymore know from being here, talking to you, that meant she had to be killed like a dog? What did you tell her? What did you show her that she shouldn't have seen?"

"Where's my *coffin?* I cleared the street traffic for you so you could get here to take me away! I've even supplied the shroud for you— *Where's my coffin? Why isn't it here?"* He was on his feet looking around, staring at the open door, listening, the rifle up and ready so fast it made Muldoon start back, "I'm a corpse! I've been a corpse now for almost a week! Why are you asking all these questions of a corpse? Corpses don't answer questions!" He was pacing, going backward and forward toward the door, his eyes moving between it and them, the hammer clicking and snicking as his thumb on it cocked it and uncocked it. Hewitt, shaking his head, demanded, "Where? Where is it? What's going on? Who are you people? I'm dead! I'm *dead!* Don't you know what I am? I'm *dead!"*

At a glance, he knew what he was. Engle, at the head of his troop, clearing a path through the peasantry, caught Horrible Houlihan by the scruff of the neck in midstride and, pulling him up against Manfred's flank, instantly clubbed him back down again with the hilt of his sword.

The elevators were all burning with electricity. He saw the stairs. They were for Infantry only. Engle, wheeling and wrenching the staggering creature back up again against Manfred's side, yelled at him, "The freight elevator! Where's the freight elevator with your horrible looting family in it?"

"Yerrff—*derff!"* He thought for a moment it was the Dragoons come to burn him out of his humble hovel in Ireland and speed him on his way to a better life in America. Houlihan, wriggling, kicking so as not to be clubbed again, always pleased to help the Law, yelled back, "Back of the store! Back of the store behind the crepe and mourning veils department!" Houlihan yelled, "And God bless you, sir, in your fine uniform! God speed your cause!"

God sped his cause. Hurled back through the air as the troop, yelling and whooping, charged for the back of the store, Houlihan, guiding his flight like a bird, hit the side of the cash register with his shoulder, and—God rewarding those who knew the art of being unfailingly respectful and helpful to their betters—with a clanking, grinding sound, magically, by accident, the cash drawer burst open and covered him on the floor with coin.

"Dead men don't fire guns from windows!"

"They do. I'm dead and I did, so they must! They wait for their coffins! I'm waiting for my coffin so dead men must wait for their coffins and—"

He was moving, pacing, working it out, cocking and uncocking the rifle. He was listening. He touched at his watch chain with his free hand, and then let go of it, then touched it again, and wherever he moved to follow him with Muldoon moving back and forth behind him like a pugilist ready for the blow, Tillman could not fix on his eyes and hold him. Tillman said as the man passed to one side of it, "Why the Custer picture? Why did Jenkins have a picture of Custer's Last Stand as the one thing in his house that was his—and why do you have one too? What does it mean?"

"Where's my coffin?"

Tillman said, "It's coming. We have to wait because it's very heavy, being of such good quality, and it needs a special wagon to—"

He stopped. Hewitt said in a sudden alarm, "Is it expensive? *How* expensive?"

"Very." He had stopped for a moment to stare at him. Tillman said quickly, "Where did the—"

"But I burned all the money!"

"You can pay for it out of—"

"But I burned all the money!"

"Where did the money come from?"

"But I burned all the money!!"

"Dead men don't need money."

"But they do! They need it to pay for their expensive coffins!" He brought the rifle up and in that moment Muldoon almost killed him. He lowered the gun to explain. "I can't go back down there and get more because it doesn't belong to me and they'd know I took it!" He was shaking, desperate. Hewitt, taking his hand off the hammer of the gun for an instant to press it against his forehead in horror, said, "They know what's there! They know what Rosie stole! They sent Jenkins to—"

"Who sent Jenkins?"

"They did!"

"Down *where? Where* can't you go down? *Where* do they know what's theirs?"

His finger stabbed at the floor, "Down *there!* They—" He was shaking, horror-struck, pointing down at an angle to the far side of the room, moving first two paces one way and two paces the other, and in the room, his hand dripping sweat, Muldoon could not follow him quickly enough with the muzzle of the gun to keep a bead on him. Hewitt, pulling out his watch and looking at it, said, ruined, *"I thought the coffin would be here by now!"* Hewitt said in terror, hearing something they did not hear, "Oh, no! Oh, *no!"*

It was bells. They were somewhere inside the walls. It was a telephone bell. Shrilling, echoing, hidden in a recess somewhere where the open voice hoses to the entire store were, echoing, shrilling in them, it rang and rang and rang without ceasing.

The smell of horseflesh and perspiration and purpose in the elevator was all he ever wanted in the world. Engle, mounted on his horse with three of his best men on their best chargers next to him, his sword in hand, hauling down hard on the rope that drew the heavy freight elevator inexorably up, said with his teeth clenched, "Remember Monty. There's a crowd gathering outside in the street. Show them what the Broadway Squad does to people who slight them. Show them just who protects their city for them. Show them what real men are made of!"

He was thirty-two years old, born in New York of Prussian immigrant parents, and he had never been in a war; all his medals were for long service or good conduct or for rescuing women or old people or children from runaway horses in the street.

He had moustaches the size of the wings of marble cemetery angels. Engle, hauling, gritting his teeth with the effort, said as an order, "If he runs and leaps across the void to another roof—whoever he is, whatever he is—ignoring the fire and the Devil take the hindmost, boys, like steeple-chasers, don't balk: *out, like lions, after him!"*

Hewitt said sadly, standing stock-still, "Oh . . . oh . . ." He touched at his face. He was weeping. He looked at the moisture on his fingertips and seemed surprised. Hewitt said softly, sadly, "Dead men weep. I didn't know that."

"What does the society do?"

He touched at the gun. He was listening to the bells. There was nothing else.

"What is it called?"

Muldoon, facing the man, his mouth drawn tight, the revolver held hard in both hands, said warningly, "Don't lift that . . ." The rifle was coming up. Muldoon, his arms outstretched, sighting down the barrel to the forehead, said with the sweat dripping out between his fists, "For the love of God, don't—"

"What did Rosie . . . *see?*"

He was listening to the bells. Muldoon, standing with his legs apart, anchored to the ground like a shooter on a range aiming for the bull in a scrap of paper so close he could not miss, said, pleading, "Don't . . . don't . . ."

"Where did the wedding rings come from?"

"Anything that moves!" The elevator doors to the roof were coming open on hidden counterweights. Engle, his sword out and glittering, his brain full of horseflesh and glory, his spurs ready to kick into Manfred's flanks, said fighting for his breath in the headiness of the moment, "Anything that moves, boys—*cut it down like a cabbage head!"*

"Where's my *coffin?"* He was running, running from the bells toward the open door, the rifle up and cocked. There was sound, movement. He heard the coffin coming across the roof through the bushes and the flowers, cutting them down. He heard—

"Stop him, Ned!" Tillman, off balance, almost knocked over by the rush, his head full of the sound of the bells, reaching under his coat for his Lightning, shrieked, "Ned, don't shoot him—catch him!" The bells were ringing, echoing, ringing through the entire building, insistent, unstoppable, shrill and piercing. There were horses on the roof, and mounted men: the Broadway Squad cutting through the garden like a swath, their faces in terrible martial rictus; at the head, Engle with his sword out and up, shrieking and whooping—and suddenly, in the midst of them, Hewitt, an old man in old-fashioned clothes, yelling for his coffin, and, not seeing it—

They saw him. They saw a maniac with a gun coming at them. They were exploding out of the elevator, not onto an open roof but into garden beds, trees and pots, statues of satyrs and sirens, fountains—

They were wheeling, turning, wrenching back on their reins to halt, drawing their rifles.

There were bells ringing, shrilling, piercing. There was a madman with a rifle screaming about coffins. There was a lunatic with a buffalo gun who killed horses.

"Boys! *Shoot!"*

There was a single volley that cut Hewitt in half where he stood.

There was glory in it.

There was, fired by all the troopers at once, a single, overwhelming, echoing volley that rang across all the roofs and streets and stilled, in that instant, even the ringing bells with its violence.

He had only ever been close up to one before, the one in Jenkins' house, but he had read in the newspapers how Mr. Bell said his electric speaking telephone should be used to get the best results. "Hello" was something Mr. Bell abhorred. He preferred "Hoy! Hoy!"

Holding the earpiece a little out from his head, standing, as Mr. Bell also recommended in the newspapers, three feet back from the speaking nozzle, Tillman yelled at the machine that talked back to you when you talked to it, "Hoy! *Hoy!*" The speaking tube to the store was open. His voice echoed through the building like a lost, angry child's.

There was utter silence. There was an S-shaped black metal handle on the side of the box set in the cavity of the wall behind a false panel, but he did not want to touch it in case it broke the machine or was live with electricity.

Tillman yelled, "Is there anybody listening? You—the bell-ringer!—can you hear me?"

There was utter silence, and then, suddenly, a crackling and a rustling and a buzz of something that sounded like sparks escaping that made him wince and almost drop the earpiece.

There was only a crackling, a hissing.

He glanced out through the open door and saw Engle coming.

There was only, in the earpiece, a hissing sound. Tillman said as an order to Muldoon, "Stall him, Ned, for God's sake!" He drew his pistol and held it by the barrel to make it a hammer.

Thumping on the mahogany box hard once with the gun butt and then dancing back to get three feet away, he listened. Tillman yelled, "Hoy! *Hoy!*" He saw Muldoon going to the door to stop Engle getting in.

Nothing.

He danced forward and whacked the box again.

"Hoy! *Hoy!*"

He whacked. He yelled. He got too close for Mr. Bell's liking and, yelling and hitting, tried to make enough noise for the person at the other end of the wire to hear him.

The telephone apparatus was hinged in a cavity in the wall, set back a little in the darkness.

"Hoy! *Hoy!* HOY!"

In the awful, ruined room full of death, as he smashed and yelled at the crackling, hissing, buzzing, stone-deaf box of wood and metal and wires, suddenly there was a sharp *click!* and it fell—

Silent.

* * *

Down there . . . There was no down there in Hewitt's store: there was only a basement full of rats.

Down there . . .

But he had not pointed straight to the floor of his rooms when with the big rifle in his hand he had pointed to the corner of the room and down.

Down there . . .

He had pointed out and down, at an angle.

He had pointed in the direction of Broadway directly outside the entrance to his store.

. . . He had pointed to the sidewalk.

15

Well done, thou good and faithful servant! Sorry about the loss of one leg, the left eye, the recurrent back trouble and a life of loneliness, misery, despair and shuffling, not to mention the nightmares.

No, not at all . . . he would have said in a clear ringing voice—if he hadn't taken a face wound at Antietam that made his tongue still loll out of the side of his mouth after twenty years— It was worth every terrible minute of those four years of the War Between the States to make the Union strong. He was that kind of man.

He was Heini Grimm.

He was the kind of man who had the common decency not to wander around during the daylight hours and upset people; at 1:30 A.M., reaching the corner of Broadway and Warren Street, bent almost in half, shambling with the help of two heavy walking sticks, his tattered coat covered with the medals and decorations and unit badges of the Grand Old Army he had fought for, ever considerate, he paused out of the circle of light on the pavement from the electric lamp burning near where an expensive closed rich man's carriage was parked and looked up at the sky.

There was a red glow in the west. He thought in his muddled state it was the glow of Atlanta and he touched at his torn and broken forage cap with a shaking finger, almost toppled over with the loss of balance and the right-hand walking stick held up, and said so softly that no one heard nor was reminded of what his generation had gone through—he needed no thanks from a grateful nation, merely, in due time, a gentle rest from God—*"Bless you, General Burnside!"*

He looked around for a helping hand. He needed no helping hand. He required, as an old soldier, no helping hand. And there was none. Except for the single carriage, Broadway—lit by lines of incandescent lamps like a Great White Way—and Warren Street running off from it, were deserted and he discommoded no one with his presence.

Outside Hewitt's padlocked and cast-iron-grilled main archway entrance, with a single tear running gently down his face (No, not true! There were no tears—he never bewept his lot! His wounds were his *honor!*)—he slipped gently to the ground.

The ground he slipped to was a flagstone marked with chalk.

The chalkmark was an X.

He touched it gently, lovingly, with his shaking fingers.

He looked up. Through his one un-eye-patched eye he saw the oiled canvas curtain of the carriage unroll just a fraction. Heini Grimm, one half of the diabolical duo that made up Grimm and Grimm, the greatest Scientific Bombers in the history of the World, rasped out to the curtain, *"Tuning fork!"*

(His medals clanked. He had perfect pitch. They were all in B flat.)

Grimm, snapping his fingers, moving his brother along inside the coach to get it right the first time, said as an order, *"Tuning fork in C!"*

Inside the closed carriage Muldoon said in horror as Martin Grimm, an exact, horrible duplicate of his brother, pulled down a secret panel and tossed out a tuning fork in C from it, "Oh my God, it's Satan's silo! It's Lucifer's larder!" In the yellow glow of the bull's-eye lanterns Tillman held in each hand to light the Carriage to Carnage he saw, clipped up to the rear panel behind the driver's box, in racks on the roof, on thin shelves held in place by India rubber, he saw—

He saw fuses. He saw detonators. He saw miniature electrical firing boxes; he saw cans of Hercules best black blasting powder; he saw masks and wigs and disguises; he saw a full complete rabbit suit with a head with big ears and stiff white whiskers; he saw—

He saw dynamite, dynamite in sticks and wads, dynamite in powder and shaped charges, dynamite in—

The inside of the carriage, behind the panels on every side, smelled like the inside of a madman's brain. Muldoon said in horror, trying to find somewhere to put his feet as Grimm Number Two, his eyes glinting, took up the carpet and floorboards of the carriage interior in a single motion and, as if they were nothing but furry wallpapered veneers—they were—folded them, under his arm and slipped them into a compartment by the off-side door, "Oh my God, this is so illegal!"

He was afraid to look down at what his feet had been resting on, what he had walked on to get in, what his very private parts on the padded leather seat rested on. Muldoon said as Grimm Number Two, moving him aside, began to disassemble it, *"Oh my God, what's under the seat?"*

It was clocks and timing devices, flares, smoke bombs, cans of magnesium and phosphorus and a box of Army mines the Army used to blow up blockhouses. Muldoon said, "Virgil, this is a mobile—" Muldoon, ducking to one side as Grimm Two reached over past his head for the little brass plaque screwed onto the side of the door that read *Constructed with Pride by Bradley & Pardee, New Haven, Conn., Coachbuilders* and, in a sound that sounded as if the plaque had not been screwed down but merely clipped (it had) said, afraid to look, "Virgil, this is a mobile bomb factory! This is Mephistopheles' Machine Shop!" He saw what was behind the plaque. It was a cavity. It was a cavity full of bottles of something paste-like and gray. It was full of bottles of priming paste, of mercury fulminate, enough to blow the carriage, the street and everything in it halfway back to the horrible little Swiss forest the horrible little Swiss black forest gnomes had come from. Muldoon thought he said, *"Oh my God, Virgil!"* He said, instead, ". . . *Ack—!"* He thought something went bang in his brain. He thought his brain got caught up in something, maybe a piece of lint or a rag or something, and all the cogs and wheels in it jammed. He thought it did. He thought he said—

Grimm Two, stripping the carriage down to turn it into the most diabolical dray ever conceived by the mind of Man, bending down in a single movement like a demented dwarf, getting something from under the floor, said quickly, "Here. Hold these!"

They were three half-pint bottles, labeled on plain strips in a cursive hand *No. 1, No. 2, No. 3.*

They were filled, each of them, with a clear, faintly yellow liquid that rolled a little like the high tide of Doom.

Muldoon said, "Ack . . ." He held the bottles, like triplets, hard against his chest. He thought he said to Tillman— He said, with his mouth stuck open, *"Arkk . . . !"* There was a click. His brain had stopped working and he only turned his eyes to the click to see what it was.

It was Tillman's Colt Lightning. In the yellow light, with the cylinder gate open, he was checking that it was fully loaded.

Muldoon said—

Grimm Two, pushing past him to get something else, said urgently, "Mind out."

Muldoon said, "Oh, sorry."

He thought he did.

He thought he said that.

In the eight-by-six cell full of the odor of sin and sudden death, Muldoon, holding the three bottles across his chest with arms that had gone strangely still, said thinly, *"Oh . . . !"*

* * *

"Tuning fork in E!"

It came flying out, and, catching it and wanging it on the sidewalk in a single motion, Grimm One, with his ear pressed against a flagstone to catch the echo, said aloud, "Hmm. A-ping . . . *pan!*" He was reporting his progress. "The old Tea Water Spring." He was very informative. "The old eighteenth-century natural spring with water so clear you could make tea with it without boiling it first to get rid of the impurities." He said to the closed black curtain, just in case they thought he was talking about something floating by in the night sky, "Down there. Under the sidewalk. Closed just before the Civil War when it was discovered the darkie servants of the rich Southern families with houses up here spent too much time at it collecting their water and plotting revolution and murder." He tapped again, "Leaking." He crawled on. He tapped at the next stone with another fork, "Ping—*inn'g!* Ah, a steam pipe line!" There was nothing *down there* that was not his. "Ah, a ping—*ingg—pan!* One of the old American Steam Company lines from the seventies, packed with lamp black, running—" He banged again, "—south to Maiden Lane." He had made a discovery. "The feeder to the exact same line that blew up in 1879 at the height of the rivalry between Andrews and the Steam Heating Company of New York when the inventor Andrews filled a line too full of pressure and blasted three tons of lamp black forty feet into the air and turned a hundred people of fair complexion into temporary Ethopians!" He said like an explorer, "Ha. Ha."

He crawled.

He tapped.

He pushed his medals out of the way and talked to the closed black curtain.

Moving on a parallel plane to the carriage, less than five feet from the side of Hewitt's store, he pinged.

Moving now onto flagstones that looked a little newer, as if, sometime in the recent past, they had been lifted and then put down again, he panged.

He ping-panged.

Trying the tuning fork in C, he rang a single hard note on the center of a chalk X mark on a newer-looking stone and, with the joy of an archaeologist, said, "A gas line!" He tried the fork in E, "And an old meter box!" In his own little world, soaring blind in the great black caverns of *Down There*, he had the brain and accuracy of a bat.

Spread-eagled on the street like a pinned, moth-eaten ancient beetle on a chalk-marked display board in a museum, Grimm One, clanking and crawling, pinged.

He pinged again.

He moved.

He crawled.

He pondered.

He ran his hand over a flagstone a little ahead of his face and stroked it. Contracting his neck into his collar, silent as a lover inching forward for his lass's breasts, he reached out with his fingertips and listened. With his ear to the ground, he heard things no other mortal ever heard.

He heard, minutely, infinitesimally, like the tumblers on a safe, all the secret movements of the Earth.

"Tuning fork in E!"

Without looking up, snapping his fingers to give his brother an aiming point, he caught it in midair as it came flying out from the carriage window.

He sat down on a box of something stenciled with a skull and crossbones. Grimm Two, just checking to see if everybody knew what they were doing, asked Tillman pleasantly, "I assume that the reason that there's nothing in the basement in Hewitt's store is because whatever you think is under the sidewalk goes through under Hewitt's basement where, if whatever is down there wasn't down there, Hewitt could have built himself a sub-basement—if that isn't what's there anyway—is that right?"

He thought that was what Grimm Two said to Tillman. It might not have been. He was holding three bottles of sudden death against his heart and it interfered with his hearing.

"Yes." Tillman said gratefully, "It's very good of you and your brother to help us out."

It was either that or twenty years in the Tombs for possession of enough explosives to blow the planet off its axis. Martin Grimm, Grimm Number Two, said pleasantly, "Anything for you, Virgil."

Muldoon thought that was what they said.

Muldoon said, "Virgil's an orphan. Family life is a mystery to Virgil so he does things no ordinary man with a family would do because he—"

He thought he said that. He thought he said, "I'm holding nitroglycerine in my arms for two mad bombers in the middle of Broadway!"

He thought he said, "For maniacs! For anarchists! For *fiends!*" He thought maybe that sounded too critical. He thought Virgil, patting him gently on the shoulder, said, "Just hold the bottles, Ned."

Muldoon thought he said, "I'm Virgil's friend."

He didn't say any of it. Grimm Two and Tillman hadn't spoken either. They were silent, waiting. He thought he said in terrible protest, the only sane man on the block, "Oh my God, *this is so illegal!*"

He didn't say that either.

In his arms, he had his three little babies, called Mass Murder, Mayhem and Massacre, to gently lull to rest.

Muldoon, in the silence of the carriage, in the quiet, steady, moving pinging of the dark, secret night, said only softly, not wanting to disturb them, ". . . *Ack!*"

Muldoon asked in a whisper so soft there was no sound at all, "What's the rabbit suit for?"

He listened. Sitting on a dynamite box, Grimm Two, reaching into his pocket for a pinch of snuff and halving it on his thumb with the side of his index finger without looking at it, sniffed it back into first one nostril and then the other.

He waited. In the cramped area inside the closed carriage, leaning forward a little with his finger resting gently against his mouth, Tillman waited.

Ping!

Outside in the street Grimm One said in an urgent whisper, talking about flagstones, "A new one . . . ! A brand-new one not dug up and replaced when something was put down or repaired or dug out, but a *new one* . . . !"

Ping!

In the carriage, Grimm Two and Tillman, gazing, yellow-lit, demented gnomes, spoke not at all.

Click! By Grimm Two's best-quality chiming gold Swiss pocket watch, with the chimes turned off, it was one forty-three A.M. precisely.

Ping!

Pang!

One forty-three and three quarters. One forty-four A.M. precisely.

Grimm One, on the street, ordered, *"Diamond drill!"* One forty-four and fifteen seconds.

He was like a cat. He had something from the cavity in the floor—something six inches long and shining like steel—and, moving, getting to the curtain, Grimm Two had it out into the night in an instant.

He sloshed, as he moved, all the yellow liquid in the three bottles in Muldoon's arms.

For the first time in that awful cave, making a sound that meant something, Muldoon made a sound that meant something.

Muldoon said, *"—Oh—!!"*

The drill bit went into the end of the right-hand walking stick. The right-hand walking stick had a twist ratchet in it. The bit touched at the edge of the brand-new virgin flagstone, and, as Grimm One pushed down on it with a hand of iron driven by sinews of steel, it whirred, and, in a flurry of dust and powdered stone, bored down at an angle of exactly thirty-three degrees into and under the stone.

He was talking as he pushed, counting it off, fixing the picture in his bat's magic mind. Grimm One said to the closed curtain, not caring if they heard or not, to himself, "Flagstone two inches thick, no splitting, above loose rock and rubble, above tightly packed earth and blue stone filling to a depth of two feet six inches, then . . ." He drilled. He sensed. "To eighteen inches of broken paving stone and—" He listened to the song of the drill. "To thick oak beams laid crossways at a depth of four feet four inches, to—" He listened, he loved: "To . . . to . . . to a *cavity!*"

Muldoon asked Grimm Two politely, "What's in bottle Number One?"
Grimm Two, looking at his pocket watch, said, "Gin."
"What's in bottle Number Two?"
Grimm Two said, "Cheap perfume."
Oh. Outside, somewhere, someone was happily drilling a hole to Damnation. He could hear him. Grimm Two, with Tillman, was at the curbside window with the black curtain up peering out, waiting for something.

They seemed like nice gentlemen, Grimm Two and Tillman and he said respectfully, watching the yellow liquid slosh as the carriage rocked with them on its springs, "Please. Excuse me . . ."

It was just a little question, but he couldn't get his babies to drop off to sleep without knowing the answer.

Muldoon, speaking softly, asked politely, "Please . . . someone? *What's the rabbit suit for?*"

He saw through the held-back curtain, coming fast into the circle of light the electric lamp on the corner cast, a figure in a blue uniform, and, as his heart jumped into his mouth as the curtain was pulled back closed in an instant, Muldoon, finding his voice, said in a gasp that sent the contents of the three glass bottles sloshing and rolling like tides, "Oh my God—*it's Clubber Simpson of the Sixth!*"

It was 1:45 A.M. precisely. At 1:45 A.M. precisely, on the steady progress of his beat, Patrolman Ruben Simpson should have been exactly at the corner of Broadway and Warren Street.

In the carriage, Grimm Two closed his watch with a snap.

On the sidewalk, getting up, Grimm One, bent over, his face in his chest, said loudly to the approaching Simpson,

> *"Here y' are— Black your boots, boss?*
> *Do it for just five cents;*

Shine 'em up in a minute,
That is if nothin' prevents."

Grimm One, nodding and groveling, said,

"Set your foot right on there, sir!
The mornin's kinder cold—
Sorter rough on a feller
When his coat's a-gittin' old.

Well, yes—call it a coat, sir;
Though 'taint much more'n a tear;
Can't git myself another—
Ain't got the stamps to spare."

In the coach Muldoon, in alarm, demanded, "What's going on?" He saw
Tillman's face. He saw the face of Grimm Two. Muldoon, holding the
sloshing bottles hard, demanded—

"Are you *insane?*" Patrolman Simpson, rocking back on his heels,
letting the horrible, ragged creature see the brass buttons shine on his tunic,
reaching for his billy club, roared, "You're not a bootblack, you're some
sort of crawling cockroach!" Patrolman Simpson, looking around for a
crime to report, demanded, "What are you doing here, you evil ragged
creature?" Simpson said, moving forward, drawing the club, "I bash
people like you." He glanced at the rich man's coach at the curb. Simpson,
raising his voice to make it carry, said, "I keep people like you in their
places so respectable people can use this city without being importuned by
people like you crawling with infection!"

". . . Make as much as most of 'em—
That's so; but then yer see—
Them other bootblacks got only one to do for—
There's two of us—Jack and me . . . !"

In the carriage, Grimm Two, his face tight and hard, with a strange tone
in his voice, said in a whisper, "Get ready."

Muldoon said, *"What's going on? Why is he quoting poetry? What's
going on?"* Muldoon said in sudden horror to Tillman, "Virgil, *what have
you arranged with these lunatics?"*

"Young Jack, he used to be round sellin' papers,
The streets here was his lay,

> *But he got shoved into a horsecar,*
> *Under the wheels one day."*

Muldoon said, *"Virgil, these people are only helping us so they can get Simpson!"*
He wanted to get out to Simpson.
He had the bottles in his arms. He could move nowhere. Muldoon said in extremis, "Virgil, this whole thing is a *setup!*"

> *"Yes, a copper did it—*
> *Gave him a reg'lar throw—*
> *He didn't care if it killed him,*
> *Some of 'em is just so."*

He was bent over, not looking at Simpson. Grimm One said,

> *"He's never been quite all right since, sir,*
> *Sorter—bent and queer—*
> *Him and me go together,*
> *He's what they call cashier."*

Simpson said with rising fear, reaching for his club, *"Who are you?"*

Grimm Two was gone out the off-side door with the three bottles and the suit. In the carriage Muldoon said in alarm, *"My God, Virgil, they're going to kill him!"*
Tillman said, "No." He was ready at the curb-side door, tensed. Tillman, shaking his head, said suddenly now not too sure of it himself, "No. No, they aren't."
"You knew this was Simpson's beat! You knew he'd be here! You told the Grimms what you wanted them to do and you told them in return they could murder Simpson and get away with it, and you—"
Tillman, shaking his head, said, "No. No, I didn't agree to that at all—"

On the sidewalk, he had an old coat covered in medals. He had in that coat tuning forks, a diamond drill—he had explosives and guns and knives and God only knew what else. On the sidewalk Grimm Number One said tightly,

> *"High old style for a bootblack—*
> *Made all the fellers laugh—*
> *Jack and me had to take it,*
> *But we don't mind no chaff."*

If he was really Swiss or German or foreign, suddenly he didn't sound like it. Suddenly he sounded like he had grown up in the streets of New York. Grimm One said,

> *"Trouble? I guess not much, sir,*
> *Sometimes when biz gets slack,*
> *I don't know how I'd stand it*
> *If 'twasn't for little Jack."*

"Who are you?"

Grimm One said mildly, shrugging, "Me? I'm nobody. I'm just somebody who is nobody with a family that's nobody with a boy of eighteen with a twisted back who's now nobody—"

"If I hit some ragamuffin guttersnipe, it was only because I was being merciful and I didn't report him!" Simpson, his club coming out, demanded, *"Who are you? What are you doing here? I'll report you! My word will stand up in court!"*

Grimm One said, tight, tensed, shaking,

> *"Why, boss, you ought to hear him,*
> *He says we needn't care,*
> *How rough luck is now here, sir,*
> *If some days we gits Up There—"*

Simpson, roaring, thundered, "What have you got there under your coat?" He looked. He saw. His eyes fell out of his head. He saw in the man's hand something that looked like part of a clock with wires and springs sticking out of it, and— Simpson said in a shriek, "My God, it's a *bomb!*" His eyes raced to the carriage. Simpson said in a gasp, going mad, "My God, a giant white rabbit!" Simpson, reaching out for Grimm One but being reached out for first by Grimm Two and finding his neck caught in a grip of steel, said in horror, *"My God, you've come to get me! You've—"* Simpson screamed, *"Who are you?"* Simpson shrieked, *"I'll report you!"*

Grimm One said softly,

> *"All done now—how's that, sir?*
> *Shine like a pair of lamps;*
> *Mornin'—give the money to Jack, sir,*
> *He looks out for the stamps."*

Grimm One shrieked, *"You vicious, uncaring, miserable, cowardly son of a bitch, you beat my child senseless for getting in your way when he was only eight years old!"*

There *was* a white rabbit outside the coach door. Looking in for an instant, wrenching the three numbered bottles from Muldoon's grasp, the white rabbit ordered Tillman and Muldoon, "Get ready—!"

Grimm One shrieked, "Report me? *Report me."* Grimm One shrieked, *"Report this, you honest copper you!"* He squeezed. He pushed. He hurled the man back. He ducked as the white rabbit, like a baseballist, threw the first of the two bottles and smashed it dead center on Simpson's chest. He winced as the smell of gin exploding from the bottle almost made him gag. He ducked as the second bottle, filled to the brim with cheap whore's perfume, smashed the man on the side of the head. He took cover, as—as Simpson, falling back, saw it all happen—as there was a pop! a bang and then—

And then there was a blast that blew the flagstone open like a hinged door, filled the street with smoke, and then, the smoke instantly going down into the ground like a whirlwind, there was a second detonation and a jet of flame from somewhere in the bowels of the Earth that sent rubble and stone and bits and pieces of blackened wood up like an eruption.

The White Rabbit screamed, "The Keepers of the Portals!" Through the smoke there were two people running, one of them carrying a Colt Lightning and a bull's-eye lantern, the other, bigger, loping along after him looking confused. The White Rabbit shrieked, "Tonight we *open* the portals to send vile coppers to *Hell!"*

Grimm One roared, *"Report that, you drunken, perfumed, white-rabbit-seeing policeman!"* Grimm One, hopping up and down with the sweetness of revenge, screamed, "Report *that!"* He would have given his life's savings to have been at the Precinct when Simpson went in to explain.

The father of a son crippled by a policeman's club, he would have given his life.

Jumping up and down with glee, making sounds of animal release he had kept pent up inside for almost nine long years, Grimm One, wrenching the third bottle from his brother's hand, dashed it to the ground, and, as Tillman and Muldoon, jumping down into blackness, disappeared below the level of the street, hit the edge of the flagstone and the edge of Simpson a glancing blow with the sloshing half pint of pure, distilled, best-quality nitroglycerine and, in a concussion that made all the windows in the street shake and the horse in the traces of their carriage rear up in terror, blasted both the flagstone and Simpson simultaneously: the flagstone in an arc exactly back where it had come from as if it had never moved, and

Simpson, his hat and tunic reduced to rags, twenty feet back down the road.

They were the greatest Scientific Bombers in the history of the World.

On the street, a man-sized white rabbit and a tattered old soldier in rags, dancing, hopping, shouting triumphant, they embraced each other and, uncontrollably, sobbed with joy.

16

Ten feet down Muldoon hit something hard and slid on it like a toboggan in a shower of splinters and falling debris, stones and broken beams and planks.

He was in a hole, a tunnel: he was sliding down feet first into a tunnel into blackness, and as Tillman's lantern somewhere behind him lit him up, he fell off whatever it was he was sliding on with a thump that he thought for a moment broke all the bones in his shoulders, hit something hard and solid and was rolled over full length on his back.

He reached up and felt wood. He reached up and ran his hand along the wood and felt the edge and, getting his fingernails deep into it, cutting a groove into the rotten material, hung on to it like a bat.

He saw Tillman's lantern light, above him, coming down and Muldoon craning to see where he was, saw he was on a flight of polished wooden stairs, every second step smashed where he had slid down it, with a storm of clay and earth falling down, cutting off the air.

He had his own lantern held hard in his right hand, pointed down and he twisted and shined it down to his feet, then up in the air above his face. Through the ray, everywhere in the tunnel, dust was falling like rain. All the steps above or below him were rotten or broken or coming off their risers. All around them were endless tiled walls, filthy with dust. The smell of the dust was overwhelming. It was the smell of something ancient, abandoned, left to rot, the smell of a tomb, the smell of—

"Where are we?" He was twisting, turning, trying to find something to hang on to to get some purchase. He was rolling over like an upturned beetle. Muldoon, feeling as huge as an elephant in the tiny space, demanded as something he reached out for—an upturned stair—gave way and turned to dust, *"Why the hell didn't you tell me what we were jumping into?"*

"I could have been wrong." Higher up, Tillman stepped carefully over a gap and tested his footing. It was not solid. He stepped back and flashed the lantern down and found a steel support for the stair.

Wrong? If this was right— Muldoon said as something his bulk rested on gave way, *"Whooa!"* Muldoon roared, "What do you mean, you could have been wrong? I know you—you looked it up somewhere! You let the Grimms blow up Simpson because you knew you were right! You *knew* this was here! Where the hell would we have landed if you'd been wrong—*the center of the Earth?"* He saw, in the light from Tillman's lantern, the curve of the tiled roof. It was ten feet above him, going down, then it went down another fifteen feet and then, getting suddenly higher, all the tiles covered in dust and filth, it became fifteen feet high like an archway and turned off to the right. Muldoon, getting to his feet, his boot smashing through more rotten wood but, mercifully, finding a metal support underneath it, demanded, "Virgil, *what in the name of God is this place?"* Above, the Brothers Grimm had sealed the flagstone like the stone slab of a sarcophagus. Muldoon roared, "They blew Ruben Simpson twenty feet into the air."

Tillman said tightly, "Ruben Simpson deserved to be blown twenty feet into the air." He ordered Muldoon abruptly, "Stay against the wall!" He was edging himself down a step at a time with his back against the tiles. Tillman, pointing the light down, at first to Muldoon's face and then to his feet so he could see where he was, ordered him, "Don't stray out onto the stairs. They're all rotten. Stay against the risers and keep your back on the wall." He could see the tunnel turning away at the bottom of the hole. Tillman, flashing the light, said in triumph, "It turns off to the right under Hewitt's store." He was a shadow behind the ray of light, lit up in the back lighting of it against the curve of the tiles. He was slight, tiny. He weighed nothing. He was a flea. Tillman, coming down, moving the light from side to side, said encouragingly, "Just stay where you are and I'll come down and get you."

The tiles his back had rubbed against had little blue and yellow flowers on them. They were part of a descent, a staircase in a corridor with straight walls of tiles and a curving, vaulted ceiling. The tiles on the ceiling here and there had designs on them—stars and moons and all the planets. Muldoon, reaching out and grasping something hard behind his back on the wall, said as his feet anchored themselves on something hard and precarious, but solid, "Virgil, where—? *Where are we?"*

The light from the approaching lantern lit him up and he twisted to see what he had his hand on and saw a brass handrail embellished with dolphins, bolted to the wall by little brass figures—mermaids—set three feet apart.

He saw that, once, the broken and rotted stairs had been polished mahogany or cedar. He saw where once, still glowing dully under the dust, they had all been French-polished and inlaid with roses.

He saw, in the light at the end of the descent, where the roof became no longer curved but vaulted, a long, carved stone bench with glass ball-and-claw feet for all the people who had walked on those polished and inlaid stairs to sit on.

He saw, down deep, going deeper, the tiled, vaulted tunnel turn sharply away to the right into blackness.

It opened out at the bench. At the bench, the curved tunnel became a room, a landing exactly fourteen feet by fourteen square with all the flowered tiles gone and the brass handrail replaced by a line of mosaics set in the wall at eye height showing the labors of Hercules and the death of the Minotaur in its cave.

QUA PATET ORBIS. It had been laid in in onyx below the labors. It meant As Far as the World Extends. It had been laid in, in English Gothic, one letter at a time.

Depeyster Ironmongery Company. It was on a little copper plaque on what had once been a gas fitting for a light on the vaulted ceiling, but had long ago either given way and fallen down or been stolen.

THIS WAY → It was a rectangle of colored glass screwed to the wall at the end of Hercules' labors and the death of the Minotaur so the people fresh from their rest on the stone bench would know what direction to take next.

They were thirty feet below the surface of Broadway, at 1:58 A.M., in the heart of the modern city of New York.

Going down into the blackness, the second flight of stairs curved away and to the right at an angle for easy walking of exactly thirty-five degrees.

The stairs, this time, were stone.

Along the walls, this time, clean where the dust and decay had not got to them, there were inset ceramic delft tiles of scenes from New York—Dutch houses with smoke rising from their chimneys and sailing ships with bunting and pennants, and here and there, Manhattan Indians on bluffs watching as the ships came in or, on hills, looking down into the vales where the houses were.

There was a tile of a man in the costume of an sixteenth-century soldier, all leather and lace, his head encased in a wide, feathered floppy soldier's hat; in his hand, ready with a wisp of smoke coming from the slow match at the pan, a matchlock rifle.

He seemed, in the flickering light, to have a peg leg.

Pieter Stuyvesant, Rex. It was a depiction of the first Dutch Governor of New York. It was an ancient tile, from someone's collection, a tile made in the late seventeenth century showing the man as the King of America.

Beyond that, the walls were, again, all flowers and petals.

Tillman said softly, "Almost there . . ." He had his lantern held stiffly against his side. The ray, stabbing downward, lit up all the stone steps.

Tillman, getting ahead of Muldoon and taking the first stone step, lighting up the arcing, disappearing passage as he went, gripping his gun hard in his hand, said so softly in the sudden silence that Muldoon had to strain to hear him, "Almost there . . ."

They were at least thirty feet below the surface of the sidewalk.

They were deep—God only knew where—in the bowels of the Earth.

He was six steps ahead. He was almost at the bottom of the stone steps with the light stabbing ahead of him into the blackness. Tillman said, "Look! Look!"

It was a blackened panel set into the walls of the tunnel, blocking it off, with two panes of colored glass on either side of it covered in filth and dust.

It was made of what looked like cedar, in two sections, secured by something black and filthy that looked as if it had once been a piece of chain.

Above it, in perfect condition, washed clean by moisture or protected from the slime by the little niche it had been set into, there was a sign. The sign, decorated and surmounted by a motif of blue and yellow flowers, read in a flowing hand-painted Irish signwriter's hand:

* *Please Note* *
THE LADIES OF THE UNION HOME FOR THE
ORPHANS OF SOLDIERS AND SAILORS
RECEIVE THE BENEFIT OF ALL ADMISSION
FEES.

The sign said, in a smaller script, under that, THANK YOU.

The sign said, ADMISSION 25¢.

The sign said, so tiny that Muldoon had to squint to read it, *"O'Heeney, Signwriter, Maiden Lane."*

"Virgil—*where are we?*"

He was so close he was out of breath. Tillman said in a whisper, "At a door. Under Hewitt's. *At a door!*" The light from the lantern lit up the rotting wood and reflected the glow back into his face off the glass at the sides. He reached out with the hand holding the Lightning and, turning it slightly, pointing the barrel up, touched at the door with the edge of his palm as if, through the grain, he could feel something beyond it.

They were twenty feet below the basement of Hewitt's store, *Down There.*

He listened, but he could hear no sound at all.

It seemed to Muldoon a long time, but it was not: it was instantaneous.

Tillman, stepping back, bringing up the gun and the lantern, holding them out, said as a single command, "Ned—" and in that instant, he had charged the door and, in a crash that sounded like the crack of doom and sent dust falling all around him, he had broken down the door and, disappearing into the darkness, was instantly through it and gone.

17

They were inside a cathedral of space, an enormity of height and width and breadth, blind and lost in anotherworld—in a world of color without form—in a Universe, a cavern, a cathedral of glowing, palpable, glittering cobalt light.

They were lost like errant comets in the shimmering vastness of the Universe, in a roofless cavern deep beneath the Earth, in another dimension, another part of the spectrum—they were, suddenly, caught like spiders in a prism of deepest, pervading opaque blue.

He could see nothing. He could not see half an inch in front of him. Muldoon, fishing his half-inch pocket lantern out of his coat and lighting it, holding it up to his face to see its glow and seeing nothing, said in a gasp, "My God—!" The air was like a blanket. It was acrid and thick and it burned at his throat. It was the same light he had seen at Rosie's. Muldoon, lost, staggering, shaking his head like a dog, his eyes and throat burning, said to where he thought Tillman's lantern light was ahead in the blanket of color, "Virgil! *Where are we?*"

Around Tillman's lamp there was a halo, a fizzing. The color was moving in layers, efflorescent, like fox fire, emitting its own lumination, thickest on the hard ground he stood on, moving like fingers through the carbide gas and wick of the bull's-eye lantern and making it spark and crackle. There was no echo to the sound of the lamp or Muldoon's voice: the sounds went away, disappeared into an enormity of distance in front of him.

His throat hurt with whatever the light was; it went dry and burned as particles of the dust or the chemicals that were in it lodged in the back of his mouth and under his tongue and dried out all the moisture there. There were specks of the stuff moving in layers in the fluorescence, falling like ash. Tillman said as an order, "Stand *still!*"

He could see nothing. He could not see the lantern in front of him, could not feel its heat. Tillman, getting down onto his knees, holding the lantern far out and away from him, trying to orient himself to turn to where he thought the man was behind him, ordered Muldoon, "Don't move, Ned. Stay where you are." He heard Muldoon coughing, trying to clear his throat. He had his gun out in his hand, held by the top strap, running his fingers along it, afraid to lose contact with it, walking his fingers along it for the muzzle to turn it to use as a hammer. He heard Muldoon hacking at the dust in the air. He got the muzzle in his hand and, pushing—he hoped—the tinplate lantern out in front of him like a cave explorer searching for an opening, rapped hard on the ground with the revolver's butt.

The ground was stone. The echo was dull. He had no idea in what direction he was pointed, or how far away Muldoon was, or where he might have strayed. Tillman, inching forward, rapping at the ground in front of him as if the next foot would bring him to the edge of a crevasse, called out with his voice seeming to go nowhere, to be muffled and lost, "Forward! Go forward a step at a time!"

He rapped and the sound was different, sharper, as if there was something like fired terra-cotta there. (He thought he saw, just for an instant, a speck of color—of yellow.) Tillman called, "Ned? *Can you hear me?*"

He inched forward. He rapped and there was no sound at all and, putting his nose to the ground like an Indian smelling a train, he rapped again at it, hard, and twisting the gun in his hand, felt for what it was.

Tillman, not believing it, not crediting the touch of it at his fingers, said to where he thought Muldoon was, *"Carpet—!"*

"Marble!" He was down on his haunches like a runner poised on the blocks, ready to run. Muldoon, all the muscles in his thighs aching, reaching out with his free hand, feeling something cold and damp, blinking, seeing for an instant something white on the ground and actually getting down to smell it, said, "Marble! Marble laid in bricks!" There was a fizz from his carbide lantern and, in the blue, like a pinhole through thick satin, he saw the whiteness on the ground and, at its edge a line of black, "Marble laid in hexagonal bricks!" He swiveled back and could not see the door they had come through. He could not see in any direction. Muldoon, moving forward, listening, his throat burning, smelling and touching at the stuff, said as if he did not believe it himself, "Laid marble like a church!" He could have been crawling to the rim of the world. He heard a sound. He felt moisture running on the palm of his hand where he pushed it across the ground.

Muldoon said, not knowing whether he was moving toward it or away from it or anywhere near it at all, "I can hear water bubbling!"

* * *

The blue light was the glow of niter. It was a glow on the ground and on the walls and on the ceiling. He could smell it. It was the smell of gunpowder, of the acrid potassium nitrate component of gunpowder. It was the smell of mold and dust and chemicals come up from the earth in particles—it was the bitter vetch of decomposition and acridness. The niter, wherever it was deposited, on whatever it clung to, was blinking and glowing in the darkness. It was everywhere. It was on his hands, and when he pulled back the gun and twisted it to wipe his face with the side of his hand, he felt it rub against his skin like emery paper.

He got down and rapped for the carpet again but it was gone, and as he rapped at something hard instead the lantern in his other hand flared with the dust and chemicals getting into its combustion chamber and he saw a flash of color in the blueness—a green and then a brown—and then the sound of the rapping changed again and he was crawling back on carpet, and then it had changed again and the floor was hard.

Muldoon, at the end of something, the limit of something, feeling something solid and built up from the ground in front of him, said to locate himself, "Water! I'm at the water!" It was like a solid, curved wall to his touch, cold and moist. "I'm at some sort of object." He could not get any light from his lantern at all, even though he felt the heat on the tinplate handle in his hand and knew it was burning. Muldoon, getting up, pulling himself up on the wall or the column or whatever the object was, called, "Virgil, I'm at the water!"

He had veered off. He crawled one more foot with the gun out exploratorily in front of him and he felt, in a moment that sickened him to the pit of his stomach, the barrel and weight of the gun go down, connect with nothing and almost drag him over.

He felt in the swing nothing but air, and, crawling back in the direction he thought Muldoon's voice had come from at the object, Tillman yelled in alarm, "Stay there! Don't move to your left! Stay on the line you've got!"

His free hand went into water, into bitterly cold water that was bubbling and moving, and, pulling it back through the stuff, reaching for the inside of the marble wall, Muldoon, holding the useless lamp up an inch from his face, feeling its heat, hearing it spark and crackle, stood up and leaned forward and saw a face.

Muldoon shrieked, *"Oh my God!"*

It was a dead face with the eyes open with no pupils in them. It was a green face. It stared at him. It was a body erect in the water with a green, pupil-less face and a hand out with something in it that was stiff and green and—

It was a statue.

It was Mercury, the winged messenger of the gods.

Muldoon said in utter, total astonishment, his mind reeling, "It's a statue of— *It's a bronze life-sized statue of Mercury in the middle of a marble fountain!*"

He was at a wall. Somehow, through the cobalt, he had crawled away from the left, passed in front of or behind Muldoon, and reached a wall, and, for an instant, like a small child touching home, touching something real and familiar and comforting, he leaned against it and felt through his shoulders its solidity, its realness; and then he moved a foot and the solidity, the plane of it, was gone and he was loosened from his hold on it and falling over, hitting the ground in his blindness and fighting to hold the fizzing lantern up in the air where he thought it would be safe.

He had found no wall at all. He touched at it with his fingers, searching out its shape in the darkness. It was crenellated and round and it was a Doric column of marble. Tillman called back behind him and to his left, "*Ned! Where are you?*" There was a sound like a taut wire breaking—a ping!—and then there was the sound of something heavy scraping, and then as if someone with hands like hammers wrenched at something delicate, there was a crackling sound of wood and then, again, the sound of the wire drawn tight and giving way.

At the column, moving right, going for a wall, Tillman called out, "*Ned—?*" He saw a flare of yellow light and thought for an instant something had caught fire, then it flared again, fizzed and crackled, and what was fizzing and crackling was his own lantern two feet out in front of him as the falling niter found a way into the combustion chamber and ignited. He felt the lamp jump with the detonation. Tillman called urgently, "*Ned!*"

"It's a grand *piano*. So help me God, it's a goddamned—" Muldoon said into the blueness, into the nothingness, in the direction of the flaring circle of yellow lantern light growing brighter by the second, "So help me God, just in front of the fountain with the statue in it, on a raised marble dais, there's a goddamned *concert grand piano!*" He felt a push in his hand that made his arm jump and then there was a glow of yellow light. Then, in the glow as if it was alive white sparks, then yellow, then, like tiny comets lights spitting up, and he felt a feeling of sudden power and inflation at the end of his hand and he knew—

He knew, in that instant, what it was.

By the piano, hurling the fizzing, spitting thing away behind him, Muldoon yelled in horror, "Virgil, my lantern—it's starting to *explode!*"

His lantern, too, was sparking, pulsing, hissing. He was at a wall—he was sure it was a wall—moving along it with his shoulders pushed back hard against it and he saw, where his own outstretched hand was, the lights and sparks jumping in the combustion chamber. He saw a yellow light somewhere ahead of him, heard a thump as Muldoon must have taken cover somewhere, and then as something hit the ground there was a shower of sparks and a corona of brilliant white light and, looking not at that, fighting to look away in the direction he was going, he saw suddenly on the floor, on the hexagonal marble inlays in front of him—where the line of green and brown carpet went away to his left into infinity—a plinth, a pedestal, and he saw something set into it flash with a reflection and then fade, and then, from somewhere, from somewhere near the piano or the fountain or the statue or the column or some other thing that was there in the darkness, he heard Muldoon roar like a Stentor, "Virgil! Your lantern's going too—*I can see it sparking!*" and pushing hard against the wall, speeding up, feeling the heat in the lantern box surge, he was going fast for the plinth, the pedestal or whatever it was, opening and shutting his eyes fast in the blue light to sear its position into his brain in case the lamp went and he had to find it in the darkness.

"*Virgil!*" The light from Tillman's lamp was pulsating, surging like a volcano, like a bomb filling with power. Down on his haunches against the legs of the piano, he saw it moving and he thought for an awful moment it might not be Tillman's light at all. He was down against the piano with no idea what was around him or coming for him at all. There was a ping as another of the piano wires inside the decomposing grand piano must have broken loose from its retaining hook and snapped. There was a fizzing from the lantern, a leaking bubbling from the fountain, the sounds of— He was below ground, blind, like a mole. He was—
Muldoon screamed, "Virgil! Virgil—"
He saw a flare.
Muldoon, up on his feet, steeling himself to charge in the darkness to where the light was, roared at the top of his voice, "For the love of God, throw the goddamned lantern *away!*"

The lantern was burning. It was burning through the tinplate with the heat, the carbide source of gas in the chamber at the base of it bubbling and melting as the niter in the wick burned through it, set the holder around it on fire and then, burning through the tin and the black paint, got to the handle and made it red-hot.

He was at the plinth. He saw, in the light, metal and wood and lines and bars of brass and copper and recesses and holes for wires and pipes, and he knew what it was, knew he had been right, and as his hand started to burn, as he felt the heat on all the tinplate radiate, surge toward a detonation, he had his gun back in his holster and his fingers were searching, pushing, looking for something he knew would be on the plinth that he could not find.

"Virgil!" He saw the lamp flare. He saw it reach an intensity his own had not reached when he had thrown it away and it had exploded. Muldoon, starting to brace himself to run toward the lantern light to wrench it away from the man, yelled, *"Virgil—!"*

"Stay there!" If the lamp went, if the explosion blew him off his feet and he was blind in the color, he would never be able to find the plinth again. He could only find what he was looking for on the plinth now, while the lamp was still lit. Tillman, his hand starting to sear, running out of time, the lamp almost useless—*but having nothing else if it went*—yelled, "Stay there! Don't come! *Stay there!*" and in that instant, as the lamp started to go and he flung it away from him into the darkness as far as it would go, his fingers closed around a chain with a handle on it and, almost going over as the lamp, roaring and burning, hit the ground twenty feet away and rolled like a fireball, he pulled the chain so far out it broke off in his hand and in that same instant, on the ceiling of the place, along the full one-hundred-and-twenty-foot length of that vaulted ceiling, one by one, in a series, in a line, in magnificence, each of the twelve zircon-powder-powered crystal chandeliers came on and bathed the cathedral, the cavern, the six-hundred-square-foot place, in a brilliant, wonderful, tinkling, breathtaking white light.

. . . Muldoon, staring across at Tillman at the control plinth, discovering him, staring at him as if he had never seen him before in his life, said with his eyes wide and staring, "Holy . . . Holy *Jesus* . . . *!*"

He could not believe, in the enormity of the place, what he saw.

Tillman said in a whisper, "My God . . ." He could not credit in that place, in the light, what he saw with his own eyes. Tillman said, not comprehending it at all, "My God, I never thought for a moment it would—"

At the plinth, staring hard at Muldoon and seeing him not at all, Tillman said in a whisper, lost in the enormity and magnificence of it all, "My God, I never thought it would look like *this!"*

18

It was, thirty-five feet below the surface of Warren Street and stretching across Broadway to Murray Street a distance of some three hundred and twelve feet, Alfred Ely Beach's wonderful, majestic, magnificent, derelict Underground Pneumatic Railroad.

It was the waiting room of the Warren Street end of the system. It was a salon one hundred and twenty feet long with murals and terra-cotta friezes on the walls, leather armchairs and sofas on the carpeted floor, Doric columns, fountains, statuary, a white Steinway piano with a marble dolphin-shaped seat set on a marble dais for the entertainment of commuters, and, for children and the scientifically curious—set into the walls under the friezes, beneath the light of the line of twelve gold and crystal chandeliers hanging from a plaster ceiling painted with all the flowers of the forest and murals of Pan, of Mercury and Zeus—fish tanks for the scientific display of specimens from all over the world.

It had been, when Beach had opened it, the greatest single step in the transportation of people in history. It had been, sootless and smoke free, the greatest step forward in the propulsion of the locomotive train since the invention of steam. It had made the steam train obsolete: it had run solely and exclusively—unbelievably—on nothing more than air. It had had as its rails, no rails at all. Like a bullet in a gun barrel, the car that seated—as the forerunner of even greater, even bigger things to come—twenty-two people in elegant comfort, was simply, suddenly, blasted down the length of the nine-foot-diameter tunnel that was the transit system by two great steam-powered twelve-foot-diameter fans delivering, at maximum power, over one hundred thousand cubic feet of compressed air a minute.

Built over two years, dug with a hydraulic tunneling machine of Beach's own invention, the entire system excavated in fifty-eight nights from the basement Beach had rented from old Mr. Hewitt, it had been, on the day it was announced in the pages of *Scientific American* Beach owned and edited, a project of monumental illegality, without city charter, without reference to the weakening of the city's greatest thoroughfare above it, without concern for sympathetic cave-ins of the land on which places like Trinity Church and its graveyard stood, and without concern for the Astors who owned the land it tunneled through below the streets or the Democratic machine under Boss Tweed whose permission to reap profits it sought not at all.

It was Beach's small-scale patent model for a system that one day would stretch from the Battery to the Bronx.

It had cost, up to the day it opened in February 1870, a mere three hundred and fifty thousand dollars.

Three years and one month later in 1873, brought down by Tweed and Astor, it had cost almost one and a half million dollars in lawyers' fees alone, and it had cost Beach his health and his fortune and it had cost him his confidence, and, broken, he had simply had the entrances walled up and faded away to obscurity.

It was like a wrecked, sunken treasure galleon hidden for centuries beneath the sea, full of riches.

Like a galleon, eaten through by mold, glowing with the niter that fed on it, in the sudden new air, in the brilliant white light, before their eyes, it began to fall to pieces.

"But there's nothing here—!" He was like a moth moving about the place, touching at it, looking down at it, examining it. In his dark, dust-covered suit, moving about the place like a tiny moth, there was nothing but damp wood and peeling paintings and leather sofas turned to dust. The ornamented portal to the tunnel was open. In it, perhaps twenty feet along its barrel, the circular wood car was jammed with its back doors hanging open, the gilt lamps inside broken free of their retaining screws on their cedar stands and leaning like drunken skeletons against the upholstered benches, the front doors open and staring down a void of blackness speckled here and there with the blue lights of niter glowing on the walls. Tillman, like Beach, a ruined man, yelled in the echoing cavern of the waiting room, moving, his shoes raising dust in the frayed and rotten carpet as he went, *There's nothing here!"*

He had thought "Down There" had meant—

He touched at the marble retaining wall of the fountain and it gave way, all the masonry rotted, all the mortise long gone, and the water, clear at the top where the zircon lamp machine had moved it, black and seeping out like mud.

He pushed at the glass of the fish tanks, and they were vile, green, covered in slime, the lead mountings holding them rusted to powder, inside the tanks only slime and mud. *"Nothing!"* There was nothing down there except what had been down there since 1873—there was nothing. The niter was the niter of ten years of total, utter darkness. The stink, the acridity that had burned at their throats was the stench of neglect and ruin and rot and decomposition. There were sounds of wood and metal starting to fall away from each other, the sound of dust falling, things coming apart.

Tillman, tiny in the cathedral, lost, not knowing which way to turn, shrieked at the top of his voice, "There's nothing down here!" Everything: Lily, Rosie, Jenkins, Hewitt—it was all for nothing. Tillman shrieked, "There's nothing here!" He saw Muldoon start to come toward him, picking his way through the carpet coming apart at his tread in chunks and he stopped him with his hand, "Look! *Look!* There's nothing down here at all!"

He was less than five feet four tall and slight. In that place, beneath the ceiling, he looked like a tiny child gazing up with his hands locked together in front of him, lost for words or excuses. All the light from the chandeliers had been was the residual zircon in fuel chambers. One by one, fizzing to the end of the fuel, the chandeliers began to go out until there was only—probably the least used in the three years the system had run—only the fading white light from the chandelier that lit up the fish tanks and murals of heroic deeds by the far wall.

He touched at his face with his hand. He ran it across his thick black moustaches.

Tillman, shaking his head, like Beach a destroyed man, said, "God Almighty, Ned—God Almighty, I lied about the way Jenkins died, I had those maniacs the Grimms blow a hole in the middle of Broadway to get into here—! And now we're going to have to smash or blast or shoot another one to get out!"

Tillman said, slapping at his head, starting to giggle, "God Almighty, Ned, God Almighty— *How in the name of all that's likely am I ever going to be able to explain that one to Headquarters?*"

"We don't have to be cops all our lives."

Tillman said, "No."

"We could open a beer joint."

"Nobody would come."

Muldoon said, "Okay then, a brothel."

He was still giggling. Tillman said, "Nah." Tillman said suddenly, amazed at the stupidity of it, "Are you crazy? If we couldn't make a living selling beer, how much do you think we'd be able to make selling *broth?*"

They were sitting on the side of the fountain by a wall mural of Atlas holding up the world.

Muldoon said, "By the way, did I tell you I bought a dog recently?"

Tillman said, "You bought a dog recently?"

Muldoon said gravely, "Hmm. A recent dog, but my dog ain't got no nose."

Tillman said, "What? You bought a recent dog and you discovered your dog ain't got no nose?"

Muldoon said, "Right."

"Your dog ain't got no nose?" Tillman said, appalled, "If your dog ain't got no nose, how does he smell?"

Muldoon said, *"Terrible!"*

He giggled. He roared. He slapped his hand into the slime in the fountain. Muldoon, guffawing mightily, yelled, "On the stage! On the stage! We ought to be on the stage!"

He could not stop giggling. Tillman roared, "On the next one straight out of town!"

Muldoon said, "Ho! Ho!" He had his hip flask of best Old Republic whiskey in his pocket. Taking it out and unscrewing the cap and handing it to Tillman for a swig, Muldoon said conspiratorially, working himself up to an Irish joke of monumental obscenity, shaking with anticipatory glee, "Now, it seems there was this traveling salesman, see, and his horse throws a shoe just outside this English dairymaid's home just outside of Dublin, see, and this dairymaid—she's an English dairymaid, see, and she—"

It flickered. Burning at the last of its zircon fuel, the chandelier by the far wall glowed no longer bright and white but yellow, like limelight.

Like a camp fire in the hills, in the falling darkness of the world, it was a single failing glow that suddenly moved.

It swung. It swung with no motive force as if somewhere, suddenly, there was a vibration.

It moved, swung.

In the darkness, it swung and moved with all the other eleven chandeliers all along the ceiling as if, above it, with a monstrous tread, something passed above it in the earth.

It tinkled. All the crystal lamps it supported on golden mountings tinkled.

It tinkled, it rang. On the walls, on the floor, like stars the blue began to twinkle in specks.

There was, somewhere unheard, unseen, a movement, a vibration of something heavy, monstrous, moving, passing by.

Along the painted, peeling ceiling, too high and dark to see, as whatever it was approached steadily, unhurriedly, all the crystal shades on all the swinging chandeliers began to ring in concert.

* * *

The sound stopped, but whatever it had been, it had been in the earth itself. The chandeliers, still swinging, were still tinkling.

The final chandelier, running out of fuel, was flickering, fading to yellow with all the stars of blue niter twinkling around it on the ceiling.

The sound had come from above. It had come from inside the walls, in the ceiling. The light was fading, starting to splutter. In the growing darkness the blue color was coming back, the specks of material glowing in the absence of light. The chandelier, as if there was still something happening that could not be heard, was tinkling, tinkling—then there was what sounded like a sharp crash and the chandelier, blazing suddenly with light, creaked at its chain support on the ceiling, and then, as the light in its lamps flared bright white there was a snap and all the crystal lampshades on one side of the assembly failed, cracked in sudden black lines and exploded in a shower of falling, glittering fine glass.

The mural of Atlas holding up the world was fading to blackness in the going light, becoming flecked and speckled with stars. Whatever was moving was behind there. Behind there—behind the wall—there was the sound of something metal hitting a buffer, then, as the scene faded into darkness, was eaten up by the blackness and the appearing stars, there was a silence.

The twinkling stopped. Burning only half its lights, the light fading, going yellow, there was, suddenly, darkness.

He had his Smith and Wesson out. Back from the mural, Muldoon, the pistol out in front of him in two hands, said into the darkness, "Straight ahead, Virgil—straight ahead at the wall!" It was a tiny little gun shooting little thirty-two caliber pills that suddenly seemed hardly enough to stop an enraged cockroach, and Muldoon, letting go of the grip with one hand and feeling for his lead-filled club to check it was there, said with Tillman suddenly lost to him in the darkness, "It's behind the wall!" He listened for the sound of Tillman cocking his Colt Lightning and heard nothing. Muldoon, getting down into a crouch, taking the two-hand hold on his pistol again, ready, if nothing else, to at least let whatever it was have everything that was in the little gun, said, "I'm ahead of you—be careful where you shoot—" There was a hissing sound from behind the wall and then something that sounded like a little pop, and, in darkness, stepping back another pace, Muldoon, hearing nothing else, said in sudden alarm, *"Virgil, where are you?"*

There was another pop and then a different hissing, and then, from behind the mural, from behind the wall, a single metallic ring.

"Virgil—" Muldoon, stepping back, his hands hard on the gun, trying to locate Tillman, said tightly, "Virgil . . ." There had been no sound of the gun cocking, "Virgil, *have you got your gun out?*"

At the mural—where in the blackness the mural was—there was a sound. There was a flash.

There was a creak as if something, exploratorily, moved.

The lamps were gone out. They were cooling. One by one the glass in them began to fault in cracks and lines and shatter, falling in shards.

There was a flash. It was behind the wall. Then a sound, a shuffling, then, as something moved, the flash was a yellow light moving like a snake up the wall and Muldoon, his hands running sweat on the gun, moving it in his palm to get a hold, saw—

Behind the mural there was a space. It was the space below the elevator wells on the first floor of Hewitt's store. In the floor of one of the elevators there must have been a little trapdoor, and below that, stairs.

There was a sound, a click, as, behind the mural, in the well below the elevator, in the hidden space, someone slipped a catch that moved in an oiled barrel. There was a flash of light from a lantern. There was another sound as the mural moved on its hinges, and he knew what it was, and suddenly, six feet from the door, facing it, his entire body was shaking and he had gone cold and he could not get his voice to work.

"Virgil!"

There was no answer. At the mural Tillman, shaking, his mouth dry, could not take his eyes away from the moving, probing light in the crack the opening door made at the wall, and he could not get his voice to work. He could not tell Muldoon to put his gun down. He could get no words out at all.

"—Virgil—where are you?"

He could not breathe. He had come so far. The door was opening, opening to the light and he knew what was there.

"Virgil—!"

And he saw, in that instant, in the light from the lantern as whatever it was in there was clear and out in the open, he saw, as the figure shimmered in the light like a specter . . .

He saw—

He was standing in the full beam of the lantern, lit up by it, and he saw, there, looking at him—he saw the face, and he saw—

He did not think, shaking, gone dry, with his eyes filling with tears of relief that he would even be able to get it out, but it came, it came out, as he stood full in the light with his hands down by his sides, quietly, calmly—it came out as if it was something merely ordinary.

"Virgil—?"

He saw her face in the light. Tillman, in the light, looking at her, his voice a whisper, said softly so as not to cause her any alarm at all, as if it was merely a greeting, "Rosie? Rosie Seymore?"

It was a soft, warm voice.

He thought for a terrible moment he might not be able to control himself and reach out and embrace her.

In that place, in the light, with the stars of niter flickering in the subterranean darkness all around him like sky, Tillman said with no emotion in his voice at all, only warmth, "Miss Seymore— I'm very glad to see you, indeed."

19

She came at him with what he thought was a knife. She had the face of an angel with uncombed auburn hair cascading down over the shoulders of her white shift.

There was a flash of steel—something that glittered in the light like the clipped-back blade of a Bowie knife—and then there was a flash that burned at his eyes, lit up the elevator shaft and the metal steps in it in a brilliant white light and he felt the concussion of the shot and thought he had been shot and blasted down to his knees. There was a bang as something hard, the lantern, hit the cement floor beside him, exploded in a yellow ball of fire in the still pulsing whiteness and then, as he scrabbled to his feet, a click and then an explosion and the room and the sight of his eyes were wiped out in exploding white light that burst out into the waiting room and turned all the glowing blue niter yellow.

Tillman, on the ground, on his hands and knees, shaking his head like a dog to clear his eyes, shrieked, "Ned! For the love of God, *don't shoot her!*" He heard clicks—with his eyes gone and streaming tears they were muffled, dull—and, reaching out, grabbing at anything like a drowning man, he felt the bottom of the metal steps up to the elevator trapdoor and held on.

It was a gun. It was some sort of huge pistol with its barrel and frame polished bright nickel. She had fired outward. She had fired straight out the open door and lit up everything in the waiting room in an instant and turned all the shadows white and the light in the room, the legs of the piano, the water in the fountain, black. He heard Tillman yell. He heard him on the floor. He heard his hand hit the metal stairs with a bang. She was in the center of the room. She must have known where he was. Muldoon, pressed hard against the mural to one side of the open door, his revolver up against his face in two hands, held in a grip of iron, waiting for the shot, yelled, "Virgil! *Get out of there!*" He heard clicks. He heard a series of hard, fast clicks as if the gun had jammed and she jerked at it to clear it. He had seen

149

her for an instant—seen her face and eyes, eyes like a doe, brown and pupil-less and staring—he knew where she was in the room. She was a little over five foot two tall. He was six foot three. Pressing hard against the mural, trying to work it out, bringing the gun down to his midriff and jamming its butt in hard against it for a point-kill shot, Muldoon yelled, "Get out! *Get out!*" He heard the metal of the stairs ringing as someone must have grabbed at it and hit it hard, then a scrabbling and then a clicking, and then as he moved fast past the open door to get the shot in there was an explosion of white light that came out the door like a fireball and he saw her in the far corner of the room with the gun out with Tillman not three feet away from her on the ground climbing the stairs on his hands and knees.

There was clicking. She was moving. Against the mural, pressed into it, gritting his teeth to listen, Muldoon heard her move. He heard a scrabbling. He heard something ring on the stairs. Muldoon, at the top of his voice, yelled, *"Police!* We're the *Police!"* and then there was a blast of white light and a concussion as she fired that he thought must have destroyed the room she stood in entirely and he was briefly blind with exploding white suns everywhere in front of his eyes.

Muldoon yelled, *"Police!"* and then, in that instant as his eyes cleared everything went white with a second blast, and, going backward, he fired all the six shots in his Number Two revolver into the lintel over the room and shot it to pieces.

In the room, Tillman was crawling. He was down on the cement floor below the level of the pistol, crawling around in a circle like a blind man trying to locate her. All he could hear were the clickings and a residual sound in his ears of a sound like burning, crackling paper and maybe he was going nowhere, finding nothing, and she was above him with the barrel of the gun inches above the back of his head drawing back the hammer for the killing shot and—

And then, in that instant, his outstretched hand touched something soft and then—

Then there was a blast of light that erupted from the open door like white lava and engulfed him, sent him reeling and Muldoon, at the open door shooting rapid fire, shrieked, "You goddamned whore bitch, now I'm going to explode your head like a watermelon!" and he saw in the light that turned everything into whiteness, a pulsating shadow like a ghost cower as the walls above her head exploded dust with the bullets.

"Rosie! Rosie Seymore!" He was shouting at her at ground level as if she was lost in the bushes of a wood somewhere. Tillman, reaching out for her, yelled to Muldoon, "Don't shoot!" He heard a click. She was above him, beside him. He heard a click and felt her presence. He heard Muldoon yell something. He heard him reload. He heard a click. He counted out his life in seconds. Tillman shrieked, "Don't shoot her! For the love of God, don't shoot her!" And then, out of nowhere, his eyes cleared in a square of bright light and he was looking down a long white-tiled passageway lit along its length by Edison incandescent lamps strung on a wire and he saw, in that square of light, a door with a key hanging from it on a piece of string and he shouted to Muldoon at the open door, "A passageway! She's got through to a passageway with a key!" She was running down the passageway with her hair streaming out behind her and the huge silver gun held down at her side as if it was almost too heavy to carry, and Tillman, getting to his feet, reeling, screamed at Muldoon as he burst in ready to kill, "Her gun's a photographer's flash powder pistol! It's not a real gun! It doesn't have any bullets! It's a photographer's *flash powder pistol!*" and, without pausing, all the strung lights bright yellow above him as he ran, covered in soot, he was after her, running her down, reaching out for her, shouting something Muldoon, only a foot behind him with his pistol still out, could not make out at all.

"Jenkins is dead!" If he lost her now everything was lost forever. Tillman, his voice echoing and distorting off the tiled walls, crying out to her, exhorting her, yelled, *"Jenkins is dead! And Hewitt!"* She was at the far end of the passage running into what looked like a blank tiled wall. She had a knife. It was some sort of spring bayonet set on the end of the pistol, a spike the photographers fixed to their flash powder pistols to protect themselves from muggers.
Tillman shrieked, "Jenkins is dead! Jenkins is dead!"

The passageway was the workings of the great railroad itself. Everywhere along its length there were little alcoves and tunnels branching off all filled with what looked like donkey engines and extractor fan machines and cables. The Edison lights newly strung above the old, rusted-out zircon lamps on the wall turned all the seized-tight machines yellow and gold with rust.
The passageway, at the end, went nowhere. It went nowhere into a blank, tiled wall.

"Rosie—!"
It went nowhere. She was six feet away from the blank wall at the end of the passage, not stopping, not slowing, her arm outstretched in front of her to touch it, and when she touched it the momentum was going to crush her arm like a concertina. The momentum was going to split her head open like an eggshell.
He knew the sound a human body made when it hit something. He knew

the sound it made when it fell from a building onto pavement, the sound it made—the thump—when it was hit by something unyielding, monstrous, like the metal of a streetcar. He knew the sound it made when— Tillman, stopped, his gorge rising, every nerve in his body tensed, said to deny it, *"Oh, no—Jesus . . . !"* and then, in that instant as the wall opened as a door at her touch, she was gone with a slamming sound as the spring-loaded hinges snapped it back into place.

It was a door.

It was a secret door at the end of the recently strung Edison lamp–lit passageway.

It was Hewitt. It was Jenkins. It was Rosie. It was—

It was *Down There.*

In the silence and stillness, his feet making no sound on the ground as he went, Tillman, taking exactly eight paces and pushing at the wall with his outstretched hand, opened it up and went in.

She was like a trapped, terrified animal trying to escape from a blockaded corner of a room.

The room behind the door was a huge paneled salon lit beneath a stained-glass ceiling of winged war horses sailing across the heavens as Thor, on a cloud, struck sparks from his hammer on an anvil. Fifty feet by twenty-five, the walls of the room were paneled from floor to a foot below the glass, bordered in oak beams, the panels themselves carved with scenes of heroic medieval and mythological battles, hung with tapestries of gold and crimson thread, the carpet on the floor a single portrait of great Prometheus with his flaming torch: Beach's office at the height of his grandest expectations. There was a single massive oak table with carved gothic legs in the center of the room surrounded by eight high-backed leather-upholstered chairs.

She was at a carved and paneled armoire against the corner of the room, pulling at it, stabbing at it with the spike on the end of the pistol. The twin doors were jammed. She was stabbing at them, pulling and wrenching at them to get them open.

He had his gun out. Tillman, looking, searching, hearing the wood splintering and breaking as she cut and pulled at it, ordered Muldoon, "Get her!" The room was lit up behind the stained glass only in the center above the meeting table: he saw in the far corner an ottoman and a low credenza, more cupboards against the side, and then, where the tapestries joined behind him against the rear plain-paneled wall, a leather sofa, a spare chair for the table, and above the mock fireplace, all marble and gilt wood, curtained in red velvet like a window out in the world, Mulvany's picture of Custer's Last Stand, six feet by six feet, hung on a golden chain.

Tillman ordered Muldoon, "Get her!" She was ripping, tearing at the wood, making no headway against the locks that held the twin doors tight. He saw Muldoon, with his Smith and Wesson out, look back, then look down at the gun and holster it. He saw him take out his club. He saw him look at it and then push it back into his belt. There was no one else in the room. At the cupboard with her back to him as if she did not recognize their presence, twisting, pushing, slashing, she was like a specter, a chimera. There was a crack as the blade of the knife smashed through something and then, as she wrenched back at it like a hysteric, a snapping sound as the blade lodged hard and broke off.

Tillman roared, *"Take her!"*

As Muldoon moved, in the light from the illuminated scene in the center of the ceiling, he saw in the far side of the room a line of cabinets, like changing rooms at a bathing beach, each built of polished mahogany, glassed-in, curtained with velvet, each marked with an engraved brass plaque.

In the light from the illuminated scene in the center of the ceiling he saw the word on the first of the plaques, the first in the line of seven.

It was a word he knew.

That word, deeply engraved—as if it was the name of the person who lived in that cabinet or owned it or changed in it—was *Oubliette*.

She was still a woman. She was tiny, her hair hanging down her back, her hands as they jerked at the door, like the hands of a child.

He had never hit a woman from behind in his life.

The blade was broken, snapped. All there was on the empty, harmless gun was a jagged broken blade that bounced off the black hard wood as she struck at it. It was blunt, useless.

She was tiny. She was like a tiny child in a white nightdress trying to escape a nightmare. Muldoon, advancing, reaching out for her with hands the size of hams, said to calm her, "Now, Rosie . . . Rosie . . ."

The doors to the cabinets were all closed. They were in line, like changing rooms.

Oubliette.

Embrasure.

Donjon.

Palisade.

Portcullis.

They were all curtained, deserted.

Archer.

Bailey.

There were brass handles on the doors, cast like dolphins.

Oubliette—
In the room, in the half light from the ceiling, his left hand on the handle and his right ready with the Lightning, Tillman wrenched open the door of Jenkins' cabinet to see what was there.

"Rosie . . . ! Miss Seymore . . . !" She was the one in the filthy pictures, she was the one from the rooms in Crib Alley, she was the one from— He heard the door of the cabinet against the wall fly open with a bang as Tillman wrenched at it, and, advancing, closing his fists, Muldoon, reaching out to grasp her and squeeze the life out of her until she dropped the gun, roared at the top of his voice, "You wanton, unashamed, godless trollop— *Turn around when I talk to you!*"

It was a telephone. It was a telephone with no speaking nozzle, only a listening trumpet and, on top of its cedar box, a bell to summon the listener.

In Jenkins' cabinet there was only a telephone, nothing else. In the cabinet marked *Embrasure* there was another, in *Donjon* there was another and then, in the cabinets marked *Bailey, Palisade, Portcullis* another and another and another.

There was nothing else.

"*You filthy whore bitch!*" He had her, he had her hard. He had her in a bear hug, jerking at her, pulling her hands and the gun and the broken blade away from the cupboard she held on to like a cat with claws. She was kicking, fighting. Muldoon, pulling her off, shaking her, straining, breathing hard, using all his strength to break her hold, yelled, "Let go! Let go, you—you filthy, disgusting, degenerate little whore bitch—let go!" and then, as the twin doors of the armoire gave way and something cascaded from the cupboard like a torrent from a burst dam he was knocked down, gone over on his back with the girl still kicking and fighting on top of him.

There was nothing in any of the cabinets but telephones!

The cascade from the armoire was coins—silver one-ounce Austrian Maria Theresa talers, thousands of them—and stones: diamonds, emeralds, sapphires and wedding rings, rings that flowed out of the packed cupboard like a river.

"*Ma-ma!*" She was screaming, fighting, kicking to get free, breaking his hold, reaching for the rings with her fingers out and flexing.

"*Ned!*" He saw Muldoon's face. Running, getting to her as Muldoon, rolling over, drew back his fist to poleaxe the squirming, screaming creature on the ground, Tillman shrieked, "Ned—*No*—!"

He saw her face. He saw her face looking at him. Muldoon, his fist in midair, his face twisted in hate, shrieked, "You filthy whore bitch! You—" He saw her face. He saw her eyes.

Muldoon said in a gasp, "Oh, my God—!"

She was the lowest of the low, a street slut, a poser with her legs apart for dirty pictures.

She was—

She was on her knees in the cascade of wedding rings, reaching for them, putting rings on all her fingers, rocking, crooning to herself, singing.

Muldoon said, not to Tillman, but to his still closed fist, wishing he could cut it off, "Oh, my God—!"

Muldoon, lower than the lowest crawling thing beneath a rock, said in the voice of a small, lost child, "Oh, my God, Virgil— Oh my God, she's *simple!*"

20

Her parents had perished in a fire when she had been a small child. Her wedding ring was all she remembered of her mother.

Her eyes were soft, brown, but they were not like the eyes of other people: not hard, watching—they were eyes that somehow, from somewhere deep inside, did not focus. Outside the all-night pawnbroker's on Chambers Street where they had gotten her a coat and shoes and a hat with a veil and where they had bought the shotgun, Muldoon said gently, "God will protect you; God and Virgil here who's a good man, and the twelve-gauge sawed-off Greener Mormon Streetsweeper he's got on a strap under his coat." Muldoon said softly to Tillman with his mouth tight, "I'm glad Jenkins died like that—slowly." He had a long nightclub in his belt, the leather lanyard hanging down in knots. The club had also come from the pawnbroker's. This morning, he and the pawnbroker's club were going visiting Quinney. Muldoon said gently, pushing back a strand of the thick auburn hair from the smiling, unfocused face, "God, Virgil Tillman and Ned Muldoon—you're safe in their hands now."

It was a little after 6 A.M., half an hour till dawn, two and a half hours until Quinney opened his photographic store, his filth house, for business. He could wait. He would walk and think and wait.

Muldoon said softly, nodding, looking down at her, "You're in good hands now, me darlin'."

He said gently, "God bless you."

He said touching himself on the chest, "Ned Muldoon—that's me."

—He could have sat down on the pavement, cut off his hand with a rusty knife, and wept.

She looked at him the way she must have looked at Quinney and at Hewitt, especially Hewitt. They were on Baxter Street on the Lower East Side of the city, during the day the densest populated area on Earth, China not excluded. In the growing light the street, lined with tenements, was full

156

of rags and trash, iron-rimmed pushcarts chained together in doorways or against poles, bollards and hitching posts like broken iron staircases. In the gutters of the sidewalks there was trash in piles, linked up like the trails of snails with oozing liquid running one to another. At the water hydrant at the end of the street there were thin and fat women in aprons and hats, Poles, Germans, Italians, Jews, filling their buckets for the day. There was a tall beggar in tattered clothes by the hydrant, brushing at the wooden sandwich board he wore around his neck on a rope. The sign read as he brushed and rubbed at it, BLIND SINCE '52. He twisted it on the rope around his neck and considered the other side. The other side read, PARALYZED SINCE THE 20TH DECEMBER. This morning it was PARALYZED. He set it square on his chest, closed his eyes for a moment to get into character, let his shoulders sink, and limped off toward the uptown part of the city.

He was out with her on the street before dawn, alone, unchaperoned, moving north. She had soft brown eyes below the wonderful auburn hair, but the eyes did not focus and the mouth was not still, but moving, forming words that did not come out. She had the face of an angel. She could not read. She saw nothing of the signs on all the stores and the paper advertisements pasted on walls, nothing of the blind, paralyzed man's sign—she moved only through the colors and the smells and the sounds. BY THE SWEAT OF THY BROW THOU SHALL EAT BREAD—it was a sign painted on the side of a delivery wagon that passed but all she saw were the colors of the wheels and spokes and the horse and the tired man with his hat pulled down over his eyes asleep on the seat. It was an empty baker's cart, with all the bread and the smell of the bread gone. He saw her look at the horse and be happy. Tillman said softly to the eyes, "Your sister Lily is dead." Tillman said as she watched the horse, "It's a baker's cart. It delivers bread." He saw her face look at him with pleasure. Tillman said, knowing the question, "I don't know what the horse's name is." Tillman said, "Your sister's dead."

All along the street doors were opening as the beggars put out their deformed children naked to defecate on the sidewalk. They were naked, boys and girls between the ages of five and thirteen. Each of them was malformed, askew, bent over from the spine with an arm or a leg against their body or their head as if it had been glued there, as if their arms or legs grew there.

On the street, naked, defecating, they were like lumps of ghastly failed test pieces of human beings. They were the vase children: the props for begging families kept in open clay vases from birth with their rubber babies' limbs set at crippled angles and cultivated like vines by their Italian breeders until the bones had set and they were of good marketable quality.

Covered everywhere with the dark blotches of bruises and cuts and whippings, trained from birth to be silent, they made no sound.

She looked at him. She wondered who he was. The wonderful auburn hair was spilling down a little on her shoulders. Tillman said to answer her question, "I was an orphan. I have no one, like you. I was taken to an orphanage a few hours after my birth with blood on me where either my mother or my father, or maybe someone else, had stabbed at my heart with something long and thin like a skewer and, like you, I have no one." He saw her look at him the way she must have looked at Hewitt. Tillman said, "Your sister is dead. You are alone. You have nobody. You have no heartfelt greetings or goodbyes to offer people you love and you have loved for a long time; all you are is someone no one loves."

Her mouth was moving, forming words. Her hands were long and soft. She touched hard at her face with her fingers as if she was dumb. She nodded at him to tell him she was pretty. She nodded to show she had a pretty face. She looked hard at him, examining his eyes, moving her head slightly back and forth to catch the faint morning light and see what was there in them. He looked away down to the sidewalk. She had to lean in toward him to see his face.

Tillman said, "Like you, as a child, I only lived on out of spite!"

It frightened her. She hit her chest hard and held her breath. It was how she had once had the picture of her name on a poster on the wall of Bunker's Dime Museum. It was how she had lived through the drowning.

Tillman said, "Jenkins is dead." He saw her mouth move, trying to form words. Tillman said softly, "Jenkins called himself an Oubliette. Hewitt— 'Oubliette, Embrasure, Donjon, Palisade, Portcullis, Archer'—which one did he call himself?"

He saw her lost. He saw her mouth forming words, but he saw that the words wherever they were coming from, came not from behind the eyes; he saw in there, inside her body, two different people. All along the sidewalk, like dogs, the vase children were urinating and defecating, rocking back and forth to keep their balance, making no sound at all.

It was a little before dawn in the city, all the colors changing, all the unbroken windows in the unending lines of tenements starting to flash and go white; the sky, for another day, clearing and becoming deep predawn blue.

"In the name of all that's right and true, you're a human being with a God who made you!"

Unchaperoned, alone with her on the street, all he ached to do was possess her.

Tillman said, shouting at the eyes, "In the name of pity, didn't He leave in you *one small spark of understanding?*"

* * *

On Canal Street she watched the lines of old women waiting outside the cracked and peeling doors of the palmists and stargazers, the fortune-tellers and predicters. It was a rumor gotten from somewhere, perhaps from the countries they had come from—Ireland, Poland, the tiny countries of Eastern Europe, the workless and hopeless villages of all those places— that the color blue for the year of 1884 was the lucky color and glass, an element anyone could see through, the symbol of being able to see through what there was into what there could be.

In the lines, like dung beetles, like the vase children, making no sound at all, they waited, all the calcium gone from their teeth from childbearing, touching at their mouths with their mittened hands to keep the cold from getting into their gums, the women wearing blue, carrying bottle shards, anything small made of glass, waited. Along the lines, in the gutters, there were rats moving like shadows up and down from one pile of trash to another, making rustling sounds.

It was too early. There were no carts or wagons or horses on the street to look at.

Tillman said as she looked at the rats with no interest, as an everyday sight, "The Irish originally settled in this area. They settled from here all the way down to Water Street. Some of these women are the wives of the first wave of settlement, the wives of the drunken and the idle who, unlike the families who worked, could not make sixty cents a day to have enough put by to move to the new area of Harlem for the laboring jobs on the farms there. These are the ones with no pride—the ones who could not even steal a length of rope for a clothesline to string between their tenements to keep themselves and their children clean in the midst of filth and apparent hopelessness, and who killed off all their hope and the hope of their children." Tillman said, glancing up the street toward Centre Street, "They moved into poverty and, without the great civilizer of a single clothesline, turned it into destitution. Now, all they hope is that the stars support them." They were waiting for their fortunes to be told. "All they hope from the stars is a lie to get them through one more day."

She was forming words with her mouth, her face contorted with the strain. She was like a doe in the forest, beautiful beyond description, and alone with her on the street, like Quinney, like Hewitt, he could have done with her whatever he liked.

The eyes registered not at all whatever it was the mouth was trying to form.

He had his hand in a fist between them, pleading with her, entreating her. His voice was a whisper, a voice like the fake voices from behind those cracked hopeless doors, a message from another world—a message from *out there*.

Like a pugilist, a trainer, touching at his moustaches with his shaking, trembling fist, Tillman said to the mouth forming the words, the brow contorting, to the battle going on in there, "Fight! Fight! *Fight!*"

"Did you always do everything you were told to do? By everyone who told you to do it?"

There were moving toward Hester Street, the Jewish part of the city. He stopped and held her briefly by the arm. "When Quinney told you to take all your clothes off and lie on his ottoman with your legs apart so he could take his photographs, did you just look at him as if you were dead or smile at him because, briefly, he was nice to you or paid you money, and do exactly what you were told?"

In Hester Street, the Little Mothers—children of no more than eight or nine themselves—were at the hydrants, washing the soiled linen of their baby brothers or sisters as other girls held the babies two at a time against their chests and sang to them. They were all spotlessly clean, the children, all with their shoes polished and their black stockings gartered tight on their thin legs. During the day, as their mothers and fathers worked in the sweatshops sewing and cutting, they would keep the babies with them at school, feed them with warm milk heated on braziers, and then at the end of the day bring them home again. They were the Jews. They were the Families. Tillman said, "I lived on out of spite and with the hope the nuns who took me in gave me." After the washing, the Little Mothers on the way to school would stop at the Flower Triangle at the far end of the street where someone, someone who had escaped and become someone had done a *mitzvah*—a good act—and bought a small spot of land where flowers could be grown, and dream their dreams. Tillman said, *"Do you just walk around like a dog hoping for any casual pat on the head from a stranger?"*

She was watching the children, "Hon—"

"Those children don't know that rhyme!"

"Hon—" As if she drove the horse on the bakery cart, with her hands snapping at reins in front of her, she drove herself. Rosie said, hurting to get it out, "Hon—"

It was the rhyme from the roof above Grammelspacher's. It was Lily's rhyme. It was one of the games of the city streets, of Brooklyn, where she had been a child. Tillman said, "Hon-pon—" Tillman said, "The wind blows East,/The wind blows West,/The wind blows over the Cuckoo's Nest./Shall he go East?/Shall he go West?/Shall he go under the Cuckoo's nest?" In the street, urging her, fighting at her, trying, trying to move the eyes, Tillman said in desperation, "Hon-pon-kuck-a-da-hook! Hon-pon-kuck-a-da-*hook!"* He was shouting, accusing. In the street, Tillman yelled to move the eyes—to make them react, "Maybe nobody on Earth now knows the rhyme except *you!* Now your sister's dead, now that you have your feet firmly on the road to Hell, maybe on Earth, *nobody knows anything about anything you ever were except you!"* He was talking to a dumb creature from the forest. He was talking to someone lost. In the street, not caring that the children at the hydrant ran to get their charges inside away from him, Tillman not touching her—fighting to keep from taking her in his arms, from touching her hand—shrieked, "All it takes to become someone, to have honor, to have *hope* is something as simple as a length of rope for a clothesline! It requires no brilliance, no effort to succeed—all it takes is a flicker, a spark: the faintest single glimmering of understanding that we are not dogs and that there is a right and wrong and that to give up, to surrender, to seek only luck or illusion or the charity of others is a disease that wastes and corrupts and destroys!"

Tillman said urgently, *"The wind blows East, the wind blows West, the wind blows over the Cuckoo's Nest*— What did Hewitt tell you down there as he took you like a rag doll and believed that at last he was no longer his father's son but a man in his own right? What did he confide to you? Where did he tell you the rings were from? And the coins, the talers? What did he tell you the names on the cabinets meant? Did he tell you which one he was? Is that how he impressed you? Did he show you how to use a speaking telephone? *Did it ring its bell while you were there and did he let you listen to what it said?"* Tillman said with the eyes not seeing him, "For God's sake— For God's sake, *all we have is each other—"*

> *Oh, God! That bread should be so dear!*
> *And flesh and blood so cheap!*

It was a motto carved into the stone lintel above the doors of the Florence Night Mission on Bleecker Street. It was dawn, the end of the night, and in her head, as the mouth still moved to form words, all there was were eddies and tides and currents. Tillman said, "It's a place run by good people."

Any Mother's Child Wishing To Leave A Crooked Life
May Find Food, Shelter, And
A HELPING   HAND
By Coming Just As She Is, To The Florence Night Mission.

Tillman said, "It's got a cat named George that lives on goat's milk from a nanny goat in the yard and a dog called Betsy that's always having lots of pups and hides them in the girls' rooms, and a—" He saw her smile. In her head behind the beautiful face there was nothing. Tillman said, "And the dog, the dog—Betsy—" He could not think of what to say, "And the dog Betsy"—he smiled back at her—"It's a good dog, a nice dog."

"Hon-pon . . ."

Tillman said, "It's a tireless dog, always ready for a game, unless—unless it's got its pups and then it's a sleepy dog and it—" He saw her eyes. From inside the place there was the sound of crockery and metal saucepans being moved. There was the warm smell of cooking. Tillman said, "And the cat—well, the cat, like all cats, is anybody's and nobody's and, and—" He had no idea at all what he was feeling, but he could no longer look at her. Tillman said, "And the cat, and the dog . . ." Tillman said, "There are girls from everywhere in the world here: from Ireland and England, Scotland and Germany and Sweden and Wales, and some girls who can't speak English, and others who—" Tillman said, "Go in. Please."

"Hon-pon—"

Tillman said, "Please go in."

"Hon-pon-kuck—"

"Please go in!" He had nothing to give her. He had only under his coat the two guns, and, across his vest, his watch and chain. Tillman said, not looking at her, "Jenkins is dead, and Hewitt, and—" Tillman, unclipping the silver-plated chain from his pocket watch and handing it over in his cupped palms, said, "Here. Take this. Take it as a collar for the dog and maybe it'll be your dog and—" He said softly, entreating her, "Go in." It was dawn, the end of the night, and everywhere on the street there were people coming out of doors unchaining wagons and carts. There were Negro bootblacks from Broome Street starting to set up. Tillman said, "You're safe now. Go in." He wished Mrs. Wooldridge who ran the place would come out, but she was busy with the breakfast. Tillman said softly, wanting to go, wanting Mrs. Wooldridge, wanting even the dog to come out to the stoop to see who was there, wanting not to think about what he wanted to think about, "Go in—please." She would not go. She was blinking, thinking, trying to arrange all the eddies and currents in her head, rocking slightly, waiting, knowing what came next because it was what came next and that was the way she got things like the chain and rings and money.

Tillman said desperately, *"Go in!"*

"Hon-pon-ka-a—" She reached out and touched his face with her hand to please him. She could not read what the sign said above the door, but inside there were dogs and cats and there was the smell of warmth and cooking and it was a good place and something she wanted, like a child, to have. Rotary Rosie said, "Sit there! Open legs! Yes!" It was what

Quinney had said to her and she had made him happy and he had given her money. Rotary Rosie said, "Beautiful man! Important man! Powerful man!" It was what Hewitt had told her to say and when she said it to him it had made him happy and he had given her things. Rotary Rosie said, "Cat. Dog. George and Betsy—" She looked at the man's face. Rotary Rosie said, "God and Virgil here who's a good man!" She took her hand away and slapped at Tillman's coat where the shotgun was, "Mormon Streetsweeper under his coat!" Rotary Rosie said, raising her hands up and out above her head to mimic the man's size, *"Ned Muldoon—that's me."*

"Go inside, God damn you!"

"Ding! Ding!" It was the sound of the speaking telephones under the ground in Hewitt's store. It was what would please him. Rosie, grinning, nodding, said with the chain still in her hand, paying for it, *"Ding! Ding!"*

"God damn you! Go inside!"

She reached down to pull her dress up, but the little man in the street slapped her hand away. The little man in the street said with an expression on his face she could not read, with what looked like sudden tears in his eyes, "God damn you! Go!"

She did what people told her to do—she remembered what people said or told her to do so, to please them, she could do it again. The watch chain was bright, glittering—she wanted it. Rosie, shaking her head, trying to remember, remembering everything, said nodding, sure this time she had gotten it right, "God. Ned Muldoon—Virgil here—*all we have is each other!"*

She thought, in that moment, his eyes filled with tears, but that could not be right. Rosie said, looking up, remembering something that must have been important to him because he had said it so slowly and carefully, "Your sister Lily is dead." It meant something. It was the name of something. Rosie said to please the person who owned it, "Hon-pon-kuck-a—" Rosie said, "It's a baker's cart. It delivers bread. I don't know what the horse's name is—"

"Mrs. Wooldridge—!"

"Did it ring its bell while you were there—?" It was important to him. He had asked. She remembered. Rosie said, "Ding! *Ding!"*

"Mrs. Wooldridge—!"

He was going to take the chain away from her. All she remembered of her mother was a wedding ring. She wanted. She wanted. She had her hands in fists. Rosie, holding the chain said, *"Want!"*

"Mrs. *Wooldridge!"*

There was a dog in there and a cat. She stamped her foot. Rosie said, "Want!" He was not listening. He was at the bottom of the steps calling to someone. He was not satisfied. She had not pleased him. He wanted the chain back. Rosie said, "Ding! *Ding!*" but it was no good. Rosie said, "Jenkins—*Oubliette!*" She saw him turn and face her. Rosie said, "Hewitt—*Palisade.*" She saw his face. She saw his eyes. Rosie said happily, earning it, winning the chain, giving pleasure, remembering everything the old man under the ground had told her in the room full of rings, "Oubliette, Embrasure, Donjon—" He had said the words one at a time as he pointed at the boxes and speaking tubes in the glassed-in cabinets in the room where the rings were. It must have been the names of the cabinets or who owned them, or something, but as he told her he smiled and looked happy so it made him happy and it must have been important—"Palisade! Portcullis—" She tapped her chest and pulled at her Hewitt's beard, "Palisade—that's me: Mr. Hewitt, Donjon, Portcullis—"

He had stopped calling. In the corridor at the top of the steps, coming, there was a slight woman wearing a wedding ring that glittered under the still burning gas lamps on the wall, and in the street, for a moment, she thought it was the wedding ring of her mother and—

She saw the dog. It was a dog full of pups that had no collar.

Rosie said to the dog, holding the chain up, "Collar!" It was almost hers to give.

On the street, Rosie said in Hewitt's voice to finally make it her own to give, "Archer—Ha, ha! No need to find a secret name there—Archer—ha, ha—!" She stroked her Hewitt's beard, "Archer—ha, ha! Silas Archer, ha, ha! Just leave that one as it is!"

Her heart ached for the dog, but she was working and until she was certain it was hers to give the little dog was not going to get the collar because someone might take it back.

She gave pleasure.

She saw the man's face on the steps and pleasured him.

"*Ha, ha! Poor little dumb creature, you don't understand a word, do you?*" It was Hewitt's voice. Rosie, rocking like a man, tapping herself on the chest, said in a deep, important voice, "Mr. Hewitt—that's me. Oubliette, Embrasure, Donjon, Palisade, Portcullis, Bailey, and Mr. No-new-name-required Silas Archer—these objects are *telephones.*" Rosie said, "Custers. The Custers. After the late General himself, that's us: The Custers!"

Her heart ached for the dog.

Full of pups, its eyes sleepy and deep, as she bent down to give it the shiny collar, wanting nothing from her at all, it cocked its head to one side and, wagging its tail, loved her.

21

O noise!

O chaos!

O the promise of the nineteenth century not merely kept, but honored, celebrated, toasted, provendered to repletion!

It didn't just sweep trash from the streets, it *ate* it.

It didn't just gather it up in little piles by the curb for laborers in collarless shirts and broken shoes to shovel into handcarts: it ingested it, gobbled it, gulped it, gorged it, snaffled it, sucked, bit, broke up, bashed, bruised, beheaded, brained, blew to bits, hacked, sawed, sliced and *sautéed* it.

Garbage, trash, effluvia—bottles, barrels, ash, cinders, rocks, rubbish, rags, canine corpses, cats, cast-outs—twenty-two feet long, fifteen feet wide, standing a full eighteen feet off the ground from the rim of its six-foot-diameter iron-tired wheels to the belching funnel of its brass donkey engine working pulleys and belts and cogs and wheels and whistles, it hit garbage in the streets like an engine of war, like a Christian knight in armor brushing aside a Saracen, slurped it through twin serrated-edged oblong suckers an inch from the pavement, swirled it down chutes with a blast from a vacuum pump to twin buzz saws with tempered teeth working at the impossible steam-driven speed of two thousand revolutions a minute, chopped it to chips, blasted it through a pipe to a holding tank at the rear, thumped it to a bale with twin trip-hammers falling down like the wrath of God, baled it with baling wire from a self-fed spool, then—with a belch—ejected it out the back.

It was in Mulberry Street. It was at the end of closed-off Mulberry Street where Mulberry met Bleecker. It was a gift from the Commissioners of the Police Department to the new Department of Street Cleaning to mark the end of an era—the passing of the broom, the laying down of a burden—the march of Progress.

It was the Ellis-Mifflin-Jackson-Swan Infinite Capacity Full Patent

Protected Street and Avenue Sanitizer, Appliance Number One. It was drawn by two matched Clydesdale horses recently retired from the Fire Department. It was, painted in black and gold along the full length of its oak wagonside, *The New York Whale*.

It was magnificent. It glittered, it gleamed, it shone—it was in its parade livery, carved with whales and dolphins, brass-engraved panels of knights slaying dragons, pictures and portraits of scenes from the Plague, the pestilences—it was all framed by a gold signboard bearing a single motto.

IMPROVEMENT!

In the street the children of St. Phillip's Church and School for Boys roared, *"Hurrah!!"*

In parade order outside Police Headquarters, the Marble Palace hung with bunting for the occasion, Desk Sergeant Fitzgerald, in medals and honors of the New York Police, Union Army and rosettes of the Hibernian Society, roared to his coppers, *"Cheer!"*

The church and school had a kettledrum and fife band. They kettle-drummed and fifed.

There was a sty of street sweepers drawn up behind the great beast, all the buttons on their white coats (issued for the day) shining like gold. One of them yelled to the blue-uniformed driver on the *Whale*, way up in the sky, *"Steam whistle!"*

He whistled. He blasted off not a whistle but a shriek that set every window in the street to shaking and steam-cleaned every shirt, chemise and stone in the place, loosened bowels, set teeth on edge and set horses to snorting and stamping. Up in Heaven, like God on His great painted and portraited throne with panels of all the Police Commissioners who had made the great gift possible, Ellis Mifflin Jackson Swan—for it was none but he, the *Inventor*, who this day rode the Great Gobbler—touching at a control that set all the trip-hammers and the saws and the vacuum working in concert like the clappers of Doom, standing up, an Admiral in the armada of antitoxin, roared with the cross of God on the spire of St. Phillip's framed behind him, *"Garbage! Garbage!"*

Shaking, the whole street shaking, with the accumulated filth and grime of a century falling from buildings and filling the street with dust and debris, the Pilot of Soon to Be Pollution Past roared to the Police Commissioners, the Superintendents, Inspectors, Captains and assorted frock-coated dignitaries from the City and Sanitation all ready to make speeches, "With no filth in the streets to cut short his life, Man could be *immortal!*"

Buildings shook, mortar cracked. Birds fell down dead from the skies. Windows shook and shattered. Men quailed. Small children fell to the ground convulsing. White coats went black.

Mere seconds from the apocalypse, his voice lost in the roaring and thumping and slicing and pulverizing, in the destruction of all life on Earth as we knew it, aching to move the brass lever in his hand from *Idle* to *Power* in a single sweep, the Saviour of Mankind's Mess yelled at the top of his lungs to the two horses that drew the terrible thing, "Giddy-*up!!*"

"*Jaisus, it's an Earthquake!*" In the Rogues' Gallery photographic studio on the second floor of Police Headquarters Horrible Houlihan, being blown out of the iron-rack chair he was screwed into for his new photograph, hitting the stone floor and disappearing in a shower of masonry dust from the ceiling, shouted to his Horrible Houlihan family being held by Matron Webb from the Lost Children Department on the fourth floor and four huge detectives from the second, "Jaisus, my wife and children! God's sent the end of the world to punish them for all they've put me through! It's the Banshees! It's the Banshees that signal the end of a good hardworking, honest man like meself at the hands of an ungrateful family!"

There was a scream of terror from the Horrible Houlihan harridan, a howl of horror from Horrible Harry, a hog-holler from Horrible Henry, a hooting sound from Horrible Henrietta and from baby Fred, some subhuman honking.

There was a rumbling like the tumbrils of Doom that lifted all the mats on the floor, smashed the camera off its tripod and buried it like an artifact in an Egyptian tomb under a thousand years of dust. There was a crash as the door to the place flew off its hinges. There was a creak as the bricks behind the plaster on the walls split and the walls started to open up to invite everyone in the room inside them out for a little eternity in the nether regions.

Horrible Houlihan, rolling over, hitting something hard, looking up in the dust and dismay and seeing the stern face of God looking down at him, said, "It's them! It's been them all me life! I wanted to be a good man, but they always conspired against me!" God was dressed in a cutaway coat edged in braid with a derby hat pulled down over his ears. God stood almost six feet tall. Houlihan screamed, "I wanted my little girl to be a nun, but the day I took her in to the good Sisters to put her name down for it, me wife ducked into the church next door and took all their plate!"

God roared, "Jesus!" It was not God at all. It was *God*. It was Inspector Thomas Byrnes of the Detective Bureau. Byrnes, ducking as the combined work of three years' comprehensive photographing, filing, and Bertillon measuring of the dangerous classes of all New York flew out of the mahogany Rogues' Gallery cabinet in the corner of the room, giving Houlihan a kick in the face that sent him reeling, yelled to his detectives being rolled across the floor by the moving, swaying building, *"All my work is being destroyed by idiots who use police money to buy street sweepers!"* He felt cold, bony hands plucking at him. *"Fools! Morons! Oafs!"* The cold, bony hands were Houlihan's cold, bony hands.

At the window, trying to break Houlihan's arms with a series of scientific heel kicks to the back of the elbows, Byrnes, his hat flying off and disappearing into the steam and smoke of the street to be disintegrated by whatever the morons on the Civilian Police Board had let loose on an unsuspecting populace, roared at the top of his voice, *"Muldoon! Ned Muldoon!* If you're down there, shoot that man on that contraption! Shoot the Commissioners! Shoot the—"

He was hopping mad, going red in the face.

There was a pause, a sudden silence. It was the moment for the voice of reason and authority.

It was there.

At the window, hopping, jumping, his beautiful uniform with all its ribbons and honors a wondrous, authoritative sight to behold, Chief Inspector Thomas Byrnes, the protector of the City, roared with his life in tatters and Horrible Houlihan's face and neck not in the best of shape either, "Somebody! Anybody! Shoot it! Shoot now! Shoot that damned *machine!"*

He had forgotten about the echo-effect. He had tested the *Whale,* not in the stone canyons of the city, but in an open field. In the open field he had set up a barrel of ash and turned the lever to *Power* and the fire horses had clopped up to it, the serrated scoops at the front of the wagon had ingested it, the counterrotating saws had sliced it to matchwood, the blast of vacuum power had propelled it through a chute, jammed it against the stop-wall, the two trip-hammers had come and smashed it to minutiae, the baler had baled it, and, with a bang as the swing door at the rear had opened, the bale had been thrown out twenty feet and landed with scientific precision on its side on a rock ready to be carted away.

Two grazing cows had watched with interest.

That had been in a field in New Jersey.

The cows, after a little while, had wandered off to sniff the gentle giant.

That had been in Old Farmer Frank Frick's field near Florham.

There had been two painted cows a-cudding.

This was Mulberry Street, New York.

There were four frock-coated and bemedallioned police commissioners up their dais a-dementing.

In the echoes, in the destruction, in the steam and smoke and crying of tiny children, in the mashing of fifes and drums and fleeing of feet, *The*

New York Whale, belching smoke, hammering helmets, baling bricks, what looked like bits of bodies, brooms, batons and boots, hit the iron fence of the churchyard, gobbled it up like licorice and, the pressure safety valve on its monstrous engine howling like a siren, turned the dais to matchwood, distributed the commissioners evenly in a row and, making a sort of preprandial burping sound, roared forward unstoppably to eat them.

It was a tale told by an idiot—a simpleton—signifying, probably, nothing.

In the basement that housed the Police Telegraph Office, a warlock's cavern of glass bottles, wires, glass cases, keys, dry batteries in lead boxes and wet ones in demijohns of acid, Tillman demanded as the shaking in the street turned the room to soup, *"Why? Why* can't you show me the listing of Silas Archer in a telephone book?"

The soup was Science. It was being boiled to barbarism, turned back to the Dark Ages, filling with smoke and dust. It was shaking, falling apart, being held together solely by the outstretched arms of Harry Roebuck.

At the far end of the wall, going for a shelf and catching it in mid-collapse, Roebuck screamed back at Tillman, "I can't show you the telephone book to find someone called Archer because I don't have the telephone book!" There had been no Silas Archer listed in the telegraph books or the electoral rolls or the business gazette. "The only person who has a telephone book—and even then I haven't seen it—is Inspector Byrnes, and he keeps it in his safe because if he didn't any fool could contact all the important people in it and get their attention without a personal appointment and drive them mad or extort them or—" He didn't have arms wide enough to hold up both ends of the eight-foot-long shelf loaded with little glass-topped bottles of spare keys and wires and connections. Roebuck screamed, "You don't even know there is such a person as Silas Archer!" The shelf was nothing. The telegraph room was nothing. They were only his life's work. Roebuck screamed, "And 'The Custers'—what the hell are 'The Custers'? General Custer has been dead for over eight years!" He saw Tillman going for the door. He saw the knob of the door, as the entire building shook, fall off. Roebuck, scrabbling on the ground to find perhaps one bottle from the shelf that wasn't broken, finding none, yelled as the ghastly object outside in the street made a sound like a dinosaur taking a bite out of a cave to get at the cavemen inside, "Possessing a telephone book without lawful excuse is a ten-year offense!" There was a sound like a mountain falling down and all the buzzing keys under all the smashed and splintered glass cases went dead and all of New York City was cut off from the police telegraph (the *Whale,* missing the Commissioners by a hairsbreadth, had eaten, instead, three of the telegraph poles in the street and the terminal on the side of Headquarters). "All of

Custer's command were killed at Little Big Horn! Custer was a hero in the Civil War, a hero at Little Big Horn, but, but—" He knew the feeling. Roebuck shrieked, "—he was cruelly massacred by savages!"

"Is there any other listing of names? Anywhere else I can look?"

"No, there isn't!" Roebuck, running for an upright demijohn of acid with his hands out like a father to stop it falling, said, "No one will let you look at a telephone book unless you've got written authority from the Mayor or you're rich enough and therefore trustworthy enough to have a telephone installed in your house or your office! They're secret—the numbers and addresses—it'd be like giving a criminal the number of your bank account and a copy of your signature to write checks on it with!" Roebuck, grasping the bottle and holding it to his chest as part of the ceiling fell down around him, yelled in rising hysteria, "Only rich and powerful people have telephones! Criminals don't have telephones!"

"They do now!"

"Then ask Inspector Byrnes to show you his telephone book!"

"For all I know, Byrnes is one of them. Byrnes earns three thousand dollars a year as the head of the Detective Bureau and everyone from the Mayor to the lowest beggar knows Byrnes has a fortune of over three hundred thousand dollars because, on a regular basis, every year, he's questioned by one investigating panel after another about how the hell he got it!" Tillman, getting to the man and grasping him by the collar, shrieked into his face with all his hopes ebbing away, "Harry, whatever these people are doing is so awful that when one of them—Hewitt the storeowner—discovered the full extent of it, he lost his mind and wanted to *die!*"

It was a tale told by an idiot—a simpleton—signifying nothing.

All he had was what Rosie had told him. Other than that, he had nothing.

On his knees, pulling at the man, entreating him, weaving from side to side to avoid the falling ceiling and rising lethal fumes, the knees of his pants burned away by the soup of acid moving in currents on the floor, Tillman, shouting above the roar of the *Whale* destroying the street outside, begged the man with no shame at all, "Harry, *please*—where in the name of God can an ordinary man like me get a telephone book so he can look up the name and address of somebody listed in it?"

"Big rabbits . . . coach . . . cockroach . . . hole . . . sidewalk . . . two people . . . big *bang!*"

He thought, off duty, he might go to Headquarters and tell Mr. Byrnes about it all.

"Rabbit . . . sidewalk . . . *Bang!*" He turned off Houston Street into Mulberry.

Patrolman Simpson, wandering happily into the steam, said smiling to himself, "Carriage . . . hole open in sidewalk . . . two people go down . . . cockroach . . . rabbit!"

He grinned. He hummed to himself.

Clubber Simpson said happily into the steam, *"Here y' are— Black your boots, boss?*

"Shine 'em in a minute,

"That is, if nothing prevents."

Nice job, bootblacking: simple, uncomplicated. Maybe he could get it.

Smiling, humming, Clubber Simpson, limping a little, wandered into the center of the street where the police commissioners in their full uniforms seemed to be having a little prayer meeting with the rector of St. Phillips's and a few of the children crying and howling with happiness, to ask them where he might apply to get it.

"Get my photographs!" In his pride and joy—his gallery room—Byrnes shrieked at his horrible, ragged-looking, dust-covered detectives, "Those bastards are stealing my *photographs!*" Horrible Henry was on the floor scrabbling about in the archaeological ruins of what had once been the Bank Robber portraits, hurling them over one by one to Horrible Harry at the Fallen Women file, the Houlihan harridan at her own pile of Blackmailers, Female, looking for mementos of all her friends and stashing the thrown cards down the front of her horrible bosom. He could not see Matron Webb and baby Fred. Baby Fred had crawled into the actual photographic storage cabinet—the hand-built, gilt-finialed best oak fifty-three-compartmented, swivel-based photographic storage cabinet he had had copied from a picture in a book of the item of furniture the Borgias in old Italy had kept all their poison bottles in. He was in there eating something. He was eating photographs with Matron Webb on the other side of the cabinet—all three hundred pounds of her—shaking him out. Byrnes shrieked, "Kill him! Draw your revolvers and shoot the whole revolting gob of spit in the face of old Ireland dead in his tracks!" He never carried a pistol himself. He was almost six feet tall, the most celebrated policeman in the country, and his authority and slow purposeful walk were alone enough to cow into submission any man on Earth.

Byrnes, his eyes popping out of his head, shaking his boot and smashing in a few teeth as he went across the room to the window with a horde of the Horrible Houlihans dragging along behind him, flailing his arms about, yelled, "Oh! *Oh!*"

Byrnes, as a humble request to Heaven, cried, "Help!—POLICE!"

* * *

From his window Byrnes screamed, *"Shoot the horses!"*

Ellis Mifflin Jackson Swan screamed back from somewhere, "I can't!" He appeared on his driving seat out of the steam at the top of the machine like a man climbing out of a cloud. There was what looked like confetti falling down from the window by a man who had two horrible-looking children by the throats and was working away at dashing out their brains by bashing their foreheads against the window jambs. The confetti was bits and pieces of photographs of awful, rat-faced people. It was being thrown by a horrible snake-faced girl. The snake-faced girl was being clubbed by a huge matronly woman with a snarl on her face. The clubbings didn't seem to change the expression on the snake-faced girl's face at all. Ellis Mifflin Jackson Swan yelled, "The lever's stuck on *Power!* They're Fire Station horses! They're trained to go in the direction of a disaster! They're already in the middle of the disaster so they're just walking around in circles, grazing!" There was a thump as one of the trip-hammers tripped, crushed an iron spear-pointed church railing to arrows and then, with a burp, baled it and spat it out. Ellis Mifflin Jackson Swan screamed in apology through the steam, "I can't see the Police Commissioners anywhere! I think I killed them all in the first pass!"

It was no time for good news. Byrnes roared, *"Do something!"* There was a crash as the horrible machine lurched forward and hit the curb, sucked it in, sawed it up, bashed it to dust, and then baling it, ejected it like a naval shell. Ellis Mifflin Jackson Swan screamed, "It's *turning!"*

It was. Under the steam and stink and smoke and smog, the beast turned.

Man and Mammon, Cathedral or cop-shop. It was deciding.

Cop-shop.

Slowly, with a sound like a tidal wave changing course in mid-ocean, sucking, sawing, hammering, compacting, baling and ejecting, it turned in the direction of the Headquarters building and Byrnes' window.

"Everything's smashed! Everything's smashed and broken and ruined!" In the basement Telegraph Office Harry Roebuck, pointing, hopping, dancing up and down to point out the destruction, cried bootless to Heaven, "All my work! All my years of begging and borrowing and making do and convincing the damned Commissioners that they should spend mites on Morse while they're spending millions on Misadministration all wasted, all for nothing—*all defeated!"* His life, like his Telegraph Office, was in smithereens. He held up something that looked like an armored snail with wires and shook it, "See this? See this? This isn't an issue Police telegraph repeater box that I should have been issued, this is a repeater box from a naval ship of the line! Do you know how I got this?

I *stole* it! I stole it because the City Commissioner needed that money to defend himself in Court against the accusation that as Commissioner in charge of allocations he wasn't allocating money to anyone but himself!" Roebuck, grabbing Tillman by the lapels and putting his face an inch from his, screamed with his eyes staring and hopeless, "Now I have to go back to him, to people like him, and beg for more money to *rebuild!* And you ask me to tell you things about *telephones?* About rich people—and you're not even officially sanctioned? You're asking about powerful people and you're not even asking me on behalf of a senior officer who'll give me credit for telling you anything: you're asking because you think something's happening and you think influential people are involved and you—" He let go. He flapped his arms. Roebuck said in desperation, "Are you *insane?*"

"Harry—"

"Are you *mad?* Are you *demented?*"

"Harry—"

"You're alone! Do you know what that means?" Roebuck shouted, "Do you know what I hear on the telegraph? What I know? Do you know how this city is *run?*" Like an antenna, one of the wires sticking out of the repeater box quivered. He reached down and, with his eyes wild, ripped it off. Roebuck said, "Hee." There was another, a smaller electrical wire sticking out of the other side. He ripped that off too. Roebuck said, "You want me to tell you how to find the names and telephonic connection numbers of rich and powerful people so you can let them know you exist—so they can know you're there asking questions: is that what you want?"

"Silas Archer may not even be important. He isn't on the electoral roll of voters so he—"

"People don't have to be on the electoral roll of voters! People who are on the electoral roll of voters are only the people who *vote!* The people who may not be on the electoral roll of voters are the people who *rule!*" Roebuck said, "I'll never replace all this. I'll never get any of this back—*ever!*"

He was finished, his life gone. All he had left was what he had left.

Roebuck said sadly, "Virgil, this is Science. This is Progress. If someone powerful wants to know who's looking for him—this man Archer—and he offers me money to rebuild all this in return, what am I to do?"

Roebuck, alone in his room, the last survivor of the ruins, said desperately as outside there was a roar and a concussion that broke even the last of his demijohns under the broken shelf, "Virgil, I'm not Edison, not Bell, not Otis, not Roebling—I'm an ordinary man. My dreams are small.

I have a wife and children. *How?* How can I get through a life like this *unprotected?"*

"My beautiful Police Station—!" On the steps, Sergeant Fitzgerald, holding his arms out like Moses, roared, *"Get away from my beautiful Police Station!"* All the rosettes from the Hibernian Society were in tatters. The Ellis-Mifflin-Jackson-Swan Infinite Capacity Full Patent Protected Street And Avenue Sanitizer, Appliance Number One was turning in the street in a miasma of red and gold and steam and smoke and ejected curbstones. It was turning for the front steps. It was going to eat the front steps, turn them to mulch, hit the door jambs and tear them to toothpicks, mash up the marble in the front lobby, bite benches, gobble guard rails, chomp, champ and chew up the charge room and then, belching, roaring, shaking, lurching, it was going to go straight for his beautiful hand-hewn bog-oak Irish Desk Sergeant's desk and masticate it to matchwood.

Ellis, Mifflin, Jackson, Swan: they were English names.

He hated the English.

He had hated the English through his family in Mayo for six hundred years.

On the front steps, Fitzgerald, ripping his rosettes off and holding them up like crucifixes in the presence of the Devil, screamed, "You filthy horrible Protestant bastard of a machine, *get your bailiffs and stinking English soldiers away from my family's beautiful little farmhouse!"*

He had emigrated to the New World to be free too. On the steps, looking as if he had been run down in the first rush (he had), Muldoon, standing shoulder to shoulder with Fitzgerald, Meath to Mayo, yelled to the ghastly turning Colossus, "Halt! Halt in the name of the Law!" He heard someone shout behind him, "Rabbit! Hole! *Bang!"* and he thought for a moment it was a man from another county come to help too. It wasn't. It was Simpson. Simpson screamed, pointing, "It was you!" He heard a roar, a thunder as the great engine belched something out in a cloud of steam, cleared its entrails for more conquest and, slowly, turned. He heard a whine as the saw started. He heard a thump as the hammers hammered, a whizz as the baling spool baled. It was Science: he heard it. He hated Science. He saw a horse, and then another one. He was a Meath man: he knew horses.

He had, down by his side, a brass hand bell from the school. He had, beside him, that great and good man, Fitzergald. He had, staggering up to his feet and starting to point an accusing finger, Clubber Simpson of the Fifth. He didn't want Simpson.

He hit with his mighty mitt, Simpson, and floored him.

He raised, like a torch illuminishing the way back to the Age of Eden, his bell.

He looked at the horses.

Nice horses.

Brigade horses.

Standing like a sentinel, ringing at his bell, Muldoon roared to the nice Brigade horses dragging the awful instrument of destruction toward him, "Fire— Fire!"

Muldoon roared at the top of his lungs, ringing the Station house alarm, "—FIRE!!"

In his basement, beyond reason, Roebuck screamed, "Get out!"

"These 'Telephoners'—what sort of people are they?"

Roebuck screamed, "For the love of God, Virgil, in the name of charity, get out!"

They got out. They reared. They snorted. They were old Fire horses and in that instant they came alive, snorted, pranced, tore at their traces to be free.

He was up on his perch, rolling over it, trying to get off. Ellis Mifflin Jackson Swan, seeing what was happening, roared, "My *Machine!*" It was turning, being dragged off its wheels, things, cogs, fan belts coming off, going over, being dragged, machine fighting muscle, Science fighting life and sinew and soundness of wind, fighting two fire horses, fighting—

"Fire! *Fire!* Fire!" On the steps, in falsetto, Muldoon screamed, "Help! *Save my little children!*"

It fought Soul.

"Fire! Fire! *Fire!*"

It fought freedom. It fought the wind. It fought fire horses.

It lost.

It had in its heart no dreams, no hopes at all. It had no *duty*.

On Mulberry Street, beating its brow with its hammers, gnashing its teeth with its saws, a-wailing, a-thumping, a-puffing, a-roaring, it lost, and, as the great beasts broke loose and with a clatter of their hooves that struck sparks from the cobblestones, and like all living things and not machines sped to their appointed, God-given duty like chargers, it sat down in the middle of the road and, slowly, sinking down into the depths, puffing, grasping, pumping, sucking, slicing, solidifying and sighing, sat down like the dinosaur it was and, with no brain at all, with no regrets, simply because that was all it could do, turned itself on the first bright morning of its creation utterly, scientifically, and completely—to trash.

* * *

In his ruined room in the sudden silence, Roebuck shrieked, "Get out! Get out! *Get out!*"

In his ruined room, Roebuck, in the silence, in the scheme of things, a no one, a nothing, shrieked at the top of his voice, "I don't know! I don't know! I don't know! I don't know *anything!*"

22

Fear. He felt it tingle at his wrists like electricity.

In his glassed-in office on the second floor of the Metal Tympanium Electro-Magnetic Speaking Telephone Company on Fourteenth Street, Mr. Adam Drawbaugh said in a gasp, *"What?"* Outside his office, he could see his massive banks of black switchboards all lit up, his boys in their shirtsleeves running at top speed between them with wires and pegs in their hands connecting up one line with another. He could hear humming, crackling, clattering: he could hear the sounds of the boys' boots through his floor as they ran. He could see young women at chairs with the bustles of their dressed protruding from them with earphones on their ears taking calls, answering questions, calling to the boys with bundles of pegs and wires in their hands. He could hear shouting, calling orders—he could see Leyden jars fizzing and bubbling, copper wires running like cats' cradles across the ceiling of the place, he could smell the smell of electricity and chemical reaction and the sweat of hard work. He could smell the smell of his waxed, wonderful moustaches with their carefully combed curls at the end. He could feel the laundry stiffness of the expensive shirt and collar he wore with his latest-style dark coat and striped trousers.

He could feel, smell, taste his world coming to an end.

Mr. Drawbaugh said, *"What?"* He stared at the little bowler-hatted man sitting at his desk. There was a huge brute of a man standing by the little bowler-hatted man at his desk, but he could not get his eyes to set on him. Mr. Drawbaugh said, "The *what?* The *who?* The—" When he had let them in he had thought they were the police. The big one had shown him a police badge. He had thought they were the Boiler Inspection Squad, the Sanitation Squad, the Employed Unmarried Women's Welfare Protection Squad; he had thought they were— Mr. Drawbaugh said as the small man with his bowler hat pulled down too far over his ears, wearing what looked like stiff, brand-new pants and coat, opened the burlap bag onto his desk and began taking out objects, *"Who* are you?"

177

Tillman said for the second time, "I am Mr. Lucius L. Lippincott." It was a high, thin voice, "N.A.D.A.B.L." He took from his bag a Bible and laid it on the table in front of him, touched at it twice, adjusted its placement so it sat square in front of him, and nodding, the voice even higher and thinner, said indicating Muldoon, "The large gentleman with me is a policeman." He took from his bag a can of red paint and a two-inch brush and, adjusting both these objects twice on the desk, reached in and removed a pewter traveling inkwell and pen. Mr. Lippincott said, "He is a member of the Anti-CUR Squad—Crimes of Unspeakable Repulsiveness."

He reached in yet again and removed the last object from the bag and placed it on the Bible—a .38 caliber short-barreled Colt Lightning revolver, well oiled.

He did not look at Mr. Drawbaugh's face at all.

Mr. Lippincott, busying himself, removing a leather-covered notebook from the inside pocket of his coat and, placing it to one side of the inkwell—uncapping the inkwell and taking up the pen—said, for the first time looking at Mr. Drawbaugh's face and giving him the faintest of wintery smiles, "Mr. Lucius L. Lippincott, National All-Denominations Anti-Blasphemy League. Mr. Drawbaugh, let me ask you now for the record so your defense may be fairly stated from all the pulpits in all the churches in the city this Sunday: just exactly how long have you been in league with the Devil in this supernatural, black-magical, anti-Christian practice of yours called *'Telephoning'?*"

"Are you insane."

Was he? He doubted it. No, he wasn't. He was the calmest of men, the most solid of men, and—he might add if it was not already obvious—the most patient. Perhaps he croaked a little, but that was merely from spending too much time rooting out the evil that lurked in places where men used strong drink and smoked tobacco. Mr. Lippincott said calmly, patiently, "No, sir, I am not insane, for it is not the Lord's work that sends men mad, it is Satan's." He made a little mark in his book. "Since you did not answer my first question when it was put to you I shall ask you a second: is it true, and do you and your necromantical coven draw pleasure from the fact that Mr. Alexander Graham Bell, the acknowledged earthly inventor of this system of sinful slavery, *used a human ear disinterred from a Christian grave to amplify the messages all around us from the Darker Regions?*"

Mr. Drawbaugh said, *"No!"*

Mr. Lippincott said to Mr. Muldoon, "He says 'No.'" He made a note of it in his book.

He was a fair man too. Muldoon, trying to take his eyes from the bustles and the breasts that heaved each time one of the female Central operators leaned forward to snap a peg into place on the switchboard or leaned around to yell at a boy—said, "For the sake of accuracy I think, Mr. Lippincott, that after the words 'He said no,' one should add perhaps in parentheses 'Emphatically.' " He smiled at Mr. Drawbaugh.

He was a married man, with children. He had a house and a garden and a set of garden chairs for quiet Sunday afternoons, and a garden table to put pitchers of lemonade on. Mr. Drawbaugh said, "Mr. Bell used the bones from a human ear to test a device that registered the patterns of human speech on a square of smoked glass so the deaf might read what was being said!" Mr. Drawbaugh said, "He was a *teacher* of the deaf! He did not set out to invent the telephone, he set out to invent a kindly, humanitarian machine to give the power of communication and understanding to those God had—had accidentally not made whole in His great—in His great manufactory of Man in Heaven!" Mr. Drawbaugh said, "The ear bones, I am sure, were from a person who had kindly and without profit to himself donated his parts after death to the furtherance of—" Mr. Drawbaugh said, "I am almost certain Mr. Bell did not dig anyone up!"

TO RETAIN THEIR EMPLOYMENT, OPERATORS MAY NOT MARRY, ASSOCIATE OR COMMUNICATE WITH, ANY OF THE FOLLOWING (ON PAIN OF INSTANT DISMISSAL);

(1) Beggars
(2) Musicians
(3) Stablemen
(4) Gossips
(5) Criminals
(6) Foreigners, Lunatics, or Politicians.

It was a framed sign on the wall of the far side of the great humming room above what looked like a frothing, foaming vat of acid. Mr. Lippincott said, glancing at it, "I see you employ females in this 'Company' of yours."

Muldoon said for the sake of accuracy, "Young, unmarried females with firm breasts and rounded derrieres and an unladylike desire to earn cash money." He nodded. He looked at Mr. Drawbaugh with raised eyebrows.

"I employ young women from good Christian families of gentle manner who, unlike the boys, do not shout at people on the lines or swear at them or try to form indiscreet liaisons!"

"There are many indiscreet liaisons to be formed in this wicked world, but the worse of them is with the Prince of Darkness who whispers along the copper wires of corruption!"

"I employ girls because they don't say to an unsuccessful caller, 'They won't answer' as if the receiver of the call is angry at the caller and trying to avoid them, but say instead, 'They *can't* answer'—"

"Why? Because your Satanic Master is busy with them on another line?"

"Because there is nobody home!"

"Oh?" He made a note. "Where are they then?"

"How the Devil should I know?" Drawbaugh, starting to sweat, shouted, "I'm not *God!*" (Mr. Lippincott, writing it all down, said, "Indeed not.") Drawbaugh said, "I have enough trouble teaching the people who *are* home how to use the instrument the way it was meant to be used without knowing where people are when they *aren't* home!" He heard what he said. It sounded insane. Drawbaugh said, "Why am I explaining that I don't know where people are when they're not at home? We have over eight thousand subscribers! Why am I—" Drawbaugh said, *"This is what the Vatican did to Galileo!"*

Mr. Lippincott said, "Ah, Galileo." He wrote it down.

Muldoon said, looking away from the girls, "Ah, the Vatican—" He nodded.

Mr. Lippincott said calmly, patiently, "Tell me—" for he did not miss a thing— "If you have only eight thousand subscribers, why is it I see telephone wires everywhere in the streets? Why is it even people like mere policemen in Brooklyn have them, persons on Broadway, persons in tunnels below Broadway—?"

Tillman said without looking up, "Tell me, what is it, on these telephones, that Satan, the Great Corruptor, *whispers to all these people?"*

Mr. Drawbaugh said tightly, "What's the red paint for?"

Mr. Lippincott said, "Why, sir, to paint the letter B for blasphemer upon your forehead so all in the Tombs prison and in the Court of Christianity on Duane Street will know who you are and in whose evil service you work!"

Mr. Drawbaugh said tightly, calmly, steeling himself, "The telephones are not all our telephones. There are at least five other companies in the city of New York alone who operate a service at least as large as ours, and in some cases larger." A strange, Galileo-like nobility in the face of ignorance had come over him. As he spoke, his eyes raised themselves to thoughts of Truth and Science and the joys of quiet Sundays in his garden, "There are, and I name them in order of subscriber numbers, the Bell Company at Number 18 Broadway, the Metropolitan at 126 Liberty Street, the New York Telegraph and Telephone Institute, also at 18 Broadway, the Tympanic—here—and the Resonating Telephone Instrument Company of Number 23 Wall Street." His voice was calm and strong. Mr. Drawbaugh said, "And apart from those—and I do not even attempt to list these for there are too many—there are a myriad of other smaller back-room operations that build merely closed-circuit loops of lines from a single house to a single factory, from a single house to a store, from one house to another, and for all I know, from house to infernal *dog kennel!*" Mr. Drawbaugh shrieked as he saw the pen poise, "Do not write down *'Hound of Hell'!* Of course no line goes to a dog kennel!" Mr. Drawbaugh said, "And sweetheart lines—" Mr. Drawbaugh said, "Don't write down *'Immorality'!* They are lines that go from one private house to another and no further!"

"And what exactly do you charge for this service from"—he cringed at the words—*"from dog kennel to sweetheart?"*

His face was set like stone. Drawbaugh said, "Fifteen cents a call or one hundred and eighty dollars a year, whichever is the lesser."

Muldoon said, "That's very reasonable."

Mr. Lippincott said, "It seems expensive to me."

Muldoon said, "I refer to the taking of the lesser charge."

Mr. Lippincott said, "There *is* no lesser charge!"

Muldoon said, "You mock me, Mr. Lippincott."

Mr. Lippincott said, "I do not mock, I *educate. I educate that another charge once thought reasonable was the selling of Faust's very soul to the Devil in return for worldly riches!* And I question! I question temptation and hellishness. I question the contract between Man and Monster—I refer to the Force that whispers down the line of the Metal Tympanium Electro-Magnetic Speaking Telephone Company's instrument without the knowledge of the Church—I question that on the 'Telephone' when there is no voice speaking what can be clearly heard are the wails and screams and cries of the Damned roasting in the Pit!"

"That's just the weather affecting the insulators!"

"I question the hideous sounds of scratchings and clawings of the cloven-hoofed gargoyles fighting to be let loose!"

"Birds roosting on the wires!"

"I refer to Instrument Number One! I refer to—"

"Not made by us!"

"I refer to—" Tillman said, "What do you mean, not made by us?" Tillman said, "I refer to Messrs. Hewitt and Jenkins and Oubliette and Embrasure and Donjon and Bailey and Palisade and Portcullis—!"

Mr. Drawbaugh said, *"Who?"* Mr. Drawbaugh said, "We didn't make Instrument Number One. We only make the Improved Instrument Number

Six. Instrument Number One was made when the company first started five or six years ago, and when we took over we cleared all the old equipment out and began production on the Number Sixes." Mr. Drawbaugh said, "Instrument Number One was made by one of the early pioneers of the Telephone—by a man called Eldridge—a farmer, a man who tinkered away in his barn and invented a better resonator than Bell's and then patented it so we could, when we bought the company, compete with Bell on equal terms, and—" Mr. Drawbaugh said, "Mr. Eldridge, I know for certain—for he was the mildest of men—*never used a human ear for anything!*" He paused. He waited. He—

He touched at his moustaches.

He said hopefully, "Yes? Wrong man? All right? *Yes?*"

Mr. Lippincott said, starting to stammer, "But—but it must follow as surely as day follows night that human nature, being what it is, temptation will inevitably arise and—"

Drawbaugh said, "Females of vile repute will insinuate themselves into the Central Exchanges and arrange trysts by telephone calls—'Call Girls.'" Mr. Drawbaugh said, "Yes, I have heard of it, but it does not happen in my establishment for I am a rock of rectitude!" He was a nice man, everybody said so. His children, each evening, waited for him on the porch to get home. Mr. Drawbaugh, stabbing his finger at it, said, *"See my sign!"*

"But—" Mr. Lippincott said, "But, certainly oaths and cursewords and Godlessness must occasionally assail the ears of your ladies—"

It was a trick question. Mr. Drawbaugh said, standing erect and still, gazing into the distance, "Perhaps you are right, sir, but it is not a problem here because my employees—both male and female—are of such gentle breeding that they would not recognize such words in the first place! They would think they were, perhaps, only Swedish."

Muldoon said, "It speaks *Swedish,* the telephone?"

"It will reproduce any sound on Earth—" He leaned forward to explain to Mr. Lippincott who had stopped writing, "Hence, sir, the sounds of little birds on the wires and the gentle heaving of the Earth itself as it settles into a more comfortable posture on its revolution. Hence the gentle whispering of the zephyrs and breezes in the air—" Mr. Drawbaugh said, "It will reproduce *music!* Our Instrument Number Six will reproduce all the sounds of a full chamber orchestra! In fact—" He leaned forward and dropped his voice— "In fact, sir, it is my dream that all those crippled and infirm, all those who presently cannot afford the rich man's service of instant audible communication, shall, once the profits justify it, have fitted to their homes, speaker pieces that will waft into their empty lives all the ecstasy and

higher feelings of music and opera and the most popular family ballads of
the day to cheer up their sad lives!" Mr. Drawbaugh said quickly, "And
educational talks by selected speakers, and sermons on Sundays!"

Mr. Lippincott, clearly moved, said in a croak, "This Eldridge fellow:
where is he now?"

"Ill. His nerves." Mr. Drawbaugh said, shrugging sadly, "Confined, I
believe, to the asylum on Blackwell's Island, the strain of invention too
much for him—but the fair price my company paid him—*for I made
certain it was so*—enough for him to spend his declining sad years in
comfort!"

He waited. He looked. He felt his moustaches stiffen in vindication. Mr.
Drawbaugh said clearly, calmly, like the man he was, "Gentlemen, you
have come to the wrong place. I am not a servant of Sin. I am a man with
a wife and children and a dream to bring joy and happiness to the lives of
the incapacitated and the elderly. I even plan to provide a home shopping
service where such people may merely list their requirements over the
wires and a messenger boy will deliver to them, from a central warehouse,
goods from all over the world at competitive prices!"

Mr. Drawbaugh said, "I am a good man, a kind man—I swear to you:
this little mix of mica and mechanism, wire and wonderment, progress and
porcelain is—" He had his eyes to Heaven every day of his life.

Mr. Drawbaugh said, filling his chest, and his eyes, "Sirs, if not from
God, whence came this great object? Sirs, This royal throne of kings, this
sceptered isle,

"This earth of majesty, this seat of Mars,
"This other Eden, demiparadise,
"This fortress built by Nature for herself,
"Against infection and the hand of war,
"This happy breed of men, this little world,
"This . . . *Telephone!*"

It made him madder'n hell sometimes, the things the little Bible-basher
bungled him into.

Muldoon of the Crimes of Unspeakable Repulsiveness Squad said
suddenly, "This is another Norwegian herring ship job! This is like the
time the National All-Denominations Anti-Blasphemy League got it into
its head that in with the crates of stinking Norwegian herring from the
North Sea there were crates of stinking Satanic literature and assorted
self-abuse appliances!" He looked hard at Mr. Drawbaugh and saw a man
who probably had a wife and children, a nicely kept garden and, for all he
knew, a set of garden chairs and tables to put pitchers of lemonade on.
Muldoon said, "This man isn't a villain! This man's mind turns only to the

welfare of widows and cripples and orphans!" It wasn't only the herring job that had left him smelling like a bottle of cod liver oil for a month, it was also the— Muldoon said, "And the coven below the Croton reservoir—!" Muldoon said, *"All there was down there was sewer!"* No, he'd had enough. This wasn't work for real men. Muldoon of the Anti-CUR Squad, a friend and aide of the N.A.D.A.B.L., but not their goddamned obedient unquestioning little slave, said shaking his head, "Mr. Lippincott, you are a good, Christian man, but you have forgotten how to march onward as a Christian soldier!" Muldoon said, "This is not the man we should be after. We should be after, to the point of exhaustion, beyond that point, not men who are misunderstood like this man, but, men like—"

Mr. Drawbaugh said, "Men like who?"

Muldoon said, "I cannot even speak his name!"

Lippincott croaked. He had his hat pulled down over his ears. He had his pen poised. He shook his head. Mr. Lippincott said in his high, thin voice, "No, I still believe this man—"

"This man is a good man!"

Drawbaugh said, "I am."

"He is not an antichrist!" Muldoon, warming to it, indicating him with a sweep of his hand, said, *"This man gives employment to the less favored in our society, like women!"*

Mr. Drawbaugh said, "I do." Mr. Drawbaugh said mildly, "I go to church with my family twice on Sundays." Mr. Drawbaugh said helpfully, "Is there someone evil in this city?"

Mr. Lippincott said, searching in his notebook for occupation, "Your wires blot out the sun—"

Muldoon said, "Progress! Damned good for the complexion, blotting out the sun!"

Mr. Drawbaugh said, "It is!" Mr. Drawbaugh said, shivering at the thought, "Cannot speak his name . . . Crimes of Unspeakable . . ." Mr. Drawbaugh said, "This . . . Unspeakable One, is he—?"

Mr. Lippincott said in a croak, *"He is my life's work!* He would be, if I could catch him, if I could bring him to book at the bar of blasphemy, my life's triumph! He would be, if I could catch him, but—" He shook his head. He gave Muldoon a look that could have killed. "But I am not the man to do this great task of the Lord. I am merely a worm—*so I content myself with people like you!"*

Muldoon said, *"But this man has done nothing wrong!"*

Mr. Drawbaugh said, *"But I have done nothing wrong!"*

Mr. Lippincott said in a croak, "That remains to be seen!" He raised his pen. The ink had dried. He dipped it into the inkwell, but the ink, like his dreams, had all turned to dust.

Muldoon said, "Mr. Lippincott, you are a Christian; you cannot persecute an innocent man!"

"I have nothing left but innocent men!" Lippincott, suddenly looking up, his eyes blazing, said in a croak, "The Lord called me to find the Unspeakable One and I have failed him! I have failed! I have searched high and low, lain awake a thousand sleepless nights, battered my brains until they were bloody, prayed for guidance and help until my knees were rheumatic and found—*nothing!* I have found only hints and whispers and—" He almost sobbed. Mr. Lippincott said, demanding it of Muldoon the encourager, "How easy it is for you to say not to yield, to surrender in the great quest! Tell me how to continue when I have nothing: no hint, no clue, no address, no—" He did sob, "No *hope!*"

Mr. Drawbaugh asked mildly, "Does he have a name, this Unspeakable One?"

"Of course he has a name! All God's children have names—if he *is* indeed one of God's children—*and he is not!*" Lippincott said, "His name is—" Lippincott snarled, "Embrasure, Donjon, Palisade, Portcullis—those are all his names!"

"They are the names of parts of a castle." He looked at Muldoon and shrugged, "I learned it in school." Mr. Drawbaugh said, "But there are no castles in America, are there?"

"There is the Castle of Evil!" He shook his head. He would not be drawn back into it. Lippincott said, "No! I will not fight again! I am one of the Lord's fallers-by-the-wayside! I will not gird my loins and don my armor and sally forth to the holy mission again for I cannot! I am only a mortal man—I cannot begin another crusade knowing success is only a chimera, a false hope, a sin of pride!"

Muldoon said, "His name is Silas Archer!"

Lippincott shrieked, "I do not wish to hear that name again!"

"Silas! Silas Archer!" Muldoon, snapping his hands apart like a trapper finished strangling a stoat, said to put an end to it, "Mr. Lippincott, we cannot persecute this good, kind, innocent man while we yet know that somewhere the Great Inflamer, the Unspeakable One, Silas Archer still lives! We cannot! Can we?"

"Yes! Yes, we can! *I* can! *I shall! I will!* I will continue with my other little tasks and put that name ever from my thoughts until I appear at the Great Interrogator and am punished for my lack of resolve!" He had a tear in his eye. Mr. Lippincott said sadly, "Yet it is a hard, hard thing, Mr. Drawbaugh, to realize that the intelligence one thought one was blessed with is an illusion and one is, really, not very bright at all."

Mr. Drawbaugh said, leaning forward, being kind, "But, sir, you have friends, allies, and you have the right on your side—surely, there is something you can still do?"

Mr. Lippincott said softly, "I confess, Mr. Drawbaugh, that—" He was practicing for the Great Interrogator, "I confess that I—" Mr. Lippincott said, "I confess I only picked on you because I know that Silas Archer somewhere has access to a telephone." He touched at his eyes. They were wet. Mr. Lippincott said to Drawbaugh, "Fine fellow that you obviously are, Mr. Drawbaugh, I confess that—"

Mr. Drawbaugh said, "Is he listed in the Directories?"

"The telephone Directories are sealed to me because I am a person of no importance, because I am nought but a private poor person who—"

Mr. Drawbaugh said, "They are not sealed to me!"

A miracle? Could it be . . . ? Mr. Lippincott said in a gasp, "Oh, sir!" Could it be . . . ? No, the age of miracles was past. Mr. Lippincott said, "No, it would not be in your Directory because—" He looked at Muldoon, "Because, yes, honest Ned, you are right and this man is a good man, and I—"

Mr. Drawbaugh said, "I have current copies of all the Directories of all the companies in the city—all of them!" Mr. Drawbaugh said, "Bell, and Metropolitan, and the NYT and T and—" Mr. Drawbaugh, standing a little straighter, said as an order, "Sir, *we are all servants of the Lord!*"

"But such things are confidential, are they not?"

Mr. Drawbaugh said, "I am a man to be trusted." He was at his desk in an instant, pulling out the books. Mr. Drawbaugh said, "Look—here they are!" Mr. Drawbaugh said, "Archer, Silas—it will be—because it is perhaps the Lord's will that the worst of men should be the first letter of the alphabet beginning his name—on the very first page!" He was riffling through the books one by one, the Metropolitan, the NYT and T, the Resonating Telephone Instrument Company. Drawbaugh, reading it, said, "Aarons! Abernathy! Ackroyd! Allen! Amberson—!" He was through the first two books and onto the third. Mr. Drawbaugh said, "Acton! Addison! Anderson! Angerstrom—!" He had even the green Government telephone book. He was leafing through it, "Abels! Achison! Alberts! Amerson! Anders—!" Mr. Drawbaugh said, *"Archer, Silas T."* Mr. Drawbaugh said, looking up, "Embrasure, Donjon, Palisade, Portcullis . . ." Mr. Drawbaugh said, "A castle, in America!" Mr. Drawbaugh said, *"Archer, Silas T.!* Returns and Records Section, Department of Immigration."

Mr. Drawbaugh said slowly, reading it, doing the Lord's work, savoring it, "Archer, Silas T., Returns and Records Section, Department of Immigration—*Castle Garden,* New York . . . !" Mr. Drawbaugh, his eyes bright with conquest, said grinning, *"Got him!"*

They had.
They had one of the Custers.
They had a living man.
They had *Archer*.

23

It was at the farthest southernmost tip of the island of Manhattan, at the spearpoint of the city, looking out toward the islands in the harbor—to Bedloe's Island where the old gibbet had been that had hanged Hicks the pirate in 1860 and a Frenchman named Bertholdi planned to build a statue called Liberty, to Staten Island with the villas and houses and forests of trees of the rich, to the deserted circles of Ellis and Governors Islands, to the quarantine islands of Swinburne and Hoffman.

It was Castle Garden.

It was the Battery.

Built in 1811 as a circular shotproof stone fort against the threat of Napoleon and the British Navy impressing American sailors into their service to fight him, it had stood ready and menacing through the War of 1812 to bring its great guns into the defense of the young nation, but, unassailed by anybody coming into the harbor from the sea, it had fired not a single shot in anger. By 1814, with its guns spiked and its gun crews posted elsewhere, it became, in peace, an unofficial place of assembly and entertainment for the city, protected with its massive blocks and fortified roof from the inclemencies of weather.

In 1850 Jenny Lind, the Swedish Nightingale, had sung there to an audience of six thousand people paying three dollars a seat each.

With none of the admission money being ploughed back into maintenance, a year later it had been closed as a fire trap.

In 1855, still unmaintained, hardly altered, it had become a landing depot for immigration.

It was Castle Garden.

It was a huge, aging, gray, monolithic, circular fort at the entrance to the New World where three quarters of the world's total immigration passed each year.

On the harbor side, blurred out by the smoke and steam of ferries and sidewheelers, launches, lighters and a forest of tiny masts from all the boats that met all the ships moored out in the harbor beyond the treeline of Staten Island, it took into its crumbling hold, into its gun turrets and ammunition storerooms, into every space that could be crowded into for processing, over five thousand men, women and children a day.

On the land side, into the chaos of the city, onto waiting wagons, buggies, chaises, stages and streetcars—without ceasing—it disgorged them.

It was Castle Garden at the extreme tip of the island of Manhattan at 4:35 in the afternoon.

Outside, in all the spaces and streets that surrounded it, it was pure, undiluted madness.

Inside, it was Bedlam.

There were bags, bundles, baskets, trunks, boxes, Babel: in the great cupola-roofed rotunda of the main hall, in every corner, in every space, in every cubic meter of air where a human being could insinuate himself, there were families with strange bone structures, strange pallors, strange smells, clothing, strange languages painted on their bundles—strange hats of every description, strange coats of every cut, boots for northern winters, strange religious symbols at necks—Greek and Russian crosses, rosaries, Jewish things like little prayer boxes on arms. There were tassels hanging down from under men's loose blouses, Bibles, Talmuds, papers in their hands. There were strangely clad children crying and being shushed. There were voices, voices from all nations calling and seeking, settling, soothing, shouting—and everywhere, in piles, in mounds, in mountains, boxes strapped with leather, boxes tied with string, cardboard boxes and bundles underfoot, in corners, on seats, in lines, in heaps, stacks, pyramids—boxes and bundles everywhere.

In the entire place, for the original garrison of twenty-three artillerymen, there had been five toilets.

There were no more now. There were lines where the toilets were.

The toilets had backed up and the hall had a smell like no other smell on Earth: the smells of sweat and foreignness, a smell like the smell of cats, dogs pent-up and sick.

There were lines where the Employment Office was: a glassed-in room at the far end of the hall below a second tier of offices reached by great metal catwalks and stairs—the line from that snaked out through the rear of the place to where the steamboats and ferries were. There was arguing, yelling, protesting at the line, but the steamboats were thumping, belching smoke, disgorging even more people for the lines, and at the end of the line, wherever the end of it was, no one could hear men in blue uniforms and braided pillbox hats yelling at tables marked ENTRY, MEDICAL,

LITERACY. They merely roared out what they wanted to say, not listening to answers and stamped papers with a steady thumping of metal stamps.

There were knots of people where the INTERPRETERS tables were, waving their hands, protesting again, then nodding, then as something more was told them, shaking their heads, thrusting papers and explaining something.

There was a crushing, a clattering, a cacophony of voices from the MEAL ROOM where a thousand people a day were fed; there were shrieks of horror from the closed-in CLINIC where the doctors examined something spotted by an official—a trachoma of the eye or a face without the light of intelligence. There were shrieks as the doctors in there explained that the sufferers would be sent back.

There were signs, placards, exhortations in all the languages of the world how to locate railway stations to the west, where to find carts that could be hired to go into the city to the north; there were ghastly warnings and illustrations of venereal diseases and trachoma of the eyes and notice of terrible penalties posted under law for their concealment—there was, everywhere, the terrible, unearthly smell of the toilets, the luggage, the sweat, the humanity.

Up in the rotunda, running all round it, there was a second level: glassed-in offices and metal catwalks above the entire circumference of the place like the gun platforms of a prison. Up there, there were more men in blue uniforms, men with papers and bags, boxes of bureaucracy and business, and, here and there, uniformed police from the Commissioners of Emigration looking down, pointing at something, shaking their heads, nodding to the blue-uniformed men as they hurried by.

Up there were the offices of Customs, of Immigration, of the Police, of the Commissioners, of clerks, counters, compilers, comptrollers.

Up there, there was the Office of Statistics. All the rooms were of glass and looked down on the pandemonium.

Up there, behind his great window with his name and title printed on it, was the COLLECTOR, RETURNS AND RECORDS SECTION, PRIVATE. DO NOT ENTER.

He was a man of middle height and build in his late fifties, wearing a blue uniform with braid on its sleeves, and on his clean-shaven face, frameless eyeglasses held on to his nose by a black-lacquered clip.

From the center of the rotunda, looking up, Tillman saw him. He saw him look down, and shaking his head in a sigh, run his hand through his hard slicked-down hair and look away to do something.

COLLECTOR, RETURNS AND RECORDS SECTION, PRIVATE. DO NOT ENTER.

The door, in large, clear letters, had his name painted on it.

MR. SILAS J. ARCHER.

He was a living man.

In his office, standing by the glass window looking down, as Tillman and Muldoon watched, as if in response to a summons, he picked up the earpiece of a telephone and, after listening to whatever it was the caller said to him by way of introduction, leaned down to where the mouthpiece must have been on his desk below the line of sight of the window and, doing the work he did each day, began speaking unhurriedly, nodding as he talked, back into it.

Outside, along all the walkways and paths where the immigrants streamed out, there were coffee wagons, iced-milk wagons, waffle wagons, even popcorn wagons painted in fantastical rainbow designs of irises and Indians as the introduction to the bizarre, rare treats of the New World, and a line of painted, inside-seating lunchwagons belching smoke and the sharp smell of frying oysters from their funnels.

In the first coffee wagon, Tillman, not knowing he was doing it, drummed his fingers on the square of table in front of him, and waited.

He glanced at Muldoon with his coffee cup full of Old Republic whiskey opposite him.

Muldoon said, offering, "I can get a few toughs from the old Strong Arm Squad together and we can lie in wait for whoever goes into Beach's tunnel to get the money and pounce on them."

Tillman said, "No." From his stool by the window, he was watching the people. He was watching their faces. He shook his head, "No." Tillman said, "No, they won't go back there now. It's not safe anymore—not after what happened to Hewitt."

Everywhere, there were the immigrants. At the end of the walkway an entire muster of them must have cleared and they were streaming out from the open stone archway of the gray building into the light. They were men, women, children from all the races and nations on Earth. Tillman said softly, "We'll wait here for Archer to finish work and come out."

The immigrants had all of their bundles, their possessions, their precious boxes and crates and bundles held hard in their hands. They held them and their children and gazed at the city.

Muldoon said suddenly, "Virgil, we don't even really know that this is the place. It could be just a fluke that Archer works here. *Donjon:* I looked it up—it means a great tower. There isn't any tower here. *Palisade:* it means a fence of stakes. There isn't any fence around Castle Garden, just docks and gardens and—" Muldoon said, *"Bailey:* it means an outer wall—there is no outer wall!" He needed a drink. He took one. Muldoon said, "This could all be a fluke—it could have nothing to do with the immigrants and it could just be a fluke that Archer works here and it could be a fluke that—"

Tillman, not listening, kneading his hands, said in a whisper, "Look at them, Ned! Look at the faces—look at the way they look!"

"*Virgil, we've told no one what we're doing!*" Muldoon said suddenly, "What *are* we doing?" Muldoon said, "Virgil, look at the people we keep coming to: Hewitt, Archer—even Jenkins." Muldoon said, "Virgil, we're not playing around here with common criminals, with the dangerous classes—what we're playing with is *power.*" Muldoon said angrily, "You're right—they won't go back to the tunnel to get their money and jewelry, not because they don't want to save anything in there or because of what we're doing, chasing after them, but because they don't *care!*" Muldoon said, "Virgil, these people are rich! And they kill. These people use people like Jenkins because he killed for them like a slaughterman, without pity, as a *job!*" Muldoon said, "I'm not a coward, but I've got my parents still living on Hudson Street and—" Muldoon said, "We could walk away from this."

He was not listening. Tillman said as if Muldoon had not spoken, still watching the people, "Look at the *hope!*"

"If you had a family—if you had ever had anyone, you'd see things clearer—you'd see that maybe to walk away from this now—"

He was transfixed. He had grown up an orphan. He had no one.

Tillman, at the window looking out, watching them, said in the wonder of a small child, "Look at them—Ned, look at their *faces . . . !*"

He was like a lover, shaking his head in awe, a strange half smile on his face, a look of awe. Tillman said, watching them, watching them as, like an army, conquistadors without weapons, like men before a mountain, at the first step of a great, arduous adventure, thinking of their children and their children's children not yet born, they came to conquer and succeed—"Look at them! Look at the light in their eyes! The energy, the hope, the *resolve!*"

"We can walk away from this now and no one will ever know!"

"No."

"This Archer may not even be the one we're looking for! It may not be him! You don't know it's him!" Muldoon said as an order, "Don't look for something to die for! It's a curse every Irishman knows from birth! Don't look around like a lover for something to die for because all you'll end up dying for is the future and the future will forget you!" Muldoon said firmly, "We have to tell someone what we're doing, what we've got, because if we don't—"

"*Who? Who can we tell?*" The immigrants, the newcomers, were like men before mountains, flexing their muscles. They looked up at the city, at buildings five stories high, at work and labor and hope. They looked at *passion*. Tillman, demanding, said, *"Who? Who can we tell?"*

"We can tell *Byrnes!"*

"We sure as hell *can't* tell Byrnes!"

"We can tell someone!" Muldoon said angrily. "Don't die out of nobility! Irishmen are sick of people dying out of nobility!" Muldoon said, "And it's blasphemous!" He tried a little joke, "And, as that little inquisitor Lucius L. Lippincott of the National All-Denominations Anti-Blasphemy League would be the first to point out to you—"

Tillman said with his face set, "It's them! Whatever's being done, it's being done to them!"

"You don't know that!"

"Look at them! Look at their *dreams!"*

"Look at your own!"

Tillman said quietly, without rancor, "Go if you want to."

"Virgil—" Muldoon said desperately, "It'll all work out without us. God will see it all works out! That's the lesson a belief in a good God—God always sees it right in the end!" He saw Tillman look away. His mouth was dry and he needed a drink. Muldoon said, "Virgil—Virgil, you do believe in God, don't you?"

He believed in what he saw.

He saw, suddenly, at a side door in the place, Silas Archer come out, glance up at the sky and, taking it from his vest, snap open his watch to check the time.

He saw him start for the street.

He saw his face. He wondered what, in that instant, all the other faces of the Custers looked like in the street.

He saw Muldoon looking at him. He saw the faces, the bundles, the boxes, the hope. He saw Muldoon's face. He saw Archer. He saw him go.

On his feet, touching gently at Muldoon's shoulder, Tillman said in a whisper, "After him, Ned— After him—"

He saw Muldoon's face. He saw what was there.

"All right, goddamnit—!"

Tillman, moving, so sure, so certain, so near, said wrenching his chair back to get out, in triumph, near conquest, "Ned— *After him, Ned!"*

24

He was so near they could almost smell him.

He was in the third seat back from the front in the ten-seater Whitehall Street stage under a glowing yellow gimballed oil lamp lit at half wick for the approaching evening. He was just across the aisle, one seat up.

It was Archer. Rocking a little, his shoulders moving up and down with the rhythm of the horses and the spring suspension on the iron-wheeled wooden stage, he was so close they could see every hair on his head, every crease and rumple in the blue uniform, every curlicue of gold-thread braid. He had his pillbox cap held loosely in both hands on his knees, so close that Tillman could see the reflection of it in the glass pane of his window, so close he could see the brown leather sweat band inside it and the silk lining, and, in gold with a heraldic shield around it, the monogram of the maker's name.

It was Archer. No one else had boarded the stage at Whitehall Street, nor hailed it to stop on Broadway, and, at Fulton Street, going north, there were only him and Tillman and Muldoon on either side of the aisle behind him. Atop the outside seat the driver of the stage was just a dark shape and a hand resting on the hole in the roof coachwork where he reached in to collect his fares.

It was Archer. He touched at his eyeglasses, adjusted them on his nose and glanced out the window, registered nothing on his face, and then looked down again to set the cap straight on his knees.

BROADWAY LINE
Whitehall Street—Canal—Cooper's Union
Timetable for 2nd Quarter 1884
Fare   5¢   Throughout

Mind molds matter. The face was tight, smooth, clean-shaven with only the faintest blue of new growth at the cheeks and neck. Above the open collar of his tunic and tight white shirt and soft official black bow tie below it, all the muscles of his neck in profile were loose and untensed. The face, in profile, in the reflection in the window, had no expression on it at all. The ears were standard, not criminal types, the sideburns cut carefully and recently by a barber, the hands holding the cap ungloved with neither long nor short fingers showing neither strength nor weakness, the nails cut on the left hand in careful half moons, on the right, because he must have been right-handed and not vain enough to have them done, cut by himself with scissors, uneven and unsymmetrical.

The eyeglasses had a black-lacquered nose spring holding them in place, positioned square with the eyes for both close reading and distance. He had no wife—the collar on the shirt had been laundered. He had some routine or a calculated number on shirts for his week's work—the shirt was still clean after a day's labor and had not been worn the day before.

He was so close he could almost smell the oil on his carefully slicked-down hair. He had a routine: the barber trimmed it each morning when he had his shave—it was neither too short from a recent monthly cut nor too long due for it, nor cut in a fashionable style. He was about fifty-five years old: he had his hair cut in the style of ten or fifteen years ago, parted in the middle with no wing tips at the ends and he had had it cut that way since he had begun work, without change, so he had no women he wanted to impress with his youth as he grew older.

It was a face, in profile, with no expression on it at all.

In his seat, looking straight ahead, balancing the blue pillbox, braided cap on his knees, traveling north, it was Silas Archer.

It was one of the Custers.

Under the glowing yellow light, he touched at the eyeglasses on his nose to set them straight.

Cleopatra's Infallible Egyptian Hair Curlers
LADIES! The Secret of the Siren of The Nile!

It was a framed advertisement above Tillman's head with a painting of a great snake appearing from a golden amphora and twisting itself about the letters.

They were at Vesey Street. No one else had gotten on the stage. Outside, with the approaching evening and clouds coming in from the west as Muldoon watched the yellow lights of all the oil lamps in the stage began glowing brighter in intensity.

He had his revolver on his knees under his hat, his hand curled around the butt with his thumb on the hammer. He watched.

He listened.

He watched Tillman in his seat across from him and, alternately, the back of Archer's head.

He listened, sitting a little forward in his seat for the sound of a click.

He did not appear to be armed. Under the coat there was no shape of a revolver, nor, in the slit pockets of the black silk vest with lacquered buttons, any sign of a pocket pistol or a derringer. The boots were laced up tight: there was no sheath there for a boot knife, and in the watch pocket only a watch and chain. There was no wedding ring, no jewelry of any sort, and the uniform was the standard uniform of the New York State Commissioners of Immigration Bureau and had not been tailored other than shortened an inch at the cuffs and perhaps, judging by the faint bunch of blue material at the crotch, taken in a little.

Mind molds matter. There was nothing on the face in profile, no expression or set of past events at all. It was a bland face, like the face in a posed, formal portrait, with no clues to a past existence at all, no sign of what, behind the eyes that looked straight ahead, the owner thought.

BROADWAY LINE
Whitehall Street—Canal—Cooper's Union

He stared past the man up at the sign in its cedar frame, watching.

He saw suddenly out of the corner of his eye, as he became aware of something, the man glance out the window.

He saw him move. He heard a click. In his seat, his thumb tight on the hammer, Muldoon—

It was his pocket watch. In his seat, without turning around, in a tight motion, Tillman shook his head to Muldoon to halt him.

It was his pocket watch. He saw him take it out and, at fob pocket level, snap it open the few degrees it took to see the face, glance out the window looking uptown, then close the watch again with a snap and, holding it, look for an instant at something on the corner of the street coming up.

He looked past him to see what he saw.

It was, on the corner of Warren Street, Hewitt's store. He saw Archer look at it for a moment with no expression on his face at all.

He saw him put the watch back in his pocket without looking at it and take the side of his cap back with his hand and settle it straight across his knees.

He saw him turn around to look across the aisle at the man watching him. He saw him take in an unmannered clod, wearing his hat inside the stage, looking up at the timetable above him.

—he saw him look away again.

The eyes were light blue, uncurious. They had passed over him and he had sensed nothing, felt nothing, and they were merely eyes that had passed over him, taken him in, made no or little judgment about him, and all they were on that face with no expression at all, were eyes.

He was like a painting, a picture of a man, like something from a past time, an icon of a petty official who had lived, worked, died, had a drawing made of him somewhere as part of something larger, more important, and then, after that moment, after that single nonexpression on his face had been captured—perhaps the details of his uniform of more interest to the painter than the face—had disappeared into the dust of history as if he had never lived.

He was a nothing, a zero. He was a face in the crowd, an unmarried, unsensational, unmoving, petty uniformed bureaucrat with, in his eyes, no meaning or clue to his character at all.

He was a man who wore his shirts once and then sent them out with the collars to be laundered, had his hair trimmed with his morning shave and cut his own fingernails probably when they scratched him, with a small pair of scissors he could not wield properly in his left hand.

BROADWAY LINE
Whitehall Street—Canal—

It was above his head in a little cedar frame.

In his seat, Tillman glanced down from it and the man, without warning, with the pale blue eyes steady and unblinking behind his bifocular eyeglasses was looking directly at him.

"Das ist fur—zum ausweglernen—ja?" They were a confusion of words. They were all he could think of. He indicated the timetable with his thumb and grinned. Tillman, the unmannered foreigner still wearing his hat and holding the seat in front of him with his hands in case he fell off, said, asking the nice man for information, starting a conversation, *"Ja?"*

The eyes did not blink.

He nodded moronically, intimately, two travelers together. Tillman said, pointing, grinning, *"Ja?"*

The eyes did not blink, and there was something in them seen full on that he had not seen in profile, something, behind the glasses that passed across them, lingered for an instant and then—and then did not go.

Tillman, nodding, grinning, his mouth gone dry, said, *"Ich bin ein auslander. Ich kann nichts—"* The eyes held his. Tillman said, nodding, *"Das—"* He meant the timetable, *"Das is für alles tags und . . . ?"* It was all he could think of. Tillman said, *"Ja, bitte? Ist er? Bitte?"*

He had his eyes on the back of Archer's head.

In his seat Muldoon, straining every muscle and organ, listened for the click of a weapon.

They were moving, moving. He felt in his spine, the steady rocking motion of the springs.

The eyes saw him.

His thumb was locked in midair, indicating the timetable, his body stiff in the seat with the terrible, pale eyes looking at him with nothing in them: no expression, no curiosity, no life.

They looked at him as if he was part of the seat.

He was so close he could see every hair on his head, every rumple in his uniform.

He was so close he could almost smell him.

The eyes looked at him.

They were the eyes of a man who had his shirts laundered, who had his routine, who had his hands held loosely around his uniform cap to balance it and did not move it even the faintest fraction of an inch as he looked.

Mind molds matter.

". . . Ja? Er ist—er ist für alles tags— Ja . . . ?"

. . . He saw him, with no expression in those eyes, not even contempt, look away.

"Driver!"

Outside, in the street, it was raining and dark.

Outside on the street, somehow it had become dark and it was raining.

Outside, on the street, somehow, it was the Bowery.

"Driver!" Standing up, rapping on the wooden ceiling with his knuckles, Archer, not looking again, called, "My stop, if you please!" and he was passing back through the vehicle to the back door, not looking down at Muldoon as he passed, and turning the lever to open the rear door to get out.

It was the Bowery. It was the corner of Houston Street and the Bowery and all the lights in all the buildings were starting to come on and, somehow time and distance had passed and it was night and it was raining and they were on the Bowery at Houston Street.

* * *

"God Almighty . . . !" It was a gasp. It was Muldoon. As the stage passed on he saw Archer walking across the street in the rain. He saw him turn into an alley, halt in front of a little iron-grilled gate to a laneway and go in. He saw, behind him, another man. He saw the man look up.

Muldoon said in a gasp, "God almighty, the man behind him—the man going in after him—it's *Chief Inspector Byrnes!*"

He saw Byrnes go in. He heard a crash. He saw Tillman burst out through the open swinging door of the stage onto the street.

He saw him out on the street reaching in under his coat for his gun.

He saw him with his revolver out in front of him running for the laneway.

He saw him reach the iron gate, wrench it open with his free hand, and—in that instant as Muldoon got to his feet and went for the still open rear door of the stage—disappear instantly into the rain and the darkness.

25

*J*esus, Joseph and God Omnipotent!"

In the basement of the place the door, smashed off its lock, came flying inward in a shower of splinters. The basement was thick with smoke. Byrnes, by a table by the back wall with two Chinese, one of them wearing a long silk gown and pigtail, the other in a suit and derby hat, dropping a sheaf of papers in his hand, roared, "Jesus, Joseph and Mary—Tillman! What in the name of all the Saints—"

It was a Tartar Hell. An opium joint.

"Don't you move!" Through the smoke there was an archway leading into another room. In there, through the stink and fog there were more Chinese bending over the outlines of men on layettes. There was the smell of burning gum opium. Tillman, the gun out in both hands, aimed at Byrnes' head, ordered the man, "Don't you even *blink!*" He saw the derby-hatted Chinese in the suit reach in under his coat. Tillman, turning the gun on him then back to Byrnes, commanded him, "Don't you even think of moving!"

"Are you *insane.*" The Chinese in the suit and hat was the translator and bodyguard for the pigtailed man in silk. The man in silk's eyes were wide. He was stepping back, looking to his bodyguard. The bodyguard had his hand flat across his vest waiting for the order to reach in for his gun. The man in silk caught Byrnes' eye. The man in silk said quickly to the bodyguard, *"Mo— Mo ah—"* and the bodyguard's hand relaxed. Byrnes, recovering, drawing himself up to his full height, demanded, "What the devil do you want here?"

"I want Archer! I want you! I want you and Archer and I want Archer now!" He was a bear of a man, Byrnes, at almost six feet tall and two hundred and fifty pounds, with his moustaches and cutaway coat, someone he had only ever seen with awe when he was passing in Headquarters, someone everyone always talked about. Tillman, the gun steady and pointing, said with his breath coming in sharp gasps, "I want Archer! I

200

want *you!*" He saw the Chinese in the next room stopped in the fug of smoke. They were watching, listening. Tillman, seeing the suited Chinese take a step to one side, said to Byrnes' face, "I'll kill him on the spot if he takes another step." He ordered the man in the suit, "Do you understand? Tell your master I'll kill both of you on the spot if you move another inch!" He was holding at gunpoint the most famous detective in America, the Chief of the Detective Bureau. Tillman, his mouth gone dry, his breath coming in spurts, said with his hands starting to shake, "Which one are you, Mr. Byrnes? 'Embrasure'? 'Palisade'? 'Portcullis'? 'Bailey'? *Which one of the Custers are you?*"

"What in the name of hell are you talking about?"

"I'm talking about Hewitt and Jenkins and Rosie Seymore! I'm talking about dead people and money and jewelry and rings! I'm talking about—" His finger was shaking on the trigger. Tillman, out of control, ready to kill, shrieked at the man's face, "Which one are you? Where's *your* telephone? *Which one of them are you?*"

"I don't even know what you're talking about! I'm in here doing business on behalf of the Police! I don't know anyone called Archer or—or whatever the other names were! There's no telephone here!" He saw the silken Chinese catch the eye of the armed man in the derby hat. He shook his head once to him to stop him. "If there's anyone in here called Archer and you want him, take him!"

"He's in here! There's nowhere else he could have gone!" He could see only shapes and outlines through the fug of smoke, "He's in there! In the layette room!"

"Then take him!"

"Where's your telephone?"

"There is no telephone in here!"

"You came in with him—I saw you!"

"I came in with no one! I came in here on Police business—" Byrnes roared, *"—which I don't have to explain to you!"* Byrnes, pointing, said tightly, "This gentleman with the pigtail is Mr. Lim. The other man with the gun and nervous hand is Mr. Lee." He reached out and took Lee's wrist in a grip of steel and lowered it down from his vest. Byrnes said to Mr. Lim, nodding for Lee to translate, "This is one of my detectives." Byrnes, unafraid, looking not at the gun but at Tillman's eyes, said as a directive from the chain of command, "If there's someone in here you want then do your duty and take him." Byrnes, turning again to Lim as Lee muttered the words in Chinese, said to complete the introduction, "This is one of my detectives—one of my Spartans—one of my bulldogs who, once they bite, never release their jaws."

"What the hell are you doing in here?" The gun was hard in his hands. It pointed at Byrnes. It did not waver, *"Why are you here?"*

He jerked his finger into the fug of the layette room. Byrnes, dropping his voice, said to encourage him, "If you want a man in there, City Detective Tillman, take him."

"Who the hell are you?"

He heard him. Without taking his eyes from the sights of the gun, Tillman ordered him in the open doorway from the laneway outside, "Ned! Stay out of here!"

"Muldoon?" He heard him too. He heard the sound of a revolver hammer being cocked. Byrnes said, "Is that you, Muldoon? Is that you out there?" He saw the great shape in the open doorway. He saw the upraised gun suddenly drop to the man's side. He saw Muldoon run his tongue across his lips in fear. He saw Tillman's weapon, steady, unwavering. Byrnes, glancing at Lee and nodding hard to him to translate the words to his master, said in answer to the question, loudly, so everyone could hear, *"Who am I? Who am I?"* He looked hard at Mr. Lim, touched himself on the chest with his finger and held it there as the words in Chinese came spilling out of the derby-hatted man's mouth in simultaneous translation, "I? I am Chief Inspector Thomas Byrnes. I am the Emperor, the King, the Lord! *I am the Caesar of This City!"*

He had taken over. With no gun, no club, no weapon, he had taken over because of who he was. Byrnes, looking not at Tillman, but at the round staring face of Mr. Lim, said quietly, "I am no horse trader or chairmaker or sailing boat fitter-outer—no Commissioner appointed by his friends to milk the city for every penny that should be spent instead on the maintenance of peace and order—I am Thomas J. Byrnes, the world's greatest detective and undisputed master hunter of men." He jerked his thumb back over his shoulder— "And these are two of my men, two of my protégés, two of my Chosen: men who will demur at nothing, fear no one—two of my Spartans at the Pass—two, two only, of the force I worked body and soul, day and night, to create—two only of the great engine of order I have created so that honest men and respectable women can walk the streets in safety and harmony: two of my Forty Immortals!"

The pointing gun was of no interest to him. He had his back to it. It was as if it did not exist. Muldoon, taking a step forward and laying his hand across the barrel to lower it a fraction, said warningly, "Virgil . . ."

He turned back, but he still had his eyes on Lim, still heard the translation spilling out from Lee, *"You ask me who I am?* I am the man who, in spite of the Commissioners, in spite of the corruption and thievery—in spite of the waste of thousands of dollars each day—I am the man who, singlehandedly, makes this city a safe place to live in, to work in, to do business in—I am the man who gives this city its *nobility!*" He paused for a moment to let Lee finish muttering the words to Lim, "I am the man who created the Deadline: the line below Fourteenth Street where any miscreant may be assured he will be picked up on sight, beaten to a pulp, and then sent north to his rat hole to find another bailiwick to plunder! I am the man who solved the great Wall Street robbery! The man who created the Rogues' Gallery—a model to police forces all over the world—the man other policemen from all over the globe come to for advice! I am the man who, notwithstanding ship fitters and stable men and chairmakers appointed to be the Commissioners, the evil and base and dangerous live in constant fear of!" He turned to Tillman and Muldoon, "Who do you think *pays* for all this? Who do you think pays for the daily running of the police, for the Rogues' Gallery, for the—" He shrieked at Tillman, "Who do you think pays when there is no money left in the Police budget because the Commissioners have spent it on street-cleaning machines? Who do you think pays for administration, for upkeep, for rewards, for information, for your *wages?* Where do you think such money comes from?" He stabbed a finger at Lim, "It comes from *him* and people like *him!* It comes from citizens, honest men, merchants paying for their warriors the way the great lords of Europe paid for their armies! It comes, in dribs and drabs, from—"

"This is an opium house!"

"This is a business that, balanced against the evil of the true criminal element in this city, does no harm to anyone!"

"You collect excise dues from saloons as well!"

"Yes, I do." Byrnes said to Muldoon, "Yes, I do. Don't I, Muldoon?"

He shrugged. Muldoon, trying to be mild, said quietly, "Well, yes, sir, I have heard that—"

"You've only heard it? You haven't *personally* collected any for me?"

"Well—" Muldoon said warily, "When I was with the Strong Arm Squad, once or twice I collected for you from Billy Lawler's on Bleecker Street and Hanrahan's on—"

"You did. And was there ever any trouble at either of those establishments thereafter? Or was there always cooperation with the Police? Was there always—always—"

Muldoon said, "Well, certainly, no one ever seemed to complain, Mr. Byrnes . . ."

Tillman said, not letting go, "You collect protection money!"

"I do. I collect it for the protection of the city." He was doing it now. He was in the opium joint arranging regular payments from Mr. Lim. That was what he was doing. That was what the papers on the floor were.

Byrnes said, "Yes, I do. *And every penny of it goes to the forces of law and order!*"

"You keep at least a quarter of it for yourself!"

He was in control. He smiled. Byrnes said to Mr. Lim, "Actually, half." Byrnes said quietly to Lim as Lee translated, "I will not weary you with the Byzantine details of the administration and ethos of this City, Mr. Lim, but suffice to say I was not born to a chairmaking fortune nor a readymade stable of fine horses, nor even Father's fine braided uniform hanging in a cupboard; I was born a poor man in Ireland, trained as a gas fitter and what I became I earned." He had read up on the Chinese before the meeting. "Far better to deal with a man whose corruption is human than a god whose face is ever built of cold marble. Far wiser to employ the servant in your kitchen whose service is good, but has an appetite of his own than the ascetic who eats not and believes you should also be an ascetic and not eat either."

Tillman said, not letting go, "You and Archer—you came in here together!"

"I know no such man. If he entered here he did so before me and I am acquainted with him not at all."

"T.G. Hewitt and Patrolman Billy Jenkins are dead! And a simpleton girl driven out of her mind with fear and a stage driver on Broadway who—"

He raised his finger. Byrnes said quietly, "Tell me nothing."

"People are dead!"

"No." He was the emperor, the Caesar of the City. He was a huge man with hands like paws, eyes that looked straight through men's lies and into their souls. He was the Hawkshaw of the Force. Byrnes, his voice a whisper, moving past the barrel of the gun as if it did not exist and laying his hand gently on Tillman's shoulder, said shaking his head, "No, tell me nothing at all."

He had his arm around Tillman's shoulder, turning him, showing him to the two Chinese, "This is one of your men—one of your Army, one of your Immortals." He held Lim's eyes as Lee translated in a mutter, "He says to me that innocently you are harboring in this establishment a man he wants for some terrible crime and I tell him: take the man. I tell him that you, as the owner and proprietor, tell him to take the man too." Byrnes said softly, "I tell him that because I know you. I know where your heart is—I know that because over the years, the many years, you have aided the Police in the detection of people like that man; for I have proof in the contributions you have made from your labor, from the sweat of your brow, that you wish only the streets to be safe for you and your family and your race to walk in without fear." Byrnes said, "Fear not. Look! Here before you is one of the men who keep you safe!" He turned the little man slightly to show him full-on to the two Chinese. "Look at him! Nothing will slow nor halt him for he is a Spartan, a Roman, an Immortal!" He swept his hand in the direction of the layette room. Byrnes said open-heartedly on behalf of the Chinese, "Archer? You seek a man called Archer? *Take him!*" Byrnes said, squeezing at Tillman's shoulder, "Body and soul. I chose men like you. Body and soul! Heart and mind! My detectives! My people! My creations! My *immortality!*"

Byrnes said quietly, "The telegraph room at Headquarters is badly in need of refitting after the Commissioners' latest little attempt at administrative innovation, and Mr. Lim here has kindly agreed to assist in its rebuilding."

He dropped his voice. He was the greatest man of his age. He was Caesar building Rome from marble. It was rumored he had eyes that looked into men's souls.

His voice low, glancing at Lim as, nodding, the man made a little bow to signal the deal was done, Byrnes said softly, intimately, into Tillman's ear, "Fear no man. Tell me nothing. Take Archer."

He knew of Archer and the Custers not at all.

Byrnes said with his hand pressing at Tillman's shoulder, shaking with strength, "Get me a victory. Get me, get us all, as the legion of Rome, honors."

He glanced over at them to make sure the two Chinese could not hear him.

Byrnes, looming over Tillman, his voice shaking with emotion, said as an order, "Fear no one. Stop at nothing. For me. For me—*Be a success!*"

26

He had him. He had him free and clear. He had one of the Custers. He had Archer. He had him with Caesar's blessing. In the vacant lot behind Lim's Tillman shrieked at him, shaking his head, *"You hog vomit, everybody connected with you is either dead or in hiding!"*

He had Archer in what looked like an old rotting glasshouse or bird aviary that ran the entire length of the two-hundred-and-fifty-foot lot. Outside the cracked glass and decayed wooden frames of the place it was still raining, the moon behind dark clouds, the only illumination the light from an oil lamp from Lim's Muldoon held up above his head.

In the lamplight, it was not disdain or contempt or superiority in Archer's eyes, it was opium.

Everywhere in the deserted lot there were shadows and shapes of ruined buildings, broken fences. It was used as a garbage dump. It smelled of decay and rot.

He had an axe handle from the pile of broken tools and sacks at the door to the glasshouse. Tillman, advancing toward the man with the light behind him, the axe handle held in both hands, said still shaking his head, "You bloodless bag of guts and giblets inside your brass-buttoned suit—you decayed, degenerate roach shit—you're one of them—one of the Custers— you, Jenkins Oubliette, Hewitt Palisade, Embrasure, Donjon, Portcullis, Bailey: you're one of the stinking crew meeting below ground like maggots under Broadway *to do what?"* The man was staggering, reeling, out of focus, touching at his eyeglasses. They had gotten to him after only half a pipe, but his head and lungs were full of the opium smoke. Tillman, halting, standing solidly on the soft, wet earth inside the place, getting his footing right, raising the axe handle to waist height, said with his eyes blazing, *"Who are they? Who are the Custers? What do they do?"* He saw the man's face. He saw the eyes blink. He saw strength start to come back into them. Tillman, swinging the handle out and to one side like a baseballist and exploding glass from the panels all around him and

206

showering Archer with splinters, screamed at him above the sound of the rain suddenly beating in, "You degenerate, scum-licking reprobate abattoir offal, *who are the Custers?*" He had the axe handle back and to one side of his shoulder like a cavalryman ready to slash. Tillman, swinging the four-foot-long length of hickory to the ceiling and raking it across glass and wood and bringing down a shower of spinning, glittering glass like daggers, shrieked, taking another step forward, "You rabid dog! You poison viper secreting yourself below ground—*who are the Custers? What are their names?*"

He was in a nightmare. He put his hand up to push it away.

"Which one of them are you? 'Archer'—is that you? Is that what they call you in their clever little play on words?" He had the axe handle up in front of him, held in both hands, his fists shaking with strength, "Hewitt was Palisade, Jenkins Oubliette, but you—'Archer'—is all they called you down there, isn't it?" Tillman shrieked, "Well, 'Archer,' Jenkins is dead and so is Hewitt! And so is a black man who drove a stage and sang songs and—" He raised the axe handle. He took a step forward. Tillman, his body shaking, his mouth twisted in hate, said tightly, "And now, so are you." Tillman, smashing at the glass above Archer's head and cascading it down on him in an explosion of glass and wooden splinters, getting in front of him as he tried to weave to get past, shrieked, "Embrasure, Donjon, Portcullis, Bailey—who are they? *What are their names?* Where did the money and the wedding rings come from?" He saw the man slip on the wet earth and as he reached out to catch hold of a support disintegrated it in a falling wall of spinning, glittering daggers and powder around him. Raising the axe handle for the death blow as Muldoon behind him said in sudden warning horror, *"Virgil—!"* Tillman, his breath coming in short spurts shrieked, "Tell me! Tell me now! *Who are the Custers?*"

He reached out but there was nothing to hold on to. In front of him there was a madman shrieking at him. There was rain and darkness, wet earth, glass everywhere. He was in some sort of glasshouse with no exit. There was a light behind the madman, the demon, but he could not clear his head to understand who he was. He was reeling, unable to set his feet firmly on the ground. He was in a nightmare. He was in an unstoppable opium nightmare and he— Archer, going back, slipping, almost falling, his mind a swarm of bees, fighting the axe handle off, afraid to touch it, trying to form words, shouted, "Who are you—?"

"I'm Death! I'm Punishment! I'm the worst thing you ever imagined in your childhood terrors! I'm the thing you wake up terrified to find in the darkness of your private room!" He had the axe handle up high. Raking it, he brought down panes of glass all around the man's head like scythes. Tillman, taking a step forward as Archer put up his arms to protect his face, screamed, "Either you're a fiend or a weakling, but in either event you won't leave this place alive!" The man was trying to rise, get to his feet and he bludgeoned at the glass to his left and exploded it around his shoulders. Tillman roared above the sound of the rain and the falling glass, "Rosie—Rosie Seymore—*are you the one who ordered her killed?*"

"I don't know anyone called Rosie Seymore!"

"Rosie Seymore is the simpleton girl you ordered murdered like a dog!" He smashed at the glass by the man's head and sent it cascading, "Rosie Seymore is the person whose lungs exploded in a bath and who was held down by someone who would not let go! Rosie Seymore is—" The man was on his knees, scrabbling away. Tillman, walking after him and raking at the roof and bringing down panes one by one after him, shrieked, "Rosie Seymore is the simpleton girl Hewitt used and you had Jenkins *murder!*" Tillman, getting ahead of the man and holding the axe handle in two hands, smashing at the roof of the glasshouse and smashing pane after pane of it with reports like gunshots, roared, *"Rosie Seymore is the simpleton girl who lived in the basement room in Crib Alley who Jenkins went back to burn to ashes along with me and my partner and anyone who got in his way!"*

"Jenkins is dead!" He was coming out of it, his heart pumping blood through his body like a trip-hammer, clearing his head. He knew where he was. He was in some sort of glasshouse in the lot behind Lim's opium house. He was— Archer, getting to his feet, wavering, drawing himself up, yelled in protest to make it clear, "I'm Silas Archer. I'm the Collector of Returns and Records at Castle Garden at the Battery! I'm an important person, a government official! I'm—"

"You're *nobody!* You're *nothing!*" Tillman, smashing at the glass everywhere around the man, making him cover his head in terror, shrieked, "You're less than nobody! You're something underground and vile and hideous and not fit for the light of day! What you are is a robber of dreams! What you are is—" He twisted the axe handle up in his hands and smashed at a line of panes by the man's head and shoulders and pulverized them to powder, "What you are is the power of uniforms and braid and caps with badges on them! What you are is—" Tillman, lifting the axe handle ready for the final blow, said with his voice tight and cold, "Who put the telephones in under Hewitt's store? Was that you? Was that what you did for the Custers? Was that *your job?*"

"The telephones were already there!" He saw the axe come up. "Jenkins! *Jenkins put them in!*"

He shook his head. It was a lie. Tillman said, "No." Tillman, taking a step forward, shaking his head, said calmly, "Now you're going to die."

"Jenkins put them in! I don't know who put them in! They were already there!"

"Who melts down the gold rings?"

"Hewitt! Hewitt has a casting pot in his shop's repair department and he—"

"Where do the rings *come from?* Oubliette! Embrasure! Donjon! Palisade! Portcullis! Bailey—Archer! Where do the rings and the money and the jewelry *come from?*"

"I've got nothing to do with it! I'm an important Government Official! All I do is—"

"All you do is *collect* them! All you do is—"

"All I do is keep records! All I do is send in returns and statistics to the State Bureau in Albany!" Archer, blood from the falling glass running down his neck and onto his collar, said desperately to explain it all, cowering, "All I do is check off numbers! *All I do is sign forms and check off numbers!*"

"No, it isn't." His voice had gone quiet, calm. He shook his head. Tillman said, looking down at him, "No. Maybe that's what Hewitt thought you did or even thought he did— Maybe that was what he told Rosie Seymore he did when he was showing her all the money he'd made to show her what a successful man he was without his father—maybe that's even what all the other Custers thought they did—but it isn't what Billy Jenkins thought he did. But it isn't what Billy Jenkins did, is it? *What Billy Jenkins did was kill people!* And Billy Jenkins, once he knew that Hewitt had told somebody about what was being done—once he knew Hewitt had told Rosie Seymore what he thought was being done—Billy Jenkins went out to kill her!" He was shaking with anger. He was so close. "—And what Billy Jenkins *then* told Hewitt what the Custers did—not sign forms or check off numbers!—what he then told Hewitt the Custers *really did* was enough to send Hewitt out of his mind and insane with horror!"

"I just fill in *forms—!*"

"No."

"It's my *job!*" He thought for a moment he could get past. He saw the lantern. He saw the huge figure behind the man with the axe handle holding it. He was trapped. He touched at his eyeglasses, but his fingers were all bleeding, *"All I do is fill in forms and count up numbers!"*

"Who are the other Custers? What are their names?"

"I don't know!" Archer, searching for a way out and finding none, his hands covered in his own blood, said with no hope at all, "I'm Silas Archer! I'm an important government official! I'm *bleeding!*"

"What do they *do?*" Tillman, his voice cold with contempt, looking down at the man, raising the axe handle for the death blow, shaking his head said sadly, "You're a liar. You're a liar and a weakling and a degenerate and, for all I know—"

"Billy Jenkins and Tom Hewitt—"

"Billy Jenkins and Tom Hewitt are dead!" Tillman said, "So is a black man of no account who sang songs and knew all the history of Broadway, and so is a girl called Lily who fell from a roof in a drunken stupor!" Tillman said, ice-cold, "And so are you." He raised the axe handle, getting close. There was blood on his knuckles and wrists from the glass. Tillman said in a whisper. "The money, the rings, the jewelry—*it came from the immigrants, didn't it!*"

"*All I do is fill in forms!*"

"Who is Embrasure?"

"*I don't know!*"

"Donjon?"

"*I don't know!*"

"Oubliette?"

"*Jenkins! That was Billy Jenkins!*"

"Bailey?"

"I don't—"

"Palisade?"

"*Hewitt! That was Hewitt! That was Tom Hewitt!*"

"Portcullis?"

"*I don't know!*"

Tillman said, " '*Archer*'!"

"Me! That was me!" He was on his knees. He was weeping, cowering, the rain through the smashed and shattered glass on the roof falling down on his face. Archer said, "*Me! That was me!*"

"The Custers—how long have they been in existence?"

He was in a nightmare. He was on his knees in shards of glass, his uniform and vest and neck and face covered with it. He needed opium. He needed it to get through the nights. He saw the axe handle in Tillman's hands. He saw it come up. He was Silas Archer, Collector, Returns and Records Section. He was PRIVATE. DO NOT ENTER. He was— Archer said with his eyes jammed shut and his voice like that of a man with his throat dust-parched for water, "*Five years! Five years at least!*"

"Who are they? What are their names? What do they *do?*"

"I don't know!" He was sobbing. He was no longer as he had been every night for five years, afraid. He had gone past it. In that terrible place in the rain, no longer afraid of the death blow, but simply because he had no one else to tell and no more opium, Archer said as the truth, the awful truth, "I don't know! I don't know what they do! I don't know anything!" His uniform was covered in glass and rain and earth from the floor. He touched at the brass buttons with his thumb and forefinger, but in the light they did not shine at all. *"I don't know!"* Archer, at the end, his days and nights without the smoke and the forgetfulness stretching away into awful eternity, said in final, last desperation, *"I don't know—"*

Archer, on his knees, promising it, laying his soul on it, horrified by it, said in a scream, "The others—Embrasure, Donjon, Portcullis, Bailey—the others—the Custers—"

Archer said, "I swear to God! I swear to God! Apart from Hewitt, Jenkins and—and me—*I don't even know who they are!*"

Tillman said, *"Liar!"* He reached out with the axe handle like a sword and laid its point in the center of the man's chest. His hands were shaking with strength. Tillman said, *"Liar!"*

"All I am is a functionary, a little man! All I am is—"

Tillman, drawing the handle back an inch, holding it in both hands, his knuckles white in the light from Muldoon's lantern said with his voice a whisper, "You're a liar!" He touched at a pane of glass with the weapon, then brought it back to within an inch of the man's face, "The grave or the madhouse. Five minutes of this about the head—applied systematically and without mercy—and it's either the grave or the madhouse." Tillman said, "Five minutes of this and the hearing goes first, then the eyes, then the brain, then—"

Muldoon said in horror, *"Virgil—!"*

"This isn't the truth! This is a goddamned defense plea!" Tillman, half turning, the axe still aimed at Archer, shrieked above the sound of the rain, "He knows who we are! He knows we're cops! He knows who we are and this isn't the truth, this is a defense plea for the goddamned Courts! This isn't the truth! This is—"

"It is the truth! All I do is fill in forms and count up numbers! It's the truth! That's all I ever did! That's all I do now!"

Tillman said, ". . . just hope that the first blow shatters your eyeglasses and sends a shard of glass into your brain that kills you instantly . . ." He raised the weapon.

"I did nothing! I hurt no one! *All I ever did was invent the names of fictitious people who'd been stopped on the immigrant ships for infectious diseases and refused entry to the country by Quarantine!*" He wanted to take his glasses off, but he was afraid to touch them. Archer, his hands bleeding as he brought them up, shouted, broken, finished, *"All I did was falsify returns so it looked like people who didn't exist had to be sent back on the ships!"*

"Liar! You goddamned *liar!*"

"It's the *truth!* I split the deportation allocations with the captains! I had six ships with captains I knew and I falsified deportation forms that nobody read anyway and I collected the deportation fares from the State Government in Albany and paid it to the captains for passengers who didn't exist—for space they'd already sold to someone else—and I had an arrangement with them to split the money fifty-fifty!" Archer, trying to explain, said to show the pure simplicity of it, the temptation beyond resisting, "It hurt no one because nobody reads any of the forms except me! I'm fifty-six years old and I've spent my entire life filling out forms and counting up numbers and sending in returns that nobody reads anyway!" Archer said after a lifetime of futility, "It was government money! It was money from the government. They were going to waste the money anyway! They waste it all the time. If they reach the end of the financial year and the money allocated for deportation passages hasn't been used up they sit down and work out what to spend it on just to prove to the auditors that they've spent it so they can get the same allocation next year! So I helped keep the Bureau of Immigration in funds! All I did was send in forms so they could use up the money they had to use up anyway!" Archer, taking the initiative, one servant of the people to another, fellow members of an arcane brotherhood, demanded, "Doesn't it happen to you in the Police? Doesn't money have to be spent on one thing or it will be spent on another? Don't you have to invent your own importance? *Don't you have to fill in forms in order to show that you need to have the money to be able to purchase more forms to fill in?*" He had gone loose, slack. Archer said sadly, "I hurt no one! All I did was split the return passage money for people who didn't exist so they could be sent back to countries they never came from!" Archer said to dare him, "Hit me! Kill me for that! All the Custers did was tell me to keep on doing what I'd been doing already! All they asked me to do was to keep filling in forms. I fill in forms! That's what I am—a form filler! I don't know who they are because they never needed to tell me who they were!"

"And you all meet together regularly in Beach's railroad under Hewitt's store—"

"I only ever met with Hewitt and Jenkins. Hewitt was Palisade. Jenkins was Oubliette. I was Archer. I only ever met with them!"

"And you filled in forms and split passage money with the same six captains—"

"Yes!"

"And you made money from it—Government money?"

"Yes!"

"The rings and the jewelry aren't from the Government! They're from real people!"

"It was from the Custers. It was for—"

"Where did it come from? Who gave it to you?"

"It was just left in there! It was left in the cupboard in there for us and we sat at the table and divided it!" Archer said before he could ask, "They recruited me by telephone. They knew what I was doing and they contacted me by telephone and, for just doing more of what I'd already been doing they offered me what I wanted—more money, and they told me by telephone when to go to Hewitt's to collect it and when to fill in the forms and—"

"What forms?"

"The same forms I'd always been filling in: forms for deportations by reason of determination of infectious disease and—"

"The people you were sending back were fictitious! The money, the rings, the jewelry are real!"

"They sent back real people who were undesirable!"

"And robbed them!"

"They were going to die anyway!" Archer, gaining confidence, dropping his voice, said intimately, as a little-known fact, "Have you any idea how many people deemed at the end of a long passage to America to have infectious diseases make it back to their own countries alive? *None!* None at all! Less than none because, at sea, what the captain of each ship does, in order that his ship isn't stopped at every port he makes on the way back, is drop the dead over the side at night the instant they expire and take their names off the ship's manifest!" Archer said, "It was an opportunity that hurt no one! The people the Custers sent back were already as good as dead, and everything they had would have been stolen by the ship's crew or the other deportees anyway! All I ever did—all I and Hewitt and Jenkins and whoever else the Custers are ever did is take money and goods and jewelry that would have been stolen anyway!" Archer said man to man, "And you know what sailors are like—*they would have just wasted it all on women and drink!*"

Archer, man to man, acolyte to acolyte in the terrible mysteries of the arcane rituals of bureaucracy, of service to the public, of a lifetime of thanklessness and filling in forms, said moving toward them with his hands out to show the simple sense of it all, the opportunity beyond refusing. "You. You two in the Police: with your hands on your hearts, tell me that you have never taken, never once— Tell me—and swear it—that you have never—never once—solicited a bribe—*or taken money from a dead man who no longer needed it!*"

27

Tillman said softly, chanting it, "I met a man who wasn't there. He wasn't there again today . . ."

Tillman said, raising the club, ". . . Liar!"

He brought the axe handle down hard and, chopping at his side with it, swept the advancing man to the ground into the mud and glass as if he had been poleaxed.

Tillman, standing over him, his face twisted in hate, waiting for him to get up so he could knock him down again, shrieked, "Liar! *Liar!*"

In the rain and the darkness there were shadows and shapes out in the vacant lot: broken fences going nowhere and what looked like broken stone and wooden buildings with no roofs. They were everywhere, unused, derelict, sinking under the piles of garbage and clumps of vegetation and hard grass. The light in Muldoon's hand was a yellow glow inside the glasshouse that penetrated the outer darkness not at all.

Tillman, raking at the glass and frames above Archer's head and exploding it into shrapnel screamed at him, "Liar! *Liar!* What happens? Does Quarantine board the vessel, choose the people who seem to have infectious diseases at top speed—*making sure at the same time they don't have any relatives who care about them*—line them up on deck, rob them blind, fill in all the forms and then—and then *what?* As the rest of the passengers are discharged into the waiting lighters and steamboats for the trip to the Battery, *chain them down and order the captain to get up steam, put the goddamned ship into reverse and sail back to whichever port he came from?*" Tillman said, "Ships don't just turn around! Ships have to be recoaled, crews have to be found, cargos have to be unloaded, galleys have to be revictualled—even the goddamned latrines have to be pumped out!" The man was getting to his feet, He raised the axe handle against him.

Muldoon said in alarm, "Virgil—!"

"No." He held the handle ready. Tillman, watching the man, targeting him, waiting to get the blow in, said shaking his head, "No. He's a bureaucrat, a form filler. There are lots of ways to fill in forms. There are spaces between the lines, gaps, ways of phrasing." Tillman ordered the man, *"Get up!* No, that isn't what happened at all! That isn't why Jenkins tried to kill Rotary Rosie Seymore in a goddamned bathtub! That isn't why Hewitt went mad and thought he was already dead! That isn't why—"

He was desperate. He could not think straight. Archer, afraid to get up, afraid to stay down, yelled to explain it all, "It happened on the quarantine island—on Swinburne! It all took place on Swinburne Island after the Quarantine boats had landed them!"

"And what? The plague carriers were taken off again once a ship was available? How? Half dead? In stretchers? Seething with disease, with plague, with diphtheria—with God knows what?" Tillman said tightly, ready to strike, "And what ship was that? What ship took them off? A ship with other passengers? What ship was that? What exact little bit of water did that sail on—*the River Styx?* How did that come into its port in Europe even assuming the plague carriers had died and been thrown overboard— with all the crew and other passengers and even the rats in the hold running with pestilence?" Tillman said, "Try again. Find another form." Tillman said in a rasp, "Choose a form that has real, living people in it, not one where numbers and statistics exist in a comfortable vacuum—*pick a form with real people in it!*" Tillman, raising the axe handle, aiming for the head, said as a death sentence, *"Get up!"*

"All I know is—"

Tillman said with disgust, "You weakling. You lying, cowardly, decayed, degenerate weakling . . ."

"I take orders! I don't know what's happening! All I do is take orders!"

"From who?"

"From—" Archer said, "From—" Archer said, *"All I do is take orders!"* Archer, scrabbling, looking up, watching the butt end of the club, and, trying to look away, not succeeding, said weeping, "I did nothing to hurt anyone in the beginning! All I did was invent people who didn't exist and pocket the money! We meet three at a time in the place under Hewitt's! I don't know anyone else! All I did for years was—" His hands were bleeding. He looked at them in horror, "All I did—" Archer said suddenly, "Suddenly, one day, the voice was there on the telephone and it knew everything about me! Suddenly, one day—" Archer said, "All I ever heard—all Hewitt or Jenkins ever heard—*is a voice on the telephone!"*

Tillman said, *"Lies!"*

"It's the truth! It knows! It listens! It knew all about Hewitt and how his business was failing: it listened; it listened when he talked on his telephone! It knew all about me and it knew the names of all the captains I'd conspired with and talked to on telephones at all the shipping offices and it knew— It probably knew all about Jenkins and whatever he had to hide too!"

"It listened in on your phone calls from your telephone in your office in Castle Garden?"

"Yes!"

"And on Hewitt's telephone in his rooms above the store?"

"Yes!"

"And on Jenkins' telephone?"

Archer said, "Yes!"

Tillman yelled down at him, *"Jenkins didn't have a goddamned telephone until all this started!"*

"He was the police telephone man at the Fifth Precinct; he was posted to the 'Owl' night duty on the police telephone after he had an accident in the Steamboat Squad that put him on light duties for almost eighteen months! The voice listened in!" Archer said, "It's everywhere, like a spider on a web, listening! And he knows! He knows everything! He knew everything about me, about Hewitt, about—about Jenkins, and he—" Archer said, getting up, menacing them, *"And he probably knows all about this!"*

Muldoon said in a whisper, "My God, Virgil, Byrnes is probably talking to one of his cronies on the telephone back at Headquarters now—about us! About—"

"Who is he?"

"I don't know who he is! He's the Custers!" Archer said to the lamplight, to Muldoon, "He's like God. He listens. He's like God. *He knows everything!*" Archer said, "The truth? The truth is that—" He was on his feet, staggering, gathering himself, looking for a way out past the lantern and the shadow of the brute holding it. Archer said, on the offensive, touching at his brass buttons and twisting them hard between his fingers, "The truth? The truth is that all anyone is doing—anyone—is choosing a few undesirables—not people with diseases, but *undesirables*— from the ships who would have been turned back anyway, and informing them clearly that if they want to stay here, if they want to come in and lord it over true-born Americans with their money and their plans for stores that put good, honest people like Hewitt out of business with their sweatshops and armies of cheap labor, then they had better—"

He stopped. He smiled. He put his open hands out in front of him and took a step forward. Archer said, holding it in his hands to offer it to them as a gift, "All we're doing is telling them that it's well within our power to deport them with a phony disease back to the pest-holes they came from and if they want to stay in America—if they want to start a new life—then, by God, they'll start the way everyone else did in this country—*with nothing!*"

Archer said as if it was the most obvious thing in the world, "This is America, where all men are equal before God. All we're doing is cutting out the rich wolves from the pack—wolves who plan to exploit even their own countrymen in sweatshops and child-labor factories and sinkholes of depravity and sin—and landing them, like everyone else on the ships they come on, with nothing."

Archer said, dropping his voice, his hands out as if to receive their congratulations, moving toward them, "All we do is cut out the scum, the lowlifes, the exploiters with their gold and jewelry and money, tell them they're on the list to go back with trachoma or diphtheria or the fever, and—"

Tillman said, "And make them pay everything they have to stay."

"Yes." Archer, smiling at the thought of it, said, "Yes. Yes!" Another two feet and he would be past Tillman and the brute and out into the rain and air and freedom.

Archer said, grinning, "Yes! *Exactly!*" Archer, grinning, nodding, taking off his glasses for a moment and almost winking at Tillman man to man, said in triumph, the master of morality, "We do the country a favor! That scum with their gold and their jewels and their money waiting to give the country nothing, but only to pillage it, rape it, use it, exploit it to make themselves fat and oily—by God, after they've come up against *us* at their first landfall in the New World, after we've taken everything they've got—by God, those evil, foreign bastards . . . Those evil foreign bastards . . . By God, they start off life here—in America . . . By God, they start off life here as goddamned *peasants!*"

"And you've been doing this since the beginning—for five years—since you were contacted by a voice on the telephone, since you became one of the Custers?"

Archer said grinning, moving forward, "Yes."

"—*Liar!*" He clubbed him with all his force against the side of the head and smashed him into a glassed-in wall in a shower of exploding panes and wood. Tillman said, grasping the man by the scruff of the neck and dragging him up to his feet, "Liar! That isn't what Hewitt thought was happening—not at the end! That isn't what he found out was happening—not at the end! That may have been what he thought was happening at the beginning, or the voice told him was happening, or he wanted to believe was happening, but that isn't what drove him out of his mind and made him dress himself up in a shroud to wait for the undertakers!" Tillman, shoving the man backward and raising the axe handle for the head, shouted at him above the sound of the rain, "At the end he knew what was happening because he'd made the mistake of involving himself with a whore like Rosie Seymore, and Jenkins, after he'd gone out and killed her, in order to still his protests, to bring him out of dreamland and into reality—told him what was really happening, what the Custers he was part of really did and, in his horror, sometime over the five days on the edge of madness he teetered on after what he thought was Rosie's murder, from his telephone in his room, he called *you!*"

"No!"

"Yes! It was you on Hewitt's telephone the day he died. It was you letting it ring and ring! He'd told you on the telephone he was dead and he was waiting for the undertakers, expected them momentarily—he even may have told you the streets were crowded and he was going to clear the way for the hearse with a goddamned *buffalo rifle*—and it was you at the other end of the telephone trying to stop him!" Tillman said quietly, evenly, "I find it extremely irritating you think me so stupid as to believe the first or even second story you make up." He pushed the man back scientifically into position and hit him across the head with the side of the handle so hard it made his hair fly up and drew blood from his ears. Tillman said in a voice taut with anger, "Am I supposed to believe that after five years—after *five years*—not one of the people you supposedly landed on these shores with nothing hasn't become even vaguely successful—because if they had money on the ships they must have been at least vaguely successful in their own countries—am I supposed to believe that not one of them has ever come back full of hatred and revenge in order to kill one of the people who robbed him of everything? Am I supposed to believe that? Am I supposed to believe that not one of the God knows how many people who you did this to, didn't even come back to get you for the theft of their wife's *wedding ring?* Am I supposed to believe they were all civilized men and happy to accept robbery and ruin as part and parcel of the New World and that not one of them—*not one of them*—came back looking for justice?"

"That was what Jenkins was for! Jenkins was the strongarm man!"

"Jenkins was a killer! Jenkins was Oubliette! Jenkins was the hole simpleton girls and fools like Hewitt were thrown into! Jenkins was—"

Muldoon said, "Jenkins couldn't have done anything. Nobody announces in advance they're going to get even, especially not foreigners. What they would have done is—"

Tillman said simply, "What they would have done is shot someone like you—their bitterest enemy—from a distance. They would have worked for the years it took to put their lives back together, to feed their families, to deepen their grief and their humiliation and their sense of outrage and then—"

Archer said in desperation, "I don't know what Hewitt thought was really happening!"

Tillman said softly, "Your victims: they would have worked and planned and festered until they were in a position of power and safety, and then, one night, one night in the rain—"

He thought, for an instant, the man was one of them. Archer, seeing the axe handle come up, tensing for the blow, said alone, with no help for it, no longer the power but the powerless, "The voice on the telephone is everywhere! It hears everything! It knows—it can read minds! It knows what you're going to do before you do it! It hears! It hears every pulsebeat in the city! It—" Archer said, "I don't know who he is! I don't know who the other Custers are! I don't even know why he calls them that! I don't even know—" Archer said, "All I do is fill in forms and count numbers! All I do is what I'm told! He tells me numbers and I make up names and I— For five years I simply went there under the store and with Hewitt and Jenkins I collected my money!" Archer said, "So much of it—" Archer said, "So much of it!"

"What did Jenkins tell Hewitt the Custers really did?"

Archer said softly, "So much money . . . !" Archer said suddenly, "I never thought I'd see so much money. I always thought if I ever—" He was sobbing, but no tears came. He was empty, spent, played out. Archer said, "I always thought that if I ever had so much money, I—" He looked up. He saw the figure standing over him with the axe handle. Archer, shaking his head, starting to laugh and cry at the same time, said, "All I use it for now is for the opium to make me forget I ever coveted money in the first place!" All his life had been nothing but a hollow joke. Archer said, shouting, protesting, searching for something, anything, to raise him above the level of a mere loyal dog, "I knew what they were doing from the start! I've been an officer for over twenty years! I knew they weren't just robbing people and sending them back! I knew they weren't making the immigrants pay to stay here because—" Archer said, ever the bureaucrat, "Because, as you say, they'll come back and there's paperwork to be discovered and—" Archer said intimately, "You see, you have to make sure that the file is closed. Even if you make up names for the files you still have to make sure the file is closed. You have to be certain that when you stamp it CLOSED it really is because—" Archer said, "Hewitt was stupid! His father knew he was stupid and he *was* stupid! He was stupid enough to believe anything anyone told him and all he did with all the money was put it back into a failing store in order to prove to himself—to his dead father—that he was a man! He was so stupid he even had to tell some whore about it to prove what a better man he was than his dead father! He had to—" Archer said, lost, gone, on the edge, "He told Jenkins about the whore and what he had told her so Jenkins told him where the money was really coming from, how it was being made—and it sent him mad! He told him why the whore had to go! He told him not the lie, the stupidity, but the truth about what the Custers did!"

He was so close to it he could barely form the words. Tillman said in a whisper, "What? What did he tell him the Custers did?"

"He told him the truth. He told him the truth I'd already worked out for myself years ago. He told him—" He looked up, the eyes gone, blood running from his ears and the hands he held up toward them in simple, open, honest explanation. Archer said, sobbing, "At first, because I never had it, *all I wanted was just once the feel of money!* All I want now is the opium! All I want now—" He raised his finger and pointed it trembling into the little man's face, into the darkness, into the rain beating down on the blackness of the lots behind him. "We're all dead anyway! We're all finished, dead, pointless anyway—all our plans and dreams and hopes and lives, sooner or later, are all for nothing anyway!" Archer, wiping at the blood running down his face, said sadly, "What do the Custers do?" He shrugged. "I've already told you." Archer said, "Diphtheria, trachoma, consumption, syphilis—" Archer said softly, sadly, "So simple, so simple . . . so easy, so uncomplicated—"

Archer said desperately, trying to make them comprehend, "Don't you see? The Custers, me, Hewitt, Jenkins—the rest of us—we're taking money to let them in." The thought had driven Hewitt mad. It had driven Archer to opium.

Archer said, pulling his hands away from his face, his eyes wide in horror and realization, "Don't you see? Don't you *see?* They're all infected and dying with the diseases they brought with them from Europe! We're letting them in for money!"

Archer, his head ready to explode, shrieked at them, banging his fists on the ground and tearing them into bloody stumps in the broken glass he could no longer feel, "It's only a matter of time—it could be happening now—until the entire city, all of us, until the entire city is gripped by contagion!"

Archer said, "Swinburne Island, the Quarantine Station in the harbor, it must be done there. One of the Custers must be there." His voice was dull, lifeless, merely reciting, "I'm contacted by telephone and given a number. That number is the number of people I'm supposed to say were deported. I can make up the names."

"When was the last time you were contacted?"

"This evening." Archer said, "The ones they choose are left on the ships all night to think about their options." He shrugged, "I guess, in the morning, on Swinburne, they pay." Archer said, "Thirteen. I have to think up thirteen names by tomorrow—"

He fell silent.

He drew a breath like a dying man.

Archer said in a whisper, "Thirteen."

Archer said softly, like a child, "I can make up the names. I only need the numbers."

He touched at his brass buttons. Archer, grasping the buttons on his uniform, pressing at his chest with his bloody hands as if inside there something had broken and he had to hold it together hard, said pleading, sobbing, "For Jesus' sake— In the name of mercy—please, *please*, let me get back to my *opium! Please!*

"Please . . ." On the soft earth, Archer blubbering, weeping, shrieked, "Don't you see? Don't you see? How long before they accidentally or on purpose let someone into the city with *Plague?*"

"Take him back! Take him back to Lim's! Take him back and tell Lim to fill him with enough opium to keep him asleep for a week!" As if it had once been something important, as if, once, somehow, it had meant something to him, hacking and chopping, clubbing, unable to stop, he swung and bludgeoned at the glass as if it was not inanimate, but something living, something that would not die. Tillman, showering himself in glass, shrieked at Muldoon in the lamplight, "Take him back now!"

"We don't know who they are on Swinburne! We don't know who any of them are—" Muldoon said in horror, "But, by God, Virgil, *they know about us!*"

"*Now!*" Tillman, unable to stop, swinging the club to destroy every vestige, every trace of the place, everything it had ever been, ordered Muldoon in a shriek, "Get this man away from me before I kill him!" He could not bear to look at the cringing man and he destroyed the glass and wood as if it was bone and flesh and living tissue.

"Now! *Now!*"

Hacking, smashing, in the rain and glass and splinters, Tillman, out of control, unable to stop, shrieked at Muldoon as an order, "Get him back to Lim's! Get him back to his goddamned opium! Get him back! Get him away! For the love of God, *now!* Get him away from this place *now—!*"

28

I hate this!" The rain had eased slightly, but as he stood outside the ruined glasshouse in the darkness it was still heavy enough to be running down his face in streams. He had dropped the axe handle. It lay in the mud at his feet. Tillman, his face being lit up by the yellow glow of the lantern as Muldoon, coming back from Lim's, reached him, said not looking at the man, "God, how I hate this!"

Down at his sides, Tillman's hands were still bleeding from the glass. Muldoon touching him on the shoulder to encourage him, said gently, coaxingly, "Come on. You're soaking wet. You'll have to go home and change your clothes." He sniffed at his own shoulder. He smelled like a wet dog. Muldoon said, "And me too."

He would not be encouraged. He did not move. The rain ran down his face. Tillman, a tiny figure in the blackness, said with sudden vehemence, "God, how I hate people like him and what they do and what they make other people do! God, how I hate—"

"You had to hit him. What else could you have done?" Muldoon, thinking that as wallopings went it had not been much of one, said to console him, "He isn't hurt. You just bruised him up a little. He's back in there now, full of smoke and smiling." Muldoon said to cheer him up, "By God, some of the thrashings old Inspector Williams used to hand out before they transferred him to the Tenderloin—by God, those were things to see! That man just didn't know the meaning of fatigue. He had an arm on him like a lumberjack. I remember once when he had one of Harry Hill's saloonkeepers who wouldn't pay his excise fee in his whacking chair—"

"I hate what they're doing—whatever it is they are doing—if any of it I beat out of Archer is even true! I hate the way they envelop people in it! I hate the way they've enveloped me in it!"

"You're still free to—"

"I'm not free to do anything!" Tillman said suddenly, "I could be one of them—one of their victims! I have no idea who my parents were! I have no

222

idea why they left me! I have no idea what they were like, what they did, what was done to them!" Tillman said, "I'm free to do nothing! They make people free to do nothing! They take freedoms away! They stand like sentries at the gate and they take people who come with hopes and dreams looking for freedom and before they even step ashore, they take all their freedoms away from them!" Tillman said, shouting, "Rights and freedoms are given, aren't reluctantly passed over, granted—rights and freedoms are supposed to be self-evident!" He turned suddenly and pointed into the darkness at the shapes and shadows, at the ruined glasshouse, "Do you know what this place was once? Do you know what all these buildings and glasshouses were? Do you know what this place was?"

"No."

Tillman said, "It was Martin's Celebrated Zoological Institute and Bowery Menagerie! It was a circus!" Tillman said, "From 1828, it was the premier circus and amusement in the city. It was where P.T. Barnum got his start—it was where he started work as a boy writing advertisements. It was where, once, in the days before electric light they turned night into day with a thousand oil lamps strung on wires and ropes between all the buildings and the aquaria and the aviaries and the tents and, on the hour, every hour, a carbide cannon fired a thousand balloons into the air, all blue and red and white and yellow and—" Tillman said with his voice wavering, "And a thousand thousand ribbons . . ." He touched at his mouth with his clenched fist. Tillman said, not looking at Muldoon at all, "After Martin's son died in 1871 Barnum took it over and turned it into the P.T. Barnum Museum, Menagerie and Circus, Polytechnic Institute and Hippodrome." He smiled at the thought of it, "It was a place children came to." The rain was still running down his face. "Before the days of telephones and terror and listening to men's souls—before all that—it was a place children came to!" The smile went from his face. Tillman said accusingly, "We're going to have to kill people, aren't we? Or they'll kill us! These people with their telephones and their evil enveloping everyone—these people whose names we don't even know—who don't even know each other—we're going to have to kill them or they're going to have to kill us, aren't they?"

Muldoon said softly, "Yes. Maybe."

Tillman said, "I knew Barnum. I knew him. Here, before he went bankrupt with his imported lions and tigers and pygmies and George Washington's childhood Negro servant who turned out to be an eighty-year-old woman from New Jersey with a lot of wrinkles—" He smiled at it. Tillman said, "I knew him. I worked for him as a boy. My first job when I was seventeen years old was here."

"It wasn't?"

"Yes." He pointed back at the ruined glasshouse, "That was Barnum's Aviary—it was where he had his birds from all nations—all freaks—his spotted crisscrossed Map bird with a miraculous natural chart of all the peaks on its wing feathers so it would never get lost as it soared above ranges, and his unique South American upside-down jungle parrot that had what looked like little parasols on its feet so that when it flew upside down its stomach didn't get wet and make it too heavy to continue, and his—the *pièce de résistance*—his Bornean toad catcher with legs like flippers so it could bury itself with just its legs sticking out of the ground in a toad patch and strangle passing toads and frogs without—" Tillman said, "All done of course, with paint and plaster and papier-mâché and—" Tillman said sadly, "All done with balloons and ribbons and—"

"What did you do for Barnum? Did you—"

Tillman said softly, "I was a clown."

"You never were!"

"Yes, yes, I was." He glanced across the darkness of the lot, all derelict and overgrown and ruined, running with the rain. He stood up straight and looked Muldoon in the eye, "I was El Hobolino—" Tillman said smiling at the thought, "P.T. Barnum, the Prince of Humbug: he couldn't even get his Spanish right!" Tillman said, "I juggled. I got hit with a slapstick on the rear end. El Hobolino: the Little Tramp." Tillman said, still smiling, "Big shoes, on the wrong feet, baggy pants and a derby hat with a big blue paper flower in it—and I thought, with the balloons and the ribbons and the lights and the children—I thought it was the most wonderful job in the world." His hands were still bleeding. He put them under the armpits of his coat and felt the two guns there—the Colt Lightning in its shoulder holster and the sawed-off Greener shotgun held by a strap. He looked down at the axe handle on the ground.

Tillman said hopelessly like a drowning man being sucked down to the bottom of a deep, deep pond, "My God, Ned, look what I've *become!*" His face was blanched with the rain.

Everywhere they were listening, listening. Everywhere, there was only desolation and ruin, terror and death.

He could not believe in that instant he stood on the same planet as them.

He could not look at the man's face. Everywhere, gone wrong, there was only desolation and death.

Tillman said in a whisper, lost beyond redemption, "Ned—Ned, if any of it's true—if only one tenth of it, one hundredth of it is true—all those rings, the money . . . what in the name of God, what in the name of Evil—what are those people, the Custers, *doing* out there on that island?"

29

Dawn.

On that island, on Swinburne, eight miles out in the harbor, what they were doing was consigning everything except human flesh to the flames of a furnace.

It looked like the breath of a dragon. The furnace was at the northern end of the island just inside the high wire fence on the shoreline. In his open steam launch the ferryman, moving his brass control knob to *Stop* and ungearing the propellor shaft, saw the smoke roar up like the explosion from a gun barrel. He saw the three white-coated, black India rubber–masked stokers at the three doors start back. He saw the smoke and boiling flame reach its apogee, hit a wind thirty feet up in the air, and, breaking up, start to descend as cinders. He saw the black plague flag on the summit of the island, the rows of lines of brick buildings around it. He saw disease, death. His twenty-five-foot-long open steam-powered ferry launch was named *Connemara Kate,* after his wife. It was all he had. Running up to the beach below the wire fence with Tillman and Muldoon with their backs to him in the bow, all he had to do before the keel struck sand was—

He heard the control knob move. Muldoon, turning, roared at him, *"Don't you reverse!"* Muldoon, glancing away as Tillman went over the side with the bow anchor in his hand to ground it in the sand, ordered the man in a hiss, "You stay here!"

There was a roar.

There was some sort of automatic device connected to the furnace, a compressor from a steam boiler somewhere, and there was a sudden roar as it cut in, then a banging and ringing, and then, as the metal doors came open and the masked stokers toiled to fill it again, a slamming, ringing sound, a thumping as the air pressure was built up again, a hiss—and then a burst of boiling flame and smoke as everything inside the crucible was destroyed.

They were burning clothes, night attire, bed linen, bandages, pads,

225

bedding, blood, sputum, human feces in the furnace: the ferryman could smell it. He saw the complex of brick buildings up on the summit of the island, the black flag. Up there was disease, death; he could almost taste it. Everywhere on the island . . . His boat was only grounded at the bow, rolling slightly with the turning of the tide, moving athwartships from the stern with the sea to bring itself around into deep water and all he had to do was . . .

"Stern anchor!" It was the little man. He was on the beach grounding the sand anchor, hauling the line in tight to snub it.

All he had to do was . . .

Muldoon, standing up in the bow, his eyes on the ferryman, said as a command, "Throw out the stern anchor!" There were black cinders falling down from the sky with the wind. He could smell what they were. Muldoon said as another order, "Put your hat on." He watched as the man stood up with the anchor in his hand and jammed his captain's hat down on his bald head. Muldoon said, "Throw out the anchor!" He looked back to the beach. He heard a splash behind him and then the sound of the rope being pulled tight through a metal ring. He felt the little boat snug out tight against the gentle thrusting of the water.

He looked back to the ferryman. Muldoon said with his eyes hard and unblinking, pinning the ferryman's soul, *"Don't you leave!"* He saw Tillman on the shore brushing sand from his coat and looking up toward the heavy wire fence set into rock and grassy earth twenty feet in from the long, deserted beach. He saw him start as suddenly, unseen, the furnace, full to capacity, roared like a beast and sent a plume of flame and smoke high into the air. He had a pair of wire cutters in his belt for the fence. With the black cinders falling down around him and the boat like rain Muldoon saw him go toward it with them ready in his hands.

It was a little after dawn, misty, on Swinburne Island eight miles out in the harbor from Manhattan. They had nothing, only the name of the man who ran the place, and that they had gotten from the 1883 City Government Statistics Report as any ordinary person could.

There was a click as, at the fence, Tillman on his knees, glancing back and forth along the beach to check no one came, cut through the first strand of the fence.

Muldoon said in a hiss to the ferryman, "For God's sake, man—for the sake of your family . . ." Muldoon said to the ferryman with what he thought was softness in his eyes, "For the sake of your family"—he saw the ferryman's face—"For God's sake, find a tarpaulin and cover your head while you wait!"

The cinders were falling like black rain. He heard them hiss as they hit the water.

He heard a click as Tillman, at the fence, cut through another strand.

He could wait no longer.

At the bow, standing up, drawing a breath, aiming for the sand, Muldoon, pushing back the bow against the anchor line hard with the sudden force of his released weight, jumped for the shore.

They had nothing. All they had was a name.

On that island, in the sudden silence of the terrible furnace drawing breath, all there was as Tillman at the fence cut through another strand, was a *click!*

30

In his office at the end of the first brick building on the hill, Dr. Hans-Martin Bergmann, opening the door and seeing what was in there waiting for him, said in a gasp, *"Mein Gott in Himmel!"* He felt something grab him from behind, at the scruff of the neck, and then there was a tremendous kick at the back of his knees that knocked his legs out from under him and he was being held with his nose against the floor. He was still wearing his black India rubber surgical mask, gloves and his white coat. He was spreadeagled like a crucified man, his loose gloves flapping on the floor. He could not breathe through the mask. He heard a click and then from the furnace outside there was a blast of power as the gas and air incinerated everything inside its crucible. The noise, through the floor, roared at his ears. He could not breathe. He could not bend his arms. On the floor, Bergmann, held in Muldoon's grip as in a vise, being forced down, screamed as a dark figure came forward to him, his boots an inch from his staring eyes, *"Who are you?"*

It was a hard whisper, a rasp. Tillman said, "I'm Oubliette." He knelt down beside him and touched the back of the man's naked neck with the cold muzzle of his gun. "I'm the second Oubliette. I'm the other one, the one you never knew about. I'm a liquidator. I'm liquidating all the assets of the Custers on the order of the management. Jenkins is dead, and Hewitt. I want all the papers and records and assets you hold of the firm. Oubliette, Donjon, Palisade, Portcullis, Archer—we want everything you've got. We want all the papers for the thirteen people coming today—I'm here for that!" Tillman said as a matter of fact, "And then I'm here to kill you."

There was a click from the gun. He felt it through his neck.

Tillman said, "Tell us where you keep the money."

"I don't know what—"

Tillman said in the same rasp, "And the rings and the jewelry."

"What rings and—" There was a roar through the floorboards as the

228

furnace outside sent a ball of superheated fire up through its chimney. Bergmann, his rib cage and heart starting to pull apart with the pressure on his arms and dislocating shoulders, shrieked through his mask, "I'm a doctor! I'm Dr.—!"

"Give us the money!"

The muzzle of the gun was pressing. Bitterly cold, it was pressing hard into his neck. Bergmann, unable to get his breath, said, "What money? There isn't any money here! All I've got in my pockets is—" Dr. Bergmann, running out of air, his eyes bulging, his mouth full of rubber and heat from the mask, his life disappearing in gasps, shrieked, "I've got two dollars in bills and change in my pocket! Take it! Take it!" It was not enough. He knew it was not enough. Dr. Bergmann shrieked with his heart starting to jerk in his chest in spasms, "What money? What *money?*"

"The money you take to let the sick and dying into the city to infect people! And the papers—the papers you forge to make it all right! And the jewelry—the jewelry you take from the sick and the dying who beg you on bended knees not to send them back to the places they came from!" Tillman said tightly, "The Custers are closing their operation. They've contracted us to clean up all the loose ends like you, and retrieve all their records. Embrasure, Donjon, Palisade, Portcullis, Bailey, Archer: everything is being wound down. The Custers are being dissolved." Tillman said with no tone in his voice at all, "We're just contract labor. There's no personal interest or human feeling in it as far as we're concerned. All we want is the money and the papers." Tillman said, "The thirteen people due today from the ships won't be processed. All that's finished."

"I don't know what you're talking about!"

He had the gun hard against the man's neck. He had it cocked, loaded. All he had to do was— All he could see was the man's naked neck above the collar of the coat. He could see a living pulse there. His hand holding the gun was shaking, trembling. He could not get his breath. He felt his heart thumping in his chest. He could see the man's living pulse beating. Tillman said, "The money. The papers." Tillman said, "Thirteen. There are thirteen people due today." He could not keep his hand from shaking. He could not catch his breath. Tillman said with his finger closing on the trigger, in a rage he could no longer control, "You scum—you're the goddamned Prince of the City, *aren't you?*" He could see the pulse. "What do they do when they come here—the sick and the diseased and the dying? *What do they do?* Do they *beg* you? Do they fall down at your feet and cry and grovel and sob? Do they stare at you in incomprehension and then—when you tell them they're going to be sent back—do they plead with you for the sake of their families? Do they offer you everything they've got? And then what? Do you relent for the sake of suffering humanity and tell them that, well, maybe, given the right circumstances, maybe something could be done? And then do they love you? Do they worship you? Do they adore you? Do they—" Tillman said, "The Prince, the Duke, the King—*the Prince of the Goddamned City:* do they swear eternal loyalty to you and swear also to keep their mouths shut and then, then do you rob them of everything they've got and send them into the city to die—*is that what you do?*"

He could not speak. His chest was heaving, running out of air, his heart running out of control and he could not speak.

All he had to do . . . "Is that what you do? Is it? *Is that what you do?*"

"*Virgil—!*" The voice was the voice of the man holding him down. On the floor Bergmann, for an instant, felt the pressure go. Bergmann, trying to get his head up, trying to see the man's face, pleaded at the end of his life. "*Don't kill me!*"

Tillman said in a whisper, "The power. Is that what you like—the power of it? Is that what you—" There was a roar like the doors of Hell opening as the furnace outside burned everything inside it to vapor.

"*Don't kill me!* For the love of God, *ich kann nichts—*" In the last moment of his life he could not force his brain to think in English. Behind the mask he could not breathe. His eyes, suddenly, were running with tears, "For the love of God—for the love of God—" Caught, pinned, about to die, blind and unseeing, his voice high and desperate like a woman's, Bergmann pleading, shrieked, "For the love of God—all these lives on this island—for the love of God, in the name of mercy—*there's no one else here but me to help them!*"

It stopped. The furnace stopped and there was only a heavy bubbling sound from all the pipes around the walls of the room: boiling water being forced from a boiler somewhere underground or in a cellar. There was a hissing coming from behind one of the doors that led off the office to the wards; there was the smell of carbolic as it was sprayed out somewhere in a fine mist.

It was a whisper. It was a whisper an inch from his face as Muldoon held the man hard against the back wall, his coat twisted and held in a stranglehold in his mitt. Tillman, his face an inch from the man's eyes, pulling down the India rubber mask to expose his face, said in a whisper, "We're the cops. We're City Detective Tillman and Ned Muldoon from Headquarters in Mulberry Street—we're the cops." He saw the face of a guilty man, a thin, high-cheekboned Slavonic or German face with no moustaches, the eyes flickering and afraid, worn, weary. Tillman, his hand shaking, touched the man's chest with his fingertip, "We're the Law—*and we know what you've been doing!*" He stepped back in the half light of the drawn curtains and touched at the desk with his fist. Tillman, grasping at the handle of a drawer, wrenching it out and spilling its contents—its stationery, silver-plated instruments, tongue depressors, parts of what looked like syringes, cylinders, pumps and bottles of colored liquids in profusion onto the floor, roared at the man, *"Where is it?* Where's the *money?"* Tillman, grasping the next drawer in the stack and pulling it free, wrenching it out so it smashed against the rear wall below the drawn curtains of the window and spilled its contents out everywhere on the floor, roared as Muldoon twisted harder at the coat and made the man's eyes bulge, "Which one of them are you? Embrasure? Donjon? Bailey? Portcullis? *Which one of them are you?"*

"I don't know what you're talking about!" He could not get free. Bergmann, being throttled, strangled, unable to twist free, shouted, "There is no money! There's no money here!" He was on his knees like a condemned man, about to be killed. Bergmann shrieked, "What money do you want?"

He was standing at the desk, rocking gently back on his heels as if he was coiled, as if any moment something was going to snap and he was going to take the gun and— Tillman, his neck tight, held rigid against the explosion coming up from his chest, said in a whisper, in a final warning, "The money you take to let the sick and the diseased into the city. The money you—" He put the gun flat on the table and put both hands on it to steady himself. His voice was a rasp, "The money you take not to deport the sick and the—"

"I deport no one!"

Tillman said, "The money you take to—"

"I take nothing! I deport no one!" Bergmann, trying to twist free, said, "I—"

"Hewitt, Jenkins, Archer, you— Who are the other Custers?"

"I don't know what you're talking about! What money are you talking about? What deportations? I deport no one! I—" Bergmann said, suddenly pushing free, getting away from Muldoon's grip and shrieking at the man at the desk, "I deport no one!" He saw Muldoon reach out for him but he squirmed away from him and fended him off with his hand, "I deport no one!" He raised his fist to Muldoon to keep him back. He saw the question coming. Bergmann shouted, "I bury them if they die! I burn their belongings and their linen but I deport no one! I send no one back!"

"You send them into the city!"

"I do!" He was on his feet. Bergmann said, "I do! I have done! I will do again!" Bergmann said, *"I do!"*

"And do they beg you for that and—"

"They don't have to beg me for anything! Every time, here, they either die or get well and if they get well—" Bergmann, fending Muldoon off, said, "The law? To hell with the law! The law says the moment one of them is pronounced cured he goes into the city to work!" Bergmann said, "The law? The law takes into account not at all that a man or a woman recovered from disease needs time and care to regather strength. The law says that a man pronounced well, pronounced cured, must be thrown into the city the same day as if he was a two-hundred-pound navvy fit for labor! The law says that that man's family must spend everything it has saved and scrimped for for years for *private* convalescent care in the city! The law says—" Bergmann said simply, "So they hang themselves: the men. Rather than taking everything their families saved for, they hang themselves!" His eyes were moist with pain. Bergmann said in a whisper, "Sometimes, first, they kill their children and their wives to spare them the pain of loneliness!"

"What are you talking about?"

"The *law!* I'm talking about the *law!* I'm talking about how I break it! I'm talking about why you came here! I'm a criminal! Arrest me! I break the law! I keep people here long after they are cured, to convalesce! I keep them longer than one day to recover, to gain strength, to—" He shook his head. "I regret I have nothing to offer you to bribe you to keep quiet about it. I have spent all the Government's money on it, and all of my own, and I have nothing left to offer you except"—he saw on the floor all the glittering instruments—"except maybe those things there—maybe you could sell them for something."

He saw the face of the man at the desk.

Bergmann said in desperation, "Don't you see? It has to be done! It has to be—*and there's no one left now on this island but me to do it!*"

Tillman said, "The Custers—"

"I don't know what you mean."

"Hewitt, Jenkins, Archer—"

He shrugged. He did not know the names. Bergmann said quietly, sadly, indicating the closed door to the ward with his open hand, "Diphtheria, yellow fever, cholera, typhus—they come here from the ships on the point of death with their families, left on the pier like bundles by the Quarantine boats. And we can do nothing except give them care and sunlight and feed their families and— And the ones we cannot cure, die." He shook his head. Bergmann said, "It is a fault of character: disease. It is God's punishment—like the law. And the law says that the moment God forgives, the moment the disease has run its course, then the curse is lifted, the character is firm again and a man must work." Bergmann, shaking his head, said, "No. That is not God's law as I see it; that is Man's law. God's law says—"

"Thirteen new cases are due on this island today! This morning! The returns you send to Castle Garden show *deportations!*"

"I send no reports to Castle Garden. Someone there is an unknown benefactor and I received a note years ago that he, whoever it was, would write my reports for me and I was not to bother with—"

Muldoon said, *"Archer!"*

"He said in his note—" Opening his hands in a gesture of hopelessness Bergmann said quietly, "Years ago I came here myself, to this place, with smallpox. The doctor who cured me died. He died by his own hand here, in this office. He sat in this office the morning I staggered like a ghost toward the boat to take me into the city along with a line of other cured men and women. He sat in the chair watching and knowing—*knowing!*—what he was sending us all to: to the slow degrading hopeless destitution of all our families in rooms somewhere in the gutters and he could endure no more and he took poison and he died." Bergmann said with strength in his voice, unshakable, "Like him, I cure or I bury, but no one hangs themselves anymore. The families of the dead I keep until their strength and their will have returned, the cured I keep until they are ready to work, but no one hangs themselves here anymore!" Bergmann said, "I staggered to the boat with the rest of the procession of the cured and ready to work but I could not board it and I came back." Bergmann, trembling, said, "I checked. I found out: every person who boarded that boat that morning, within a month of entering the city, was dead by their own hand or by starvation and their families along with them! I checked! I found out!" He was shaking, trembling. Bergmann said, "We the people! We the people!" Bergmann said, "If not me, then who? If not me, then who?" Bergmann said, "Money? You ask if I take money to send people into the city who are sick? I use every penny I can get to keep them out until they are *well!*" Bergmann said violently, "We, the People . . . God in Heaven, it is why we all *came* in the first place! We, the People! *We, the People!*" Bergmann said challenging them, "I have nothing to give you to bribe you to keep silent. I cannot ask the sick and the suffering to pay you because I—We, *the People!*" Under the white coat, his clothing was old and frayed, the cuffs of his shirt in tatters.

It was not the sound of boiling water in pipes. It was the sound of people in the next room with their lungs full of cholera and typhus and fever drowning in their own fluids.

Bergmann said, glancing at the curtained window, "Out there in the great, shining city—out there." Bergmann said, "Eight years . . . eight years—"

Bergmann said with the sadness of realization, shaking his head, "Dreams, lives, dreams . . ." He had been a young man when he had come.

Bergmann, shaking his head, said, "God in Heaven, in all that time, I have never even been there!"

31

. . . If not him, then no one . . .

If not that, then nothing.

If not Swinburne, then—

On the beach, gazing out at the ships, all the ships moored in the harbor, Tillman said with his jaws clenched tight, "It's them, I know it is. It's the immigrants. It's *them*." On the shoreline, the boatman in the *Connemara Kate* was out from under his tarpaulin looking over the side of his boat at the tide changing on the sand. Tillman, not looking at him, a man standing on the rim of the world, said, not to be moved, *"It has to be them!"*

He felt ashamed. Up on the island at the furnace the white-coated stokers were still packing bloody packages of bandages and bed linen, human waste and God only knew what else to be loaded into the hissing incinerator. Up there, in the wards, there were people drowning in the fluids of their own bodies. Muldoon, not looking at the little man on the beach but up at the island, said with the water from the changing tide starting to lap around his boots, "He thought we'd come to arrest him for his compassion, or to take money from him for—" Muldoon said, "It's not them! It's not the immigrants. Everything Archer told us is a lie!"

"It's them." Out in the harbor, the day had begun. Out there an armada of little boats and ferries and launches were everywhere making wakes and columns of black smoke and steam about the anchored ships. It was the morning run. It was an hour from the Battery by sail or steam with the last of the outgoing tide, an hour to unload the ships or inspect the ships—or whatever all the officials on all the boats did—and it was an hour back on the turn of that tide and the extra speed it gave. It was a little after 10 A.M.: the morning run. Tillman, taking out his watch and crushing it hard in his hand, unopened, said, not to be moved, "It's them! They're the ones! The rings, the jewelry, the money—it's from *them!*"

"And the Custers are going to land thirteen of them here on this island?"

"They're going to land them somewhere!"

235

"That man up there told you! No one knows from one day to the next how many cases are going to be landed here!" Muldoon said in an undertone, feeling ashamed, "He thought we'd come to arrest him for his crime of being a Christian." Muldoon, only wanting to go, wanting to take Tillman by the shoulders and carry him to the waiting boat to get away, said with an effort at control, "Leave it now, Virgil, leave it . . ." Muldoon said, "Virgil, in the name of God, let's—"

"They come off *somehow!* Somehow, the Custers take them off the ships between here and Castle Garden and somehow they—"

"Maybe there *are* no Custers! Maybe it's all, like everything else—"

"It's a feint, a flourish! Jenkins, Hewitt, Archer, the telephones; everything so far is a flourish, a movement, a feint—something done by a magician to cloak the trick, to keep the eyes and the attention of the crowd on what it appears he's doing out in the open with his right hand while his left—" He could not take his eyes from the ships. "Everything so far is a ruse for simpletons and yokels gawking at black sackcloth and thinking it's satin, and at tinsel and thinking it's silver and everything is all ruse and illusion and—" Tillman, not to be moved, said, "But it's them! It's the immigrants because it can't be anyone else! They're the victims!"

"Maybe we're the damned victims!" He looked back to the island, then away again. Muldoon said as an accusation, "We came sneaking in here like criminals and almost frightened a good and saintly man to death!"

"The Custers exist! The telephones exist!"

"Everything the Custers told even their own people was a lie! None of it exists!"

"The thirteen people exist! They exist in Archer's instructions! They exist because his job was to make sure in the chaos of the bureaucracy that they were accounted for! They exist this morning! They exist *now!* They exist *today!* They exist *here!*"

All he wanted to do was get away. Muldoon, controlling himself, wanting to take the man by the shoulder and lead him away, but afraid of his own strength and anger and shame, said in desperation, "Virgil, no one is coming!" Muldoon said, "Can't we leave?" Muldoon said with his clenched fists starting to shake, "For God's sake, we've failed! We aren't clever! We're just dumb cops! We're—"

Muldoon said as an order, starting toward the little boat beached at the shoreline, "Leave it now, Virgil."

The Custers. Oubliette, Embrasure, Donjon, Palisade, Portcullis, Archer, Bailey. It was all he had to sustain him. He was a rock, staring out at the ships. Out there, everywhere around them there were ferries and launches, pilot boats with auxiliary sails turning to catch the tide, coming in on a tack toward the island to catch the windward breeze, Quarantine launches going toward other ships anchored back up the harbor, hospital ships, a fleet of what looked like whaleboats moving back to the anchored vessels loading and unloading passengers, harbor tugboats standing off puffing smoke in case they were needed for a vessel breaking loose on its mooring, fireboats blowing white steam as they kept their pumps primed in case of disaster, coalers and barges lying off ready for the rebunkering of the great ships, sidewheel ferries and—

—and, on the sand, there was the *Connemara Kate* waiting to take them away. He looked up at the fever buildings. On the sand, gazing out, Tillman opened his watch and looked down at it.

"Virgil, haven't we—" Muldoon said, entreating him, "For the love of God, haven't we done enough damage today *already?*" He had gone to midnight Mass because he thought, this day, he might have died. He had not died. He had done worse. Muldoon, looming over him, looking over him, looking past him, having nowhere to look, said shouting so loud the boatman heard him and looked up in alarm, "For God's sake, man, we're beaten! We can't win! We're too *stupid* to win!" The Custers, whoever they were, whatever they did, were as grown men to small, insignificant, crawling insects. Muldoon said, for the first time in his life not wanting to hit someone, not wanting to conquer, only wanting to slink away, "For God's sake man, for God's sake—for the sake of all those poor souls up there on this island dying in agony, for the sake of that good and saintly man we've terrified out of his wits for no reason at all—*will you leave it?!*"

On the sand, with the tide coming in around his boots, he looked out into the harbor.

Like a man on the rim of the world gazing out at the open sea and seeing nothing, he—

He thought it all a chimera, a—

Tillman said in a voice so soft for a moment Muldoon thought he had imagined it, *"One . . . !"*

"Oubliette, Embrasure, Donjon, Palisade, Portcullis, Archer . . ." Out in the harbor all the little boats were scurrying about for the turning tide, their steam engines sending smudges into the windless sky, staining it, the leading boats—the lighters and the launches—puffing hard to turn their screws at full revolutions to gain the extra few knots to assure them of a quick one hour's morning passage to the Battery and the piers at Castle Garden. On them, and on all the great ships, as the unloading was completed and they turned to gain the wind and the tide, all their flags were flying.

Tillman said slowly, going over it like a recitation, "Oubliette, Embrasure, Donjon, Palisade, Portcullis, Archer." Tillman said softly, *"One—"*

He was staring out into the harbor. Tillman said tightly, counting, *"One, Two, Three, Four—"* He looked up at Muldoon. Tillman said, *"Five,* Six, Seven, Eight . . ." Tillman said softly, tightly, "Nine. Ten—"

"It's time to go back, Virgil." Muldoon said beside him, "The tide's turning and the boatman—"

"Eleven." At each word his eyes changed, glittered. Tillman said, *"Twelve."* Tillman said tightly, starting to rise, staring out at the flotilla of boats turning toward the lee side of the island for the tide, *"Thirteen!"* Tillman, his hand stabbing out at the turning boats said as an order, *"Look!"* Tillman, his eyes burning through Muldoon as if he was not there, said, "Not the sick! Not the contagious, but criminals! *Criminals!"* He had his hand still pointing out in the direction of a steam launch out in the harbor loaded with people coming to make the turn off the island to catch the tide and the shore breeze. Tillman said, starting to shake, "Not the sick or the diseased or the dying, but *criminals!* Criminals taken off the ships by the Police! Criminals with money coming in from Europe and—" Tillman said in triumph, his finger stabbing at the boat coming toward him, "It's the Police Steamboat Squad launch! It's Jenkins' old Squad—it's the Police steamboat loaded with criminals from the ships! It's—" He wrenched at the man to make him look, "Look! *Look!"* Tillman ordered him, "Count them! *Count them!"*

Muldoon said, "Thirteen." Muldoon said, "But it—"

He was on his feet, wrenching, pulling, starting to dance on the sand. Tillman said, "Look! *Look!"* Tillman said, "Oubliette! Embrasure! Donjon! Palisade! Portcullis! Archer . . . !" Tillman said, "Look! *Look!"*

It turned. Not fifty yards from shore, fifty feet long, its open stern packed with people sitting along benches, guarded by a uniformed policeman from the Squad, it turned to take the tide.

It was an order, a plea. It was the first moment of a day he thought had had no end. Tillman shrieked, "The name of the boat, read it! Read it! *Read the boat's name!"*

Muldoon said in a voice with no emotion in it at all, "Captain Theodorus—" Muldoon said, "Bailey."

There were men, women, children in the stern of the boat, criminals, thieves, murderers, wanted or known or suspected felons and their families taken from the ships. Muldoon said, "Bailey. Captain Theodorus Bail—" Muldoon said like a man electrocuted, "Bailey! *Bailey! —Bailey!"* He could have, in that instant, taken the little man up in his arms and, embracing him, danced with him on the sand.

Muldoon, his eyes glittering, cemented to the sight, said in triumph, "Bailey! Captain Theodorus—" Muldoon shrieked, *"Bailey!"*

He thought, all his life, he had lived for no other moment than this. The police launch was fifty yards from the beach, turning away to the north. On that beach, with the boatman patting at his donkey engine to keep its brass free of the cinders from the still burning furnace, they had a boat.

Bailey.

Bailey—

Bailey!

He thought, all his life, he had lived for no other moment than this.

On the beach, starting to run, Tillman, roaring at the boatman who at first understood not a word, shrieked in that moment, in that triumph, like a madman, "The *Bailey!* It's them! It's the *Police!* They're heading for the Police Whitehall Street wharf at the Battery! For God's sake, for God's sake—"—they had at least two extra knots of speed on the boatman's launch and already they had caught the tide and were going—"For God's sake—*after them!*"

32

Do you have a glass in your boat? A *telescope?*"

At his tiller, shouting above the sound of the straining engine, the boatman said, "No! Nothing!" The *Bailey* was a mile ahead of them, starting to make the left-hand turn between Staten Island and the coast of Brooklyn into the Narrows that led to the upper bay of Manhattan. She was a converted oceangoing steam trawler at least fifty-eight feet long and of eighteen-foot beam cutting a twin wake behind her from engines that made the brass donkey engine of the *Connemara Kate* look like a clockwork toy. The *Kate*'s engine was at full pressure, the needle on the pressure dial stuck on red. The boatman saw Muldoon at the open fire gate of the furnace heaving in wood. The boatman yelled at him, "Too much! Too much pressure!" She was doing four knots, too much: he felt the iron handle of the tiller vibrating in his hands.

In the stern of the *Bailey* there were thirteen people being guarded by two uniformed policemen standing against the back of the high wooden wheelhouse. She was out of the main shipping channel, passing between the casemated fortifications and pointing cannon of Fort Wadsworth on Staten and the ruined crenellations and overgrown barracks on Fort Lafayette Island to the east, catching the sun, glittering white and then silver and then, in the heavy smudge of her boilers, being lost behind smoke. She was a mile away, opening the distance, crossing over to starboard to catch the tide for quick run to the Whitehall Street pier of the Steamboat Squad at the foot of the Battery.

She was just out of reach, by moments, getting farther and farther away.

In the stern, he could see only the shapes of the people in two rows. From where he strained his eyes in the bow of the *Kate* to see, he could see the auxiliary mast and jib of the *Bailey* only as a single pole, blurring as she moved.

He could see shapes on the forecastle where there were square things lashed down—the steamer trunks and baggage of passengers.

On the *Bailey* they were making at least six good, solid knots and whoever was in the wheelhouse noticed him not at all. Tillman, turning back to see Muldoon at the boiler, yelled, "We're losing them! We can't make up the difference!" Tillman, drumming his hands on the anchor point at the bow, pounding at it with his fist, yelled, "More speed! We have to have more speed!" He felt a jerk as the propeller at the stern of the boat must have missed a beat, or a blade buckled. He felt the *Kate* start to slew as the boatman lost control of her. Tillman yelled, "Open the valve up full!"

He could not get more wood in. Inside the furnace everything was red-hot. Muldoon, turning to the boatman, yelled, "What do I do?"

Behind him, under the water below the stern where the blade was, there was a bang, a convulsion, and, the tiller—swinging hard—came out of his hands. Its force knocked him to his knees. The boatman, reaching for it, wrestling with it as the bow of the *Kate* started to come around, roared, shrieked, "Do nothing! No more wood!" The *Kate*, named after his wife, was all he had. The boatman fighting the tiller back, feeling the resistance suddenly released as he got the rudder back in line, grabbing at Muldoon with a suddenly freed hand and pulling him down to the scuppers, yelled with his eyes wide in terror, "Let go the release valve!" It was like some sort of terrible raid on the South in the Civil War. They were a little unarmed boat passing between forts and cannons on either side of the shore. The boiler was about to explode and blast their boat in two and they were— The boatman, reaching past Muldoon and getting the pressure-release valve wire and yanking it, setting off a whistle and blast of white steam that enveloped everything, yelled, *"For God's sake, nothing's worth this!"*

He heard above the steam the little cop at the bow drumming his hand on the anchor post. He heard him in orison saying over and over, "Come on! Come on! Come on—"

The boatman shrieked, unable to stop, *"Jesus!"* and, pulsing, vibrating, charging into the Narrows like a raiding ship going for the prize between the forts that guarded it, the *Connemara Kate*, blasting steam and whistling, went on.

The distance was still opening, ever opening. The *Bailey* was cutting through the harbor by Bedloe's Island. It was veering slightly toward the grassy wastes of Ellis Island to make its run past Governors Island with its stone castle and cannons toward the East River where the Steamboat Squad's pier at the bottom of Whitehall Street was.

He could see the outline of the trunks on the white forecastle only as a blur as the boat, hitting some sort of rip or finding shallower water, rolled a little and made the turn. He could not see who was in the wheelhouse.

He could no longer see the uniforms of the two policemen at the rear of the wheelhouse. He could see no movement on the boat at all. He could see the thirteen people in the stern as only a single shadow blurred out by the smudging black smoke of the funnel as the wind must have changed. He could see only—

It was no longer a mile away. It was a mile and a half. The *Bailey,* heading towards Governors Island, seemed to put on more speed and it was a mile and three quarters.

He was so close.

He was so far away.

He was never going to make up the distance! Tillman, at the bow, turning back, hammering his hands in the air, shrieked, "More! More *speed!*" Behind him the brass boiler was glowing red-hot. It was a bomb, surging and swelling. He turned and saw the look on Muldoon's face and realized in that instant that the anchor post against his hands was shaking, that all the planks were vibrating, trembling. He saw the boatman reach for the stern release valve to yank it down to bleed the surging steam pressure. He heard a sound like the power from the muzzle of a Gatling gun as steam blasted out in twin jets of superheated power like dragon's breath. He turned back and he saw the *Bailey,* passing behind Ellis Island out of sight, become a smudge of smoke, a track, a lingering trail of vapor.

The *Kate* was to the left of the island, moving in a different channel. He saw the smoke of the *Bailey* on the surface of the harbor break up and dissipate.

They were coming around on the port side of Ellis, clearing it: he saw the Battery and Castle Garden unfolding like a diorama as the *Kate* cleared it. He saw all the cannons and castles and barracks. He saw, as she shuddered, wallowed for an instant, then righted herself, the entrance to the East River, to where, two streets above the Battery, far to the right, the Steamboat Squad's pier was.

He saw the *Bailey* not at all.

He saw only, on the grayness of the sky, a lingering smudge of black smoke. He saw boats, launches, ferries all along the piers at the foot of Manhattan, the great shining city behind them.

He looked down and saw the twin bow waves of the *Kate* still churning white water as her propeller cut through the water. He saw across all the water between the Battery and Ellis Island, across the run to the entrance of the East River—nothing. From behind the buildings at the tip of the island where the Whitehall Street pier was he could not even see smoke.

He could see nothing.

Tillman, turning, holding the anchor post hard as the *Kate* rolled and surged with the bursting boiler, ordered the boatman, "Keep going!

There's no smoke! She's shut off her engine and tied up at the pier!" He saw the boatman's face. Tillman ordered him, rolling and rocking as the *Kate* ploughed on, *"Keep going!"*

On their track parallel with the Battery they were less than half an hour out from the entrance to the East River and the Whitehall Street pier. The *Kate* was cutting through the water. She could land them on one of the private piers at the tip of the island while the *Bailey* was still tying up. It could do that. It was small enough. They had time.

Then they could get by foot to the Whitehall Street dock, blocking it while the passengers were still being disembarked.

It could happen. They had time.

He was so close—so . . . *close!*

The *Kate* was not going to blow up. The pressure valve dial was holding, and, without the *Bailey* to pace her, to make a comparison, she was surging through the water.

"Land anywhere! Don't stop! Run the *Kate* straight up to a pier and land anywhere!"

He was so close.

They were perhaps not a hundred yards from the Whitehall Street pier around the corner in the entrance to the East River. He was so close.

He saw a pier almost at the entrance to the river, sixty yards from it. Tillman turning to the boatman yelled, "There! Stop there!" He saw Muldoon glance at the pressure valve. Tillman yelled, "Ned! Up here to the bow!" He turned back, felt the boat rock as Muldoon made it to the bow, then felt it stagger as he got his weight up onto the anchor post beside him and tensed. He turned and saw the boatman. He was not going to stop. The *Kate* was all he had. He was going to run it by the pier once and then—then he was going to get the hell out of there. It was on his face. At full speed as the *Kate*, not stopping, not decreasing speed passed by the edge of the pier in a cloud of steam and a roar of the bulging, seething, red-hot engine, Tillman roared at Muldoon, *"Jump!"* and so close, so close, they leapt together and hit the pier steps running.

Nothing!

The Whitehall Street pier was empty, vacant, deserted and she was gone.

There was nothing there at all.

Panting, gasping from the run, Tillman, unable to believe his eyes, screamed in protest, "Not there! Gone!" He could not believe his eyes. He stared at the long wooden pier and the buildings around it, glancing back and forth, even at the tiny spaces between the pylons as if, somehow, it had hidden itself there; but it had not, and the *Bailey* was not there and it was gone or had never come, or had—

There was no one around: the Steamboat Squad Headquarters office and 24th Precinct area were deserted with only a few hansom and brougham cabs parked in the street back from it with the drivers napping on their perches in the midmorning pause from their labors, and there was no boat, no people—nothing.

There was nothing!

There was only—

Tillman said, *"There!"*

He saw it. He saw up the river, ahead, going north, not stopping, moving at a steady five knots, the *Bailey*.

It was less than two hundred yards away. It was less than— It was going north to one of the piers at Twenty-sixth Street—there was no place else on the island of Manhattan for it to go.

He had it. He was so close.

At the end of the pier, not taking his eyes off it, so close, so close, Tillman running for the first cab on the rank—a light extension front brougham with a good sound horse held in readiness by its overcoated driver in a top hat, shrieking, yelling, holding up his police badge to show the man who he was, dragging Muldoon along with him by the coat sleeve, roared as an order that made the horse start and rear up in its traces, "There! That boat! Along the shore roads! *Follow it!*"

He had Muldoon shoved in through the door of the carriage before the driver even had time to respond.

He looked back from the open door.

He saw it. He saw the *Bailey*.

He saw on it, clearly, the thirteen people. He saw, for an instant in the wheelhouse, the glint of something metal on a uniform.

"Drive!" At the half-open door, shrieking, yelling, so near to triumph, Tillman roared as an order to the blinking, staring driver, "Drive! *Drive like hell!*"

33

He didn't have to be told twice. On his box, the cabbie, delivering a blow from his whip to the horse's flank that would have cut an oak tree in half, yelled, "Yaa—*hahh!!*" He had a police laissez-passer to break all the speed restrictions of the highway.

He had thought he looked familiar. In the carriage, Muldoon, groping for a seat, being thrown back against it by an instant acceleration, hearing the shriek change to a howl, a bellow, said in horror, "Virgil, it's Roaring Lion Lewis!" He was the worst drunk, the fastest cab driver, the heaviest-handed whipper, and the most determined hater of horses in the world. Muldoon, being thrown roof-high against the recoil of the springs hitting a pothole, sailing like a cloud a foot below the roof as the vehicle became briefly weightless and being crashed against the padded rear seat as it came down, shrieked, "Lewis!" Muldoon said, *"Oh, my God!"*

He could see it. At the window, hanging out, he could see the *Bailey* going up the East River. It was moving up with the running tide in a trail of boiling black smoke, passing a hundred feet out from the wharfs and docks of the San Francisco and London Packet Line. He saw it through the maze of rigging and masts. With his hand gripped hard on the thin wood of the door to keep it shut the latch banged and clattered as the wheels hit cobbles, struck sparks from them, and the carriage turning from Whitehall into South Street, paralleling the river, almost collided with a wagonload of barrels. Roaring Lion Lewis, changing from a scream to a bellow, made the carriage rise up on two wheels and almost cut the screaming barrel wagon driver in half where he fell.

As the carriage turned, crashing back onto four wheels, all he could see was Lewis' top hat screwed down on his head and a mighty hand plying the whip. Tillman, his voice being taken away by the slipstream, yelled, "The boat! Don't lose sight of the boat!" The river was out of sight behind the buildings of the West Indies and South American Mail Line Company, lost in the spider's web of moored steam and sail boats. It was lost in a miasma of smoke from a locomotive tank engine at the end of one of the loading piers delivering or taking off cargo. Then it was back again, the sun glinting off the glass in its wheelhouse, white water bubbling at its wake and Tillman, leaning out, trying to see it and Lewis at the same time, pleaded as Lewis, reaching the intersection of Broad Street tried to turn up, "Don't turn! Stay on South Street! Stay on the river! Don't turn!"

A voice from inside said, "At Broad Street South Street becomes a one-way street!" It was Muldoon somewhere on the floor, crawling about for an exit. His voice sounded a long way off. The voice said mildly, "At Broad Street . . ."

"Yaa—*rahh!!*"

"Don't turn!"

He didn't.

"*Police business!*" He saw coming at them on the one-way street a solid wall of carriages and wagons and carts. Tillman, trying to make Lewis hear, yelled, "Don't turn!"

He didn't.

Lewis, standing up, roaring like a lion, yelled at the top of his voice, "Yaa-*Hahahh!*"

And he didn't.

He didn't turn.

In the carriage, twisting back in from the door, searching for Muldoon in the darkness, talking to a shape, Tillman said at the top of his lungs above the screams of the owners of all the destroyed carriages behind them, "It's all a lie! Everything!" The *Bailey* out in the river was a glittering shape in the morning sun, white water bubbling astern of her as she made a steady five knots with all the figures and baggage and trunks on her lost in light. "Hewitt was a lie, and Archer and Jenkins and Swinburne Island and Quarantine and Rosie! Even everything she knew or remembered or quoted like a parrot—everything, all of it, was a lie!" He saw Muldoon drawing his revolver to shoot Lewis dead through the roof. Tillman, forcing the man's hand down, trying to grab him by the collar to stop him becoming airborne as, outside, Lewis roared under the span of the Brooklyn Bridge and made the roars echo, yelled, "The *Bailey* is taking the people from the ships up to the Twenty-sixth Street pier not because they've got plague or they've threatened to deport them because they might have plague—they're taking those people up to the Twenty-sixth Street pier to land them in the city because they're *criminals!* They're the Steamboat Squad—cops! They can board any ship in the harbor and take off whoever they like on simple suspicion!" He saw the *Bailey* for a moment through the open entrance to the Brooklyn Ferry and Long Island

Terminal waiting room. He saw her make smoke. "No ship's captain is going to ask for proof or argue with the cops in their own port and if the Steamboat Squad says someone at Castle Garden—Archer—will make the figures right who the hell cares? *No one cares!* In a daily processing of thousands of immigrants everyone is glad to be rid of them! And if the Steamboat Squad tells the criminals they've taken off that, for the consideration of everything they have, they'll let them into the city with no record at all of it, why, that's even better!"

Tillman said, "It's all a lie! Plague, deportations—everything, everything is a lie! What it is is bribery! And who cares? No one! The rich don't care so long as criminals only prey on the poor, the good and true congregation at Trinity doesn't care so long as they can keep the poor in their place! The dangerous classes prey on their own kind! Surely, it's poetic justice for the rich, the powerful, to prey on them!" He saw the *Bailey*. He saw it disappear on the river behind a mountain of coal by the empty wharf of the New London and Norwich Mediterranean Steamship Company's wharf. It was three miles in a straight line from the foot of Whitehall Street to the Twenty-sixth Street pier. Tillman, reaching for the shapeless moving mass that was the airborne Muldoon, yelled, "The Custers: Oubliette! Embrasure! Donjon! Palisade! Portcullis! Archer! All lies!" Hanging out of the carriage door, all the bones in his chest being smashed and crunched against the wood of the door and the metal of the latch as Lewis sent the horse into a turn north of Grand Street that lifted Muldoon up in the air again and then set him down, Tillman shouted— sure, certain—"It isn't Castle Garden! It's Castle Manhattan! It's Fort *New York!* It's the Custers' secret toll road through their fort into the city! It's the way thieves and traitors and killers bring more of their own kind in behind the walls *for money!* It's Jenkins' big house and more money than anyone knows what to do with! It's the criminal classes of Europe paying to enter the New World with no papers, no checks, no records—it's a new start for people who have robbed and killed their way to fortunes and are happy to pay men in uniforms and positions of power to conceal them and give them a new life!" Tillman said with hatred in his voice, "The rings and coins—the rings and coins are the stuff of victims killed and ruined a continent away!"

Tillman, the wind whipping his words away, his eyes hard on the *Bailey,* said as Lewis turned hard left with the road and made the turn onto Tompkins Street to follow the river, "This damned country—this damned country—everything everyone came here to escape from is being brought in again on that filthy boat like a rotting disease to ruin us!"

He looked out the window and saw the gasometers of the New York Mutual Gas Light Company at the end of Avenue D coming up. He saw a rough track through the place between the gasometers, full of ruts and potholes with no room to drive a carriage at full clip. He saw the *Bailey*. Tillman, not taking his eyes from the boat as it made headway, as it drew away, ordered Lewis on his seat, with no hesitation at all, "Through the Gas Light Company! Don't stop! Don't stop for anything! If anything gets in your way, *run it down!*"

All that was needed in that place full of glittering tanks and gas lines was a spark.

It got the eruption of Etna. The iron wheels of the carriage, hitting potholes, smashing bricks, destroying paths, glancing off pylons, a spear of solid flint, a fizzing firework, careered through the place toward the foot of Avenue B like a flare. Hitting a rock—or it could have been a rock-like Gas Company employee in a dustcoat—it made a sound like a bat being disemboweled and lurched in a shower of red-hot metal shavings from its brakepad and became airborne, leapt a puddle of something that blasted up like a waterspout and hissed with steam.

Roaring Lion Lewis was having a good time. On his perch Roaring Lion Lewis roared, *"Haa-Raggh!"*

In the carriage, Muldoon, at least wanting to give the impression of dying in the performance of his duty and not as a sniveling self-serving coward crying for mercy, demanded, "But *how? How* is it done? How do the Steamboat Squad know who the criminals are? How is it organized?" The carriage must have hit something. He hoped it wasn't a person. It wasn't. It was a hole. The carriage went up and then higher up and then came down with a crash that loosened all the teeth in his head and sent him flying against something near the seat that he hoped wasn't Tillman. Muldoon demanded, "Who arranges it? How would the Steamboat Squad know who to take? It'd mean there'd have to be an organization of the Custers on at least two continents! It'd mean there'd have to be someone arranging it in Europe and telegraphing names or descriptions here to America before the ships even leave!" All the coins had been Maria Theresa talers. Muldoon, his brain bouncing off the inside of his skull like a boxer's, screamed above the sound of something outside being destroyed, "There must be a thousand different languages in Europe! Who the hell can speak all those languages and arrange passages to America and pickups by the New York cops from one central point?" Muldoon, holding his head in both hands to keep his brains in, going over like an acrobat, shrieked as Lewis' roars turned into Lewis' bellows and there was the sound of him whipping either the horse or a human, "And these criminals, these murderers—*where the hell are the Custers sending them after they've landed in the city desperate and penniless?*"

* * *

He saw it. Halfway out of the carriage door as the rutted path through the gas company became a cobbled path through a grassy vacant lot and the air became full of flying cobblestones and scythed grass, he saw the *Bailey* out in the stream.

They were on Avenue B, going the wrong way down a wide street full of homes of respectable clerks and draper's assistants. He saw their nice little houses and their tended gardens, and, at the far end of the street, a little way out from the curb, their neat lines of ash and garbage cans ready for pickup by the City. He saw, through a gap between two of the houses, the *Bailey* make smoke as if she either slowed down or speeded up in preparation for a maneuver. He saw the houses and gardens pass safely by. He saw Lewis head straight for the cans. Tillman, ducking back in as the horse with legs of tempered steel rocked the cans to one side with its passage and the carriage, with its passage, detonated them sky high and filled the street with soot, screamed up at the roof of the carriage to Lewis, "Keep on! Keep on!" They were at the junction of East Twentieth Street, less than six blocks away from the Twenty-sixth Street pier. There, waiting for the passengers, there would be wagons, carriages and maybe, maybe the Custers. He felt a jerk. He felt one of the wheels start to wobble on its axle. He could see nothing through the miasma of soot. "I don't know!" There was another gas company lot directly ahead, with, thank God, a street running east of it parallel with the river: he knew it from the map—and Tillman, ducking his head out, trying to see the boat, seeing nothing, feeling Muldoon plucking at his shoulder, ordered Lewis who could not see either, "Down by the river, through the coal yards and into the grounds of Bellevue Hospital to Twenty-sixth!"

The soot cleared and they were already there: he saw the hospital. Turning back he shouted to Muldoon wherever he was in the soot, to make him feel better, "We're at Bellevue Hospital!" He could not see the *Bailey* at all. He saw smoke from the river but it seemed a long way off and he did not know if it was the *Bailey* or not. He saw the open wire gate to the hospital grounds leading to Twenty-sixth Street. He saw—

He heard a splintering sound and then, as Muldoon like a huge spider crawling about in soot shrieked, "Oh, my God, the wheel's come off!" the entire world went black and turned over as the shattered axle like a furrower gone completely out of control dug itself a hole, and spun the horse, the traces, the roaring lion, the carriage and everything inside it in a circle and, with a crash, turned all the coachwork to matchwood; and, only ten feet from Twenty-sixth Street, his shotgun somehow miraculously out from its strap under his armpit and in his hand, he was out and running and there, in the street where it met the river at a long wooden pier, where there would be carriages and wagons and all the Custers—*all of it!*—there was—

There was only the stern of the *Bailey,* still out in the stream, making headway north up the river, and on that stern where all the people from the ships should have been, had been, there was nothing.

On Twenty-sixth Street there were no carriages, no wagons, no one waiting. There had been no landing.

On the *Bailey* all the people in the stern had gone. On the roof of the cabin top there was no luggage roped down, no trunks, no bags nor bundles. There was only, as the *Bailey* moved on north up the river, smoke from her funnel. There was nothing.

There was only, behind him, a sooty, tattered shape that looked like something that had once been Ned Muldoon limping out from the hospital grounds and cursing.

"Raaa-hagghhh!" From inside the hospital grounds it was Roaring Lion Lewis at the wreck of his carriage. A lion, a hunter, a creature of the jungle—it sounded as if, at the end of the hunt, roaring his triumph, he was sitting down to eat his horse.

Minutes ago, in the stern of the *Bailey* there had been thirteen human beings. There had been, roped to the cabin top, all their belongings.

All he could see of the *Bailey* now as it went unhurriedly on its passage up the river with all the glass of its cabin shining in the morning sun was its emptiness.

They had not been landed at the pier.

All there was in the street all the way down to the pier were the little, well-tended houses of people connected with the hospital and the river.

In the street, all around him, there was not another living soul, and Tillman in that moment, like the carriage, starting to fly apart, feeling all the cement of his body swelling, exploding, the gun out in his hand ready to shoot with nothing and no one to shoot at, shrieked at the top of his voice to the shambling wreck who was Muldoon, to Lewis sitting down to eat his horse, to *anyone*—to the gods, to the sky, to the silence, to the smoke on the river—"A *boat!* For the love of God—bang on all the doors in the street and find me someone who has a *boat!*"

34

The *Bailey* was gone. It had taken twenty minutes at Twenty-sixth Street to find a boat and another twenty minutes for the boatman to get up steam to turn the prop over in his open one-lung steam launch and, by then, even the smoke had gone on the river and there was nothing but the still, clear glass surface of the tide at full flood and, far to the north, in the upper reaches of the river, clouds forming and turning the afternoon light golden brown.

In the prow of the moving boat Tillman's eyes did not move. They were beads staring straight ahead to where the *Bailey* had gone.

It had gone into invisibility. At the level of East Forty-second Street, spaced two lots apart as the city that high up thinned out, there were only warehouses, factories, coal yards, here and there set back on rises, hospices and hospitals for the dying and the fevered and the colored blanketed by smoke and the effluvia of cooking yeasts and malt from all the breweries of the city.

And there were no other public wharves or piers up there at all.

In the prow of the boat, Tillman, turning to the ancient, white-haired boatman jiggling at the controls on his engine, said, knowing the man did not know what he meant, "Where is it? Where's it gone?" He saw Muldoon rubbing at one of the many bruises on his shoulder and chest from the driving skill of Roaring Lion Lewis. Tillman, his face set, having no other question to ask, said with his eyes still squinting straight ahead, *"Bailey*— What's it mean? Captain Theodorus Bailey. I've never heard of him. Who was he?"

Two men in white coats had come down from Bellevue Hospital to dissuade Roaring Lion Lewis from eating his horse in the hospital grounds. He had had to help them. Every bone in his body hurt. Muldoon said, "He was a Police Captain in the old Metro police about twenty years ago." Muldoon, turning to the boatman, jerking his head upriver, demanded, "What's up here? After Fiftieth Street?" No one ever ventured that high on foot. It could have been the Wild West of Texas, or the Dakotas. Muldoon said above the steady popping of the tiny engine, "What's up here?" He could see the southern tip of Blackwell's Island coming, but beyond that, nothing.

"Blackwell's Island. The Charity Hospital and the Jail and the Lunatic Asylum—"

"Beyond the island?"

"Hell Gate, Ward's Island, Riker's—" It was as far north as you could go and still technically be in the City. The boatman said with a shrug, *"America."*

He could see nothing on the silver river. Tillman said without waiting for Muldoon to turn back from the boatman, "Why 'Custers'? Why that same picture in all the rooms and in the meeting room under Hewitt's?" The boat was making for the southern reaches of Blackwell's where the smallpox hospital was: he saw its gray stone buildings looming up and the warnings posted on the tip of the shore. Tillman said, "You were a soldier, Ned, why the 'Custers'?" Behind the smallpox hospital on the long, jagged spear of the mile-long island there was the outline of the Blackwell's Island penitentiary, and, behind that again, the shadows of the old Blackwell mansion that had given the island its name and, to its right, smoke rising from the female Alms House and hospice for terminal female venereal diseases. He had nothing else, "Why the *'Custers'?"*

He had no idea at all. Muldoon, watching the island, said shaking his head, "I don't know. In the Civil War I only ever saw Custer once and I'm not even sure it was him. All I know about him is that he was the youngest general in the Union Army and that he preferred English revolvers to American Colts." Muldoon said with a shrug, "Apart from that, like you, all I know is what I read in all the newspapers about how he died with all his command at the Little Big Horn against Crazy Horse and the Sioux." Muldoon said, as any male in the nation could, "June twenty-five, 1876."

"He died with his entire command of two hundred and sixty-four soldiers."

Muldoon said, " 'Troopers.' He was Cavalry. He was the Seventh Cavalry in the Indian Wars. In the Cavalry they call them 'troopers.' "

"Was he a hero?"

"So everyone says." In the Civil War at Chancellorsville he had been shot through the stomach. Sometimes at night, even twenty years later, it still hurt. Muldoon, still shrugging, looking away for a moment to the smokestacks of Schmitt and Schwunenfluegel's Original Foaming German Beer brewery up the eastern shore and smelling its product in the smoke that wreathed it, said with his own views on the glory of war, "I don't know if he was a hero or not. His command perished to a man. For one reason or another Reno and Benteen refused to move their men into the area to support him and so, unsupported, he died bravely with his men. If in death there's victory and valor, he died valorously and victoriously." Muldoon said, suddenly looking away from the brewery and into Tillman's eyes, "I don't know. To die valiantly in a hopeless battle with all your men who had no say in it is an English notion. We Irish prefer to die in bed with wailing family around us and the whiskey, not arrows, falling around us." He glanced back at the boatman and wondered if he was listening. He was an old man. Old enough to have lost sons in the War. Muldoon said, "But I don't know anything about the Indian Wars out West. Maybe it was different."

"They say he would have been President if he'd subdued the Indians. Is that true?"

"Why not? He was a Major General at twenty-nine for subduing the Rebs."

There was nothing on the river, no craft at all: they were too high.

All he could see on the still and silver river was the dark spear of Blackwell's Island coming closer and closer, and all the dark, terrible buildings on it like a fiefdom of disease and sickness, punishment and death.

"Where is it?"

All he could see was the smoke from all the scattered buildings and industries on the shore of Manhattan with all their piers and wharves empty.

They had lost forty minutes at Twenty-sixth Street and, with all the people in the stern of it already gone, they had lost the *Bailey.*

At the prow with only the dark finger of Blackwell's beginning to pass by his right, moving slowly in midstream less than five hundred feet from the smoky, obscured shore of Manhattan and the same distance from the terrible, dark silent island of madmen and prisoners, Tillman, gripping hard at the rubbing board of the little boat, staring straight ahead, said to no one, to Muldoon, to the boatman, to the Custers lost beyond finding, *"Where? Where—in the name of God—has it gone?"*

The boatman was a spare man in his mid or late sixties with thin white hair blowing in wisps back against his forehead with the vibration and exhaust from the engine. Once, he might have been a fisherman. There were deep ruts in the joints of all the fingers in his hands burned gray from the burning of the lines and the sun. Now, he was old and his strength was gone. Tillman, holding the man's eyes with his own, demanded, "The *Bailey*—where does it go up here?"

They were passing the East River Steam Kindling Wood factory on the western shore and on the right, on Blackwell's, the crenellated and turreted granite of the jail. On the island there was nothing, no movement nor sound however small. The island was forbidden territory. It housed disease and pestilence and madness and death. It housed the Prison and the Fever Hospital, the Refuge for Epileptics and, at its northern end, hidden behind walls the Asylums for the Indigent Blind and the Incurables Hospital. It housed the mad. The boatman said without looking at any of it, keeping his eyes ahead, "I don't know. I don't know anything."

"How often does the *Bailey* stop at the Twenty-sixth Street pier?"

"It stops there sometimes." The boatman, shaking his head, said, looking away, "I don't know."

"For what?"

He could smell the smell of the curing wood from the timber yard. He thought about that. The boatman, still shaking his head, said, "I don't know. To make pickups. To drop people off at Bellevue Hospital sometimes. I don't know."

"Is it a regular run?"

"Sometimes."

"Do you see the boat often?"

"Sometimes."

"Sometimes isn't often! *Does the* Bailey *make regular runs up here or not?*"

"Yes!"

"For what?"

"I don't know!" They were passing on the right the old Blackwell mansion that had given the island its name. It was a ruin, full of ghosts. All around it the grass and foliage had grown up and begun to eat into the stone like a cancer. The boatman, glancing at it, shaking his head, said, "I don't know anything about what happens on that island at all! I just do my job! I just ply for hire! I take my money, do my job and go home!" His hands were gone; he could never go back to making a living on the sea.

"Who's on that boat?"

"The Police—?"

"*Which police?* You see them regularly! You talk to people on the river—*which police?* What are their names?"

"Allison and McTeague, and Sergeant Reardon!" The boatman, glancing across at the island as if it could hear what he said, said quickly, "Allison and McTeague and Sergeant Reardon—someone just told me in a bar once." The boatman said, starting to tremble, "They've never done me any harm! I've never had any dealings with the police!" The boatman said, shaking, "Allison and McTeague and Sergeant Reardon!"

Muldoon said tightly, "Billy Jenkins' people. Jenkins' old mates from when he was with the Steamboat Squad. Reardon's been with the Squad for twenty years."

"What do they do up here in the *Bailey,* Allison and McTeague and—"

"I don't know what they do! It's none of my business!" They were paralleling the Female Alms House. They were paralleling its building. That was all they were paralleling: there was not a living, moving soul anywhere on the island. The boatman said, "I don't know! Up here, this high on the river, everything is islands and tidewaters and treachery. Anything that comes up here gets lost at Hell Gate! All the rich people with their yachts and their steam pleasure launches stay downriver where their friends can admire them from their great houses on the shore!"

"Then what the hell do you do up here?"

"I ply for hire!"

"Who takes the sick and the dying and the criminals onto the island?"

"Boats from the Office of the Superintendent of the Outdoor Poor!" He was shaking, afraid to look at them. The boatman said, "All I do is the occasional job if it isn't worth sending a big boat up! All I do is—" The boatman said, "I've got a contract with Bellevue Hospital! Sometimes, if it's not worth getting a big boat up, I take one of the lunatics from Bellevue onto Blackwell's and drop them off at the pier! Just sometimes!"

"What does the *Bailey* do up here? Where has it gone?"

They were a hundred feet out in the river, passing the Incurables Hospital and the Chapel and the Mortuary on the island. There was no movement there either. The boatman, turning the tiller slightly to starboard to get away, said, not looking at any of it, "I don't know. Up here, past here, all there is is Hell Gate and Ward's Island and—"

Tillman said suddenly, "What's that noise?"

The boatman said, "This is the end of the line!" He could hear it too. It was a low humming, a moaning. On the still air, it was coming from the top of the island where, like a castle at the edge of the known world, the Lunatic Asylum with its octagonal rotunda center rose up. The boatman said suddenly, desperately, not wanting to see it, "I just have a little contract with Bellevue! Nothing regular, just a little arrangement to make a few extra dollars to feed my family! I make a little and someone in the Office of the Superintendent of Outdoor Poor pockets a few more, but I—"

"I don't want you, or them! I want the *Bailey!*"

"I don't know where it is! It could be anywhere!" He bit his lip. The boatman said, "On the other side of the island, on the Long Island side there are plenty of little piers where—" The boatman said, "This side, all the piers are official and have their traffic checked in!"

"Is that how you do it when you land people from Bellevue?"

"I only do little jobs from time to time!" The boatman, his livelihood going, searching for power, said desperately, "It's not just Bellevue! It's everyone! Yesterday—yesterday I even dropped off someone from the Police!"

"One of the Steamboat Squad? One of the—"

"No, someone from Bellevue! Someone who—" The boatman said, "A patient! An official patient from Bellevue Hospital—someone for the asylum on Blackwell's!" He reached down and pulled aside a bilge cover. The boatman, taking something silver out from in there, said, "Look! Look! See! Handcuffs! Bellevue even gives me an official set of handcuffs to keep the patients manacled down with!" The boatman said, "Yesterday, I took a policeman up—a patrolman—a man who—" The boatman said with fear on his face, "All the way up, all he raved about were white rabbits disappearing into tunnels, and explosions, and being run down by trash collectors!" The boatman, pleading with Tillman, explaining, justifying, trying to take his attention from the rising, deepening sound coming down the river, said, "A patrolman! A cop! One of yours! Patrolman Simpson from the Sixth!"

All he could see from the boat was the high stone wall surrounding the Asylum and, running over it, moving down to the shore on linked poles and then disappearing as it went underwater toward the eastern shore of Manhattan, all he could see was—

He saw it too. For a moment, he did not even know what it was. Everywhere, everywhere, coming from somewhere, was the sound of the humming. Muldoon said, "Telephone lines!" They were at the northern tip of the island. In another hundred feet they would have gone around into the East River and— Muldoon said, "Virgil, *telephone* lines! That man—that pup in the telephone company—Drawbaugh—didn't he say—?" Muldoon said with his eyes wide and staring, "Didn't he say the man who, the man who he bought the company from, the man he claimed invented the telephone— *Didn't he say he ended up committed to the Asylum on Blackwell's?"*

"Stop here!" There was a beach landing on the island a hundred yards below the end of the stone wall around the asylum. Tillman, pointing to it said as an order to the boatman, "Stop here! Let us off here!"

"Do you see them? Do you see the wires?" From the island, everywhere, there was the sound of the humming and the murmuring. From the island, there were telephone lines running to the shore, then under the river to the world. Muldoon, wanting to reach forward and shake the little man in the prow of the boat hard to wake him up, demanded, *"Virgil, do you see the wires?"*

"I see them." His mouth was hard, twisted. Tillman said in a whisper,

"I see them," but he was not looking at them. He was looking at something else: at the looming shadow of the great Octagon, the five-story granite- and sandstone-columned rotunda that was the center of the walled city of the insane: he was looking at something on a little white flagpole that flew at its dome.

By his puffing, polished little one-lung engine, the boatman, near tears, not understanding, not knowing what anyone saw, knowing only that he had no trade to fall back on, said in desperation to stop them, "All I have is my little cash business—!"

"Land there!" It was a guidon: a little standard with twelve stars set in the corner of its blue field, its flying edge cut into a V and, in its center amid a circle of nineteen more stars, as military pennants did to denote their unit, a number.

It was a number Seven.

"Land here."

It was a pennant from a cavalry unit: the Seventh.

It was the unit pennant from the Western Seventh Cavalry. It was Custer's pennant.

High up there, above the sound of the humming, behind the stone walls of the Asylum where the telephone lines to the city ran from, like the flag of a fort on the edge of untamed Indian Territory, it flew in the darkening sky like a marker.

35

There was a terrible cry and then the sound of the humming rose, then stopped, and as Tillman and Muldoon pushed open the unlocked rusty gate into the grounds of the place, became a howling, a snarling, and they were in a melee of mad creatures terrified by the sight of them: men and women biting, wrenching, flailing at the rope and leather harness that bound them to a huge, painted flower- and shrub-bedecked iron-wheeled wagon.

In the grounds of the asylum, with the great domed Octagon looming up above them, they were men with hair disheveled and sticking up in spikes on their heads, women like hags in white shifts and no shoes, eyes wild, reaching out amid the shrieks and clenching, wrenching at the harnesses around their chests and necks holding them back like leashed dogs, tearing at their own flesh.

They were baying like dogs, convulsing. In the grounds, on the porch and entrance to the Rotunda, by the Ionic stone columns that framed it, in each of the windows of the twin single-story annexes that ran off from it, there was not another living soul, and they howled at nothing, shrieked to no one, stuck, wrenching, tearing, going nowhere.

There were twenty-eight of them, harnessed together to the painted, flowered wagon, like a single monstrous team. The wagon, made of oak wood and iron, its wheels rimmed and of colossal weight, had jammed deep into the ground and stuck. They had walked a rut, a trench in the ground fifty feet in diameter. It was a wagon, a weight to be pulled by the muscles of twenty-eight people, its wheels set to continue in a single circle forever—it was the Lunatics' Chariot. It was the suicide watch, scientific treatment: it was the exorcising of evil impulses by labor.

In all the windows in the Rotunda, in all the windows along the two wings of the asylum, of the madhouse, there was not another living soul. Tillman shouted above the screaming, "The main door! The main door leads up to the offices in the Rotunda and—" Everywhere there was decay. In the stones of the octagonal Rotunda vines and creepers had gotten in

258

between the masonry and were pushing, twisting like worms inside it, breaking it down from the inside. Tillman shouted, "Through the main door there has to be a corridor that leads to the wings!" He started for it. He saw Muldoon hesitate. He shouted amid the screaming and howling, "They're finished! They're only hulks. They're Suicides!"

Muldoon, transfixed, staring, said in disbelief, pointing, "That's Maisie O'Hanlon! She isn't mad! Her brain's just gone fuddled with the gin!" He had arrested her once for being drunk and disorderly. Muldoon, going to her, said, "Maisie—it's—" Muldoon, looming over her, stilling her cries, making her cower, said, "Maisie, it's Ned Muldoon from—" Muldoon, turning to Tillman to explain, rooted to the spot, forgetting all else, said in horror, "No, it's just the drink taken! It isn't—" Muldoon said, "Maisie, how can you have—" Muldoon said, "This poor girl's only thirty years old!"

"*Ned!*" They were the insane. There was nothing that could be done. Above the Rotunda he could see the flag flying. Somewhere in there were the Custers. Tillman, a head and shoulders shorter than Muldoon, getting too close, moving too quickly, plucking at his sleeve, shouted at him to bring him back to reality, "Ned, they're lost souls! There's nothing anyone can do!"

"*She's a good Catholic woman!*"

"Not anymore!" He saw the mad people staring at him. He saw their eyes narrow. He saw the harness tauten as they took the strain. He saw the harness jump as, in that instant, all the creatures at once exploded a single spasm of mighty strength that wrenched the wagon out of the rut, lifted it up through the air and turned it over with a crash that sent smashed wheel spokes and splinters flying.

"*Ned!*" He was at the portico to the Rotunda looking for what he knew was there. Everything was rotten, filthy, run-down, the vines and creepers moving up to the glass doors like the tendrils of insanity, eating it away, eroding it, splitting its foundations in long cracks and rifts.

"Virgil—!" They were after him. They were shrieking and screaming and wrenching, clawing at him. Maisie, her eyes wild and staring, seeing him not at all, had her hands out like claws to tear at him, to rend him limb from limb, with her toothless mouth open and slobbering, to *eat* him. Muldoon, rooted to the spot, shrieked, "*Virgil!*"

He found it. He knew it was there, and he found it. It was a water pressure outlet with a faucet tap connected to it, pointing outward, and, wrenching hard on it and turning it open full bore, Tillman, at the portico, sent a cataract of spraying water up and stilled them, froze them—by the mere sight of it, turned them to stone where they stood.

"Get back to your labors!" It was an order, a command. He had grown up in an orphanage. He knew what they did to mad people. Above him, out of sight, the little flag on top of the Rotunda was flying, flying. It was the flag of the Seventh—of the Custers.

Tillman, turning the flow off as quickly as it had come on, so close, so close, said as an order to Muldoon as he picked himself up from the ground, "Now! We're so close!" He had the shut glass doors to the terrible place behind him, both his guns—his revolver and shotgun—beneath his coat, and inches away, less than inches away, Tillman, unstoppable, stopping for nothing, all the wires and the flag in the sky above him, his heart leaping into his mouth, roared at Muldoon on his feet, "Now! In here! Inside this place! Inside this place together—*now!*"

In the huge entrance hall of the Rotunda there was only a single clock ticking, its hands at four o'clock, and here and there thinly upholstered chairs with deep scratch marks from fingernails on their arms and marks where there had been leather straps.

There was not a living soul anywhere. There was the smell, everywhere, of dampness and decay. In the light shining down five floors from the glass skylight in the domed roof above the deserted stairs that curved away to infinity like the way to the top of a lighthouse, everything was rotten and running with slime.

There was in that place no sound except the ticking of the clock.

There was the smell, everywhere, of damp.

It was the Rotunda: the center of the Asylum, the hub of Hell.

"Wather . . ." He said it in the Irish way, the way he had as a child in Meath in Ireland when his world had been secure. Muldoon, looking down, not understanding what had happened outside, seeing water in drips on the slate stones of the floor, not the same water, but a different water leading away like a track in droplets to one of the wings, said as a child to show Tillman, "Look . . . *wather!*"

It was the Madhouse.

It was a place on Earth God's hand had not touched. In front of him, still looking up, Tillman, his friend, turned to see him.

"Go that way!" His eyes had death in them. The track of water went to the left, through an archway, into one of the wings of the place. His finger was trembling as he pointed to it. Tillman said in a whisper, shaking, "You go that way!"

"For what?" Everything was lies. The *Bailey,* Archer, the Plague, deportations, criminals, Maisie . . . Sometimes, sometimes he felt his brain so inadequate for life he could have wept. "For what?" Muldoon, looking at the drops of water leading away, not understanding them either, said in hopeless confusion, *"I don't even know anymore what I'm looking for!"*

"That way!" His hands were shaking. *Thy rod and thy staff, they comfort me.* He put his hand under his coat to touch at his gun.

Tillman, so close, his voice a whisper, the ticking counting out the moments of life, said with all his purpose set, his course beyond change or variance, "That way! You go that way!"

Ahead of him, spiraling away to the roof where the flag flew, was the rotting flying staircase.

There was not the sound of another living soul anywhere in the place.

Taking the first step, making it creak, his hands clear of the banister rail, Tillman not waiting to see if Muldoon minded him or not, gazing upward, watching, listening, started—unstoppably—up.

In the corridor to the wing the drips of water became puddles. There were no windows in the corridor: it was a tunnel with a low, curved brick ceiling, smelling of damp, but the pools were not from that. The puddles were a trail, a spoor, little irregular circles on the ground as if someone had gone down there with a bucket or a pail filled too high and sloshed it as he walked.

It was a snail's trail. In the yellow light from the low-burning gas jets on the walls, it shone silver footsteps.

Water. He wondered why, out in the grounds, the lunatics had stopped at the sight of the running water.

In the corridor, moving slowly, his hand at his hip pocket where his pistol was, Muldoon, moving on tiptoe, could hear no sound at all.

He stopped.

He listened.

Everywhere, in splashes and spots and drips, held in the hollows of the worn-down stone floor, he could see the water.

He leaned down and touched one of the puddles with his fingertips and it was not water at all.

In the little melting shards and slivers, painful to the touch, it was ice.

The telephone wires had arced from the shore of the island to a line of poles and then, as they ran to the Rotunda of the asylum, they disappeared into the stone foundation blocks and were gone.

On the stairs, Tillman could see no sign of them anywhere.

If the wires went into the asylum, to the offices on the top floor of the Rotunda, then they ran behind the walls the last hundred feet, or had been hidden between the mortar of the blocks and came in at a window somewhere.

The stairs curving away to all the floors were thick mahogany, put in when the hospital had been built as an exercise in philanthropy thirty-six years before in 1848 when the duties of Christian care for the few witless creatures thrown up by honest families had been simple and clean—before the Civil War and immigration and cheap gin had filled the streets with a multitude of the demented and dangerous—and the Christians had moved on to a problem of more moderate proportions: the care and saving of carriage horses. The stairs, like the care for the mad, were in derelict state, out of style: the rooms on all the floors, as he climbed, open and empty with plaster and laths falling down from their walls and ceilings.

He thought perhaps if there was a telephone line to the top floor where the flag was, it could be live with electricity and vibrating, and, pausing a moment on the third floor at the landing, he put his hand flat against the wall to feel for it, but there was nothing and the wall was damp and loose, the plaster with the vines growing in the wall behind it starting to lose its adhesion and slide away like the plaster in all the rooms on the way up; and there was no sound at all, anywhere; and he and Muldoon were on an island and there was no help to be had.

At the bottom step of the rise to the fourth floor Tillman, leaning over the banister, looked down to the hallway vestibule.

He saw only the gray slate of the floor and a shaft of light from the skylight above shining down to it like a tunnel.

All the wood of the staircase was dark and dull with age and disuse.

He heard, from the vestibule fifty feet below, as if it came from a cavern, only the steady ticking of the clock.

At the end of the corridor—of the tunnel—the puddles stopped at a metal door and went under it, and, as he leaned forward to put his ear near it, Muldoon could hear the sound of water, and, as he listened, the sound of murmuring.

He listened to the murmuring and could not tell if it was human or animal.

He listened, and it was not murmuring at all, but a sort of lowing, something quiet and bovine, bestial, something sleeping.

The door had no lock on it, was merely held closed by two six-inch-long spring hinges at the top and bottom.

They were moist with oil, in use.

He touched at the door and it gave an inch and he let it come back on what must have been a spring somewhere on the other side of it.

His mouth was dry and he ran his tongue across his lips to keep it moist.

He heard the murmuring. He heard it like the soft, sad calls of souls lost in limbo.

He was the last of the male Meath Muldoons.

He wondered how Tillman had known about the water. He wondered what it meant.

At the door, pausing for a moment, Muldoon drew a breath.

At the door Muldoon said softly to himself, *"I'm Sullivan. I'm the great John L. Sullivan with paws like poleaxes!"*

It comforted him. It swelled out his chest.

At the door, his hands out in front of him balled into fists, ready to face whatever was in there like a man, Muldoon began, slowly, to push forward against the pressure of the spring.

Tillman was on the top floor. On the top floor only—the only one on all the floors—there was a room with a closed door.

On the landing on the top floor the light from the skylight fell down in a beam like a weight and sucked all the breath out of him, and he had to force his chest to work to fill his lungs with air.

He saw through the skylight, hanging down from its staff on the dome of the place, the flag of the Custers.

He saw, running down from the staff, its rope halyard.

It snaked, going out of sight to his left down from the top of the Rotunda, down through the domed roof to whatever was in the room behind the closed door.

He had his Colt Lightning out in his hand in front of him, the hammer cocked back, ready.

Echoing, being magnified by the empty cavern of the place he heard the clock downstairs in the entrance hall click the minute, and in that instant, leaning back to gather power, with all his force, kicking at the wooden lock mortise and smashing it to splinters, he burst open the door and got in.

He saw no telephone anywhere in the room, only a desk and cupboards and a safe set into the wall, and—

In the room, on the wall, by the hook where the end of the rope halyard came in through a skylight, Tillman, seeing not a living soul in the room, saw, sheathed in its curved nickeled scabbard, a sword—a saber.

He saw a picture, a painting: he saw Mulvany's painting of Custer's Last Stand in the Dakotas.

He saw what was there in the room and, through the curved single vista window on its side, what there was to be seen from it.

* * *

He was ready.

He was not ready for what he saw.

At the open doorway, filling it with his bulk, Muldoon, all his resolution gone, said in a gasp, "Oh, my God!!"

He saw what was there in the room.

36

He thought for a moment it was a Mortuary.

It was not a Mortuary; all the bodies were moving slightly, their cheeks billowing in and out, breathing clouds of white vapor in the ice-cold low-ceilinged hall, where, in rows and lines and ranks—hundreds of them—they lay in oak-framed box baths, held down by flat boards secured to the sides of the baths by chains.

He was John L. Sullivan: he had his fists clenched and he was in a low crouch at the open door.

There was the sound of low murmuring in the room. Line after line, row after row, there were the bloodless faces above the ends of the restraining boards with eyes like coals looking up at the ceiling and breathing vapor.

In the baths, all round the naked, hidden bodies, there was ice and ice water. Here and there, where it had been broken up from blocks, it was in melting shards and bergs on the stone floor around the baths.

There was from the white, drained faces with hair and eyes too dark to be human, the sound of low murmuring.

There were hundreds of them. The baths were coffins, chained down, and he thought for a moment that some of them were women, but they were all men.

The room was cold, like a tomb, full of the white vapor of their breath.

Muldoon, his hands locked together at his chest, his thumbs stiff in the cold, his hands rigid, locked, said because he could not think of anything else to say, "Oh, my God . . . !" He wanted to ask someone, someone in charge, who all the people were, but there was no one in charge—not a living, standing soul in the room in charge—and he already knew who the people were.

Muldoon still at the door said in a whisper, "God . . . !"

In the white, bloodless faces their eyes were like rubies, their hair was dark and flattened, like wigs. In row after row, line after line, above the chained-down body boards they were like the heads and shoulders of

265

porcelain dolls in a shop window. They were like the busts of dead people made of marble along the entrance walk to a mausoleum. With only their cheeks billowing in and out from the breathing, from the little clouds of vapor about their mouths, they made only the softest murmuring sound.

Water and ice: it was what the demented harnessed to the Lunatics' Chariot in the grounds had feared when Tillman had turned on the faucet tap at the portico. He had done it without thinking—he had grown up in an orphanage: he had done it without thinking. Muldoon, appalled at what he must have known, said with his voice becoming thin, losing its manliness, "Oh, my God!"

It was the brain-pan cooling room of the men's ward on the east wing of the Blackwell's Island Lunatic Asylum. In the west wing, there must have been another for women.

Muldoon said in horror with her face in his mind, *"Maisie . . . !"* He had arrested her. She was a fair-quality woman gone bad with the drink. He had helped send her here. Muldoon said, *"Maisie . . . !"*

He put his hand to his mouth.

He saw, in the first row, ashen and drained, the faces gazing up at the ceiling.

Muldoon, taking a single step forward, his own breath vaporizing into a cloud in the awful place, looking down at the face he knew, said with his voice a whisper, "Simpson? Patrolman Simpson? Patrolman Ruben Simpson—*is that you?*"

The top room Tillman had burst into was an administrator's office, probably the office of the asylum Superintendent. With the overcrowding and dereliction of charity establishments all over the city, it was a room that no longer boasted opulence or position. It was like the madhouse and the island itself: something shoved out of the way, rotting, forgotten, decaying with time and negligence.

In the room on the top floor of the Rotunda he could see through the picture window the lighthouse at the northern end of the island that signaled the limits of civilization. He could see, beyond it, the river turning away to where all the other islands beyond the Pale were: Ward's Island, Riker's—the prisons, the asylums, way north, out of sight, where all the other refuse from the city was—to Hart Island, where, in trenches and mass graves, the poor and unwanted and unclaimed of the city were buried.

Everywhere in the room there was the smell of damp and decay.

On the desk in the center of the room there was nothing at all: no papers, nor inkwells nor blotters. Leaning against the wall to one side of the window, mounted on pasteboard so it could be picked up for easy reference, there was only a two-foot-by-two-foot diagram of the nerve points in the human elbow.

It was the diagram used by police and madhouse keepers to locate the Bedlam Paralyzing Grip. It was a diagram of the place to reach for with the fingers that short-circuited all the nerves in the arm and, with an explosion of pain to the brain, reduced a raving and dangerous lunatic or criminal to a moaning wreck on the ground.

Apart from the painting of Custer at bay from the Indians and the sword there was nothing else on the walls of the room at all.

He pulled open the top drawer of the desk. In it there was only the empty holster of a military issue Colt Cavalry Peacemaker revolver.

There was a tiny spy window on the right side of the wall of the room, the wooden frame around it rotting with damp and black with age and lack of maintenance, but down below, somewhere out in the grounds, someone must have been burning something and he could not see anything from it for the smoke.

There were no books of medicine, nor instruments of treatment, or chemicals or drugs in the room at all.

He pulled open the second drawer and there was only a black leather-bound hymn book from Trinity Church in the city; inserted between its pages was a single sheet of paper and a photograph.

It was a list.

Running downward in a neat, orderly hand, line by line, it read:

Oubliette	*Jenkins,*
Embrasure	*Allison,*
Donjon	*McTeague,*
Palisade	*Hewitt,*
Portcullis	*Reardon,*
Archer	*Archer,*
Bailey	——

The photograph was a tintype from the days of the Indian Wars.

It read, on the back, *January 8, 1876. Dakotas.*

It had, under it, a single name: KELLOR, Saml. P. (M.D.)

The picture was of a tall, cadaverous-looking man wearing a medical coat standing proudly next to someone outside a bivouac tent in a military field hospital somewhere.

The someone he stood next to did not have his name written on the back of the picture.

There was no need.

Standing ramrod erect, his chest puffed out, in his full, braided uniform, his long yellow hair falling down over his collar, his hand resting on his doctor's shoulder, it was General of the Army and Commander of the Seventh Cavalry, George Armstrong Custer.

Muldoon shouted, *"It wasn't a rabbit, it was us! It was Virgil Tillman and me and the Grimm brothers!"* Muldoon, wrenching the chain apart with his bare hands, pulling at the board that covered the man's nakedness, reaching in and grasping the ice-cold flesh under the man's shoulders and pulling him out like a drowned corpse from an ice hole, said with tears running down his face, *"For the love of God, Ruben, we didn't know! All we wanted to do was get in under the sidewalk at Hewitt's and we didn't know!"* Pulling him out, it was like a picture Muldoon had in his mind of someone—he thought it was the Blessed Virgin holding the dead, white body of Christ across her lap and mourning with her eyes raised to Heaven. It was cold in there, like a church in winter. It was—

Lifting the man out, looking around for something to cover him with, finding nothing, wanting to take his own coat off and having nowhere to put the limp, thin, frozen body down on except the cold stone floor while he did it, Muldoon said to explain, to make it right, "I never knew! No one did! No one meant you to suffer like this!"

He had never realized how old Simpson was, how, without the uniform, he was just a thin, aging man with the flesh around his muscles going soft. He had never realized how little he weighed. Muldoon, trying to balance, getting the man up like a dead, limp body under his left arm and fighting to get his coat off with his right, said looking down at the man as if he was a doll under the arm of a girl, *"Ruben, it's Ned! It's Ned Muldoon—it's a fellow policeman!"* Muldoon getting down on one knee, trying to rest the body not on the floor but across his other knee, getting the coat off and trying to cover the man's chest with it, said with his face all covered by the vapor from Simpson's breath, "Ruben, you crippled the Grimm kid: that's why the Grimms did it to you, but they're real men and they would have fought you if they thought they'd had a chance against your uniform, but they—we—*no one ever knew this is what would happen to you!*"

Muldoon said in horror, "Oh, my God—" Tillman, at the portico, had turned the tap faucet on. He had known about such things. He had grown up in an orphanage. Muldoon said, "Oh, my God—*do they do this to children as well?*" Simpson's eyes, looking up at him, were coals in the stark-white bloodless face. Muldoon, wanting to slap blood into the cheeks but only touching, only stroking at the brow, said to rouse the comatose, lost, subdued man, "Ruben! It's a mistake! No one intended by their actions to send you *here!* The Grimms, if they thought they could have fought you fair and square, would have fought you fair and square!" The eyes, the windows of the soul, were dead as was the soul itself. He shook him by the shoulder and it was like laying his hand on marble. Muldoon, shouting, trying to wake the thing inside the body that had been put to sleep, cried, "Ruben! *Ruben Simpson!"*

"Ruben!" In the terrible, ice-cold place, in the center room of the madhouse, in the room where the souls of the mad were murdered, Muldoon, begging, entreating, shaking, his eyes running with bitterly cold tears and shame of damnation, shouted above the murmuring, his voice echoing in the stone, windowless coffin-hall of the insane, "Ruben, for the sake of my own promised place in Heaven—*wake up and forgive me!"*

Samuel P. Kellor, M.D.
Superintendent, Blackwell's Is. Asylum, 1881.
In the same neat hand, it was written across the flyleaf of the hymnal.

> *Jenkins*
> *Allison*
> *McTeague*
> *Hewitt*
> *Reardon*
> *Archer*
> *Bailey*

It was the list of all the guardians of Castle New York, Fort Manhattan—whatever it was they called it. It was Rosie drowning in a bathtub, held down until her lungs exploded and she went limp, and, like refuse, like only flesh with no soul, she was taken away and disposed of in the river. It was Hewitt already dead, waiting for his undertakers and shooting horses in the street to clear the way for their hearse. It was the room under Hewitt's store with its tables and its telephones. It was Jenkins on fire and screaming in the street. It was Archer half crazed with opium with blood running down his face in the glasshouse as it smashed to shards around him. It was Rosie's sister Lily, reeling with gin and seeing the ghost of her sister and falling, falling interminably. It was—

Kellor, Saml. P. (M.D.)
It was the Custers.

"Ned?"
He could not understand. The eyes were back, but they blinked, and he could not understand where he was and, looking down at it, touching it with fingers that could not feel the material, he touched at Muldoon's oversize coat around his chest and did not know how it had gotten there.

Ruben Simpson, all the hardness gone from his face, said, trying to understand, not yet realizing he was naked beneath the strange coat, "Ned? Ned Muldoon?"

"The telephones! All we were trying to do was find the telephones!"

"Ruben Simpson, Ned. With the Sixth. I worked with you once when you were with the Strong Arm Squad when we raided Harry Hill's Saloon on—"

"I know who you are!" He could not look into the man's face. He could not stop the tears running down his face. Muldoon, his hand soft on the man's cheek, looking away, said with his voice a whisper, "I know who you are." Muldoon said in desperation, talking not to Simpson but to God, apologizing, "All we were doing was trying to find the telephones." He could not look down, "No one knew! Not even the Grimms! No one knew that places like this were—" Muldoon, desperate, finding no God, said as a shriek, *"All we were doing was trying to get in under the sidewalk to find the telephones!"*

He thought any moment Simpson would die. He could not stop his tears. He could not look down at the man. All he could do was stroke his face. Muldoon, forcing himself to look, starting his penance, said with all the muscles in his neck tight and his voice cracked and gone, "Ruben . . ."

"In there, Ned!" The eyes were bright, useful. They were the eyes of a living man. "In there, Ned!" He had his finger up and pointing to the far corner of the room, "A door, Ned, behind that door, in there!" Simpson, his face breaking into a terrible grin, a triumph, said pointing hard, "I told them! I told them I was a policeman! I told them! I told them I was almost a detective, like you, Ned—*I told them!*"

He could not stop his tears and he almost did not hear what the man said.

Simpson, the color coming back, the eyes coming back, said, saved, "Telephones, Ned? In there, Ned, lots of them! In there!"

He had no words to say and no tears left to weep. He merely, in his arms, held the man.

Patrolman Ruben Simpson of the Sixth, happy to assist, touching at the coat covering his nakedness, searching with his fingers for the brass buttons and shield that all his life he had had to clothe him, said with his finger trembling in the direction of the closed door at the far end of the awful anteroom to Hell, "I see things! I notice things! I file things away—that's why I'm a cop. Telephones: is that what you want to know about?"

"Yes." Muldoon said softly, "Yes."

"I'm studying. All the time, at night, I'm studying, watching, listening." He had a secret. Simpson said in a whisper, "I want to be a detective, Ned, like you." He remembered his business, "In there, Ned, in there!"

His voice was a whisper. It was his secret.

Simpson, patting at the hand that gently stroked his face, said as his secret, as his whisper, "Ned, I always wanted to be a man like you."

He looked and the smoke had cleared outside the spy window and they were down there, Allison, McTeague, and Sergeant Reardon, and they were standing next to someone with his back to him and, on the foreshore of the island, standing in a circle like children at a bonfire, they were burning something.

He saw him. He saw the tall, cadaverous man with them turn and he saw Kellor. He saw the outline of the long-barreled Cavalry Colt under the tightness of his buttoned-up white doctor's coat.

He saw him turn back to the river to look at something. He saw them look.

He saw them see what it was.

"Wait here."

At the closed door in the far corner of the room, Muldoon, setting Simpson down gently on a low wooden bench with his back to the wall, leaning down to pull the coat around his shoulders to keep him warm, said in a whisper, "Wait here."

In his hip pocket he had his Smith and Wesson Number Two service revolver and he touched its butt with his left hand and felt it ice-cold.

"Wait here." He looked to see if Simpson's eyes registered what he said. He said again in a whisper, "Wait."

His hand, ready on the butt of his gun, felt like the cold hand of death.

"Wait." He said it again. And again, "Wait."

Slowly, with his heart ice in his mouth, he went to the closed door at the far end of the room and resting his free hand flat against its surface, began pushing it to get it open.

He saw, as the quartet of burners looked back down into the flames and the smoke of whatever it was they were destroying, a little way down the shore at a pier in a tiny natural cover, puffing smoke from her idling engine, ready at any moment to depart, the *Bailey*.

37

He could barely push the door open against some sort of powerful spring holding it closed, then suddenly, all the pressure was released and he was in a darkened room and the door, thrown back by tempered steel or a human hand, or God only knew what, slammed shut and he was struck across the shoulder by something that could have been a brick or a rock and poleaxed hard to the floor.

He felt his revolver fly out of his hand. Falling face down his forehead hit something soft like leather, like the leather covering of a horsehair sofa, and as he rolled on it he tried to get to one knee, got to one knee and was hit again and thrown back against the door.

He saw in the darkness as he fell, fifteen feet up in the air, two unblinking yellow eyes.

The door was padded. He felt buttons on the leather as he reached out to get a hold on it, and then, as whatever it was in the room moved toward him and swung the weapon down in an arc that whistled in the air, he was tripping over backward and the room was full of bats.

He had lost his gun. Muldoon, dodging down in the blackness, losing purchase on the yielding upholstery of the floor, screamed, *"Jesus Christ!"* He saw the yellow eyes in midair. The bats were flapping down on leather wings, cutting into his hands and folding down around his fingers as he reached up to protect his face.

He heard a buzzing, and the bats were all around him, on him, on his head, his shoulders, his legs, and, as he tried to take a step to get away from them, something moving swiped at him with the weapon, caught him a stinging blow against the hip, and as he flailed to keep the bats away, they rose up all around him and clung to him, flapped at him and sliced at him with the honed, hard edges of their wings.

"Ruben!" The room was padded, windowless, soundproof, and outside Simpson could not hear.

He heard whatever it was in the room breathe. He heard it breathe in sharp, short gasps. Then, in the darkness, he heard the breathing stop.

Muldoon, not knowing where to look, said as a command, "This is Muldoon of—" and then there was a terrible blow at his knees that lopped him down like a tree trunk, and whatever it was in the room was on top of him—tiny, half-sized, a gnome, a gargoyle—and it was flailing for his face and, missing, thudding the brick or the stone or the club off the horsehair beside him, and he was drowning, flailing out, flapping his arms away from his body like a man in a nightmare unable to fix on the object of his terror and smash it.

He reached up and felt a neck and, his hands like the jaws of a vise, strangled it.

There was a gurgling, a squawk, and then the bats at the bidding of the gargoyle and the still unblinking yellow eyes of whatever beast lived in there with the gargoyle came down in flights and, spreading their wings across his face, smothered him. They readied their razor teeth for the bite. He pulled away, pushing at the bats as they battered on his face for suction.

"*Simpson—!*" It was no use: the man outside could not hear. On his back, crawling, jerking like an upended crab, Muldoon, slapping at the floor like a downed, caught wrestler, yelled, "*—Ruben Simpson!*" but outside, ashen, bloodless on his bench the man could not hear, and in that instant, slapping at the floor, his palm touched the gun and bringing his left hand up to clasp his hands together over his chest to turn the barrel of the thing the right way around and get his fingers on the trigger, Muldoon, getting to his feet, aiming for the eyes on the wall, roared in command, "Stop! I'm Muldoon of the Police! *Stop where you are or I'll shoot!*"

He saw the yellow eyes glow.

He heard a sound, a whisper of movement.

He felt the bats fall, become helpless and drop.

All the bats were dead or exhausted, or they were—

He saw the twin eyes on the wall grow brighter, the yellowness turn to white and form circles of light on the black padded-leather wall behind them.

He saw the eyes glow white. He saw them become two gaslight jets on the wall, their intensity regulated by a long, thin brass chain hanging down from their Siamese fittings.

He saw, everywhere in the black-leather-padded room, on tables and benches and shelves, wooden and brass telephone instruments, with, like the strands of a spider's web, leads and earpieces running out from them.

He saw the bats.

The bats were manila dossiers and files, full of lined paper, thousands of them: he saw them everywhere on the floor around him.

He saw the gargoyle, the demon.

He saw, staring at him with what looked like a brick in his hand, a man in his fifties, ashen-faced as if he had never seen the sun, no more than five feet two inches high wearing, with all the buttons and badges shining in the light as he pulled on the chain to raise the gas jet with his hand, the uniform of a telegrapher.

He saw, at bay, staring at him with an unblinking stare, a madman.

In the room, with all the banks of telephones buzzing and making sparks as their mechanisms worked, seeing the pointing gun not at all, his eyes like coals holding Muldoon's, the madman taking a single step forward raised up the brick in his hands to strike.

On the foreshore the fire was almost out. Taking his watch from his vest pocket and snapping it open to glance at its face, Dr. Kellor, addressing Sergeant Reardon as the senior noncom present, said as a little reward for their help, "Go get yourselves a drink."

Dr. Kellor said, in case Reardon thought he might take a drink with them, "I have to check on the ice rooms to see no one's drowned."

Kellor said with a thin, comradely grin, "Or to make sure a few of them have."

He saw their stupid faces try to work out if that was his little joke.

Dr. Kellor, giving the ashes of the fire where all the papers and documents from the boat had been burned only a cursory final flick with his boot, said as an order, "A drink. In the Chief Orderly's room in the mess hall. One drink. A small one. Whiskey."

Allison, the younger of the two patrolmen, the one who looked a little like a terrier in his pressed, neat, parade-ground turn-out uniform, said enthusiastically, "Thank you, sir." He looked at Patrolman McTeague and grinned like a small boy.

"Very well." He nodded. He thought for a moment Sergeant Reardon, thinking hard, was about to engage him in friendly conversation.

He put an end to that notion.

Putting his watch back deftly into his pocket he turned away quickly and, without another word, began walking rapidly toward the Rotunda to come in quietly by the back door to the corridor of the east wing.

He looked up at his flag, and then, suddenly, back through a maze of trees and overgrowing bushes to where the *Bailey* was, and thought, just for a moment, he saw a movement.

He thought it was one of the Steamboat cops gone back to the boat because he was a teetotaler.

They were none of them—men in their stations in life—teetotal, and Kellor, dismissing the thought, walked on toward the wing.

He thought he heard a noise in the trees.

The wind.

He thought—it was conceivable—it was one of the ice people broken loose and escaping, but he had seen darkness in the movement—clothes—and they had none.

It was a foolish, mentally undisciplined fancy, but, touching instinctively at his Cavalry Colt in his waistband in his back, quickening his step, Dr. Kellor, the Superintendent of Blackwell's Island Asylum for almost five years now, thought he had better fulfill his charged function and check.

It was Eldridge. It was Eldridge of the old Metal Tympanium Electro-Magnetic Speaking Telephone Company before Drawbaugh's consortium had bought him out. There were telephone apparatus everywhere, listening horns and speaking tubes, wires, bells, wooden casings, telephones in states of construction, repair, maintenance. Muldoon, taking the gun in both hands and pointing it out at the man's heart, said, "You're Eldridge! All these telephones go to the room under Hewitt's store and to Jenkins' house in Brooklyn and Archer's office at the Battery!"

It was as if he saw Muldoon for the first time. It was as if, as he cocked his head to one side to stare at him, he had never seen anything like him in his life before. It was as if—

Muldoon said, *"Drop the brick!"*

He looked away.

Muldoon said, *"Drop the brick!"*

He looked down at the brick and shook it.

He tried to think crazy. Muldoon said with his voice still hard, not relenting, "It's not connected to your hand."

Wasn't it? He looked down at it. He shook it to see if it was connected. His fingers were curled around it and it could have been. He looked at the gun and did not know what a gun was. He cocked his head to look at the face above it.

Muldoon said as an order, "Let the brick drop." Muldoon said, "I'm Muldoon of the Police. I'm Ned Muldoon of the Detective Bureau, New York City Police, Mulberry Street." Muldoon, touching at it with a stiffened finger of steel, said, "This is an official police pistol, and I—"

"Muldoon?" He looked down at the dossiers. He was a tiny sparrow in the uniform of the Telegraphy Service. Eldridge, suddenly blasting air from his lungs in an explosion of mirth and disbelief, said, laughing, amused, not fooled for an instant, *"No."*

"If you value your life—!"

Eldridge said, "Ha, ha, ha, ha, ha—hah!" He looked down at the dossiers. Eldridge said in happy amusement, *"No—!"* He shook his head. Eldridge said with heavy irony, "Muldoon. 'Muldoon'?" Eldridge said, "And you're a policeman? A God-fearing man of the law?" Eldridge said happily, "Ha, ha, ha, ha, ha—hah!" Eldridge said suddenly warningly, "I'm amused and I know you are trying to amuse me, *but a lie is still a lie!"*

"Drop the brick now!"

Eldridge said, thinking about it, " 'Eldridge'?" Eldridge said, grinning, "That's a funny name. You're a comedian sent to amuse me." He thought he heard something behind him and he turned for an instant to see what it was, and—in the name of pity at last put the brick down on the bench. Eldridge, turning back, said with a smile, thanking someone, "Thank you. It was thoughtful, 'Muldoon,' but I have no need for amusement because I never tire. I cannot. It is not in my nature. I listen. I hear. I *know.*" Eldridge said, forming the word like an elocutionist, " 'Eldridge.' Oh, I have been called many things, but not that, and not that by something calling itself 'Muldoon.' "

In the little room on the island he was connected—wired—in control of every telephone machine in the entire city of New York. Everything he heard, he wrote down in the dossiers.

He stopped smiling. His eyes in the tiny, pallid, pinched little face were burning black.

Eldridge said to put an end to the blasphemy, "I listen! I hear!" He stabbed his finger angrily at the dossiers on the floor. He wanted the man's real name. He wanted it now.

In the padded room, in his web, the leaves and folders and dossiers of his Great Record everywhere about him on the floor, Eldridge said with his eyes burning fierce and vengeful, "I am God."

"Muldoon"—the word no longer amused him. He could check. Pointing hard to the dossiers, to all the prayers all men offered up to him, he could check.

Eldridge, roaring it out, thundering in the little Heaven of his room, demanded, "Well? Tell me now, 'Muldoon'—have you or have you not been *good?"*

In the corridor leading to the east-wing ice room he saw the puddles and shards of ice the orderlies had carried in for the baths.

He saw, through them, passing over them, breaking them up, the marks of footprints—not bare feet but boots. He saw where they went.

It was a raider, an infiltrator. It was a spy.

Drawing his revolver, cocking it, holding it out in front of him to shoot the moment he saw a shadow, Dr. Kellor, his shoes ringing on the stone floor, ran for the door of the ice room to instantly dispatch with no quarter whatever it was that, undetected, had gotten in there.

He ran headlong, armed and unstoppable, toward the Enemy.

38

On the shore Tillman could not see Reardon or McTeague, Allison or Kellor anywhere. Between the time he had gotten down the stairs and down to the boat they had gone.

The fire was only ashes. Whatever it was they had been burning—paper, something frail—had been totally consumed.

At the little pier the *Bailey* was lying heavily in the water with eddies and currents in an incoming flow of water from the western side of Astoria and Ravenswood slapping at her white painted oak sides. Somewhere, north in the river at Hell Gate between Yorkville on the island of Manhattan and Astoria on the mass of Long Island there must have been winds and currents working: she slewed at first one way against her mooring lines, then seemed to be pushed back, then, as the current or the air masses moving above the land changed and the water changed with it, she pushed forward, strained against her ropes and, pushing abaft, sluggishly thumped against the kapok-filled canvas fenders protecting her woodwork from the pier and then pushed out again.

She was fifty feet long, a converted steam trawler with auxiliary mast and sails, her name *Captain Theodorus Bailey* painted in black on her bow in letters six inches high.

With her engine turning over below decks, there was only the puffing sporadic spume of white smoke from her funnel. The sun was low in the sky behind him, not reflecting, and at the wooden railing, peering in, he could see through the three square windows on her port side into the wheelhouse.

All the brass in there—her gimballed lantern and binnacle and ship's clock and barometer—was polished brass. Like exhibits in a museum they shone in the dull light out at him.

He could see no one anywhere in sight. Behind the east wing of the Rotunda there were what looked like low dormitory or mess buildings with barred windows set back behind a high chain wire fence. The grounds between the buildings and the fence were deserted and if Kellor and Reardon and Allison and McTeague had gone there, they were in behind closed doors and he could see nothing of them.

On the pier he waited for a moment, but if anyone saw him from the dormitories they did not report it or remark on it, and no one came.

On the *Bailey* there was no sign at all of the trunks or boxes that had been lashed to her cabin top when he had seen it from Swinburne. Perhaps they had been merely thrown overboard into the river.

There was from the *Bailey* the sound of the engine turning over at low revolutions, the shaft disconnected from the propeller being revolved by the steady thumping of the piston.

He listened but he heard above the sound only the creaking of the hemp lines that held the boat moored to the pier.

There was not another living soul anywhere to be seen.

He drew a breath and listened.

Listening hard, he could hear no sound at all except for the creaking of the ropes and the engine.

She was like an exhibit in a museum, clean and polished and still— deserted, like something excavated from the ground and set on display. She was a lifeless, gently moving ship.

He glanced back once to the dormitories.

He did not even know, on that shore, on that ship, what he was looking for.

There was a closed gate in the railing just a little back from the closed, polished mahogany door to the cabin, and, slipping its bolt back to free it and pushing it inward on oiled hinges, taking hold of the railing on either side to give himself purchase, stepping up from the pier, he boarded the *Bailey*.

Around the spoked wooden wheel where the pilot stood the wheelhouse was full of instruments and implements: boathooks set in clips on the curved, oiled ceiling, grappling hooks and lines coiled and lashed with sailor's knots against the rear wall, lanterns and running lights in their places in hollowed-out shelves along the floor, Winchester rifles and flares and ammunition in what looked like an arms locker below the ship's clock and barometer, here and there brass hooks screwed to bulkhead sections for uniforms or lifebelts, charts and maps of the harbor rolled in tubes, and clipped up on a panel, unused on a river boat, two full sets of navigator's instruments, hand compasses and navigator's rulers and, set in a line, all sharpened to needle points, a dozen pencils and an eraser for removing the marks the pencils made on the charts after a voyage was done.

There was no sound anywhere except for the muffled turning of the engine and, in the cabin with the beam of almost eighteen feet to cushion it, no movement of the current outside or sound of the river slapping at the hull.

She was empty, deserted.

"Tillman. Detective Bureau." Below the cabin room, she was a labyrinth of holds and bilges and cramped dark spaces accessible only from closed hatches on the planked, polished deck.

"Tillman! Detective Bureau!"

He said it loudly in that empty wheelhouse to prove that he could.

He heard from below, from all the places under his feet, only the steady thumping of the engine, and, taking a polished brass signal lantern down from its place on the shelf, carrying it by its brass loop and hearing the lard oil in the reservoir slosh as he went, he went back out of the wheelhouse cabin and onto the deck behind it to lift up a hatch and get in.

"Bell!"

He took a step backward. *"Bell!"* He thought, for an instant, it was the vexatious litigator of telephone patents come to kill him. Eldridge, reeling back and colliding with his table, knocking telephones and telephone earpieces, telephone wires, magnets, armatures, telephone speakers and telephone cogs and wheels, fuses and switches, connectors and disconnectors everywhere onto the floor around his feet, said in horror, "Bell! You're Alexander Graham Bell come to get me!"

In the padded cell Muldoon screamed at the man, "Are you *crazy?*"

Yes, he was. He was a crazy man in a padded cell in a lunatic asylum.

Everywhere on the floor were the burst-open files and dossiers, the names of the subjects written over and over in ink to make the letters big, the dossiers crammed to bursting with handwritten pages.

Muldoon, advancing, saw on one a name.

Jenkins.

The Custers. It was them.

He was six feet two, monstrous, huge in the tiny room. His shoulders hurt like hell from the brick.

He was God. He heard the tiny man's breath catch. He heard him gasp.

He saw him, at his table of Infernality, cower in fear.

All Tillman could see below the hatch was a flight of six steps leading down to what looked like a tiny, silver-metal-lined compartment.

He saw it by the light of the sun, kneeling on the deck with the hatch cover held back in his hand, then, as he leaned down into it, all the light from the sun was lost and he peered into blackness.

There were six steps down.

There was only the sound of the muffled, turning engine.

Lighting the lamp on deck, shielding its wick with his body as he got it going, closing the glass and brass globe down on it once it glowed yellow and grew, Tillman, drawing a breath, sliding his foot carefully onto the first step, went below.

It was a compartment lined with soldered zinc the full width of the boat, six feet long with perhaps five feet of headroom, and in the halo of the lamp, he could see nothing stored down there and no fittings.

It was an old fish storage hold from the time when the *Bailey* had been a trawler. In the halo of light from the lantern he touched at the zinc and felt the pits and fissures on it from long exposure to seawater.

Crouching, he threw the light down to the floor and touched at that too. It also was lined with zinc, striated with black streaks from the acid of long-dead fish.

There was no smell: the odors had all been scoured out, the corrosion stopped, and, here and there where there must have been a particularly bad acid burn from the iodine of the fish, the zinc had been scoured bright like a dinner plate.

There was no sound other than the sound of the water on the hull outside, but that was muffled by the zinc, and the sound of the engine turning over was only a gentle rumble.

He could not stand up, and, crouching down a little, he had to hold the lantern out at an angle to illuminate the beam of the place.

With storage space at a premium on any boat, it was big enough to have accepted the trunks from the ship, but they had not been stored down there, they had been lashed to the cabin top, and there were no marks where anything, trunks or anything else had been pushed or pulled across the zinc to snug them into place.

There was nothing.

It was an empty space.

There was nothing in there except . . .

Except the sound, suddenly, of something moving.

Ahead of him, somewhere ahead of him in the darkness, he heard it breathe.

"Who are they? Who are the Custers? What do they do? Who built this place for you?"

In the ice room, Kellor heard it. The man Simpson, half naked with the oversized coat hanging down on him like a giant's shirt on a dwarf, was at the door at the far side of the room, straining to get it open, and he heard it through the half-open door as Simpson slipped on ice on his bare feet and fell flailing and yelling to the floor.

"Who runs this place? Where is he now?"

Running, past all the baths with their pale, dead faces staring at the ceiling, past all the murmuring, through the vapor of breath, Kellor, his gun out, made for the door.

He saw it. Moving with his Colt down at his side in his free hand, Tillman saw through the open bulkhead entrance into the main hold, a shadow. He heard something, metal on metal, click as it stirred.

He could see in the light from the inadequate lantern only the zinc floor glittering up at him. He could see in the two-foot circle of light as he held it out only his own hand feeling ahead as he passed through the kennel entrance into the hold.

He could hear, now, nothing at all.

In the hold ahead of him, in all of Creation, there was only the gentle fizzing of the lamp and, somewhere ahead, somewhere behind walls in another part of the boat, the engine turning over.

He heard the breathing sound again not at all.

He went forward.

He wanted to get it out. It came as a rasp, a whisper: "Tillman. *Detective Bureau!"*

He had the Colt Lightning down at his side. He was crouched over and he could not bring it to bear.

"—Tillman! *Detective Bureau!"*

He heard no sound at all.

He heard suddenly the click of metal as whatever it was readied itself for him in the darkness.

"JENKINS."

He had the file up from the floor in his hand. Muldoon, tearing at the pages upon pages, notes upon notes held inside the cardboard covers and thrusting them at the cowering little man, roared, "These are all records of conversations on the telephone—dozens, hundreds of them!" He saw a date, "Going back for years!" He saw a notation, "From when Jenkins was the night telephone man at the Fifth! From—"

On the floor, he saw on the cover of another file, another name. He saw "HEWITT." He saw—

Muldoon, advancing on the man to bash his brains out, to beat him to a pulp, roared in the presence of Sin too awful to contemplate or have a name, *"Why? Why are you doing this? Why are you writing down everything that anyone has ever said?"*

Muldoon shouted, wanting an answer now, "Who? *Who are you doing this for?"*

He saw on the cover of a file, the name "ARCHER."

In the lantern light he saw a shape, a shadow, and for a moment he thought he had been wrong about the sound and there had been no sound at all, and the shadow, the thing in the darkness at the end of the hold was only a pile of discarded rags.

"Tillman! Detective—"

He saw the rags move. He heard in the darkness, once, definitely, sharply, the sound of metal on metal.

He heard a sound. It was Simpson trying to get in.

Muldoon, turning, already shaking his head to warn the man off as he opened the door, said with his voice as gentle as he could make it, "Ruben, this isn't—"

He saw in the open doorway the muzzle of a gun. He saw the face behind it.

He saw, he felt— Muldoon, his brain stuck, said to finish the sentence to Simpson, "Ruben, this isn't something you should be involved in because—" and then there was a flash, a detonation, and his brain, not forming the words, but only sighing, regretting something, told him he had been shot, and he fell backward to the padded floor and was still.

He saw, in the lantern light, what the sound of the metal was.

He saw the rags, the shadow.

He saw, glittering in the light in a pile on the floor, the heavy, milled gold Maria Theresa coins of Europe.

He saw, behind them, in the darkness, their eyes wide and staring, men, women, children.

He saw on the fingers of the men and women, wedding rings.

He saw there—huddled, terrified of him and his light in that awful place—the people from the ships.

39

*W*_{*ho are you?"*}

He could hardly see them in the circumscribed light from the lantern. He went bent down, hunched with the lack of headroom in the hold and he could not raise the lamp above the level of their faces to see them.

"Who are you?" There were thirteen of them: four men with beards and cheap narrow-brimmed felt hats and ill-fitting coats with shirts with no collars, men with high cheekbones and staring, unblinking dark eyes, four women between them in long, enveloping dark dresses and head scarves hiding their faces, holding children in their arms, one of them a baby in swaddling clothes.

"Who are you?" In the darkness with their scarves tight about their heads, he could not see the faces of the women at all. They could have been lunatics. There was the deep, sweet smell of perspiration about them, and from the babe in arms and maybe on the clothes of the cowled and hidden woman who held it, the smell of urine soaked into clothing. They could have been lunatics. They were all stock-still, frozen in the darkness looking at the light.

"Who are you? *Where do you come from?"* He was crouched down, leaning a little forward like a lion trainer in a cage trying to coax a tensed, watching lion from a corner. In the hold there was almost no air. What there was was heavy with sweat. "What ship did you come from?" He took a step forward and they sat still, like stone. The men were big men. They had the shoulders of men of strength. *"What are your names?"*

If they were diseased he could not smell the smell of sores and they did not cough or grasp for breath. He thought for an instant they did not breathe at all. The sound of metal had been the clinking of the gold Maria Theresa talers being laid out on the floor in front of them. He glanced down at them and tried to count them, but they were in a pile, *"What is this money? What is it for?"*

If they were criminals, unlike criminals, they looked at him straight in the face. They were men, women, children—families. Perhaps they were lunatics. Perhaps they saw him not at all. Perhaps—all of them—merely stared like moths into the light in their madness and the light was not a light held by a living man at all, but a light that—

The steamer trunks and boxes the *Bailey* had had lashed to its cabin top were no longer on the cabin top. They were not with the people. He wanted to holster his pistol but he could not bring himself to do it. He tried to see the men's faces and the expressions on them, to calculate the violence on them, but all he could see were shadows. "Where are your trunks? Are they still on this boat? *What's in them?"*

"Tillman. *Polizei!"* Maybe they were Jews. *"Shammes!"*

He wanted to see them. He wanted to see their faces but in the light they did not move. They did not, in that awful place, watching the light like lions, even breathe. Even the child, the baby, was silent and still. He saw the coins glitter on the silver zinc. "What are the coins for?" He saw the gold wedding rings on each of the four women's fingers. He saw bands on the fingers of two of the men. *"What are the coins for?"*

They could have been lunatics, or criminals, or plague carriers.

He saw one of the men—the biggest, the shadow in the center around the swathed women and children—move.

"English? No English? Do you speak English?"

"Don't you move!" It came out as a croak. He had his gun out and pointing. It was all he did have.

"Don't any of you move!"

He heard a sound, a scraping. He heard it everywhere in the hold.

He heard it behind him, above him.

He heard it coming from above and behind him on the deck.

It was one of the ironbound steamer trunks. In the forward hold ahead of the cabin it had moved, and as they got on board and made the deck of the boat rock slightly, they heard it scrape.

With the coming dusk the river surface was starting to run shadows and Sergeant Reardon, touching at his chest to help a belch along from the Chief Blackwell's Orderly's Room whiskey caught in his windpipe, standing by the open door to his wheelhouse, watching Allison and McTeague resecuring the trunk in its hold, glanced at the water and calculated tides and times.

He was a man getting on in years, passed over for promotion, his jowls on either side of his moustaches and muttonchop whiskers getting flaccid and loose like the jowls of an old hound.

McTeague and Allison, his patrolmen, his crew, were both younger dogs, thin and wiry and quick-eyed like terriers, and Reardon, when he could, consistent with safety and sensible routine, let them do things.

He let them do things now.

Belching gently, he waited until they had finished at the forward hold before he gave the order. "Ready to make way."

Touching at his chest, rubbing at it, letting them move to the task of easing off the heavy lines from the pier, he went into the wheelhouse with a sigh and shut the door tight closed behind him.

"Simpson!" He had the half-naked man hard by the lapels of the enveloping coat, dragging him to his feet, and, drawing back his hand and swinging, hit him full across the face with his open palm. Dr. Kellor, dragging him back, pulling his face into his own and holding it two inches from his eyes, shouted at the blinking man, "Who was he? Who was that man I shot?" He saw Eldridge a little behind him reach out to pluck him by the sleeve, and Kellor, turning to him with his eyes burning, shrieked, "Stand there! Do nothing! Say nothing! Stand there or I'll have you in the ice room with all the rest!" Simpson had sunken down in his grasp and he pulled him up. "That man—in there—he was a cop, *wasn't he?*" He had his Colt rammed into the pocket of his white dustcoat. Holding Simpson in a grip of iron in one hand, he reached down for it and stuck it in the blinking man's face. "Who was he? Was he alone? Are there others here on the island? *Tell me the truth or I'll blow your eyes out through the back of your head!*"

"*I'm a policeman!*" Simpson, blinking, shaking his head, said in a small voice, "I'm a police officer, I'm a—" Simpson said, "I'm Patrolman Ruben Simpson of the New York City Police, charged with the sacred duty and responsibility of—"

He heard the gun's hammer click back. He saw Kellor's gray-green eyes. He saw the eyes cold, like ice.

He was a man, a policeman.

He was a man who, once, because he had irritated him, had crippled a child for life.

Simpson, cringing, going back, trying to pull away, said, "Muldoon! Muldoon of the Detective Bureau! There are two of them! They work together! Ned Muldoon and Virgil Tillman! Tillman's a little man and he always wears dark clothes because he's—he's a detective, a shadow! If Muldoon's here on the island Tillman has to be too!"

He said a moment before the barrel of the gun came back and, smashing at the side of his head, poleaxed him naked and sprawling onto the stone floor of the vapor-filled room, "Oh, please! *Please!* I'm a policeman, an officer of the law! *Please, can't I have my uniform back to wear in this awful place?"*

They were still huddling in the darkness, unmoving, silent, listening to the sounds on the deck. They were shadows in dark clothing and head scarves in the shadows and darkness of the hold. They were lions in a den—at the back of a cave watching the light moving back and forth, watching what he did.

There were thirteen of them: four men and four women and five children, one a babe in arms, silent as if it had been drugged. They were like a statuary group in the farthest secret corner of a church, all their clothing heavy and draped, the women in front of the men, nothing but outlines, silhouettes, the men, each of them young and strong with beards and hats covering their hair.

The children were merely shapes, dark, tiny figures in their mothers' arms.

"Who are you?" He said it softly, but he did not take a step forward to approach them. He saw them, like statues, stir not at all. There was a musty smell of old clothing and, sharply, from the baby or one of the children, the smell of urine on rough material. There was the smell of sweat. There was the cold, icy smell of the zinc metal on the floor and the walls and the roof.

"Where are your papers?"

The papers had been burned on the shore. He heard, on deck, the scuffles and footsteps of the men who had burned them.

"Where are you from? What ship? What country?" Tillman, moving forward, his hand on the grip of the revolver, said with his voice a croak, "What name your ship? Your country? What name your country?"

Whatever it was the three Steamboat cops on the deck had seen when they had boarded the ship—when they had lined up all the passengers for inspection—he could not see it at all.

He could see nothing. He could see only outlines and shadows and faces and a tableau of people like wax. Tillman said softly, soothingly, "Nobody wants to hurt you." He took a step forward and felt, like electricity, a tensing and he thought, in that instant, that one of them might spring, and he stepped back.

He said, starting to entreat them, "Tillman—Detective Bureau . . ."

They made not a single sound at all—nothing—not even the sound of breathing.

"Who are you? Where are you from?" He wanted to reach out and lay his hand on the shoulder of the baby in the woman's arms and feel through the swaddling its warmth, but it was still and silent, unmoving. He wanted to touch at the baby's hand and have it grasp him around the thumb and not be afraid.

He saw the dark eyes of the men watching him in the light. He saw no emotion in their eyes at all. Tillman, going forward, said calmly, quietly, as if to dogs watching him from their kennel, "It's all right . . . everything's all right . . . it's all right . . ." He holstered his gun and looked up in the light to the eyes of the woman who held the child and it was a fine, clear face with soft, dark eyes, and on it, no sign of illness or disease at all.

He reached out. He touched a little at the baby's hand with his finger to caress it, to calm it, and, unafraid, it squeezed back at his hand and made a little cooing sound.

He released his finger and, with the lantern out to see the faces of the men, squatted down a little before the woman and baby.

"*Who are you?*" He asked it in a whisper.

Off balance, unprotected, his gun locked away and impossible to get to in time, raising the lantern up as high as it would go to illuminate not the faces of the men to him, but his own to them, Tillman said softly, "*Friend.*"

He saw, next to the woman with the child a huge, bearded man in a waistcoat watching him.

"*Friend—*"

He put out his hand for the man to take it in his.

He took his hand: he felt its warmth. Tillman, drawing the hand back a little toward his own chest, said softly, "Tillman," his name. He saw the soft eyes of all the women watching him. He said to them, "*Tillman.*" It was his name.

He felt the hand in his own. He saw, one by one, the other three men in the group raise their own hands slightly to be next in line to touch him.

He saw the hands. He saw the plumpness of the baby and the glowing health of the children as the light moved on their faces. He saw, in the light, their rough clothes, their swaddling, but he saw also in that light their hands. He heard a sound, a motion on the deck and he saw as he turned to look back to see it, all the talers laid out on the zinc floor. He saw that they were for him.

He saw the hands, and the talers, and the eyes. He saw the cheap, rough clothing. He saw what Reardon and Allison and McTeague, trained to see, had seen.

Tillman said in a gasp that made the man release his grip, "*Oh, my God!*"

He saw their hands, their disguise: he saw that their hands—the hands of men from countries with no name—he saw no roughness or calluses on them at all. He saw, where they came from, they did no physical work.

He saw the talers on the floor and all the gold wedding rings on all the fingers.

Tillman, starting back, said in horror, "Oh, my God, you people, traveling with all the other immigrants, dressed like them, pretending to be like them— Oh, my God, you people are *rich!*"

He heard a crash as, up on deck, someone must have checked the hatch and, lifting it a little from its flanges to reseat it, dropped it down hard. He heard a click, a snap.

Up on deck, he heard someone fit a padlock to the hasp on the closed hatch cover and, as the engine cut in and flailed the propeller hard into the water to make headway, with a sound that echoed in the empty zinc-lined hold as if it was a tomb, seal them all in.

40

He was not dead. He was in a pool of blood on the padded floor. The half-ounce soft-lead bullet traveling at eight hundred feet a second had broken at least one of his false ribs and, deflected by it or them, had flattened and spun upward to lodge in a muscle or sinew under his lung on his left-hand side. The room was full of acrid white smoke, particles of unburned powder in it fizzing and spluttering as they were ignited by the flames of the gas lamps on the wall.

He could not get his breath. Muldoon, getting to his feet and trying to flex his body to somehow move the bullet inside him—turn its edges—bellowed like a wounded bull. His flank was running blood and, pressing his palm to it, reeling and turning, he fought to articulate his body and move the bullet.

All the telephones were sparking and making sounds: voices. There were little wire bridges and gaps flashing blue flame between their junctions, and Muldoon, dragging his red handkerchief from his pants pocket and wadding it, forcing it under his suspender to stanch the blood, his hand coming away running and sticky, ordered all the voices on the telephones, "Shut up! Say nothing! Keep your secret thoughts to yourself! People are *listening!*" The blood from his side was not crimson—the wound was not a mortal one to an artery—but he felt as if his feet were numbing; he felt a coldness in them.

He stamped. He roared at the fizzing telephones, *"Shut up!"* The blood was running down inside his pants and getting over his boots and onto the leather floor and he slipped, reached out for the workbench against the wall, and brought the telephones down in an explosion of wires and sparks. He was Muldoon. He was John L. Sullivan. He was a Colossus, a Phoenix rising from the ashes. Muldoon, going for the door and wrenching it open, slapping his palm to his face to make his eyes find the knob, roared, "SIMPSON! WHERE THE HELL ARE YOU, SIMPSON?"

* * *

He was down for the count. He was down against the wall of the ice room with his face a swelling bruise where someone had hit him hard, and he was no use to man or beast.

He hit him anyway. Muldoon, reaching down through a wave of pain, dragging the unconscious man to his feet and jamming him against the wall, raising him off his feet like a hanged felon, roared, "SIMPSON!" Muldoon screamed in his face, "You cowardly kid-crippler, who did it? Who shot me?" Whoever it was, he had gone. Whoever it was, he had taken Eldridge with him. Whoever it was— Muldoon, having to leave off execution to press his hand against his side, grabbing the bleeding man in one hand by the throat, turning him, spinning him, getting his face pointed to the wall so he could smash it again and again against the masonry, shrieked, "Where's Tillman? Did Tillman come down here after me? What happened to him? Where is he?"

He turned Simpson into the crook of his elbow like a sheaf of wheat and held him an inch from his face.

Muldoon, his eyes going, losing focus, seeing only a blur where Simpson's face should have been, feeling the blood draining out of him, bellowed at the man, "He was upstairs! He would have heard the shot! Where is he? *Where's Tillman?*"

Muldoon shrieked, *"Virgil—!"* He was at the bottom of the flying staircase in the entrance hall, standing in a halo of light from the skylight, the stairs stretching upward and away into infinity and silence, and he could see nothing because there was nothing to be seen, hear no one because there was no one anywhere to be heard.

And he was slipping, falling down, losing rigidity, beginning, like a rag doll, to sag at the middle and slide away, and he was—

Muldoon roared in the silence, *"No!"* Turning inward, holding himself tight, searching through his body down all the veins and sinews and muscles for something hard, something that was his life's center—something that would not break—Muldoon, stamping his feet, yelled in the dying place, "No! I'm Muldoon! I'm Muldoon from County Meath!" He screamed as an order, *"Virgil, get down here!"* The wad against his side was slipping and he rammed it back into the wound with fingers sticky with blood and flexing, drawing strength, getting to the door to the outside and wrenching it open, shrieked at the lunatics at their wagon in the grounds like a banshee, "Where is he? Where's the man who shot me? *Where the hell has everyone gone?*"

He heard the lunatics howl in horror at the blood all over his face. Muldoon screamed, *"Shut up!"* He saw Maisie, harnessed to the chariot like a doll, open her mouth to shriek and then throw herself to the ground in terror, and, passing her, waving his arm at them all to dismiss them, Muldoon, heading for the iron gate and the trees beyond it, roared, *"Shut up! Pull yourselves together!"*

He saw the trees. He saw them as a blur of green, as something to aim for, as somewhere to arrive at and lie down amongst and let the pain pass into nothingness, and, for a moment, his mind drifting loose from his body, he thought they were the oak and chestnut trees of Ireland and that, behind them, raised up, there were the old burial places of the ancient Celts, the tumuli, and that he . . .

But he was not going for the trees. He was going around in circles. His eyes cleared and he was in the asylum grounds in front of the Octagon and he was circling it as if he was spinning, seeing high up on the dome the flag, then not seeing it, and he was circling in the ground amid the lunatics and they were all on the ground cowering and screaming and he was—

Muldoon cried out, "Holy God, *help me!*" and suddenly, the holy God helping, transporting him, the screaming was gone and he was in a forest of trees going over a path, going somewhere.

He saw an oak tree. Muldoon, half turning to it, all his sight gone, seeing it only as a blur, entreated God, "Help me, God. Don't let me stop. If I stop I'll sit down against a tree and die!" He could not remember what Tillman's face looked like. Muldoon, stopping, pausing for just a moment out of respect and because he had to explain to God why he was unenthusiastic at the idea of entering Heaven, said reasonably, "My friend is in trouble, Lord, and I have to keep on going to find him." Muldoon said, "God, it's almost nighttime and I haven't finished my work." In the Civil War he had been shot hard and lain all night in the grass at Chancellorsville looking at the trees and the sky. He had thought he was going to die that day too. Muldoon said, "Oh, Lord, I've tried to be an honest man!" He was, somehow, at a river. Muldoon sang in a whisper, "Shall we gather at the riv-er . . . ?" He saw a boat. He saw at the shore in an inlet, a cutter rig sailboat and, by it in the shallows, a whaleboat. He saw buoys, moorings—he saw some sort of little hidden harbor—and he saw, on the cutter rig sailboat, Eldridge.

He saw on the boat, working at the mast to raise the sail, a tall, white-coated man with a long-barreled Cavalry Colt stuck in his waistband.

"Jesus, Joseph and Mary and all the Saints in Heaven—help me!"

He saw upriver, going north, the *Bailey.*

He felt the bullet inside him move.

He felt God's hand touch his.

Muldoon, a Celt warrior rising up from the earth, leaving the cold dampness of his dying and swelling, filling with strength, closing his fists and turning all his muscles and sinews and life to steel inside his chest, turning back to the Octagon to get back to where the lunatics were, bellowed in thanks, in glory, in triumph, "—*URRRR!!*"

On the river, the *Bailey* must have hit something floating and as it lurched and then righted itself he lost his footing and, reaching out to save himself against the ceiling, dropped the lamp and saw it roll over the coins on the floor like a fireball and be saved at the last moment from exploding by the man whose hand he had taken.

In the light he saw the man hold up the lantern for an instant and start to reach out to return it to him.

The hatch was padlocked shut. On the floor, starting to slide with the motion of the boat, were all the coins.

He saw the man look down at them. He saw him nod for him to come forward and take them. He saw him raise the lantern and look down at the children. He saw him think something, try to understand—in his own language inside his head—try to make sense of something.

The engines, thumping to make way in heavy water, were roaring, deafening and the man, shaking his head, could not think for the sound of them.

He saw him shake his head, tense, pull back. He saw him grasp the lantern hard in two hands.

He saw him decide.

Tillman, his Lightning out in his hand, shrieking above the sound of the engine vibrating in every pore of the boat, ringing in the zinc that covered all the walls and floor and ceiling of the sealed-in hold, ordered the man, "Sit! Sit back down again! *Don't you come any closer!*"

Like something from their delirium, he came out of the trees and into the grounds like a demon, his face and body covered in blood, a huge thing of terrible, unstoppable bulk and burning eyes. He was roaring, bellowing. He hit the center of the chariot and, crashing into it, colliding with it, overturned it with his momentum. Muldoon, caught up in the harness, wrenching at it, his eyes demented and staring, yelled to Maisie, fallen on the ground and cowering, "He's on the *Bailey*! Tillman! Where else would he be? *He's on the* Bailey!" There was a poor old man in a ragged shift with medals pinned to it caught up with him in his harness, and Muldoon, wrenching him aside and knocking him down, knocking all the lunatics down in turn with him like domino tiles, screamed as he pulled at the leather that bound them all together, "They're going north! *North!*"

He could not undo the harness. It was riveted together. It was padlocked at the pivot points. Muldoon roared, *"Arrgghh!"* He got his hands around the central padlock and pulled. He could not move it. Rolling over, he got his back against the oak wagon and, grunting, straining, his eyes bulging, pulled at the padlock.

"Arrgghh—!" It did no good. The lock would not come apart in the hands of a mortal man.

"Maisie—! *Maisie—!"* He roared for her to stand clear.

He was unstoppable: a Muldoon.

He had his Smith and Wesson Number Two revolver still in his hip pocket.

Hauling it out, an armed, bloody, roaring giant in a madhouse, he put its muzzle against the padlock and blasted it in a shower of spinning, red-hot shards of metal, straight to Hell.

The mainsail of the sailboat was up and filling out, and it was a colt of a racing cutter and it could catch the *Bailey* before it got to its destination. It was his own boat, rigged for single-handed sailing, and, at the helm, Kellor, turning the tiller with one hand and pulling on the winch handle to free the foresail to get the bow to come around, ordered Eldridge as it came out with a snap, "Stand clear of the sail!"

He could catch the *Bailey*. He could see the smoke from her as she thumped up the river to turn east at Ward's Island and, hitting the currents and eddies at Hell Gate, rolled and lurched with the turbulence.

He could catch her. He had been an officer in the Seventh, a gentleman. He had been an officer with Custer and he had all the accomplishments and it was his boat and he could catch her.

"Get back here, Eldridge, to where I can see you!"

He had his Cavalry pistol on the seat beside him.

He could kill the man Tillman on the boat in midriver and weight his body down and sink it forever.

On his feet in the stern, tightening the lines, making the boat fly, Kellor, his eyes flitting from the smoke in the sky to the gun and then to Eldridge and then up to the taut singing rigging. rapped out as a single, military order, *"Get back here now or, so help me, I'll shoot you where you stand!"*

They were no longer huddling, but gathering, swarming in the light from the lantern, gaining strength, resolving—and they could not understand a word he said.

"Keep back!" They knew he was an enemy who did not want the money, and in the din of the engine they were swarming, humming, making sounds like animals, gathering courage.

"Keep back!" The hatch was padlocked and in the zinc-lined hold there was no way out and they could neither hear nor understand a word he said.

They had children. They were men and women with children.

He saw them watching him.

He saw a man rise in the lantern light. He saw him, huge, bent double against the cramped roof, look down to the man with the lantern.

He saw them decide what to do.

He was at the little harbor where the sailboat had been, herding them at gunpoint like cattle. There were twenty-eight of them, men, women, all demented, shrieking, full of muscle and mad, ticking, sparking nerves and sinews throwing their arms and hands out like dolls'.

In the shallows, waiting, ready to go, there was a whaleboat with all its oars shipped and gleaming, and Muldoon, pushing, shoving, getting in with them and thrusting the wooden blades into their hands, looking to the smudge of the *Bailey* and the white sails of the boat after it, harnessing them, setting their machine of madness onto a single, mighty, thunderous course, screamed at them, *"Row!"*

He slipped the mooring.

He heard the maniacs, unleashed with it, shriek like banshees. He saw the oars tear into the water in an explosion of foam.

With no pain, with all the pain in his body gone, full of power, Muldoon on his feet in the stern, a Viking whipmaster in a dragon boat at last with something simple, something elemental to be done, roared as a single commandment to his crew, "Row, you lunatics! *Row!*"

41

He was in a darkened metal box: a windowless, doorless rabbit trap lined in scoured smooth silver zinc, and as the boat rolled in one swell after another he could not keep his footing and there was nothing to hold on to.

The engine, at full bore, was thumping, roaring in the chamber of the hold, vibrating through the walls and through his boots on the floor, and he could not hear what the huge man said to the others as he bent down by the lantern to talk to them.

He thought for a moment they were Russians: he thought he heard the sound of the language, a snatch of it. He saw the face of the man with the lantern react to what was said—he saw his face in the light look confused, undecided, unsure, and then he saw him look to a heavily bearded man at the end of the line and ask him.

He saw the bearded man shake his head, and then, reaching out and pulling the lantern man by his shoulder, try with his face screwed up and intense to talk some reason to him, put some sense to it, warn him not to act rashly.

He saw in the spilling glow of the yellow light one of the women—the one holding the baby—lift her face up and say something.

He saw the lantern man—the male lion of the pride—silence her with a shake of his head. They were all related. It was one family: they were all brothers or cousins or— He heard the woman say in alarm, in terror, "Nyet—!" and they were Russians and he had not one word of the language and they understood him and he them not at all.

"Rouffler!" It was what it sounded like to him. It was the man with the beard: seen in the light, the second oldest, the second in charge, the father, by the way he drew the woman with the child in toward him with the crook of his arm, of the baby. "Rouffler!!" He said it again to the man with the lantern. They were all faces moving in and out of the yellow light of the lantern, coming and going like ghost faces at a séance.

The man with the lantern shook his head.

He had his Lightning still out in his hand, but maybe they could not even see it, or did not even know what it was. The boat was rolling, lurching in a swell of heavy water, and with the sound of the engines he could not think straight, and he had not a single word they could understand.

They were terrified people trapped in a sealed box at sea, and they did not know who he was, what the gun was for, and it was going to be only moments before they decided they were going to have to fight for their lives.

"Rouffler!"

He thought that was what it was.

He had not a single word he could say to them that could make them understand.

"Rouffler—skizyet!"

He knew only in Russian the single word *"Da."* He thought it meant "Yes." He had no idea what they were talking about, no idea at what point in the talk he would add his "Yes." He had no idea what—

"Geld!" It was the man with the lantern. Turning, he roared it above the sound of the engines. He roared it at the man with the gun. He had the lantern up, pointing, accusing, his left hand out and stabbing into the darkness.

"Geld!"

It meant, in German, in maybe the only word he had in any language on Earth other than his own, *Gold.*

It meant, *Money.*

He meant, as his finger stabbed at them, the Maria Theresa coins on the floor.

He meant, as he came forward with his free hand flat on the low roof to steady him, as the light came forward with him and lit up the walls of the hold foot by foot as he approached, the glittering golden coins everywhere sliding and rolling with the movement of the boat.

"I don't want to shoot you!" He took a step backward, but there was nothing behind him but darkness, nowhere to go.

"Geld!" He was at the center of the strewn coins, picking out all their glitterings with the light, pointing down at them, his face twisted and desperate. *"Geld!"* He was prepared to die. In his voice there was a catch. He stabbed at the coins with his finger, *"Geld!!"*

"I don't want your money!" Tillman, taking a step forward, lurching, reaching out for the wall to steady himself, shouted above the engines, "Can't you understand? Can't you understand who I—"

"Geld!" The man was on his knees, rolling and lurching with the *Bailey's* motion, gathering the coins up like dust, not caring how many he got, but getting enough to show, getting sufficient to offer, holding them

out, pushing them forward with his hand, *"Geld! Geld!"* His eyes were full of tears and streaming, *"Geld!!"*

"For the love of God—!" Tillman, coming forward, in that moment reaching out with his hand, said softly—but the engines drowned him out—"In the name of . . ."

He saw the pleading man's face look up at him.

The man with the lantern, the leader, the head of the family, said with his heart broken at the loss, the loss not of the money, but of something dear: his family, his child dying there at the hands of a stranger, *"Geld . . ."*

His eyes were running tears and he kept trying to sniff them back and be a man.

"No . . ." He was above him, looking down, seeing his face, like a child's, looking up at him. Tillman, sinking down to his knees in front of him, said to convince him, to soothe him, to assuage him, "No . . ."

He had the man's hand in his own, and he felt in it warmth and life and— Tillman, straining forward, getting close to the man's face as if somehow they could read what was in each other's eyes, said to explain, "No, I'm not who you think I am . . ."

He had the man's hand. He had it in his. He had it carefully, gently, with no force, and all that he could think of to say was . . .

Tillman said softly, only his mouth moving above the sound of the engines, making no words at all, but only mouthing them, "No . . . Please . . . No—" He turned the hand and, to make it clear, turned it over and let all the coins spill out into the light and fall into the darkness on the floor.

He holstered his gun and shook his head. Tillman said, shaking his head, "No . . . No . . ." and in that instant—

—And in that instant, out of the darkness, roaring and snarling, all the other men were upon him and, as the *Bailey* hit a heavy swell and lurched and then wallowed in the water he was going over backward, being punched, ripped at, kicked, rolling over and over as, grunting like animals, in that terrible place as one man the pack tore at him to kill him.

The *Bailey* was in the center of the Hell Gate section of the river where it opened up and diverged right and left around the south edge of Ward's Island, rolling, lurching, fighting the currents, the smoke from its funnel blasting hard and uninterrupted as its engine worked at full pressure to keep it in midstream away from Mill Rock and Flood Rock and the reef at Frying Pan that could rip its bottom out like paper.

She was stern on to him, and all Kellor could see of her was her smoke.

All he could see beyond the smoke was the growing darkness of the regions to the north, of the coming night.

"Eldridge!" He saw the man look up in terror. He saw him huddled in the cockpit on his hands and knees, in his madness look around to see where he was. He saw him look up and see the sails winched in tight running the boat close up to the wind. He saw him look startled, look ill, want to be sick, "Hold your guts together or I'll throw you overboard dead!"

His hand jumping on the tiller with the power of the speed, Kellor glanced at his gun on the seat beside him, and locked it down tight with his knee.

Hard over, close up to the wind, making only a swooshing sound as the deep keel cut through the water, his colt of a boat, sailed by an expert, ate up the distance between Kellor, his gun, and the *Bailey.*

The *Bailey* was in the east stream of the East River, and as the hull cleared the currents at Hell Gate, the flow of water under the keel became smooth, and Sergeant Reardon, at the wheel, took out his pocket watch and, snapping it open, looked at its face.

Allison and McTeague were on deck at the bow, looking for obstacles.

"Allison! McTeague!" Pulling it down a fraction, he called to them from the port-side window of the wheelhouse.

There were now, at this point in the journey they had all made a hundred, two hundred times, no more obstacles to be found.

"Stand by—!" With one hand on the wheel, still at the half-open window, he watched the seconds hand in its own little dial on the face of the watch ticking away the moments.

"Stand by now!" He watched the seconds. He saw, ahead of him, the coming night.

He counted, one by one, the seconds to the exact, scientifically calculated instant to give them the order.

His head hit something on the wall, and whatever it was it came loose and sliced at the side of his neck like a razor, and then, as the snarling pack kicked at him and he rolled away, whatever it was hit the zinc floor and bounced up into the air like India rubber.

It was some sort of square of flat, hinged metal like the lid of a stove with a blued-steel spring attached to it, and for an awful moment he thought one of the snarling men kicking at him caught it and was going to bring it down and decapitate him with it. The lantern light was somewhere behind the pack, held by someone moving back and forth and screeching—a woman—and as he rolled and rolled into darkness the object hit the floor and flew back up into the air, and he was being mauled, kicked, and in the darkness he felt a blow to his chest that knocked all the wind out of him and made his head swim with pain.

He heard a buzzing. He heard the children, the baby, shrieking and crying, and he was on his feet reaching in under his coat for the pistol or the shotgun; but they found him, hit him again in a wedge of bodies, and he went down, shielding his face from their blows.

His shoulder hit something hard and sharp, and he was on the other side of the hold, sliding on the zinc floor, and whatever it was he hit came away and flew free, and was another of the hinged plates, but as he got his hand to it, tried to lift it up as a weapon, it was still attached to the wall by the spring and had only buckled in its cavity. He felt behind it a tube, a pipe.

The *Bailey* was slicing through still water: his fingers, twisting around the thing in the wall, holding on to it, felt a flange, a rim on the edge of it, and, his boots slipping on something that could have been his own blood on the floor, using every ounce of his strength, he pulled himself up by it.

He saw for an instant at the far end of the hold the lantern light flash, make a halo, illuminate all the children and women, and he thought in that instant, getting himself up, that the men had gone, but then, out of the darkness they were on all sides of him, punching, clawing, and, struck by a fist against the side of his face that missed his eye by a fraction, he was poleaxed back down to the floor and his grip on the flange or the tube or the pipe or whatever it was was gone.

There was no way out. The hatch was padlocked and he was in a cage of lions and there was no way out. They understood not a word. Anything he said meant nothing, was only a sound, and as he tried to squirm away from them to get his pistol out, to at least terrify them, to at least do *something,* they had him hard, and one of them—a huge bear in the darkness—had him by the shirt and, grunting, straining, lifted him off the ground and with a blow that he thought must kill him, butted him like a goat head-on in the center of the chest and propelled him against the other wall.

He felt something hard and sharp strike him in the small of the back and he thought he had been thrown against a meat hook or a spike and been sliced through, impaled on it like a moth.

He was bleeding from his neck and his eye felt swollen to the size of a hen's egg, and he could not get his breath as he slid down from the object like, in the picture of it his mind gave him, something slack and ruined and dead . . .

His legs were gone, turned to jelly at the knees. He saw the light coming toward him in a circle, eating him up with its brightness. He saw, above him, the huge, bearded man reaching down for him with the strangest, saddest look on his face, and Tillman, reaching up for him and grasping him by the back of the neck for support, wrenched him down and, lashing, smashing out and upward, broke his nose with his fist and made him stagger back.

He felt blood, but it was not his blood; his legs, as if they were replenished by it, worked again and he was on his feet ready for the next of them.

His hand worked. It had strength. It had hit out and worked and he got it in under his coat and caught the grip of the Colt Lightning and started to pull it free. The boat was steady, moving through clear water, and he got a firm foothold on the floor, braced himself against the wall, and drew the gun. He heard the screaming of the children. He heard— He shrieked to stop them with the gun out and pointing, *"Stop!* For the love of God—*stop!"*

He felt against his back the object set in the wall. He felt what it was. He felt in it movement, a vibration. He felt— He heard, in the darkness, the pack coming for him.

He shrieked, not to them, but in the sudden horror of realization, to no one, to anyone, to the panic there suddenly in his brain, "Stop!"

He felt through his coat at the end of the pipe in the wall against his back, under pressure, water.

He heard the pack come.

He shrieked, he roared, but they had not a word of English and all they thought he made were screams.

"Stop! For the love of God—Stop!!"

Time. In sight of their destination, it was time, and Sergeant Reardon, snapping his watch cover closed, gave the order.

He had done it a hundred, two hundred times before and he thought no more of it than that it was time to give the order and he had, now, given it.

Tillman screamed in English, "It's water! It's water in pipes in the wall! It's water!" He heard in the engine noise, a different sound. Tillman shrieked, "Seawater! All the pipes in the walls are inlet pipes for seawater!"

They understood not a single word, but it stilled them; something in his voice stilled them.

It was a rectangular box below the waterline of the boat, a storage place from when the *Bailey* had been a trawler: a closed, sealed cavity lined in scoured zinc, a tomb.

"It's a wet hold!" Tillman, trying to go forward, trying to stop them, trying to—trying anything—screamed at them, "Understand for the sake of your lives! *It's a wet hold and they've sealed us in and there's no way out!*"

"Pressure." On the deck, Allison, watching the needle rising on the gauge at the midships steam pump, said as a formality, "Pressure." He glanced at McTeague by the single brass lever by the wheelhouse it took to open all the valves and flood the hold with water.

"Pressure." It was a formality, a routine done a hundred, two hundred times before. At sea, an order was always responded to twice to make sure its direction was clear.

"Pressure." At the lever, McTeague said it again.

It was clear. A good sailor doing his job with no personal feelings about it at all, Steamboat Patrolman McTeague of the *Bailey* opened the lever full on.

42

They were at the mouth of Hell Gate in the river, the whaleboat rearing up from the bow with the current and sudden winds, the lunatics screaming, the oar blades slashing at the surface of the water, missing it, skimming it, slicing it, sending explosions of foam and spray up around the hull like the burstings of cannon shells.

And they were not afeared, the mad people. In their soaked rags, their eyes glittering, shouting, screaming, keening, they were hacking, carving at the water with the oars like shovels, the air in their hair, their faces washed clean by the exploding, stinging, wakening water, full of joy, released.

Wind, current, water, power—in the bow, standing up, sliding, slipping as the boat kicked and bucked and rolled, Muldoon had no need to shout any order.

In Hell Gate, full of meaning, direction, purpose, the lunatics, free of all their fetters, screaming in triumph, without ceasing, rowed.

They rowed for the sailboat flying through the water a mile and a half ahead of them.

Free, liberated, not beasts, but people of purpose, part of the earth, the sea, the sky, with no fear of death—fearing that least of all—in Hell Gate, the lunatics rowed.

They rowed like hell.

Sailing heeled hard over, he had made it through Throg's Neck and the northern islands of East Chester, and, coming around into the bay, he saw the *Bailey*, saw her clear, on track, less than a mile from her final destination.

He saw himself as if he was God, standing straight and ramrod stiff at the helm of his sailboat with the wind in his hair and his moustaches, and he saw coming, the final moment, the blooding, the charge, the moment of glory.

Kellor, Samuel P., Superintendent, Blackwell's Island, New York.
Kellor, Samuel P., Major, Custer's Seventh Cavalry (Ret'd).

He thought briefly about killing Eldridge and pushing him over the side, but his long-barreled Colt was not for that. He looked only ahead, his heart beating in his thin chest, only to the *Bailey*.

He looked up only upriver at the *Bailey* smudging smoke in the darkening sky.

On the *Bailey* now, briefly out of sight as she went behind City Island for the last run of her destination, Sergeant Reardon would be easing off the engine and, disengaging the prop shaft with a single ring from his telegraph, setting it on STOP to let her drift.

He saw it in his mind's eye.

He saw in his mind's eye all the little figures—Reardon, Allison, McTeague—going about their business on the deck and in the wheelhouse like ants.

He saw in his mind's eye the black mass of the *Bailey*'s hull, ever so gently, list a little to the side and slowly, ever so slowly, as if its holds were all filling up with water, start to lower from the stern.

He came around the edge of City Island and he was there, not seeing it in pictures, but there, seeing it.

He saw the gently drifting boat make contact with the bottom as she ran the last few feet up onto the foreshore of her destination—the final island.

He saw her tremble as her keel, running out of depth on the beach, scraped hard and locked her tight at the bow.

He saw beyond the bow of the boat, on the little island where she lay, going quickly toward her in the last dying light of the day, the yellow blazing lights of torches, of beacons, of burning flambeaux held by running, dark-clothed, bent-over dwarfs.

He saw, as if suddenly, all at once, her holds flooded with water and weighed her down, the *Bailey* start to settle.

43

In the hold they were screaming, panicking. The water, from the outlet pipes behind the hinged covers, was gushing out in torrents. There were eighteen pipes, nine on each side of the hold: the water, under pressure, foaming and roaring, was exploding, coming in in fountains.

In the hold, sealed in, losing their footing, being blasted off their feet by the force, they were all drowning, slipping, going under and then surfacing and then, with no headroom, nowhere to stand up, being caught bent over and being driven back down again.

The boat must have beached at an angle: at the stern the woman with the baby slid backward with the lamp and the child in her arms and, as Tillman was hit by a blast of water and salt driven by the pump like the jet from a fire hose, she disappeared into deep water. She surfaced again, seemed for an instant to float, then, flailing, was knocked sideways and sent crashing against the zinc wall, the lamp, knocked from her grasp, floating away on the boiling surface.

The lamp was a sealed deck hand's lamp, waterproof. For a moment it bobbed on the surface, spun over and over like a buoy cut loose from its mooring—and then, from nowhere, someone had it, holding it up in the darkness, dragging the woman with the baby up to her feet and holding her.

The men were all together in a knot reaching out for their children, their women, slipping, sliding as they tried to get a firm foothold. He heard someone roar above the screaming and give an order and then, as the lamp seemed for an instant to go out and there was utter blackness, the men were all thumping and punching at the ceiling, scraping at it with their nails to break through it and then someone hit him from below the surface and swept his feet out from under him and he was going down into the turbulence, turning over and over, grasping for holds and grips that were not there, turning like a cork.

He surfaced and the lamp was a yellow glow somewhere a thousand miles away and he struck out for it along the wall, not knowing which way he was going. He saw suddenly, at the stern in the lamplight, the baby held high like a sacrifice to God.

He saw the woman holding it go under. He saw someone—a blur, a mass, something bellowing like a lion—wrench her to the surface and the lamp, all there was, was floating free and rolling, fizzing, starting to go out.

He saw, above the screaming, the roaring, above it all, the face of the child drowning. He saw it, held up like something on a spit, writhe and convulse as its tiny lungs filled with water. He saw the man with the beard reach out for the child and grasp it from its mother's hands.

Then the entire boat seemed to shake and everything was dark and he was swimming, thrashing toward nowhere, and, as he reached up to grab hold of something his hand no longer broke free above the water up to the elbow, but only to the wrist. All the air, the space, the life, was being eaten up by the water and there was almost nothing left but the ceiling.

There was nothing left but the lamp. The lamp was all there was, and it was nothing but a glow, a yellowness, and too far away, with every muscle in his body thrusting, he freed himself and turned to where he thought the hatch was. He struck something, a body, was spun around by it, came up between the rising water and the ceiling twisting his face to it to breathe, and then, in the darkness, in the force, he was through the bulkhead, away from the maelstrom, and he came up at the far end of the hold where the hatch was and he was upright and he had a foot of air above his head.

He reached up and touched at the oak hatch.

He heard the baby cough and start to die.

He heard it vomiting back water.

He heard, as the boat must have shifted with the weight of the water, the sounds of thirteen men, women and children sealed in a hold, in the last pocket of air, shrieking and hammering on the zinc ceiling, drowning like rats.

The whaleboat came around the back of City Island into the last bay on the river and he saw the island.

He saw the lights on it, the torches. He saw the *Bailey* beached up on it. He saw the sailboat with Eldridge and the white-coated man who had shot him running up to it, letting go the sails to reach it—he saw what island it was. He saw, there in the dying light of the day, the place at the end of the world: he saw what island it was.

"Row!!" Muldoon, at the bow, saw even the lunatics start. He saw what was on their faces.

"*Row!!*" He had his gun out. They were a mile away, too late. He saw on the deck of the *Bailey,* figures moving. He saw, on the beach, Sergeant

Reardon moving to where the sailboat would land. He saw, coming down to the beach, lit by flaming torches, dark-clothed men who looked like dwarfs.

He saw the *Bailey* shudder as if below decks she filled with water.

"Row! *Row!*" He was a nightmare, covered in blood, swinging his gun wildly.

Muldoon, a worse terror than any terror behind or ahead of them, roared like a madman to his boatload of staring, gaping, trembling already mad people, *"Row!* For the love of God—*Row!!"*

He almost got his hand to the hatch.

Then there was a renewed torrent as the pumps must have picked up and he was hit square on in the face and neck by it and he was rolling, reaching out for nothing, sinking into the depths of the black water, being driven by it, turning over and over with nothing to catch on to.

He reached out. Spinning, out of air, flailing upward, he reached out and felt what he thought was the hatch.

It was not the hatch. It was something soft: the baby. It was the dying baby. He felt, as he tried to get its face above water, feeling for its face, hurting it, its chest jerking and all the ribs in it going, pushing, turning to rubber as the lungs died.

His ears were gone and he could hear nothing but the roaring of the water, could feel nothing but the dying child, could see nothing, and sinking, going down, dying, with his last ounce of air reached up past the baby and felt the hatch.

He felt it. He felt the hardness. He felt below it, cold, less than three inches of air.

All he had was his shotgun, but sinking, pulling, tearing at his clothing he could only get at the barrels caught up in its harness under his coat and he could not get it free and out.

The barrels were full of water. His finger was stuck in one of the barrels and it was full of water and even if he got it free of the harness there was no room to turn it upside down to run the water out. He wrenched at it, got it free and like a drowning man holding a stick got it flat and parallel with the water, held it up in the darkness where he thought the air was and twisted it hard to clear it and got the muzzles hard up onto the hatch and rammed them hard against its surface.

The baby was jammed up against him. He felt its body go into convulsions. He felt its death spasm.

Moments. He had only moments. The barrels were scraping, coming off the wood of the hatch as it ran slippery with water.

Moments. All he had were moments, and even if the gun had the power to blast it open, he could not find the end of the hatch where outside, in the air, the padlock would be, and then, suddenly, he could no longer breathe and it was too late, and he was sinking, holding the shotgun like a pole, sliding away down it, and his mind, drifting away, forgot what it was he was doing and, sinking, all there was was a muffled keening, a lowing sound, and he thought it did not matter much and at least he was not alone, and he thought . . .

. . . He thought it did not matter much anymore.

He felt the baby against him and pulled the trigger, and there was a thunderclap, a roar, and all around him the water was compressed in a sudden detonation that wrenched at him, sent him down again, and then he was in a torrent of foaming water, seeing light, and he was coming out, being projected up, and all around him there were people, legs, arms, people flailing and he saw light. He was in a waterfall, a cascade, an avalanche of water and the baby in his arms was howling, shrieking, screaming and through the blown-open hatch, in the maelstrom, he saw light.

On the beach halfway to the sailboat, Sergeant Reardon turning around, reaching for his revolver in the hip pocket of his pants, screamed, *"Allison! McTeague!"* The *Bailey* was lit up by yellow deck lights. He saw McTeague at the hatch stagger back under the lights in a blast of moving air and force and then a torrent of water under pressure roar up in front of him like a waterspout and knock him off his feet. He saw Allison at the pump lever go down in a torrent of water. He saw people escaping onto the deck.

On the island the dwarfs with their torches had stopped, staring. Reardon, wrenching his gun free, starting to run, slipping in the sand, screamed, "Kill them! *Kill them!*" He saw Allison at the pump, back on his feet, hesitate, look around. He saw people climbing out of the hatch like ants, like an army, onto the deck. He looked back to see Kellor beaching his boat. He saw a rowboat coming. He saw Muldoon. Reardon, running—not knowing which way to run and turning back, wrenching at the pistol in his pocket—screamed to Kellor, "Doctor!" He saw Kellor, fighting with Eldridge to drag him out of the beached sailboat, pull back his Cavalry Colt and crash it across the side of the cringing man's head. He saw Eldridge stagger with the blow. He saw Muldoon and an army of rowers coming for him. He saw, on the deck, Tillman with a child under his arm.

He saw his shotgun.

They were all behind him. They were alive and they were behind him, getting out. The baby was still under his arm, but he could see nothing, he could see nowhere to put it down, no one to give it to, and all he could see through the pain and salt in his eyes were lights and the foam on the decks and a shadow moving, coming toward him and he did not know who it was—then someone had the child, took it from him, and as he shook his head to clear his eyes he saw someone on the deck coming at him and it was McTeague.

It was Hart Island. It was Hell. It was all lights and torches and flames, and as they rowed with the water splashing around them, Muldoon at the prow could not make out who was running on the beach, but knew from the uniform it was one of them, and with the Smith and Wesson .32, a popgun at that range, he blanketed the running figure with bullets that kicked up sand all around him, made him turn, and, as the running man tripped and fell, he saw from the Sergeant's stripes on his arm it was Reardon. He saw on the boat two more: Allison and McTeague. He saw McTeague on the deck with something silver in his hand, but everywhere there was movement and water and running figures on the boat and he could not get a shot in.

He saw Tillman. He saw him there on the deck. Muldoon, the rowboat under his feet surging in toward the beach like a Viking longship, screamed across the distance to warn him, "Virgil—!"

He saw him: he saw McTeague raise his pistol.

His eyes were clearing. He saw lights, flames, torches. He saw dwarfs, bent-over men carrying litters, stopped in a line on the sand. He saw on the deck the water from the hold swirling around him.

On the *Bailey*, there, coming at him, his revolver out, he saw Patrolman McTeague, and, his eyes burning, stinging, shrieking, snarling like a released, maddened animal, Tillman, bringing the shotgun up, shooting for the head and blasting it into an explosion of bone and blood and brain, killed the man on the spot, and, dropping the empty gun and reaching in under his sodden coat, he went for his revolver to kill Allison too.

44

It was Hart Island. It was the worst place on Earth. It was where, in trenches, in graves, in holes, all the indigent dead of the city, the lunatics, the convicts, the unwanted and unknown, were buried in rows, in lines, namelessly, unmarked, en masse.

It was Potter's Field. It was lit from end to end by burning flambeaux and torches set in the earth, on the dunes, and in the sand of the beach. The dwarfs were not dwarfs: they were bent-over gravediggers dragging wooden litters for the drowned. On the deck of the *Bailey* McTeague was still falling in a fountain of blood, in a mist of blood and bone and brain, and all he was was a bag made of brass buttons and leather belts and serge uniform.

It was Hart Island. On the deck, his gun out, rubbing hard and fast at his eyes to clear them, Tillman could not see Allison. Allison had been at the pump. The pump had not stopped and the water, gushing from the blown-open hatch, had set the decks awash and he could not get his footing.

"Sergeant Reardon—!" It was Allison. He was screaming for help. On the deck, his eyes clearing, Tillman down in a crouch, slipping and sliding on the deck, trying to make him out saw him as a blur for'd, saw him with something silver in his hand and then he was gone with the people all around him, shouting, shrieking, trying to get off the heeling boat. He looked around for the baby and saw it in the arms of a woman near the for'd hatch, and could not see Allison anywhere. There were trunks and boxes broken loose and surfacing from the for'd hatch, starting to float down toward him, and then there was a terrible hissing as the water, filling all the compartments of the boat, saturated the red-hot boiler in the engine room astern and enveloped everything in steam.

On the beach, there were people running. Turning, looking through the steam, he saw some sort of sailboat fifty yards up the beach with people on it, fighting. There was gunfire coming from somewhere—from the sea—and then, as the families: the women, the children, the men, escaping, went over the side, the *Bailey* tipped and Tillman was sliding along the moving deck grasping for his gun to hold on to it.

He heard Allison scream for help but he could not see him through the escaping steam. He saw someone in rags, someone bent over at a litter on the sand where the people were jumping—a gravedigger, a horrible creature with a flaming torch—and then, as one of the men leapt onto him from the deck he was gone and the bearded man from the hold was pummeling at him, holding him down and suffocating him in the sand. He saw the line of gravediggers. He saw them run for the bearded man on the sand with shovels and picks raised in their hands. Then there was a shot that made the woman with the baby cower on the beach and he saw Allison behind the pump, cringing against it for support, shooting for the baby, and Tillman, roaring, snarling, shrieking at him, shot him between the eyes and sent him jerking back with his mouth open like a doll.

He heard gunfire. All he wanted to do was kill. He saw the bearded man get up from the suffocated gravedigger and then fall back down on him again to finish the job and he saw, all over the island, the lights and flames.

He saw Reardon. He saw him halfway along the beach with his gun out. He saw flashes. He saw one of the gravediggers run into the line of fire and snap in half like a hinge as one of Reardon's bullets hit him in the stomach. He heard him scream. He saw the man flail into the water at the edge of the sand and slap at it in his death agonies, and Tillman, running to the stern of the boat and leaping into the shallow water with his gun out stiff in his hand, collided with one of the ragged dwarf-men and, as he raised his shovel to strike, shot him in the heart where he stood.

He was a Viking. He sailed into a burning, flaming, torch-lit, alien enemy shore. The blood on his side and the pain was his badge and his battle standard. Muldoon, standing in the prow of the flying whaleboat, screaming for Tillman, shrieking at Reardon, saw the dwarfs on the beach turn into the water and come out wading toward him with shovels and picks like swordsmen.

He saw, in a blast of steam and exploding deck lights, the hull of the *Bailey* shudder and start to list. He saw all around it people moving in the water and on the sand and in the shallows. He saw Reardon, down in the sand, roll as one of the dwarfs ran across him to get away and he saw him on his feet, his mouth open and screaming, shoot the dwarf in the back as he passed him, and then there were dwarfs everywhere around him in the water pulling and wrenching at the sides of the boat like spiders and as the boat spun with their weight the lunatics in the front rowing seats were up on their feet beating at the heads of the dwarfs with their oars.

He was on his feet.

He took aim.

Muldoon, shooting not to wound but to kill, seeing only their heads and fingers as they wrenched at the boat, shot five of them one by one like a man shooting ducks in a gallery on the Bowery.

He could not see Tillman anywhere. He saw the *Bailey* list hard, shudder, gout steam as the water in her hit the boilers, and then as he looked back to see the sailboat and instead saw Reardon running toward it, the boat detonated in a sheet of flame and smoke and spun back, all its port side gone, sinking, falling to pieces, on fire from end to end.

There were people there. There were women, children, men, a woman running in circles with a baby in her arms, and Muldoon, too far away to help, roared to his crew, *"Way!* Get under *way! Get speed up!"* Everywhere around him in the sea, made yellow from the light of the torches on the beach, there was dark blood from the dwarfs and then it was gone in an explosion of white foam and spume as the lunatics slashed their oars into the water and almost sent him overboard with the surge.

"Virgil—!" There was a second blast from the *Bailey* and she was a pyre that lit the beach from end to end, lit up all the crevasses of the rise that led up to the flattened hill area that was the center of the island and he could not see Tillman anywhere.

"Stand by—!" He saw, instead, the sailboat with the man in the white coat who had shot him on Blackwell's. *"Stand by—!"* He was a Viking. He was a Berserker. Through flames and the sound of battle, he was awash in foam and spume as his longship, at top speed, lifted out of the water as the lunatics behind him, screaming and unstoppable, rowed like gods.

"Stand by—!" He saw Eldridge in the stern of the boat trying to get out. He saw the man in the white coat, his face like a yellow demon in the light, reach out for him, catch him and drag him back in. He saw the whippet sailboat rocking with the wind in her half-raised sails. He had his gun out. He needed no gun.

"Stand by—!"

His longship ate the distance up. She rose up from the bow and flew. Propelled by oars, by muscle and sinew, clear in a trough of deep water, the whaleboat, his longship, his army sliced into battle.

"Stand by . . ."

He saw the man who had shot him and Eldridge realize what was happening. He saw their faces. He saw the fear. He saw smoke and flames and light and death.

In the prow, like a madman, like the leader of madmen, like a man who had been shot and left for dead and only saved by the grace of the good God, Muldoon roaring, waving his arms, howling his war cry, thundered into the chaos, *"Stand by to ram!!"*

* * *

Tillman was running through smoke and darkness, through circles and pools of torchlight in the smoke and in the darkness on the sand and the shallows of the sea. He was running through the screams and cries of the maimed and the maimers; he was running with the sound of the terror of children and the shrieking above it all of a baby, half drowned, howling for life. He was running for Reardon.

"Shoot them! Shoot them!" He was running for the sound of Reardon screaming orders to his policemen already dead on the boat. He was running for the sailboat, for Kellor, for the sound of banshees shrieking as they came in from the sea. He was running to kill.

He had no pain, no thought.

"Shoot them! *Shoot* them!" It was Reardon. He was ahead of him in the smoke on the sand, standing up, shouting, and Tillman, running, running, running toward no end, no ceasing, no cessation, ran to him through smoke and the corpses of dead men floating in from the sea.

"Shoot them!" The smoke cleared and he was screaming to no one: to the burning boat hard over on its side, sliding back into deep water. He was screaming to a hulk, to dead men. He was alone but for the sailboat with Kellor and Eldridge in it, and as he turned to see it he saw a nightmare ship racing in through the shallows and he saw Kellor slice a blow from the barrel of his revolver against Eldridge's head and get to the mast to work at the sails. Reardon shrieked at him, *"Doctor! Dr. Kellor—!"*

The immigrants were not dead, not drowned. Through the smoke he could see their shadows, their forms. They were alive, loose, and Reardon, not knowing which way to look, frozen where he was like a man in quicksand, shrieked to the sailboat, "They're loose! They're coming for me! They're loose!" He had only his revolver with maybe one or two shells left in it. Reardon shrieked, "I don't have any spare bullets!"

He felt something reach him—something, someone terrible and unstoppable and malevolent—and, sinking to his knees, bringing his hands up to cover his face, Reardon, begging, pleading, howled to whatever it was—the dead, the drowned, the unfairness of it all—"Oh, God—for the love of God— *Don't kill me!*"

On the sailboat Eldridge, on his knees in the stern, saw the whaleboat coming like a scythe. He saw in the boat's bow a dead man. Eldridge, his head bloody and spinning from the blow from the gun barrel, demanded, "What's happening?" He saw everywhere in the canvas of the night shapes and shadows, fire. He was God. He had made everything. He had not made this. Eldridge, above the screaming, the cries of the wounded and dying, the howling of the demented and the evil shrieked in utter confusion, "Who are all these people? *What's happening here?*"

He was bursting, exploding, out of control, snarling like a wild dog with the fire and the night, the shrieking, the revenge, the killing. The killing was easy, elemental: it took nothing, cost nothing, required no humanity, no feeling, no mind, no thought: it took only the Colt Lightning in his hand and the Colt was charged with energy and conclusion and an end to everything and it lashed out and killed and solved and completed and there, on that beach in that night, that was all there was.

It solved and completed Rosie and pity and care and small dogs in night shelters and the feeling in his loins with her, and it solved the black man on the stagecoach with his songs and hope; it solved the Custers and the *Bailey* and the drowning of babies, and it solved Jenkins on fire and Hewitt in his shroud, and Archer pleading for pity in the glass-house, and as he saw Reardon on the ground with his gun up in his hands covering his face it would solve him too. He ran, the gun out like a knife, to destroy him, to shatter him, to kill him, to ram the muzzle into the man's face and explode it the way the shotgun had exploded McTeague. He saw him on his knees through the smoke. He saw Kellor at the sailboat. He saw Muldoon in the prow of a whaleboat roaring and gesticulating to a crew of lunatics. He saw Reardon on the sand take his hands away from his face wild with hate, and as the hands came out like talons Tillman was caught around the waist and thrown over on top of him and his gun was gone.

With the weight gone, Muldoon saw the sailboat start to slide back into the water. He saw Kellor and Eldridge running into the darkness, hand in hand like lovers, toward the rise to the hill. He still had his Smith and Wesson in his hand, but he was all out of bullets from the dwarfs, the gravediggers, and he could not shoot. He turned and saw the rowers, the mad people, their eyes wild with joy. *"A Muldoon!"* In the bow, inches from the sliding sailboat, he shrieked his war cry.

Tillman's hand, closing over where he thought the gun was on the sand, closed over nothing. He heard Reardon snarl like a wild dog. He looked back and saw him with his lips drawn back over his teeth, and as Reardon brought his own pistol down in an arc like a club, he turned back, got his hands around the man's throat, got him in a death grip and, squeezing, grunting with the power, the strength of it, strangled him, bursting all the little veins and capillaries in his brain one by one, killed him.

* * *

The whaleboat hit the sailboat bow-on and smashed it like paper, and then the whaleboat was on the sand and all the lunatics were out and running down the beach shrieking, and Muldoon, trying to reload his gun, trying to see anything in the smoke, screamed to them, "Come back! You don't know what's down there! *Come back!*"

He saw Maisie, the only one he knew by name, fleeing, going into the darkness and, losing all his spare cartridges, Muldoon, looking around, trying to see Eldridge and the man who had shot him, seeing nothing, roared, *"Come back!"*

He saw through the smoke, shadows and figures. He thought, in an awful instant, they were the Steamboat Squad. He thought they were McTeague and Allison, and then he saw their shapes, their outlines, the way they ran, and they were the people from the *Bailey*: men with children, women, babies.

"Maisie!" Reardon was still out there. He had not been shot. Reardon was out there somewhere.

"Maisie!" It seemed, in that instant, so important.

"Virgil!" He could not see the man anywhere, could not see his shape, could not hear his voice anywhere.

The pain in his side and lungs was a fire and, as he touched it and looked down, he was bleeding again.

"Maisie!" It seemed to him, in that moment, for some reason, so important, and, faltering, staggering, all his side burning with the pain of the bullet still lodged in there, Muldoon, unarmed, ran through the melee after her.

He had him. With every ounce of his strength, kneeling with him, he was strangling the life out of Reardon even after he was dead, killing him, and then, as above him there was a crash and a shadow above him, Tillman, seeing Muldoon, let go and got his hands out to kill him too.

He slapped the hands away. Muldoon roared at him, "Eldridge! That way!" He had Tillman's Lightning in his hand, shaking the sand from it, shoving it into the man's hands, pointing away up the little hill to the center of the island, but was not looking there, looking down the beach. "Eldridge—*up there!*"

"Who the hell's Eldridge?" Tillman, on his feet, reaching out for him, grasping him by the side and making him double in pain, roared, "Kellor! *Where's Kellor?*"

"Who the hell's Kellor?" In the torch's light, he saw Maisie. He saw her running down the beach like a madwoman. Muldoon roared at Tillman, "Eldridge! Up there! Up *there!*" and Tillman was gone, running through the smoke for the hill and Muldoon had lost her, could not see her anywhere and she was not safe.

"—*Maisie!!*" The pain in his side, through God's good grace, was all gone and unstopping, unstoppable, he ran into the smoke to save her.

He was some sort of maniac from Blackwell's. He was some sort of maniac from Blackwell's dressed in an ancient, bloody Telegrapher's uniform. Halfway up the dirt path to the top of the hill he was wandering among the burning torches, lost and moaning.

He was no one. He was a maniac. Catching him, grasping him by the collar and spinning him around, Tillman screamed at him, "Where is he? Where's Kellor?"

He was Eldridge. He must have been Eldridge.

Tillman shrieked, "Eldridge, *where's Kellor?*"

Muldoon roared at her, "Maisie!"

She had stopped. She had stopped where the people from the boat were on the sand and she had sat down with them—all the lunatics had sat down with them—and they were all looking at the things they had seen from the whaleboat as if, from some strange alien world, it was something they had never seen before, or had not seen for a very long time.

They were looking at the children.

"Maisie . . ." They were strange, foreign people from a country somewhere else. She was sitting among them, humming, smiling. She had the baby in her arms. Muldoon said softly, "Maisie . . . oh, Maisie . . ."

In the water, at the edge, there was Allison's dead body moving in and out with the current. Muldoon said softly to Maisie, to the people to show it was all right, "Maisie . . . Maisie . . ."

"Neddy—" She saw him, recognized him. She smiled at him with a wonderful smile.

By the light of the burning boat, in that awful place they had come to, sitting quietly on the sand, she held the baby in her arms to soothe it, to caress it, and rocking it, in a voice so clear, so young and pure, with a face like an angel, her heart full and complete again, she sang to it a lullaby from the good times, from times past, from her childhood.

"I'm God!" Eldridge demanded, looking him hard in the face, "What is it you want from me?"

"*Kellor!*" It was a rasp, a croak. "*Kellor.*"

They were in the Inferno. He was Satan. Tillman said with his voice a snarl, "I want *Kellor!*"

* * *

"Sweet and low, sweet and low,
Sleep and rest, sleep and rest,
Father will come to thee soon,
Rest, rest on mother's breast,
Silver sails out of the west,
Father will come to thee soon . . ."

It was love's old sweet song.

Cradling, rocking, all the lunatics gazing silently at the children, as Muldoon watched, in that place, she sang it gently, wonderfully, as if, all her life, she had always known what it meant.

45

He had come so far. He had come, at last, to the end of it.

"Kellor!" He was soaking wet, covered in blood and sand from the beach, his face and neck lacerated and bruised from the boat. He was a tiny, armed man with death in his eyes. On the rise, lit like a demon from the flaming torches set in the ground, surrounded by the open graves the dwarfs had dug for the night's work, Tillman, from the depths of his soul, shrieked *"Kellor!!"*

In the flickering yellow light of the torches he saw him standing with his back to him, the Colt held loosely by his side.

He saw everywhere the mounds and hills and depressions in the ground where the dead were. He saw the shovels stuck in hillocks of soil where, this day, the gravediggers had dug the holes for more. The Lightning in his hand was like a sinewed animal throbbing with life, full of power. Tillman, stopping, halting, his flesh burning with fire, screamed at the figure, at the Custer, at the monster, *"KELLOR—!"*

There was a sound behind him on the path, a panting—Muldoon and Eldridge—and Tillman, glancing at them for only an instant, not losing sight of the man with his back to him, not letting him go, not letting him evaporate, disappear, become mist and chimera, shrieked, "Get back! Get back to the people! Get back!"

He saw Kellor, ramrod straight, still in his doctor's white coat, standing like a statue. He saw the gleam of the long-barreled Cavalry revolver slack in the man's hand as if he had forgotten it. He saw him, six feet tall, the master of his dominion, of the island. He was standing in a mass graveyard of unmarked dead. There were no headstones, no crosses, merely, below the surface of the earth, everywhere, the dead. Tillman said in horror, in realization, in a gasp, "My God, how many? How many of your dead are buried here? *How many voyages like this has the* Bailey *made?"*

He would not turn around.

Tillman ordered him, *"Turn around!"*

318

He would not turn around.

Tillman ordered him, *"Turn around!"*

"You listen in! You made Eldridge—mad Eldridge who thought he was the inventor of the Telephone—connect you with every instrument in the city and like a spider you listened in from the center of your web and you heard men's thoughts and you recruited them—you enlisted them! Jenkins: you heard him at the Fifth Precinct at night on the telephone talking to his cronies, to the Steamboat Squad, to Reardon and Allison and McTeague, and you heard his hatred for anyone who wasn't like him, anyone whose life was more than his life had been and you recruited him to do what his innermost thoughts wanted him to do—to kill, and you enlisted him as your murderer! Hewitt, the boy-man in the shadow of his father, losing everything because he was afraid to change, because his father's dead hand reached out to him every day of his life from the grave, you recruited for what was under his store—for the railway tunnel and the rooms and the cover-cave—for the meeting place! Archer you recruited as the pen-pusher, as a concealer in ink and paper and columns and lines and figures of people you took from the ships! Didn't you?"

He was the lord of the island. It was as if Tillman was not there and he gazed out across it into the darkness of the river and thought his own thoughts.

"Didn't you? *Didn't you?* Oubliette, Embrasure, Donjon, Palisade, Portcullis, Archer, Bailey—you created a fort, a castle, a stronghold—*Didn't you?"* He was shaking. He could not control his muscles, and everything, all his body, everything that had been cut or bruised or lacerated or twisted, was beginning to hurt. "They were your fort's defenders—*weren't they?* And they all did exactly to the letter what you told them to do, *didn't they?* They obeyed the voice on the telephone. They obeyed until Hewitt, pathetic Hewitt, *stupid* Hewitt, wanting to be even more than what you made him—wanting to be more than merely *rich*—wanting something his father never allowed him to think he wanted—wanting a woman—showed a poor, thieving street girl who he was, what he was part of, what a man he was!"

Tillman ordered the man, "Turn around!"

He would not turn around.

Tillman said in a whisper, "So you ordered Jenkins to kill her."

He was a statue. He had his back to him.

Tillman screamed, *"Didn't you?"* His voice was quavering. He could not control it. "And the immigrants, they did what they were told too, didn't they? They came from countries so bowed down with the fear of authority and terror of the police that when Reardon and McTeague and

Allison ordered them off the ships within sight of land they did what they were told with no protest, and the captains of the ships they came from, of course, had no objection either because the numbers were made up on forms signed by Archer and whatever reason the police gave for removing their passengers didn't matter to the captains—plague or criminal record or lunacy or anarchy—none of it mattered to them because they had turned their passengers over to the authorities and earned their passage money!" Tillman said to comprehend the numbers, "Four years! At least four years! The Custers have been at their business for at least four years! How many people altogether have you taken off the ships? How many families? How many children, women, men? How many are here? How many in this monstrous conspiracy have you—"

"This *'monstrous conspiracy'?"* He turned, his eyes blazing. Close up, in the yellow light of the torches, he was like a cadaver, the skin stretched tight over all the bones and hollows in his face, Kellor, the gun stiffening in his hand as he gripped at it in a spasm, shrieked as if the thought was beyond belief, "What 'monstrous conspiracy'? The monstrous conspiracy is not *mine!"*

"Drop the gun." He stepped back. Tillman bringing his own Colt up to aim at the man's head, said as an order, "Drop the gun!"

"You ask me how many dead lie here? How many are buried here? You ask the *figures?"* He was a madman, shaking his head like a dog. Kellor demanded, "How many lie dead at the Little Big Horn? How many lie dead at Antietam? At Gettysburg? How many lie dead in unnamed places everywhere beneath the flag of our country? How may are maimed and ruined and castrated, limbless, insane, shamed? How many—" He had his hand clenched around the butt of the gun, moving it, making it shake, trembling at it, "My 'monstrous conspiracy'? I have no monstrous conspiracy! The monstrous conspiracy has already been perpetrated! The monstrous conspiracy—the true monstrous conspiracy—is what you, you ridiculous man, seek to uphold, believe in, think you now are glorying in—the monstrous conspiracy is *The Law!"*

He went on as if Tillman was not there, as if, as an orison, a chant, he said it over and over each day for the strengthening of his soul. His voice was a whisper. Kellor said, not to Tillman, but to the darkness, "I was a soldier. I was with Custer. I was with Custer in the Seventh." Kellor said reverently, softly, in awe, "God, but he was a fine figure on his horse with his uniform and his yellow hair and his piercing eyes and his white gauntlets . . . I knew him! I spoke often with him. *I knew him!"* Kellor said suddenly, conversationally, "He was exactly the same age as I, exactly, almost to the day. I was a medical doctor in his regiment and I worshipped, *worshipped* the ground he walked on!" Kellor said with his eyes narrowed, the gun still hard in his hand, but down, pointing at the ground, "Honor, bravery, duty, *glory*—the world has never seen a man of his like and never will again." He made a fist with his free hand and held it to his mouth to form, to force, the words. It was as if Tillman was no longer there. "Sometimes, late at night when he could not sleep, he would come to the hospital to look in on the men who were down with illness or wounds and, often, sometimes, at my desk, sitting like old friends—" Kellor said suddenly screaming, *"And he died for nothing!* He died, not for glory or for honor or bravery or for duty, but because miners, dirty, scratching, venal men with broken nails and filthy clothes found gold on Indian Territory, and he died, deserted because it was necessary to break the treaty with the Indians and the only way it could be done was by rousing the populace to a blood lust of slaughter and by making him a hero!" Kellor screamed, "My monstrous conspiracy! There is a monstrous conspiracy, but it is not my monstrous conspiracy! It is the monstrous conspiracy against honor and loyalty! It is the monstrous conspiracy against the nobility of a soul like Custer's! *It is that monstrous conspiracy!"*

Kellor said, as if Tillman was not there, "I begged him. I pleaded with him to let me go with him on his last expedition, his crowning achievement! I entreated him with my hands clasped together in prayer—I wept to him to grovel for the opportunity! I pleaded to be part of his nobility!" He had the Cavalry revolver down hard in his hand. He held it up as if it was not a weapon of death but a relic, an icon, "But no, he gave me this. He gave me this and patted me on the shoulder and said like a kind father, 'Next time.' But there was no next time and the next time I saw what could have been him, he was nothing but a gutted, blackened corpse and where he fell in glory there is no glory—there are only miners grubbing in the ground for wealth! My monstrous conspiracy? The monstrous conspiracy is not of my doing—it is the monstrous conspiracy of reality!"

He was shrieking. Kellor, thrusting the gun down and back in the air like a pile driver, bursting with the truth, the reality, shrieked at the pathetic— the stupid man facing him, "The monstrous conspiracy, the greatest, the most venal, the most truly, unashamedly monstrous conspiracy on the face of the Earth is this!" He stabbed hard at the ground with the gun, "This! Here! This! This place! This country!"

Kellor, roaring in the darkness, his face the face of Satan in the light of the torches, screamed as if to a moronic child, "You fool! You fool as Custer was a fool, the monstrous conspiracy is *America!"*

* * *

"You are under arrest. Drop the gun. You are under arrest for—"

"It is all true!"

"Drop the goddamned gun *now!*"

Kellor said almost sadly, "Custer and his dead command—all the brave, noble boys: all that was for an illusion. All the great battles, everything. The killing of one soldier by another in battle is but child's play, a pretense. Death in the name of nobility, of war, is a joke! In the name of peace the mine owners, the railroad barons, the canal builders, the great, the honored, rich men of our society kill not a hundred, but a thousand a day, maim a hundred thousand, cast them aside, walk by them on the street—*and think nothing of it!*" Kellor said, "You believe in America? You must believe in cruelty, in exploitation, in lying and cheating and venality!"

"I believe in the Law!"

"The Law is there to protect the exploiters! The Law is administered by the venal men! The Law in Indian Territory was administered by the gold miners! The Law, that expression of the nobility of men's minds—that bastion of fairness—changes with the seasons to protect the men for all seasons!" Kellor said, "The rich men, the Astors, the Carnegies, were the first to have the new Telephone—they were the first I listened in to!" Kellor said accusingly, "Your own leader, your own hero, your own creator of the Detective Bureau, Chief Inspector Thomas Byrnes, is in cahoots for money with opium dealers!"

"You have *killed* people!"

"*Everyone* has killed people! It is the American way! I have done nothing more than is done every day in the mines, on the canals, in the pestilent swamps of the South and in the tenements and sweatshops of the North—I have done nothing more than take the subversive and the alien—the despoilers of our nation—and placed them in the mouth of the cannon for profit!" He could not see that the man did not comprehend the simple truth of it immediately. "America is not and never was one nation: it is two nations—the exploited and the exploiters!" Kellor said as self-evident, "There is no glory, no freedom, no shining nobility! There is only profit and death!"

"An insane asylum is the—"

"It is! It is the university par excellence for the learning of life!" Kellor said, shaking with the power of the truth, "When I came to the city I was lost. I found in the insane asylum sanity! I found in bitterness and resentment and hatred and disappointment knowledge! I found among the inferior men that I was not an inferior man! I found in the weakness of my tears *strength!*"

"Jenkins, Reardon, Hewitt, Archer—"

"All believed they did what they did to rid society of inferior races. They believed it because they were inferior themselves and, finding someone to hate, they became larger, better—" Kellor said, "I have no hatred of any other race: I am an American—a true American—all anyone else on the surface of the globe is to me is labor, profits, riches!" He paused, smiling, "And they would have all died anyway of disease or overwork or hopelessness and I spared them the anxiety."

"The people on the ships—the ones you took—were the money carriers: the brightest and the best from their towns and villages—the educated! The hope of all their people! The ones chosen as the advance guard to make a place for the others who would follow!"

Kellor said mildly, "I am not a fool. There is no profit in robbing a man who has no money. On the ships it was easy to see from their hands which of them did no physical work."

"On Swinburne there is a man, a doctor, who has never seen the island of Manhattan!"

"Bergmann." Kellor said, "Bergmann is a fool."

"He shamed me with his nobility of spirit!"

"Then you are a fool." In the yellow light he gazed at the man. Kellor said, shaking his head, "Look at you talking to me—I, in your position, would have killed you on the spot, but look at you: look at you standing there desperate for meaning in your life, look at you not knowing, wondering, full of hints and clues and half-formed terrors that what I say may be true—look at you!" Kellor said in a whisper, "I know people like you. I hear them. I hear them on the Telephone. I hear them wondering, asking, seeking—and then I see them on Blackwell's when their brains burst of the not-knowing! I know people like you! You have no one, nothing! You grasp for nobility, for a cause, for one tiny shining moment—a war, a crusade, a great pursuit, a glorious venture—some little thing to make the long years of your sad, useless existence have meaning!"

"Like Custer?"

"Custer was a fool!"

"You begged him to let you come on his last great charge! Into his final shining battle!"

"Then *I* was a fool!" Kellor said, "There is no meaning. Life has no meaning! The only meaning is money!"

"There is a meaning to hope! There is a meaning to the hope of the people on the ships! There is a meaning to families fleeing a corrupt, ancient world to find freedom in the New!" Tillman demanded, "How many? How many of them have you buried here? How many of them have you killed?"

"What difference does it make whether it was one or a hundred?" Kellor roared at him, *"I tell you a great truth about life and all you ask about are the figures!"* Kellor said, "Let me put your mind at rest. Let me simplify life for you. Let me tell you the answer to the question of your nights. You are no one! Nothing! And you will die lonely and poor and forgotten! You will die—"

"You would have gone with Custer! You would still go with him now!"

"I would *not!*" Kellor, shaking his head, the gun up in his hand, screamed at him, "I am the New Man! I am the one free man in the world! I have seen the truth and the truth is that there is no great sacrifice for the greater good, no great causes or shining uniforms or long yellow hair—all there is is murder for money!" Kellor, shrieking, demanded, "If there is nobility, if there is good, tell me what good, in your life, you have done!"

"I have saved the life of a child!"

"On the boat? The life of a child on the boat? That child, should it even survive beyond this day, is fated to be worked to death in a mine somewhere or in a sweatshop or to suffocate with disease or starve on the streets—that child, if it is not the child of one of the New Men—that child you have saved you have merely saved for a life of misery! The mine owners know that, the railroad barons, the Astors, the Carnegies: they know that." Kellor said, "That child and its family merely represent what labor, what profits can be taken from it—I am greater than the Astors, than the Carnegies: I chose already rich men rather than wait through the hours, the days, the years of their labor for my profit, I take it now!" Kellor said quietly, intimately, "You have done nothing. You have merely put off the inevitable."

"All this is a lie!"

Kellor asked with his lips curled, "What were you before you became such a moral man?"

Tillman said with no emotion in his voice, "I was a clown in a circus."

"You still are!"

"Virgil—!" It was Muldoon somewhere out in the darkness.

Tillman ordered him, "Get away!"

"You moral man . . ."

"Kill him!" Somewhere out in the darkness, it was Eldridge. He was no longer God. He was a man who had been brought out to the island to be killed. Eldridge shrieked, *"Kill him!"*

"You moral man . . . !" He shook his head in disbelief at the stupidity of it. Kellor said in disappointment at the man, "You fool, I will get away with it, don't you see that? Don't you see that the laws are made by people like me? Don't you see that my peers, the good folk of the Trinity Congregation, my judges, don't you see that they are precisely what they are because they are like me? Don't you see that to save me they will destroy you? Don't you see . . . ?" Kellor said as if it was the simplest truth on Earth, "You fool! I *hear!* I *know!* To know people's secret thoughts, their dreams, is to control them! The Law—"

"The Law is made by the people!"

"Washington was a slave owner. The laws he made were for himself. The rest is merely rhetoric."

"The rest is the expression of the true nature of Man—of his aspirations!"

Eldridge screamed, "Kill him! Kill him! *Kill him!*"

Kellor said, shaking his head, "I will get away with it because I have a fortune and I can pay to get away with it!"

"How many people are buried here? How many men and women and families? How many lives and—"

"You are still a clown." Kellor asked conversationally, "Why did you give it up? Why did you become what you are now? What did you see in your nights, your dreams? What did you see that made you become what you are, as I have become what I am?" Kellor screamed, *"Four thousand! I have killed on the* Bailey *and buried here on Hart Island four thousand people!"*

"And is that more than Custer ever killed?"

"Yes, that is more than Custer ever killed! It is more than any man in history has ever killed! I see in my dreams, reality! I see in my dreams, the truth!" Kellor, taking a step forward, shrieked at him, "You failure of a man! You pathetic little creature flying in the face of the true reality of the human soul, *what do you see in yours?"*

He saw Rosie and her dog. He saw Bergmann. He saw a black man on a stagecoach singing as he drove up Broadway. He saw only senseless, pointless, inane, meaningless things. He saw only faces.

He saw in all his dreams, the glitter of a skewer. He saw, in all his nights, shadows.

Tillman said in a voice so low neither Muldoon nor Eldridge behind him could hear, "I see—"

Tillman said in an instant before he brought the gun up and killed the man where he stood, "I see— I see *you!"*

46

They came.

In the greatest mass migration of human beings in history, watching from the Battery, on all the ships, speaking a hundred languages, in rags, in shawls, in coats too large or too small, saved and sewn, with bundles and boxes and baskets of all they were, he saw them come.

They came from nights too long to contemplate, from fear and terror and the dread of uniforms and brass buttons and men on horseback with whips and decrees.

Between the years 1882 and 1884 there came, in total, one and one-half million of them, more in the years at the end of the century and extending into the new century.

They came, out of the night—wise men, fools, great men and insignificant—into the morning.

They came, each one of them on his or her own day, with the awed eyes of children, gazing toward the shore, into the morning.

They came.

Bright, bright day.

On all the ships, lining all the railings, gazing, peering, craning to see, they heard, above even the engines of the ships that had brought them, the sound of their own heartbeats.